MOUNTAIN OF FIRE

BOOKS IN THIS SERIES

Under a Graveyard Sky (by John Ringo)
To Sail a Darkling Sea (by John Ringo)
Islands of Rage and Hope (by John Ringo)
Strands of Sorrow (by John Ringo)
Black Tide Rising (edited by John Ringo & Gary Poole)
Valley of Shadows (by John Ringo & Mike Massa)
Voices of the Fall (edited by John Ringo & Gary Poole)
River of Night (by John Ringo & Mike Massa)
At the End of the World (by Charles E. Gannon)
At the End of the Journey (by Charles E. Gannon)
We Shall Rise (edited by John Ringo & Gary Poole)
United We Stand (edited by John Ringo & Gary Poole)
Mountain of Fire (by Jason Cordova)

BAEN BOOKS by JASON CORDOVA

Monster Hunter Memoirs: Fever with Larry Correia

Chicks in Tank Tops edited by Jason Cordova

MOUNTAIN OF FIRE

by

JASON CORDOVA

Set in the Black Tide Rising world
created by

JOHN RINGO

A Baen Books Original

Baen Publishing Enterprises
P.O. Box 1403
Riverdale, NY 10471
www.baen.com

ISBN: 978-1-9821-9361-4

Cover art by Kurt Miller
Maps by Violet Flores

First printing, September 2024

Distributed by Simon & Schuster
1230 Avenue of the Americas
New York, NY 10020

Library of Congress Cataloging-in-Publication Data

Names: Cordova, Jason, 1978- author.
Title: Mountain of fire / Jason Cordova.
Description: Riverdale, NY : Baen Publishing Enterprises, 2024. | Series: A Black Tide Rising Novel ; 13
Identifiers: LCCN 2024017673 (print) | LCCN 2024017674 (ebook) | ISBN 9781982193614 (hardcover) | ISBN 9781625799838 (ebook)
Subjects: LCGFT: Science fiction. | Novels.
Classification: LCC PS3603.O73424 M68 2024 (print) | LCC PS3603.O73424 (ebook) | DDC 813/.6—dc23/eng/20240422
LC record available at https://lccn.loc.gov/2024017673
LC ebook record available at https://lccn.loc.gov/2024017674

Printed in the United States of America

10 9 8 7 6 5 4 3 2 1

DEDICATION

For Juanita "Nina" Cordova
1954–2005
The brightest light in our life left us too soon.

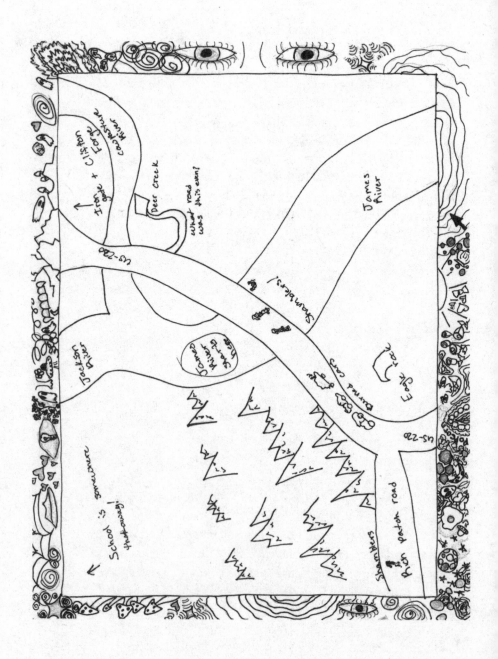

ACKNOWLEDGMENTS

First off, this book would not be possible without John Ringo and Gary Poole. When I first read *Under a Graveyard Sky* almost ten years ago, I never thought in a million years I'd be writing in the universe. The Smith family was just the epitome of awesome, and the right survival types for this sort of world-ending event. When the call came out to write in the first anthology (*Black Tide Rising*), you can probably imagine my surprise when Gary asked me to write a story, then asked me to return a second time for *We Shall Rise*.

Also, thank you to both Charles E. Gannon and Mike Massa for showing me the way. There are many stories still to be told in the Black Tide universe John created. I'm thrilled to be a part of it.

Toni Weisskopf has been a tremendous help and has offered a lot of guidance during the creative process. Having one of the best editors alive work with you on a novel was eye-opening, to say the least. Her endless patience in explaining *why* I shouldn't do some things in the book, instead of just telling me I can't, needs to be applauded.

Dr. Brent Roeder has been particularly helpful with coming up with research quotes and guidelines from the University of the South. His twisted sense of humor and helpfulness have been a boon during the writing process. Also, thank you to Violet Flores for both the maps drawn within, as well as modeling for the cover. The maps came out amazing and I hope the readers love them as much as I do!

A special thank-you goes out to Jamie Ibson for creating a timeline of the entire Black Tide Rising series and lining them up to make it all work. Through painstaking research, and one impressive data spreadsheet, he was able to help me line up events that occurred throughout the original four books, as well as the two spin-off series. There was no way I could have figured it all out without his assistance.

And one final "thanks!" goes out to the audience at LibertyCon 34, asking if we were going to get to see Catholic schoolgirls versus zombies in a future Black Tide novel. Here ya go.

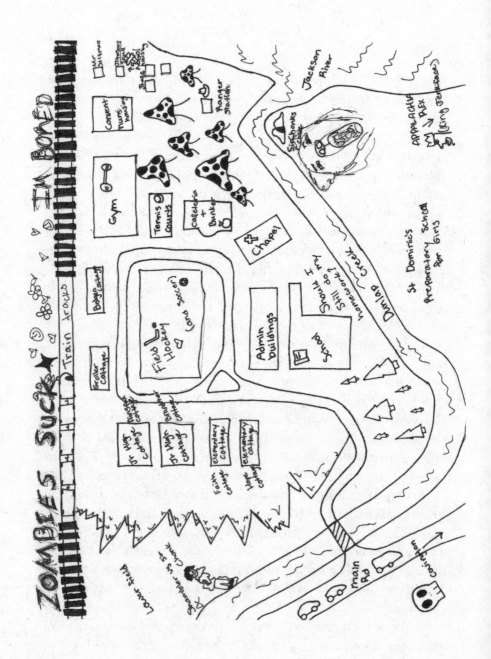

INTRODUCTION

Biomedical ethics are the moral and ethical issues associated with advances in the biological sciences and biomedical engineering. It is not just science and engineering that undergo changes, but also society. Societal changes also affect morals and ethics. Therefore, it is important to understand the changes—scientific, engineering, and societal—that contribute to our evaluation of what the ethical approach to research is.

Few things throughout history have changed society as much as The Fall. Because of the chaos inherent to The Fall, we are still rebuilding our history of not just what we lost but, more importantly, what we were able to save and rebuild. To those of you born after, it is hard to understand how easy and readily accessible individual and mass communication was to even the poorest throughout the world. We lived in an unparalleled age of information exchange.

Even the remnants of this communication ability that survived the Fall have allowed historians a trove of information ranging from official government communications to untold thousands of personal journals. To this day we continue to integrate these sources of information together to provide a record of, arguably, the largest event in human history in greater detail—and from more points of view—than any other event in history. This is both a boon, and a curse, thanks to the reputed unreliability of some narrators.

We will begin this class with a survey of the major historical events that contributed to pre-Fall biomedical ethics, and what the ethical positions were prior to the Fall. We will then move on to the history of biomedical research during and following the Fall and how that research was viewed under pre-Fall ethical positions, and how new ethical standards have evolved since then.

It is important that we look beyond mere survival, toward ways to grow and flourish. We *must* observe and record, with a dispassionate eye, the various datapoints that allowed for society to rebuild. As scientists, part of the way we contribute to this is not just by being effective in our research, but by being ethical in how we approach that research. In this way we help to move past simply persisting, with the records that show how average people rose above expectations and contributed to society rebuilding, and thriving as our guide.

Now, if you look at the timeline on your syllabus you will see that the first lecture will cover...

—Beginning of the first lecture in the course
"Grad 725—Research Methods for the Infected"
by Dr. Tedd Roberts, University of the South, 2047

PROLOGUE

My Thursday afternoon rapidly turned to crap when a zombie ripped Sister Mary's face off right in front of me.

"Move! Get to the cafeteria and lock the doors! Move it, Maddie!" Sister Ann yelled in my ear as another zombie ran at us, ignoring the fallen Sister Mary. Twisting desperately to avoid contact, it somehow missed me as I gracelessly landed on my butt. Instead of turning around, the zombie continued to charge at Sister Ann. I somehow managed to hook it with my field hockey stick and trip the zombie.

That maneuver would have been worthy of a yellow card.

As I'd been doing for the past ten minutes, I ignored Sister Ann and focused on bashing in the zombie's head. With Sister Mary down and having dispatched Sister Margaret earlier, Sister Ann was the last nun alive that I knew of. There was no way I was going to leave her outside, alone, in the middle of the zombie apocalypse.

A so-called juvenile delinquent? Yeah, that was me, before my days at St. Dominic's. But someone who bailed on a freaking nun? No way. Not even I would stoop that low.

Pivoting, I brought the full weight of the heavy stick across my former classmate's face. It impacted with a very meaty *thwack!* The *thing* that had once been Chelsea stumbled to the side, blood trickling from where I'd tried to brain her. Careful to make certain none of her blood got on myself or Sister Ann, I smacked her with my hockey stick again. The nun was unarmed. I, at least, had a weapon of sorts. One I was pretty good with. The number of yellow and red cards I'd earned the previous field hockey season would confirm this. Howling with rage, zombie Chelsea turned and tried again.

This time I was a little more prepared. I jabbed the toe of the hockey stick into her larynx, hard. Completely illegal if I'd done it in a game. Fortunately, God seemed to be refereeing this little soiree and didn't blow the whistle. Chelsea's howling abruptly ceased as she clawed at her ruined throat. I had a window of opportunity and needed to take it. Rearing back, I let loose a powerful swing.

Crack!

Chelsea dropped to the ground. Snarling as best she could through her ruined larynx, the zombie tried to push herself back up off the ground to attack. Blood was pounding in my ears but my adrenaline was spiking high. I heard rustling from somewhere behind me. A quick check over my shoulder told me it was Lucia guiding the last surviving elementary school girls into the cafeteria, with Sister Ann pushing another zombie away with a two-by-four. The weak gurgle of a snarl brought my attention back to the writhing zombie. Chelsea was still trying to crawl toward me. With tears in my eyes, I bid my classmate a silent farewell.

Crack! Crack! Crack!

The final blow split her skull open and she slumped back to the ground, dead. Or well on her way to it. I couldn't tell through my blurred vision. I felt Sister Ann gently touch my shoulder and say something to me. I think it was supposed to be comforting. There was no way to be sure, but it would have been totally in character of her. Nodding, I let her pull me toward the cafeteria and inside. The girls huddled inside were staring at me with wide-eyed horror. Or past me. I couldn't tell. I glanced back outside and instantly regretted it.

Chaos reigned. Far in the distance, the school director lay next to the front door of the admin building, dead. Two zombies were gnawing on his legs. Nearby, I spotted one of the admin workers get chased down by a naked man—Mr. Gonzalez, from the looks of it. Her screams rose in higher pitch as another zombie jumped on her. The screams abruptly cut off as more of the zombies dogpiled her. I looked away as fresh tears filled my eyes. The place that had become my reluctant home was being overrun.

Sister Ann pulled me inside, closed the metal door, and quickly tied the chain off. The heavy door was as secure as we could make it, thanks to some modifications done in the prior weeks. In the darkness, it was hard to make out faces. Preparedness had allowed the staff to board up the cafeteria, covering the windows on both the inside and out with plywood, in case the news reports of the so-called zombie apocalypse were actually real. A good idea, in hindsight. But at the moment I couldn't see anything at all.

Some of the girls were panicking. I could hear their short breaths over the sounds of someone sobbing. The interior of the cafeteria was stuffy and hot. A quick sniff of the air told me a few of the younger girls had wet their pants. Maybe even the older ones. I didn't blame any of them. If I'd had a chance to be afraid I probably would have, too. More than half sounded like they were hyperventilating. All of us were crying. It was impossible to see who was where, or even who was still with us. Outside we could hear more howls as zombies searched for a way in. There was none. The only danger now would come from within. Eventually, there might be starvation.

Maybe. That would be later. I needed to focus on the *now*. Which meant listening to Sister Ann.

"Attention." Sister Ann's calm voice cut through the noise. She clapped her hands once. All the girls quit talking immediately. Sister Ann just had that ability to get them to listen. None of the other sisters at St. Dominic's could do that as quickly as she could. Her demeanor was calm as always. "Thank you. No arguing, no discussion. I want everyone to the bunker, now."

We practiced this twice a year in case violent weather hit the mountaintop. Today was different, though. We had lost power and this was no drill. There was an emergency light near the stairwell leading down to the bunker, but it was on the other side of the door. Better than nothing, I guess. The girls hurried toward the light, more than a few sniffling and whimpering the entire way. I couldn't blame them. I'd just brained one of my roommates to death, and this was after I'd had to shoot a few nuns and my best friend, Wren, with the shotgun I'd . . . lost? Somewhere along the way I'd dropped it. Stupid of me. Real stupid. Sister Ann was not going to be happy with . . . murder? Or would she kill me for losing the shotgun?

I hoped not. Maybe I could track it down later and she wouldn't be disappointed with me losing it?

Yeah, right.

I was the last one through the doorway. Reaching up with my

hockey stick, I smashed at the light until it broke and plunged us into full darkness once more. Everything we'd seen and heard before the television went off the air said the zombies liked loud noises and light. There was no reason to give any of the zombies outside incentive to try and find a way in. I secured the bunker door and dogged the lever hatch. It was supposed to be able to withstand a bomb, but I'd settle for holding up against an angry horde of zombies.

Zombies . . . What the heck? Not how I thought my senior year was going to go down.

Descending the stairs, I found Sister Ann in the main area of the bunker tying each girl's hands in front of them. Three candles were lit, which gave her enough light to tie the knots. Though I was pretty sure she could do it in the darkness. The light was to calm the other girls down, I guessed.

"Maddie? You remember how to tie a bowline knot? The rescue knot?" Sister Ann asked me. I nodded, remembering our multiple camping trips. She'd been pretty insistent I learn how to tie proper knots. I'd made some inappropriate jokes at the time, but now I was glad I'd paid attention anyway. "Good. I need you to cut enough rope to make lines to tie the girls apart, just out of range of each other, and help secure them. Then yourself."

"Yes, ma'am," I replied tonelessly. My emotions were a jumbled mess but when Sister Ann gave a command, you listened and obeyed.

"Maddie? You can cry. It's always okay to cry for ourselves."

"I know."

"And we never apologize for our tears," she added. I nodded numbly. The skull I'd just caved in upstairs had been a friend . . . well, as close to a friend as I could have. Making friends was not my strong suit. Or keeping them, it seemed.

I found the rope in question—nylon rope, which would flex some but was very hard to actually break—and started tying off the bowlines as instructed. More than a few of the younger girls shied away but I didn't care. Once they were secured, I moved on. One after another all the girls were tied and secured. It's easy, really. Tie their wrists together behind their ankles, then to their shoelaces. We knew what turned the others into zombies had been the flu that had torn through campus two weeks before, but now it was a waiting game. The CDC had said the flu was lessening right before the lights went out. But the zombie bites turned the survivors as well. So did their blood. We had to be careful.

Were we careful enough, though? I had no idea.

A sharp scream, followed by a cry of alarm, told me we hadn't been careful enough.

"It itches! Oh my God, it itches!" It was Becca, our valedictorian. The blonde was frantically trying to tear her clothes off. She had a crazed look on her face. I'd seen it before—when Sister Margaret had turned into a zombie and attacked half her cottage. "Get them off! Get them *arrrrrrfff!*"

Her scream turned into a low, guttural howl and she lunged at Sister Ann. The nun stumbled back as Becca's rope caught on the catch. The newly turned zombie was snarling and howling, tearing at her clothing and failing to get her shirt off. It was almost impossible with her hands tied. Sister Ann crossed herself and began to pray out loud as Becca continued howling and pulling the rope binding her wrists.

Fortunately, Sister Ann had tied a good knot. It held. Becca was going nowhere in a hurry.

All the younger girls were screaming, trying to get away. Their own knots held them in place. Becca couldn't reach any of them, thankfully. I could faintly hear responding howls from the outside. The bunker was secure, but would Becca bring more of them? I didn't know. We couldn't afford this, not if we wanted to survive. Someone had to do something.

I had the field hockey stick. I'd already used it a few times to deal with a zombie.

What was one more?

I hefted the stick on my shoulder and shut my brain off. That dark part of my soul, the angry girl who had thrived before coming to St. Dominic's, reared her ugly head. Zombie Becca snarled and lunged again, but made no headway. The knots held.

Taking careful aim, I lined my swing up. The gore-covered stick whistled through the air as I swung as hard as I could, making sure to try and keep her blood from splattering about. It took me four swings to her head and neck before she finally quit moving. I checked myself over, just to be sure. None of her blood had gotten on me, or anyone else for that matter. We'd have to carefully get rid of the body.

Jason Cordova

There were some heavy-duty oversized trash bags in the bunker. They were supposed to be used for construction work, but they'd do for what we'd need later. Probably.

I looked around. None of the others would even look at me. The younger girls were still crying, dazed. One or two were staring off into the distance, not even aware of what was going on. A few of the juniors and seniors were trying to comfort the others, but failing. They couldn't reach one another. Everyone was crying. Except for Sister Ann. Her face was twisted in grief, but there was a stoicism about her that gave me courage. Slowly, I walked toward Sister Ann as she finished tying up the last girl. I didn't want her to think I'd turned by rushing. At the same time, I needed . . . something. What, though, I didn't know.

"So, now what?" I asked, since nobody else seemed willing to speak coherently. Or maybe they were unable. Who knows? Sister Ann brushed a few stray strands of hair out of my face and tried to smile. I set the field hockey stick aside as she held up more rope. I felt the old familiar friend buried in my heart recede. That angry little girl was no longer the dominating part of who I was. St. Dominic's had made certain of that.

"We survive," she replied and knotted my hands. Once I was secured and in place, she passed around two bottles of water for all the girls. Then she tied herself up as well. "After that, we rebuild."

I wasn't sure we could. Rebuild, I mean. There were fewer than thirty of us left. The school had five hundred students and staff before this. There was no way we could do any type of rebuilding. How could we? We were just a bunch of preteen and teenage girls, all alone in the Blue Ridge Mountains with a single nun.

Sister Ann, however, was determined.

Fortunately, nobody else turned that day. Or the next.

Maybe we had a chance after all?

Part One

A MOUNTAIN ON FIRE

*Victory at all costs, victory in spite of all terror,
victory however long and hard the road may be;
for without victory, there is no survival.*
—Winston Churchill

CHAPTER ONE

"This is Big Al... on behalf of all of us here at WKEY 103.5 FM... wishing each and every one of you good luck. God bless you all, and God bless America."
From: *Collected Radio Transmissions of the Fall,*
University of the South Press, 2053

Six months later...

The shambler was slowly picking its way through the woods, stopping every so often to lift its head and sniff the air like an animal. I doubted it knew I was there. Safely off the ground in one of the many tree blinds scattered around the mountain, the odds were slim to none of me being spotted. I stayed quiet anyway. Zombies tended to focus on sudden movements, loud noises, and bright lights. It was of the first lessons we learned when the aftermath of the H7D3 virus arrived on campus.

Taking slow, controlled breaths, I continued to watch as it shuffled around. My rifle did not have a scope. At such a short range, though, it was unnecessary. The green dot sight was more than enough for this sort of work. However, I hesitated with the shot. There was no reason to risk anything just yet, especially since I didn't know if there were any other zombies nearby.

The zombie was naked, as they all were, nothing more than skin and bones. It was not as well-fed as the ones I'd killed during the early days of the Fall. Still, watching what had once been a regular man

11

walk around naked in the middle of the Blue Ridge Mountains was disturbing as hell. If I had dreams, this view would have haunted them regularly.

Tracking this zombie had been a chore. It'd first been spotted by one of the lookouts a few days ago down by Dunlap Creek, which ran around the base of the mountain we were holed up on. It was almost wide and deep enough to be a river, but for some reason the locals had declared it to be a creek. The girls who'd spotted the zombie had managed to give me a rough heading and location without alerting it, which was fairly impressive, considering. The zombies tended to follow sound and light, and those two girls weren't known for being quiet. Since my job was site security—a big job for anyone, trust me on this—it was left to me to deal with it. However, this zombie seemed more elusive than most and I'd had a heck of a time tracking it down. Eventually I just decided to park my butt in a tree stand and wait by the creek. All zombies needed water, and the creek is the easiest and safest source of water around.

It'd been a few months since the lights went out. Lots of people called it "the Fall." It was difficult to remember those dark, early days. Cities burning, chaos, zombies running everywhere. The survival rate if you were in a city was almost zero. For those in the mountains or countryside, it was slightly higher. Not by much. Maybe five percent, tops. All the smart people went out to sea—and even then, odds weren't great. With the weather service out of commission, nobody knew when storms were going to hit.

For those of us on the mountain, we'd had to deal with zombies running amok, over eighty percent of my schoolmates dying, and a rapidly dwindling food supply issue. We held on, but just barely. Most of the credit for our continued survival went to Sister Ann, the last surviving nun at St. Dominic's Preparatory School for Girls here in Alleghany County. She'd been a marine during the Global War on Terror before finding her calling as a nun and ended up at St. Dom's. Since then, she'd been the glue that held us together.

We were lucky to have her. Nothing against any of the other sisters who'd taught at St. Dominic's before the plague had ended the world, but I don't think we'd have done half as well if any of them had survived and been in charge. They say God works in mysterious ways. Putting a retired marine who became a nun in charge of a girls' school in the mountains of western Virginia right before the zombie apocalypse occurs?

There's a reason why I don't really believe in coincidences anymore.

A sharp crack of a branch breaking drew my focus back down. The zombie had stopped and was staring off to the west. It was growling, which wasn't too surprising. Everything we'd seen up to now suggested they didn't talk or communicate—at least not in any language I understood. They were more like aggressive dogs, ready to attack at a moment's notice. Most of them, at least. Once in a while you got a quiet, meek zombie who'd only attack when cornered. No idea what was up with those but since they tended to not come up to the school and try to eat the younger kids, I didn't usually waste a round on them.

Okay, so I know they're not zombies exactly. Listening in on the clearance operations of the so-called Wolf Squadron on the shortwave helped straighten things out there. Everyone else called them all sorts of names—including zombies—but since Sister Ann said that was incorrect, we'd taken to calling them shamblers. Not because of the way they walk or anything, but because nothing else we thought of really fit.

The forest around me had grown eerily silent. This was normal whenever a shambler appeared. The birds always went quiet whenever one showed up. They were a handy alarm system to have. Not always reliable—they stopped chirping whenever I walked by as well—but better than nothing. Even the squirrels, always numerous, were up in their trees and motionless. It was if they recognized the danger, too.

The shambler was clearly hungry. It was locked onto a target somewhere in the tree line. I carefully aimed and almost took the shot right then and there. However, past lessons told me that if there was one near campus, there could be others. They might come running at the sound of the gunshot. I had two spare magazines, but after the horde that had come down from Warm Springs the month before, I wasn't willing to risk it.

Instead, I tracked the direction the shambler was looking. After a moment I spotted what had drawn its ire. A good-sized black bear—a chunk, truth be told—had wandered out of the forest and into the glade. This late in the season it had to be looking for food, with winter just around the corner and all. Bears have become a more common sight around campus since the Fall. They hadn't gotten into the garden yet but since they could climb, it was only a matter of time. I wasn't sure if this one had been a regular at the trash bin, or a newcomer.

Either way, the shambler was clearly not happy with the bear's sudden arrival. It howled a challenge and charged it in a blind rage.

For a moment I could almost see the thought process of the bear as it looked up and spotted the shambler running toward it. *Pink man-thing charging? Retreat. RUN. Wait, I'm a big boy. They call me Chonk. I don't run from pink man-thing. I fight. WIN.*

The bear made a strange grunting noise and backed away a few steps, swinging its head back and forth. The poor thing didn't know what to make of this strange naked human, howling like a banshee. It had to have seen humans before, but never one that actively tried to attack it like this. Hopefully. It reached the bear and tried to claw at it. The bear reared up on its hind legs and roared a challenge, or a protest. I'm not really sure. Bear-ese is not my forte. I took Latin (required by the nuns) and German (the foreign language I chose, because it was required by the state to graduate ... the jerkfaces). The shambler replied with a howl and tried to bite it.

Standing up, the bear was slightly taller than the shambler, though it was a close thing. The former man had been a bit on the short side to begin with. The black bear was definitely heavier, though, and used its weight to throw off the annoying shambler. The infected stumbled to the ground and tried to get back up to continue its attack, but the bear wasn't having any of it. With terrifying speed it swiped the shambler across the head with a meaty paw two, three, four times.

The shambler fell, growling and mewling, keening an unearthly sound that set my teeth on edge. However, its legs clearly weren't working. The chonky boi must have had some power behind those swipes and done some damage to the emaciated thing that had once been human. It tried to grab the bear but Chonk clearly wasn't having it. Opening its mouth wide, the bear bit down hard on the back of the shambler's neck and began shaking it like a rag doll. The shambler howled piteously one final time before sound was cut off abruptly.

I had a horrifying thought as I watched the end of the battle: Could a bear turn into a weird hybrid zombie thing, like the shambler?

The shambler was definitely dead now, courtesy of Chonk. The bear took a second, tentative bite of the dead shambler's head before dropping it. I shivered. The idea of a zombie bear was terrifying, but the sight of the bear trying to eat a shambler was not something I needed in my head. Not now. Not ever. I couldn't leave just yet, though. If the bear saw me, it might decide I would be fun to chase. Or not. Hard to tell. Again, caution is sometimes better than guns a-blazing. The bear's full attention was on the dead shambler lying there. It swiped the head again before rising up and bringing its full weight down on the shambler's back. I could hear the sickening *crack* of the zombie's spine from up here. The urge to vomit was there but I managed to chew it back. I could heave my guts out later.

The possibility of bagging the bear entered my mind but I dismissed it almost as quickly as it came. The 5.56mm round from "Baby" (the custom-built AR-15 I'd "acquired" in the first days after the Fall) would probably just piss the bear off more than it already was. Even a shot to the head might not kill it immediately. Besides, I figured I owed Sir Chonk one. It'd bagged a shambler and saved me some ammo.

Eventually the bear grew bored of mud-stomping the shambler into pieces and wandered away in search of more actual food in preparation for the winter. I stayed up in the blind for another hour before deciding it was safe to come down. The zombie hadn't moved during the entire time. There wasn't much to see but from what I could, the bear had done a number on it. This was something I would bring up to Sister Ann during the student council meeting that night. Bears were a nuisance and could even be dangerous, but they also apparently hated shamblers about as much as I did.

Good to know.

Like Sister Margaret had always said, nature always finds a way to win in the end.

The forest came back to life, slowly but surely. The birds sang and the squirrels bounced around on the forest floor looking for their meal. A slight breeze blew across my face and for a moment I was able to forget what I'd just witnessed. Instead, I let nature sink in and bring a calm to my soul that growing up in Southern California had never managed. The smell of the mountain air was different, sweeter. Definitely no pollution up here. I didn't miss the smog alerts we'd dealt with back in Orange County.

The moment of calm passed. I needed to get back to campus. Sister Ann would want a detailed account of what happened here. Plus, with the number of zombies—yeah, sorry, *shamblers*—we saw dropping every week, we needed to start preparing for whatever crisis would hit us next. And there *would* be one. Things were running too smoothly.

I let out a soft sigh and kicked the rope ladder down. It unfurled in a hurry and stopped two feet off the ground. Once Baby was secure, I carefully climbed around the safety rail of the blind. Using the trunk of the tree as support, I made my way down the ladder. Safely down, I scanned my surroundings. Still no sign of any other shamblers. I started back up the mountain to campus, staying aware for any signs of danger. A girl's job is never done.

My name is Madison Coryell. Everyone I care about calls me Maddie, but this isn't my story.

It's *our* story. Humanity's.

For better or worse.

Long before I removed her head with a twelve-gauge, Sister Margaret had given me solid advice: Try your best and rise above the rest. I'd always taken it to mean that she wanted me to rise above everyone else, to be better than them. It wasn't until the middle of the zombie apocalypse that I began to wonder if there was a deeper meaning to her words.

The long hike back up the mountain gave me plenty of time to think about her words. Not for the first time did I search for some kind of hidden meaning in them. But lately I'd been wondering about her words, mostly because they didn't really fit with what was going on before the Fall had occurred. Had she somehow known what was coming? I mean, everyone had been tracking the Pacific Flu when it first showed up, but what had Sister Margaret anticipated?

One of the benefits of the school was that St. Dominic's was perfectly situated to survive a zombie apocalypse. Or any sort of apocalypse, for that matter. Originally built way back before the Great Depression to provide a home for orphaned girls, St. Dominic's had morphed throughout the years to become a reform school of sorts for at-risk girls. All of us were somewhere between eight and eighteen—except for my classmate Lucia, who'd turned nineteen right after the news of the Pacific Flu broke.

The campus was situated high in the Blue Ridge Mountains of Virginia, not too far from the West Virginia border. Alleghany County was big, but not really populated. Ten thousand people, maybe twelve, tops. The nearest major city was probably Roanoke, which was over an hour away to the south. Covington was a few miles away but since it had less than five thousand people before the Fall, I guess it's not a city. Or is. Was? Eh, whatever. This entire area was weird *before* the Fall hit.

Secluded and isolated was what the orphanage's founders wanted. I don't know why. Most Catholic orphanages that I've read about in books were situated in big cities like Boston or Los Angeles. The founders of St. Dominic's, however, wanted seclusion and privacy. The original farm was supposed to be self-sustaining, complete with dairy cows, pigs, and chickens. Of course, as more time passed and technology progressed, the cows and pigs went away. The chickens remained—until the Fall, at least. None of them had survived the shamblers.

That'd been one nasty incident.

Thanks to this isolation, though, St. Dominic's had weathered the early days of the Fall better than most. Although we'd lost over ninety percent of the students and staff to the plague, we had natural borders, fresh water, well water, and some solar panels to help keep the mechanical well running.

Which made it the perfect location for a small group like ours to survive just about anything.

During the height of the Cold War, some school director had decided that being so close to the Greenbrier Resort was a BAD IDEA. The Greenbrier was where members of Congress would go in case of a nuclear attack. If missiles started flying, then it was supposed to be a place politicians could hole up and wait it out. Since the Soviets probably knew this as well, the old school director had figured it had some nukes aimed there. You know, to be thorough.

So how does one protect a school from nuclear fallout? By sinking two years' worth of the budget into building an elaborate underground bunker system across campus, and a separate one beneath the cafeteria, complete with air filtration system. This second one was what all of us girls called home now, since it was still too dangerous and nasty to clear out the dorm cottages around campus. Eventually we'd get there. Especially if Sister Ann decided we would open up the school for refugees . . . if any found their way to us, I mean.

Like a phoenix from the ashes, St. Dominic's was rising once more. Fueled by the iron will of a nun, some teenage spite, and lots of ammunition, maybe, yeah, we *could* rebuild. It was better than simply lying down and letting death come for you. At least, that was what I thought. Fortunately, Sister Ann shared my opinion.

Somewhere in the distance, another shambler gave out a keening howl. It was unsettling but didn't sound very close. I stopped and listened for a reply. None came. Just to be sure, I unslung Baby and waited. A few more minutes passed and still nothing. The shambler must have been a loner, not part of the more dangerous hunter packs that seemed to roam randomly throughout the Alleghany Highlands.

Nonetheless, I wasn't going to hang around and find out if I was wrong. We didn't survive this long by being stupid when it came to dealing with shamblers. I picked up the pace and fifteen minutes later was on the bridge that led up to the school.

Dunlap Creek was running high, though not quite enough to flood out the lower fields. The bridge sat high above the creek and was narrow, barely wide enough for two cars to pass each other on. And I mean *really* small cars. Looking at the concrete bridge, I wondered if there would be a time when we needed to block access. Or perhaps make it so narrow the only passage would be to walk through it. There were some cars up on the mountain that could work . . .

I shook my head. Figuring out Sister Margaret's advice would have to wait. I had a report to give.

I slung my rifle back over my left shoulder and walked on the right-hand side of the road. It might seem odd to note this, but it was the sign that I was returning alone and safe. If someone was forcing me to come up to the school or something, I'd walk on the left and have the rifle over my right shoulder. Simple, but effective. I just had to make very certain I remembered if I ever was coming up the main road—which I didn't do too often. This, along with the fact that it was actually quicker, was why I preferred the path by the railroad tracks on the north side of the school.

I could see one of the other girls watching me from the rooftop of the cafeteria. I rounded the main road past the ruined admin building, making sure to stay clear of the wrecked building just in case. We hadn't seen a shambler spend the night down there in months but once was enough. Not being careful back in August had cost us Tammy.

The spotter on the roof had a rifle but there was no way she would fire, even if I'd come up the road being chased by a horde of shamblers. None of the girls were willing to kill a shambler, which pissed me off to no end. However, she could give the alarm. This meant that while I would be screwed, the other girls could make it back into the safety of the bunker. I'd accepted this risk since I first volunteered to start scouting around campus, but it still sucked.

I really needed to find someone to back me up. Soon.

Sighing, I waved the all clear. There were days when it sank in just how alone I was up here. Today was one of those. Yeah, the girls lived in the bunker with me, but with the exception of the student council, nobody really wanted to deal with me. The nagging suspicion that even the others on the council detested me lingered constantly in the back of my mind.

For a moment I just . . . paused.

The quad was quiet and still. The athletic field, where we played soccer and field hockey before the Fall, was overgrown and filled with weeds. It was still green, though it'd started to turn a little brown as autumn really started sinking its teeth into the Blue Ridge Mountains. The abandoned cottage dorms of the elementary and junior high schoolers were to my left, and in rather rough shape. When the Fall had begun, many of the first-floor windows had been smashed by shamblers trying to get out or chase down anybody trapped inside. Since we weren't in a hurry to sleep anywhere but in the bunker, there wasn't a need to clear them yet. We hadn't seen a shambler anywhere near them in four weeks.

My eyes followed the curving pavement path beyond to the high school cottages. Both Groller Cottage—my former residence—and Bolgeo Cottage were in better shape than the younger girls' cottages.

They were also newer, which might have had something to do with it. Or not. Still, we'd cleared them to make sure shamblers weren't lurking in there and locked them up. Sister Ann told me we might have use for them later. I didn't know what for, but I'd learned to completely trust her judgment over the past six months.

The paved path actually made a full loop around the field. On the opposite side of the field was the gym. We'd only gone in there a few times, grabbing items off a list Sister Ann had given. We'd seen shamblers around it in the early days, but nothing recent. Still, caution was something Sister Ann preached on almost as much as the Bible. Anytime any of us went near it we were careful—especially since the hidden back trail came up behind it.

A cry overhead drew my gaze upward. There were a few ravens flying above, their wings catching thermals as they rode higher into the late afternoon sky. They were a pretty common sight and one of the other natural alarms we had for the school. Typically, if the ravens weren't flying above then there was a shambler somewhere close. They soared higher and higher, dipping and weaving as they jockeyed for position on the thermals. For a moment, I wanted nothing more than that sort of freedom. To just lift off and fly away at a moment's notice was . . . enticing.

Growing up used to be my life's ambition. To be an adult and not have to deal with people telling me what to do anymore was probably the biggest reason I started acting out in junior high school. My parents tried to tell me to slow down on a daily basis. But I knew best, of course. It was my life and I would live it how I wanted.

God, I want to go back in time and smack the hell out of fourteen-year-old me. That little girl had been one ignorant *bitch*.

The heavy door to the cafeteria squeaked open. Sister Ann's voice cut into my reverie. "Maddie? It's getting dark. Is everything okay?"

My moment of peace was over. It was time to get back to work.

"Coming, ma'am."

CHAPTER TWO

"Please . . . we need help. We're trapped in here! I can't believe it . . . Zombies? Real-life zombies? Help! Help us, please! They're everywhere!"

From: *Collected Radio Transmissions of the Fall,*
University of the South Press, 2053

After nightly Devotionals and the younger girls went to bed, the student council met in the bunker storeroom beneath the cafeteria. Counting Sister Ann, there were eight of us in total. We each had a separate job on the council, and we were pretty much the ruling body at the school. Well, Sister Ann was really in charge, but the council was an idea she had early on to help make decisions should anything happen to her, when we were first setting up our headquarters beneath the cafeteria.

There were two dozen concrete rooms leading off the storeroom that we'd turned into bunk rooms. The student council got their own rooms—thank God—and the others seemed more than happy to share. The storeroom was the best place for our meetings, since there were no outside windows. The entire underground bunker had been built this way, thanks to the aforementioned paranoid school director. It might not survive a direct hit from a nuke, but a zombie apocalypse? It made for a pretty good fortress.

See? I paid attention during history class.

Sort of.

Other buildings around campus had bunkers as well, but none

were as expansive or well-made as the one beneath the cafeteria. We could burn all the candles and lanterns we wanted and nobody from the outside would see. Plus, the back loading dock had been secured with a two-ton lift, effectively blocking the only unsecured way into the building. The lift also blocked the outside entrance to the apartments on the second floor, where some of the campus staff had once lived. Other than clearing one of them for shamblers back when we first set up in the cafeteria, though, none of us tried to live in them.

Sister Ann said it was too soon. The other girls didn't understand, but I did.

I think.

"Let's get tonight's meeting in order," Sister Ann said as Lucia Archuleta, my newest best friend, brought the shortwave radio into the room. It was mounted on a wheeled serving tray, an older one we'd found during our clearance of one of the bunker rooms, and it was more than sturdy enough to support the radio. Granted, it wasn't that big, but rolling it out had become a pre-meeting ceremony. A tradition, almost. Sister Ann was big on traditions. Routines were good for us, psychologically. At least, that's what Sister Ann said. "Lucia? On Monday you mentioned you needed to do a battery inventory. How are we?"

"Solid for another twelve months at least," Lucia reported as she pushed the cart carrying the radio until it was against the large dining room table. She clicked the wheel locks on so the cart wouldn't roll away. "Since we've cut back on listening to just twice a week, they might last longer. I was reading—"

"Liar," one of the other girls muttered. I was pretty sure it was Rohena, but it was hard to say.

"Please." Sister Ann calmly folded her hands on the table and looked down toward the other end. Rohena coughed and turned her face away, clearly embarrassed. The nun smiled sweetly. "Continue, Lucia."

"Yeah, anyways, I was reading about solar power and all that, and it said in one of those old instruction manuals these radios can run off solar." Lucia stopped and looked over at our resident engineer. Well, the one girl alive on campus who actually understood the basics of any mechanical crap. "Emily? If we find more solar panels—the small ones, I mean—can you hook it up so it's like, I don't know, permanent?"

Emily Mottesheard was a freaking genius, and one of the most reliable girls on the student council. I still don't know how or why her parents had sent her to St. Dominic's. The girl should have been at MIT or some place for smart kids, not stuck at a Catholic girls' reform school. She must have pulled some crazy stuff back home to get sent here.

"Well, uh, we *could* do that, yeah," Emily began, her tone low and slow as she thought it over. "The problem isn't wiring or anything. That's easy. We rigged the well pump up that way."

"*You* rigged it," I pointed out. "*We* just watched with a wooden broom on standby in case you electrocuted yourself."

"The problem is storage capacity," she continued, her tone a little more confident now. She only needed a gentle nudge sometimes. Like I said, she was reliable. "Car batteries might work, but I don't know how safe it would be to daisy-chain a bunch together to store the electricity the solar panels generate during the day. I mean, I could experiment, but if I fu—uh, screw it up, those batteries would be wasted."

"It's not as though we're driving anywhere, Em," Sister Ann reminded her.

"I *really* wish we still had the horses," Kayla Washington complained. She'd been at the school since the fourth grade and was well-acquainted with the animals. She also was our resident gardener, since she'd been working with the farm manager before the Fall on a part-time basis. Kayla knew more about farming and crops than the rest of us combined—and that included the two elementary school girls who were working with her. Coincidentally, she was the only girl whose hair was frizzier than mine. She had hers braided in tight cornrows. I wanted to copy her look, but since I was whiter than rice in snow and she was not, it would have looked weird on me. Kayla continued, "Yeah, they're expensive pets, but they're handy for something like this."

"Think any of the farms in the area have some?" I asked, curious. We'd been branching out and searching for supplies we could use at the school, but hadn't strayed more than a mile or two from campus. Lucia and I were the only two who went solo anywhere. Every other time we went on an expedition we had a group of at least four. It was safer in a group, usually. More eyes to watch out for shamblers.

"Maybe. But I'm not about to go farther up the road looking for any," Kayla replied. "Even the Moose Lodge is farther than I want to go."

"I could scout it," I offered. Kayla shrugged but didn't reply. I made a mental note to go a little farther out the next time I was headed north.

"So we'll put down the daisy-chain battery experiment as a 'maybe,'" Sister Ann said, guiding us back on task. She was good like that. "Lucia, start coming up with a plan to repurpose any car batteries we might have lying around campus."

"Lots of cars," Lucia agreed with a nod. "Shouldn't be too hard. I'll need some help gathering them up, and someplace to store them. If they leak, that's bad news. So it'll need to be someplace we don't go much."

I nodded. "Back storage area on the main level. By the lift? Out of the way and the flooring is that nonslip rubber stuff. Uhh... insulation, you said?"

"See? You do pay attention," Emily said, chuckling. "That sounds good. Unless the battery casing itself fails, it should be fine to run our little experiment."

"Excellent." Sister Ann nodded. "Kayla? Did we have any late bloomers in the garden?"

"No, sorry," Kayla answered as she shook her head. "I thought the string beans would do well but there's some sort of bug on them. Not like the corn, though. Ugh. Those weevils were in everything. I washed a few of the string beans off but there was nothing inside the pods. I think the bugs ate the beans from the inside."

"Not good, but not horrible," Sister Ann acknowledged. "We still have potatoes."

"Lots of potatoes." Kayla smiled at that. "We're not going to starve anytime soon, though we're going to get sick of potatoes eventually. We've got enough dried and old canned stuff to last us through the winter and well into next summer. Now that we figured out how to can vegetables, it might even last longer."

"Fantastic news. Maddie? Security situation."

"Well..." I paused, thinking it over before continuing. "I got to see a bear kill a shambler today. That was kind of cool."

"What?" Lucia stared at me in horror. The other girls looked just as shocked. I smiled and nodded.

"Oh yeah. It was pretty interesting, actually. Never seen a bear get angry like that. Usually they run away when we yell at them—the bears, I mean, not the shamblers. Oh, can bears turn into zombies? That would be bad, right?"

"Uh..."

"Probably not," Emily said, shrugging her delicate shoulders. Her eyes drifted over to Rohena before looking back at me. She smirked. "I think there was something on the radio about higher primates and the blood. I forget. But around here they're just oversized trash pandas. The bears, of course."

"Cute but dangerous, big chonky bois," I added, grinning. Emily knew what I was doing and was totally game. The girl was awesome. "The bears, I mean."

"Did he live? The bear, naturally."

"He got the better of it. It was bear-ly a fight at all. For the bear."

"Do you have to clarify whether you're talking about bears or shamblers every single time?" Rohena asked. She was clearly annoyed and glowered at the two of us. "Pretty sure we can figure it out."

"Well, since it bugs you, yeah, I kinda do," I replied and gave Rohena my sweetest smile. "I mean, is it unbearable yet?"

"Bitch."

"*Language.*" Sister Ann interrupted, her voice snapping like a whip. All arguments ceased and we looked at her. Despite her tone, she didn't look displeased. Merely... disappointed. Shame made me blush, which, considering how pale I am, made my ears and neck turn red.

"Sorry, ma'am," Rohena and I said simultaneously.

"Sorry for what?" she asked. *Oh man,* I thought. *She never lets me off easy.*

"I'm sorry for instigating Rohena," I replied. I tried to sound like I wasn't lying, but I'm pretty sure she knew I wasn't sorry at all.

"I'm sorry for picking on Rohena as well, Sister," Emily said. She actually sounded contrite, where I knew I sounded more grudging than anything.

"I'm sorry for swearing," Rohena added. She was sincere, but everyone around the table knew she'd pop off again at the drop of a hat, so it really didn't matter. Swearing was second nature to her. She was the main reason we picked up sign language in the first place—to swear at one another without getting into trouble.

It also helped when we wanted to communicate while outside and we didn't want to announce our presence in a world dominated by shamblers.

Sister Ann harrumphed. "Five Hail Marys each tonight before you go to bed. Since you three appear to be getting on each other's nerves—*again*, I'll add—you'll all also be performing a service of my choosing over the coming weeks. Rohena, you can help Emily with the battery experiment. Hopefully the energy expended carrying the batteries will remind you to watch your tongue. Emily, in your copious amount of free time, you will assist Kayla in the garden. Weeding is soothing for the soul and eases pettiness, as well as encourages you to take your time in doing any job correctly."

"And me, ma'am?" I asked, a little fearful. She normally didn't add on extra consequences like this.

"I want to speak with you privately after the meeting adjourns tonight."

"Oh, *snap*. You're dead, girl," Kayla stage-whispered. The other girls tittered, and even Sister Ann smiled. It was brief, but there. I inwardly sighed in relief. Whatever my consequences were going to be, they were designed more to teach than to punish. At least, that's what Sister Ann always told us.

"Yes, ma'am," I answered, nodding. There really wasn't anything more I could say. Sister Ann turned her attention elsewhere and I breathed a sigh of relief.

The twins, Finlay and Fiona, had nothing new to offer. Lessons were going fine, blah blah blah. They were part of the education track, helping Sister Ann teach the elementary and middle schoolers during the day in between chores. Stupidly smart girls, though they were only eleven. They were going to give Emily a run for her money as the smartest chick around one day. For now, though, they read *everything* we could find and learned how to lesson plan, then assisted Sister Ann with classroom lessons. And they remembered every single thing.

Rumor had it that the reason they were at the school was because they were suspected of being a little too fond of starting fires by the police in their hometown. No charges had been pressed, but their parents had sent their possible firebug twins as far away from home as they could. I wasn't about to hold it against them, though. We all had our little quirks. Plus, it'd inadvertently kept the twins alive when the world ended.

Once the meeting was adjourned, we turned on the shortwave and listened to the continuing adventures of Wolf Squadron.

It was another part of the routine—five o'clock, every Monday and Thursday. Initially, I'd been confused by the broadcast, but as more time went on, for us their weekly exploits turned into an ongoing soap opera drama. It was hard, though. Most of the time it was about the ships they'd come across, the number of dead they found on board, and if there were any survivors (which was rare) or infected still alive on the vessel who had to be cleared.

Grim stuff, but better than nothing.

After an hour, we shut it down. There'd been absolutely nothing on the shortwave from any form of government since four months before. Early on, there had been the occasional transmission from someone claiming to be in a secure location, but after a few broadcasts they typically went off the air. I was actually kind of happy they stopped. Secretly, I was worried someone would be broadcasting when the shamblers broke in and ate them. The younger girls would never recover from that.

Sister Ann knew this risk as well as I did. She had to. If she was concerned, though, she did a good job of hiding it. Instead of focusing on the negative, she constantly talked up the positives. The easiest one was that people were still alive. In spite of millions and millions of shamblers in the world, there were human beings still there, fighting. This helped give the younger girls some hope that one day, maybe, things would go back to normal.

All it offered me was depression.

The girls were clearing out for bed. We had enough old storage rooms in the bunker so everyone could have their own area, but most of them chose to room up with two or three others. I couldn't blame them. They still had nightmares. Rooming together lessened the nightmares.

I roomed alone. I don't dream. Not anymore, at least.

"Madison." Sister Ann's voice stopped me before I could head to my room. Exhaling slowly, I turned around. I had hoped she'd forgotten about me after the dismal broadcast, though I really should have known better. Sister Ann never forgot anything.

"Yes, ma'am?"

"How are you coping?"

Well, that was unexpected. "Uh . . . fine?"

"I speak fluent teenager, Maddie. How bad is it?"

"I'm okay, Sister. Honest."

She frowned but didn't challenge me on it. The truth of the matter was, I didn't know precisely how I was doing. I wasn't sitting in a corner quietly like some of the younger girls, but I also didn't associate much with the older ones. Lucia was probably the only girl I went out of my way to talk to, and that was because she was the one who gave me items to look for whenever I went out. So I really didn't have a really good feel for my state of mind.

"I know it's tough for you. You've shouldered the responsibilities of everyone's safety, and there's no way to properly express how grateful the other girls are."

"They have a weird way of showing it," I muttered. The younger girls were terrified of me. The older ones shunned me about as much as I shunned them. Well, Emily was okay, but the others? One of the middle schoolers had called me crazy last week. Unhinged, maybe. Crazy? I was a long way from that, I thought.

I hoped.

"They are still afraid, Maddie," Sister Ann said, lowering her voice and moving closer. Though she hardly ever wore her habit these days, even in a hoodie and jeans she remained imposing. I squirmed under her intense gaze. "They're not afraid of you, though. Constant, unending fear does things to the mind. Some are coping better than others. Seeing you go out, then returning and talking about how many shamblers you've seen? It terrifies them still. They look at you and wonder how you can do it. They transfer their own fears onto you. They're processing. Give them time."

"Time is a luxury we don't have anymore, ma'am," I reminded her. "I don't know how cold it's going to get this winter. Those woolly worm things you told me to look for? Lots of black, some red. That means bad, right?"

She shrugged her shoulders. "It was from a single research survey that nobody could replicate, but . . . maybe. But that's not where I'm going with this. We need to start thinking like those people clearing the boats at sea. Throughout history, the Church has been a light and beacon in the dark of the night. I want to start looking at ways to secure the area around campus. We've got our natural barriers, but what about elsewhere? What about those farther up the road? Are there any survivors?"

"I don't know," I admitted. I hadn't gone that far from campus yet. The desire to see random bodies of people who died in their homes was not high on my list of interesting things to do. "We're surviving here. We're safe. Isn't that enough?"

"It's not just about our survival, Maddie," Sister Ann said as she gently brushed a loose strand of hair out of my face. I looked away, embarrassed. She always managed to say the right thing whenever I was uncertain. "It's about thriving. Building. If we exist simply to survive, then we are not doing what we were put on this earth to do."

"So why am I here?" I asked, feeling a little belligerent. Once again, Sister Ann seemed to know precisely why I wanted us to stay hidden up here on the mountain. Meek, silent, unseen. Which meant no shamblers running around, and no outside threats like we heard about on the radio. She had me dead to rights, but I wasn't going to back down easily.

"You are here as a role model to the others, to show them that they do not need to be afraid of the monsters in the dark," Sister Ann said in a firm voice. She gave Baby a pointed look. "One way or the other, the girls know you're going to protect them. They might be a little afraid, and sometimes they don't show it or tell you how much they appreciate you, but at the end of the day you do not give them nightmares. You offer them hope."

Damn it. I was afraid of that.

"I don't want that responsibility."

"Whether you want it or not, Madison, you've taken on the role. You're a natural leader, and—"

"I'm not a leader," I interrupted her, shaking my head. "I don't like most of the girls. They don't like me. I don't *want* to be in charge. Why would I be in charge of people who don't like me?"

Sister Ann gave a soft chuckle. "That's called politics, Maddie. Every leader has opponents."

Oof. She had me there. "Okay, yeah, maybe. But still—"

"I want you to teach one of the younger girls how to shoot the shamblers." Sister Ann cut me off this time, her tone quiet and thoughtful. I stared at her, confused. Most of the young girls were really messed up still from the day I'd had to kill Becca in front of them. They wouldn't even come near me, for the most part. "Your penance for instigating the others. I watched how you guided Emily and encouraged her. Which, I will add, is something you all should be past by now. You need one another, even if it's difficult or tempting to make them miserable. We need a backup for you out in the field. My vows make the . . . handling of the shamblers problematic. But you need help. You can't do it alone, no matter how much you probably want to."

"Uh . . ." Did I want to be alone? I wasn't sure. The next question I had to ask myself was a simple one: did I enjoy killing the shamblers? If I was being honest? A little bit, yeah. No, that's a lie. More than a little. In my mind they stopped being humans the moment they turned. They wanted to eat me. In turn, I tried really hard not to let them.

Before I'd arrived at St. Dominic's, I had been a bit of a wild child. A lot of it was simply me rebelling against parents who never told me "no" when I was a kid. When they finally did start trying to punish me for things, I flipped out and ran away. A lot. During one of those times, I'd met a guy who was like me—I thought, at least. I opened up to him, trusted him.

That . . . would be best described as a mistake. Politely put, things went downhill from there.

Sometimes when I shoot shamblers I imagine his face. Makes me want to aim for their heads and wipe that smug look off of them. Shooting them was a lot easier when I stopped considering them humans and then gave them his face. Sister Ann would have chastised me for doing it. I didn't care. Call it therapeutic, whatever. Killing shamblers was just something I did now, with almost zero hesitation—unless a chonky bear comes along and does it for me. But I'd always assumed I'd be hunting and shooting shamblers alone, forever. Or until one of them got me before I could get them.

One good thing about the Fall? It was much easier to spot the monsters now.

Sister Ann continued, unaware of the dark memories rumbling around in my head. "I was thinking about which girl would be a good fit. It took some doing, but I think I found the right one. What are your thoughts on Ulla?"

"Ulla?" I stared at her. It felt like my brain had locked up as I tried to process her words. "*Really?* Ulla?"

"Yes. The other girls are having extra chores for their behavior. This is more of a teaching experience than anything else, Maddie." Sister Ann gave me a slight smile. "Ulla needs someone she can trust and bond with. You need someone willing to listen and who won't argue with you. I want you to start slowly and teach her how to shoot, how to move. Things you've picked up since the Fall. I'll work with both of you on precision shooting."

"Nuns with guns," I chuckled. Sister Ann might be unable and unwilling to shoot the shamblers, but she knew everything there was to know about the actual act. Apparently once you were a marine, you were always a marine. Or something, I don't know.

"So it's settled. You'll teach Ulla how to shoot, and this will perhaps teach you to not antagonize your peers."

"Fine," I agreed in a quiet tone. "I'll teach her. If she doesn't listen or starts to argue—" I stopped and chided my whining inner voice. Ulla hadn't spoken since her sister had her throat torn out by a shambler minutes before we'd made it to the safety of the cafeteria. The only thing the little girl *could* do these days was listen.

And, I had to admit, she was probably the one girl I would have picked to teach if it'd been left up to me. Shambler disposal was my job, but only because the other girls' reluctance had made it that way. The younger girl probably had a bone to pick with shamblers, once she got over her fear of them, and was a pretty good listener when given instructions. Which wasn't surprising. It wasn't like the girl was going to argue back when given a command. The young middle schooler was also fluent in sign language. Ulla . . . *might* be a good choice after all.

I snorted, amused. Of *course* Sister Ann was right. She always was. "Okay."

"Thank you, Maddie."

"Sure."

"Madison?"

"I'm sorry, ma'am. I mean, 'You're welcome.'"

She smiled. Every moment was a potential teaching one in her eyes. "Good night, Maddie."

CHAPTER THREE

"Copy, Dispatch. Unit 5-31 responding. Copy multiple reports of . . . zombies? Is this real? Dispatch, Unit 5-31. We don't have time for your jokes out here. It's a fucking madhouse!"
From: *Collected Radio Transmissions of the Fall,*
University of the South Press, 2053

There was a brief lull between when Sister Ann told me to teach Ulla and when I actually got around to it. A really bad storm swung through and dumped a ton of rain on the campus, which caused Dunlap Creek to rise almost high enough to wash out the bridge. I wouldn't have been too choked up if that'd happened, since it meant there was no way for someone to come up the campus road without crossing the creek beforehand. Unfortunately, after the rain stopped and the flooding went down, the bridge still stood.

The possibility of flash flooding in the mountains was always there, but not usually something we worried about too much on campus. St. Dominic's, after all, was at the top of a mountain. It would have to be rain of Biblical proportions to threaten us. Granted, some of the older buildings could flood—the basement of the school was one—but the mountain itself wasn't going anywhere.

Which was a good thing, too. It was a lot of rain.

Instead of traipsing around in the rain being wet and miserable, I began teaching Ulla from the comfort of the bunker everything Sister Ann had taught me about firearms safety: trigger discipline, making certain you keep the barrel pointed down and away, making certain the safety is on if you're not about to use it . . . Every little nugget of information Sister Ann had given me, I tried to pass on to her.

To her credit, Ulla was an ideal student. She soaked up information like a sponge. If she didn't understand something she'd ask me to explain more. Her favorite rifle was a bolt action that Mr. Stitmer, the retired accountant who'd become our Outdoor Activities Director before the Fall, had chambered in .270, which irritated Sister Ann even further for some reason. He had plenty of rounds for it in his safe, though there were way more 5.56. Ulla took to the weapon like a duck to water, and absolutely loved the recoil on it. Personally, it felt like a jackhammer was punching me in the shoulder, but Ulla actually had some meat on her and wasn't as affected.

Teaching her to shoot involved heading up to the roof and braving the rain, though. That part sucked. Rain in the Alleghanies was either hot and warm, like showering in mosquito-infested soup, or freezing cold. It depended on the time of the year. The plus side now? No mosquitoes or gnats.

I was glad her hearing was fine. There was no way I could have signed to her everything she needed to know.

Another problem that I should have spotted during my prep was shooting. In itself there were no problems. She wasn't shaky at all when firing from both prone and kneeling positions, and she was fairly steady while standing. The rifle wasn't too heavy so she managed it fairly well. No, the issue was in the act itself.

A gunshot is a loud noise. Rifle rounds are even louder due to traveling faster than the speed of sound. Noises like that tend to attract shamblers, which is something we were really trying not to do. Granted, if they did show up we'd simply lock up the bunker and try to plug them from the rooftop. It'd be great practice for Ulla, as well as letting us see if she could actually do the deed.

But dead shamblers meant cleanup. God, I hated cleanup. The fluids got everywhere and the smell never really went away.

So we went through the motions of shambler killing instead of doing the real thing for a few days. Dry fire, eject a casing, make certain to not let it fall in the leaves and get lost—not that there were many leaves up on the roof. Not yet, at least. The leaves were turning but hadn't started to fall. Sister Ann was strict about us taking care of spent brass. She constantly reminded me that we might find a reloading kit somewhere.

On the third day, Sister Ann joined us. I had Ulla show her everything she'd learned. Sister Ann tweaked a few minor things, mostly with Ulla's tendency to stick her right elbow out during shooting, but otherwise didn't correct much. The kid was a more gifted shooter than I was and seemed a natural fit for the rifle.

She was very pleased with Ulla's progress.

Once Ulla was "dialed in," as the former marine put it, we planned a brief outing. I'd never taken anyone this young out before, and I didn't want anything bad happening while I was teaching where the paths and trails were around campus. Good weather, no shamblers, and something simple for an objective, like teaching Ulla how to find a landmark. Sister Ann agreed, and we made plans.

For our first foray out, it was decided that we needed to go and check out the status of the Jackson River. I'd only been a few times since the Fall, and only seen it from a distance. Considering it was one of our first lines of defense against shamblers—as well as one of the biggest magnets for them—it made sense to keep an eye on it. It was also closer to Covington than I really wanted to go. However, since all the grocery stores and hardware shops were in town, eventually I was going to have to go take a look.

I had no plans for us to go alone, though. Some of the other girls would need to help me scavenge and loot—I mean, *acquire resources*—when we eventually got around to it. Experience was only achieved through action.

Sister Ann's words, not mine. But accurate.

Two days after the rains finally ended, I found myself walking along the banks of the Jackson River with Ulla and the twins, Finlay and Fiona. None of them were talking much. Ulla, because she hadn't uttered a word in six months. The twins because they were listening to me explain just why walking around the woods in our school outfits was a really stupid idea and needed to be fixed in a hurry.

"We need to clear out the admin center," I told them as we carefully picked our way along the small dirt trail of the river. The Jackson was running high again, thanks to all the rain. It'd been doing this almost nonstop since the Gathright Dam failed two months ago and flooded downtown Covington. The very edge of the river was almost up to the footpath we were on. Experience told me it would lessen a little in the coming days. In the meantime, though, we had to be aware of the mud. It was slick and, if you weren't paying attention, you could slide right into the river. "Parading around the forest in our school uniforms is just asking for trouble. At least we could have worn slacks or something, I don't know."

"Then why are we doing it now?" Finlay asked. While they were identical in almost every way, Fiona didn't have the small mole on her cheek that Finlay did. It was the only way anyone could tell them apart.

"Seems dumb," Fiona added. Ulla nodded and signed in agreement.

Though silent, Ulla had her own way of fluently communicating with the rest of us. A few of us older girls had picked up sign language as a way to swear at each other without any of the nuns yelling at us back before the Fall. It'd caught on and we'd learned all the bad words. Then the Fall happened and we had more important things to worry about. We really hadn't kept up with it after until we realized it was the only way Ulla would talk to anyone. Now we were all fairly decent at it, though not fluent—except Ulla, I mean. Most of us were getting there, though.

"It *is* dumb," I agreed and shifted Baby slightly. The tactical sling I'd snagged when I'd scavenged the rifle sometimes dug into my shoulder. It was designed for someone with muscles on their shoulders, not skin and bones like me. Still, it was better than carrying the heavy rifle in my hands all the time. "It stands out, and the shamblers would easily see us. Just another reason why we need to clear the admin building and get down to the donations room."

One of the cool things about St. Dominic's is that the local community—the entire Alleghany Highlands, really—had been hugely supportive of the school's mission, pre-Fall. They loved to donate used goods to the school, and a lot of that was clothing. Since we'd been required to be in uniform most of the time, the donated clothing was washed, folded, and placed away in storage bins. There had to be a ton of clothing in there. However, after Tammy had been killed by one of the shamblers—a rogue I'd somehow missed—after getting too near the admin building, nobody had wanted to help me clear it. Or even walk past it.

I'd only made two forays into the admin building before then, and never past the registration office. There hadn't been any signs of a shambler hiding out there at the time, but I didn't go into the basement. Instead, I'd snagged all of the campus walkie-talkies I could find and fit into the duffel bag I'd carried. I also grabbed pens and notebooks, though that was on the second trip. Sister Ann had tasked me and a few of the other girls with recording day-to-day stuff since the Fall. Kind of like a living historical diary, I guess. I updated mine every night, but I don't think the other girls did.

Something caught my eye. There was movement on the opposite side of the bank. I didn't have a good view of what it was just yet. Still, caution had kept us alive so far. Recklessness was not a part of Sister Ann's plan.

"Freeze," I hissed in a low voice. The girls were well-trained by now, having had this drill performed many times before whenever a shambler had wandered too close to the cafeteria. Nobody so much as twitched as I brought Baby up and ready. "Finlay, slowly look behind us. Is anyone behind us on the opposite bank?"

"No."

"Fiona, left? Anything?"

"Nobody."

Whatever I'd seen wasn't there anymore, but *some* type of movement had caught my eye. There wasn't a breeze and the birds were mostly silent, which suggested *something* was out there. I didn't know if it was a wild animal, a shambler, or even some regular old survivor—not that I'd seen a single human outside of the school since the Fall. My brain hadn't had a chance to identify it. Had I imagined it?

Unlikely. Paranoid, yes. Delusional? Not yet. I had a long way to go before I hit that point.

"On my count, we slowly walk back the way we came," I told the girls as I swept the far bank with Baby. Still nothing. Maybe I was seeing things after all? The birds were still quiet, though. The air was filled with a palpable sense of danger. We needed to leave. "One . . . two . . . three . . . okay, slowly."

The girls turned and slowly began walking along the path, back toward the school. I kept Baby up and carefully began to pace backward. I remembered the path had been clear during our trek in, so there wasn't anything like a branch or rock that could trip me until the bend, which would put us out of sight of the river. Still, I was walking blind. It was a risk, but one I was willing to make. If I fell on my ass, so be it.

I took another slow step back. Maybe we'd gotten lucky and it was only a wild animal, like a turkey or something. It was a possibility. We weren't that close to the Covington side of the river, and the Jackson was wider than it used to be. Even though we were in our uniforms, the only bright thing were our blouses—something we really should have stopped wearing a long time ago.

If it'd been a shambler, it must have missed us.

"Okay, I think we got lucky," I whispered to the girls. "Let's pick up the pace and get back to campus. Stay to the left, near the bushes. We might be—"

"*Hellooooo!*" a voice called from across the Jackson. I stiffened in shock. That was not the sound a shambler makes, but one that gets their attention. Only an idiot would call out in a loud voice in the middle of the zombie apocalypse. I *had* seen movement after all, only I'd been wrong about what it was. Grimacing, I half-turned and looked back. There was a burly man standing on the opposite bank, wearing full hunting gear. He had a rifle in his hand but he wasn't pointing it in our direction. Instead, he was waving at us like some idiot. "Hello! Girls! Are you okay? Y'all need help? I can come get ya!"

"*Scheisse*," I hissed through clenched teeth. "Hurry. Social security office first, then up the main road to the school."

"Why?" Fiona asked, clearly confused. Finlay smacked her arm.

"So he doesn't track us directly to the back way, dummy."

"Oh, that's a good point."

"The back way is still a secret," I reminded them in a low voice. It was unlikely the guy could hear us from across the river, but there was no reason to risk it. Ulla was signing something but I didn't have time to stop and translate. Instead, I ushered the girls along. I really wanted to get us out of there. "Hurry!"

"Hey! I just want to talk!" The shouting followed us as we quickly made our way back along the path and toward Dunlap Creek. The guy was definitely an idiot. Any shambler nearby could come looking for a snack. I kept Baby ready, just in case this happened.

There was the slim possibility the dude would try to swim the river and chase after us. Slim, but possible. Granted, he'd have better luck floating across in a boat or something than trying to swim across with all that gear he was wearing. The river was moving too fast for any old person to easily make it across. This was one of the reasons our shambler problem wasn't nearly so bad as it'd been during the early days of the Fall. As far as I could tell, shamblers couldn't swim. The shouts followed us around the bend.

"Hey! Wait a sec!"

That wasn't going to happen. There was no way I was about to acknowledge some random person calling out to us, especially when I was with three preteens. Not without talking to Sister Ann about it first, I mean.

It ended up taking us two hours to get back to campus. It wasn't the younger girls who slowed me down, no; the hike up the hill on the main road was steep. It was another reason why I preferred the back way into campus. With the high possibility of being followed, it was an easy decision to make. Even if it did suck.

Sweaty and miserable, it was almost dark when we finally made it up the mountain. The girls were on constant lookout for any shamblers while I kept an eye out for any sign of our mysterious man following us. I didn't see anything, but that didn't mean much. I was a city girl from Southern California. Locals from around here could probably walk through trees or something, I don't know. I was still finding Mr. Stitmer's deer blinds around the mountain nobody had ever known about.

Sister Ann called for an emergency meeting with the student council the moment I told her what we found. Since Ulla wasn't a council member, she would have normally been sent to the other room. However, Sister Ann didn't want her telling any of the younger girls anything before the council decided what to do, so she stayed and listened, sitting between the twins.

"Other survivors . . ." Kayla said breathlessly once I'd finished my report. She had a hopeful look on her dark face. "Like families . . . *our* families?"

Everyone started talking in loud, excited voices at the same time—except me. I remembered the news reports, and the images on the TV and internet before the Fall. There was no way any of our families survived. Well, almost zero chance. The possibility was always there, even if it was slim to none. The last images of New York City on fire before we lost power had been burned in my memory for all time.

Survivors in Los Angeles? Philadelphia? New York? Hell, even Kenosha? Wishful thinking.

But the others didn't seem to care. I could hear it in their voices as the volume in the room rose. Looking around, it took everything in me to not dash those hopes. I couldn't do that to them. As much as they sometimes annoyed me, they were my sisters here at the school. We'd survived so much. Telling them that their hope was a waste of time now, right after discovering other survivors nearby? There'd be no coming back from that.

Sister Ann must have been thinking the same thing I was because instead of shooting down the talk, she subtly shifted the subject.

"Maddie? You and . . . Lucia sneak back down to the river where you spotted the man," Sister Ann said. She was staring into the distance, thinking. We'd seen the look on her face many times before. "If he was alone, then we keep an eye out and see if he needs help."

I blinked, confused. "Sister . . . ?"

"It's our duty to help those in need," Sister Ann said firmly. "If he needs help, then we assist. If he doesn't, we leave him be. St. Dominic's has always been here to help those in need. These are dark days, Maddie. The Church has always been a beacon for the lost in the darkest of hours. A light in the darkness."

That's not what the brochure said, but there was no way I was going to argue with Sister Ann over this.

She did have a point, though. I still needed some backup. While the plan was to train Ulla up to where I was, we hadn't really gotten a chance to work on much just yet other than her shooting. Fiona and Finlay were two others who might one day be willing to shoot. For now, though, they seemed like they preferred more *extreme* methods of shambler removal.

One of them—Fiona, I think—mentioned something called Tannerite, and how effective it could be for removing shamblers permanently. I had no idea what it was and asked Sister Ann how to get some for the twins. She'd almost had a heart attack for some reason and mentioned talking to the duo, and for me to forget about the stuff.

However, I did teach them two of the most important lessons I'd learned from Sister Ann: keep your finger off the trigger unless you're ready to shoot, and never point the rifle at anything you don't plan on shooting.

Everything after that, as Sister Ann said, was fiddly bits.

"We have the housing to help out many families," she continued, her eyes back on me. "We have eight cottages sitting there. Has anybody been inside any of them?"

"Other than the two senior cottages? No, ma'am," I supplied. There'd been talk early on of clearing one of the younger residential cottages the elementary girls stayed in before the Fall, but after the mess outside the admin building with Tammy, Sister Ann had decided against it. Many of the cottages had broken windows and doors. While the likelihood of a shambler inside one was slim, it was still possible. The cafeteria had been prepped for the Fall. The cottages? Not so much.

"What about . . . you know . . . the bodies?" Emily asked, nervous. I fiddled with my hair and thought about it for a moment. I couldn't remember noticing any nasty smells coming from inside any of the abandoned cottages, but I honestly hadn't been paying attention to smells during the early days of the Fall.

"We'll handle it," Sister Ann answered quickly. "Their immortal souls are gone. Only the bodies remain. Even so, we'll treat them with the respect they deserve. We might not be able to bury them, but we can give them Rites before finding a place for them. And we *will* consecrate the ground as best we can."

Sister Ann was a better person than me. By far.

"Maddie? I need you and Lucia to go down to the river tomorrow—no, the day after." Sister Ann pursed her lips, her expression turning thoughtful. "If he wasn't alone, I'm willing to bet there's going to be a message for us."

"Message?" I asked, confused. She nodded.

"The Jackson's too wide to jump, and moving too fast to wade across. Plus, the bottom is very rocky and dangerous. Anyone trying to wade across could break an ankle."

"Still . . . they could try to cross," I pointed out.

"They could. But the man also probably saw Baby. If he has any sense, he's considering the odds of his survival against fording the river."

"The idiot was yelling for us to stop in the middle of the zombie apocalypse and standing there like an idiot."

"Fair point," Sister Ann acknowledged. "Still, my instincts are telling me that he's not alone. Nobody survived this long on pure luck, or while being immensely stupid. Two days, then go down to where you spotted him. Wear natural colors, not anything bright. No school uniforms this time. Stay hidden and keep your eyes open. Dollars to donuts there's going to be a message."

There was a message, all right. Sister Ann was scary like that.

We were up and moving before dawn, working our way down the back entrance to the school just as the darkness was changing to gray. It was a little more dangerous than broad daylight, but since shamblers saw about as well as regular people did, we felt reasonably secure. Still, I was armed, and even Lucia carried one of the hunting rifles we'd acquired from the deceased Mr. Stitmer. It was unloaded, but anyone we might run into didn't need to know this.

Instead of coming up to the site along the river, we cut down a game trail hidden behind a mimosa tree. Up in the branches was yet another deer stand—probably put there by Mr. Stitmer, but considering the school bordered on the George Washington National Forest, it could have been anyone. The ladder was gone, so I couldn't take advantage of the surprise find. I made a silent promise to fix this later and we pushed on in silence.

The brush grew thicker the closer to the river we got. Carefully moving through the thick foliage, we made sure to not step on any small branches or twigs that could make noise. This close to the river it was unlikely anyone would hear us, but we hadn't stayed alive so long by being careless.

After what felt like an eternity the river came into view. Crouching down, I surveyed the opposing bank. The sun was just starting to rise and the sky was already shifting from gray to orange. I could see clouds in the distance, but they looked like they were going to miss us to the south. Which was good. We'd gotten enough rain the past few weeks to make me wonder if we needed to build an ark.

Lucia tapped my arm twice to get my attention. She pointed at a weird-looking white square on the other side of the river, a little downstream from where we were. It was by the ruined bridge which had, once upon a time, been the only way up to the school.

It took me a few moments to realize it was a whiteboard. There was writing on it. It was small so I couldn't quite make out what it said. Lucia held out a pair of binoculars she'd found somewhere. My questioning look was answered with a shrug of her shoulders. Fine. She could have her secrets. I had plenty of my own.

It took a moment to adjust the binos. Once set, though, the words written on the whiteboard chilled me.

> To the survivors up at St. Dominic's,
> You are under the authority of King Dale the First, King of Appalachia and ruler of the Blue Ridge Mountains.
> Meet at the ruined bridge by the old motel at 3PM Friday to discuss your surrender.
> Do not resist.
> King Dale I
> King of the Blue Ridge

"What the...?" I hissed quietly. Was this guy serious? That idiot who'd been yelling at us thought he was king? He wanted to meet in three days and, apparently, fully expected us to surrender. Or maybe he only hoped we'd show our hand or do something stupid. Who knew?

Reading the sign again, I couldn't believe it. With shamblers running around and no word from the government in months, this maniac thought he could call himself king? It was hard not to laugh. We had the mountain, guns—well, okay, I was the only one willing to use them so far, but still—and the river between us. Only someone insane would pick the zombie apocalypse to try and say they were the King of the Blue Ridge Mountains. Or Blue Ridge? Was that a kingdom?

Still, there were ways to get to the campus that didn't involve crossing the Jackson. Most of them would take days to hike, but it was possible from this point. Maybe even without attracting the attention of every single shambler in a five-mile radius.

I shuddered at the thought. That could be bad.

This guy has an ego, Lucia signed. I nodded in agreement. Who in their right mind wanted to be king out here? The only thing this entire area offered—besides meth and teenage pregnancy—was the paper mill, and our school.

Time to go. First, though, I had to make sure there was nobody lingering around. The odds were pretty good this so-called King Dale would leave someone in a safe place to see who checked out the sign and how they reacted. They could possibly follow us back, to see if we would show them something if we were careless.

Sorry, Dale. No gnashing of the teeth or wailing today. The panicky girls didn't survive the Fall.

Still, we ended up taking the *looooong* way home, making sure we ducked inside the old abandoned ranger station at the base of our mountain to see if anyone was following us.

Just in case.

CHAPTER FOUR

"B.E.R.T. was a necessity for our continued survival, and every single participant was given a pardon—posthumous and otherwise—by the President of the United States on behalf of a grateful nation and world. To go back and argue they should face consequences, that this was inhumane, smacks of idiocy, Madame Senator. You lived through the period. You should know better. You should remember. Have you no shame, Madame? Have you no dignity? Using the sacrifices these individuals made in order to score political points, to attack all we've accomplished since? Life is not theater, Madame Senator. President of the Senate, ma'am, I'm not sure how they did this back in the day, but I make a motion to have the honorable senator from the state of Washington censured..."
—Minutes from the 124th Congress, March 10, 2056

That night's student council meeting went about as well as it could have.

Which is to say, not very. When I'm the voice of reason in a discussion, you know we're in trouble.

News had spread quickly about the sighting and a few of the elementary school girls were excited. They thought we were being rescued at long last. None of the high school girls wanted to break the news to them before we had a council meeting, so we didn't say anything other than there were people still alive on the other side of the river. The middle schoolers were a little more reserved at the idea.

The elementary girls, after seeing how the middle schoolers were reacting, changed their mind. That shut down the rescue talk real quick.

Of course, then Sister Ann had to explain what some of the other terms meant. There aren't enough words in the world to express just how grateful I was that it was her and not me. She was born to lead and teach.

Me? Not so much.

"Do we barricade?" Emily asked once the rest of the room settled down a little. She tucked her hair behind her ears and looked around, nervous. "*Can* we barricade the road? I mean, I could design one with the cars..."

"Can we destroy the bridge over the creek?" Lucia looked at Emily. She was trying to play it cool but I could see she was just as terrified as the younger girls. Unlike anyone else, she'd seen the sign. Granted, there hadn't been mounted heads or skulls scattered around it, but the neat, precise writing had unnerved her.

"Maybe? I don't know. It was built to handle flooding from Dunlap Creek, though, so not without a lot of explosives."

"We're not allowed to play with those anymore," Fiona said in a wistful tone. Finlay looked over at Sister Ann meaningfully but remained silent.

"Crap." Lucia crossed her arms and frowned. Secretly, I think she wanted to blow something up as badly as the twins did.

"I'll go and meet with them at the time they want," Sister Ann said in a soothing tone. She looked at the other girls gathered around the table. It was times like this I was glad there was a student council and nobody had decided to put me in charge. Still, Sister Ann's idea was pretty stupid, if anyone had bothered to ask me.

"That's a bad idea," I warned Sister Ann anyway. The other girls all nodded in agreement. For once they weren't looking at me funny. "What if they just start shooting at you?"

"Then I die, and the council is in charge of the school," Sister Ann replied calmly. She wasn't kidding, either. I had to hand it to her. A lot of people could talk the talk, but Sister Ann walked the walk. "But I don't think they're going to shoot. No, I think they want to negotiate. Next time you're out on patrol, don't wear the school's uniform. We'll get down into the donations closet. Then you can go through and find some donations with old hunter's pants or something. After it's cleared, I mean."

"I should have been doing that from the start," I berated myself. "Stupid."

"No, just shortsighted of me," Sister Ann corrected. "We didn't count on survivors coming around and making demands. I thought . . . It doesn't matter. I should have, though. I'll meet with him, and you'll be my visible second. Let them get an eyeful of Baby. Ulla will remain up at the school on overwatch in case a shambler shows up. We have three other girls nearby with rifles standing in partial cover behind some trees in case they start shooting at us—which, I will reiterate, is not going to happen."

"Why?"

"We're no good to them dead," Sister Ann said as her eyes drifted around the table. It took me a moment to get where she was going with that. When I arrived, it was not a pleasant image.

"Oh."

"So what I want you to do, Maddie, is get there just after sunrise on Friday," she continued after a moment. "Only you. Set up in that old hunter's blind you found and see if this so-called King Dale has anybody up there watching for us to arrive. They'll probably get there a few hours before the scheduled meet. Once I arrive, give it a few minutes before you come out and stand with me. Let them know we're always watching, always ready."

"That's why you want me getting there so far in advance," I murmured. "That's smart."

"Be prepared," she reminded me. "I have no idea how our meeting with the self-proclaimed *Appalachia Rex* is going to go."

Oh, I would be prepared, all right. We all would be.

The predawn morning of the meet was cooler than it had been in months. With the loss of power, heat and humidity quickly became things of the devil at St. Dominic's. In summer, the entire Alleghany Highlands felt like a swamp, but it was finally beginning to cool off. The only saving grace was that the bunkers were solid concrete, so it wasn't nearly as bad. Autumn up here was admittedly kind of nice. The winter promised to suck, though, if it was anything like the year before.

Right now, though, the weather was being agreeable. It was so nice the gnats weren't even out yet. Maybe the day would be a good one after all.

Perched in the hunter's blind high above the ground, I watched as the swollen Jackson River moved sluggishly along. It was still mud-colored from the rain and flooding. To be fair, the entire river had remained the same ugly brown since the dam failed and, from what Sister Ann had suggested, it would probably be a few years until it all settled down.

Sighing, I adjusted Baby's sling and looked out across the river. The damn thing was annoying me again. Either I was going to develop one amazing callus on my shoulder or replace the sling with another—if I could find one. Across the way I could see the mostly destroyed hotel and a few cars that hadn't been tossed away during the flood. The paper mill to my left was a burnt, ruined mess. There was a little bit of standing water in the streets. Surprisingly, there wasn't a single shambler to be seen. With all that water in the streets, I expected to see one or two. It made me wonder where they'd all gone.

I knew they were still out there. Sometimes late at night, when I couldn't sleep and slipped up to the top of the cafeteria, I'd sit with Rohena and we'd listen to their howls. From the valleys below our mountain we could hear their strange and haunting cries. It was a terrible, unearthly sound that echoed across the night sky, and sounded both far away and terrifyingly close.

I never spoke while up on the rooftop. There was no need. Rohena typically made up for my lack of conversation by chattering nonstop.

I leaned back against the tree and sighed. So far, our so-called King Dale was a no-show. Another hour passed by, then four, and six. Still no signs of a shambler—or any sign of someone coming in early to recon us. The possibility of someone beating me there was slim, but still there. Since we had zero information on him, we didn't even know from what direction he'd come from. Sister Ann suggested our intrepid new ruler was probably out of Clifton Forge, the next town over.

Still nobody. I grumbled silently and shifted the damned sling again. I'd expected some sort of scout to show up and check things out. "Disappointed" was a word I wouldn't quite use, but it was a close thing.

The day grew a little warmer. The sun was still trapped behind the low-lying clouds but I could faintly see it through them. A faint rainbow made a circle around where it should have been showing through. I took this as another positive sign. I could faintly smell honeysuckle in the air. Somewhere nearby, a cardinal started chirping incessantly. Then another answered. The river flowed on and I took another deep, calming breath.

For the first time in what felt like forever, a sense of peace enveloped me.

It ended ten minutes later when the so-called King of Appalachia rolled up in what looked like a freaking *tank*.

Okay, I knew it wasn't a tank. It just *looked* like one. I'd seen SWAT vehicles before back home in Cali, both in person and on the news. This was just like them, but kinda cooler. It rode higher off the ground, and even had a spot where someone could stand up on the top. Sister Ann later told me it was a turret mount. Whatever it was, it was pretty freaking cool. I clicked my walkie-talkie three times, like Sister Ann had told me to when King Dale arrived.

Amusing side note: I could have wiped him and his entire crew out when they climbed out of the large, armored vehicle before they'd even know I was there. He'd sent no advance scouts, nothing. It would have been a slaughter. Sister Ann gave me explicit instructions to simply observe until she arrived, so observe I did. Besides, while I had no problem shooting shamblers, I was less thrilled about the idea of shooting a real person. Well, mostly. If they did anything to hurt any of the girls, for example, then it would be game on.

Thanks to a slight bend in the road and a large pile of debris, the men had no idea what was about to hit them. About twenty minutes after they'd arrived, Sister Ann walked around the rubble with all of the student council—minus Emily, who'd remained back at campus with Ulla and the younger girls—flanking her, each girl armed and appearing ready for action. I knew otherwise, but the men across the river didn't. Plus, Sister Ann's arrival created a visible stir across the river.

She'd ditched the whole stole-and-penguin outfit when the Fall began in favor of something a little more economical and sensible.

Jeans, T-shirt, and comfortable hiking boots made up her normal everyday wear. Now, however, she'd donned her full habit and even wore her veil, which was rare indeed. Only during Mass did any of the school's nuns wear the stiff headpieces that hid their hair. It was psychological warfare, she'd told me the night before. It was meant to send a message.

The so-called King of Appalachia stood on the far banks of the Jackson River, surrounded by his men. The river wasn't too wide here but it was definitely deep. Thanks to the dam failing a few months back, it was also nearly impassible. The three bridges that ran over it had all been destroyed when the massive wall of water had demolished just about everything in its path. Hooray for natural disasters.

Or would this one be considered man-made? I always forget the difference. Either way, it was handy.

We'd thought it was a bad thing at first because all the large stores were on the other side of the river, but it turned out to be a blessing in disguise. Not only did the zombies get swept downriver when they tried to cross, it had also managed to stop anyone else from coming to us. Other than a small community of houses near the top of the hill by the school and the Moose Lodge, our little valley and mountaintop were empty.

This was the first time I'd really gotten to get a good look at the guy Sister Ann had dubbed "Appalachia Rex." Thanks to the school's graduation requirement of knowing Latin, I understood what it meant. It was the same as what the King of Appalachia called himself, but since we were dealing with hillbillies he'd probably think Sister Ann was insulting him.

King Dale didn't look like a normal hick, though. At least, he didn't dress like one. He was tall, well-built, and actually wore what appeared to be a new sports coat with really nice jeans. Great shoes, too. I didn't think anyone from around here had that fashion sense. He also sported a giant blond beard, but since they weren't really making razors anymore I cut him some slack. I mean, I hadn't shaved my legs in months.

The girls following Sister Ann must have been a very weird sight to the men. Armed girls on a river with a nun, all in full uniforms. I know what men think whenever they see a Catholic schoolgirl. We'd heard enough during trips into town before the Fall. Or maybe the fact we were better armed than his group made us even more appealing, I don't know for certain. What I did understand, thanks to Sister Ann's "briefing" beforehand (it's what she called it), was this was the beginning of a negotiation process. The so-called king believed he was dealing from a position of power.

"Let him think this," Sister Ann had told me before I started the long hike down. Despite the early hour she had already been up and preparing for the day. Sometimes I wondered if she ever slept. "If he thinks he's in control, he'll underestimate us. If they get there early, we'll have a good measure of the man, and how those who might follow him train. And, more importantly, how dedicated they are."

Sister Ann was, and will always remain, a marine trapped in a nun's habit.

After introductions were made, the negotiations did not start smoothly.

"Why do you keep calling me Rex, woman?" he shouted at her. I'd climbed down from the blind during this, which caused more than a few of them to swear and point. They knew I could have shot every single one of them, and it terrified the men. King Dale didn't seem too impressed, though. The men around him were armed but he wasn't. Nobody was pointing their weapons at us, either, and all of them seemed to be showing good trigger discipline from what I could see. Fortunately. "My name is King Dale, and I am the ruler of Appalachia!"

"Nice to meet you, Dale," Sister Ann replied back as she raised her megaphone. The megaphone had been in the gym, and it even had working batteries still. She'd known precisely where to find it. "You stay on your side of the river now, you hear?"

"With all due respect, ma'am, y'all are in my domain, and I have right to rule," Dale yelled back. "We're gonna cross that river, and y'all need to respect that!"

"And we reserve the right to refuse, since we still live in the United States, my son," Sister Ann replied in a polite tone. It was well amplified by the megaphone. I kept an eye out for any signs of a shambler, but the coast appeared cleared. Vaguely I noticed a few of his men were keeping an eye out as well. So they weren't complete idiots. Good to know. The man we'd spotted initially earlier in the week was with King Dale, standing just to his left. I pegged him as either a bodyguard or someone high up in his chain of command. I'd make certain to let Sister Ann know once we were back up on campus. The microphone squealed. The nun gave it a solid smack before continuing. "Since we're not a confederate state in some medieval German principality, you cannot be a king in a republic guided by a legal constitution. Now please go home and leave us alone."

Dale was flustered. I was just confused. Sister Ann was really smart and sometimes pulled out historical references that had even left the monsignor of our school dazed. Her ability to defuse a situation by simply being the biggest nerd in the room was why the girls in her cottage were always on their best behavior. I couldn't even remember when the last real fight broke out in there. She had a way of just keeping the peace with only a look.

"You don't understand what I'm saying here, Sister!" Dale shouted.

"No, I understand you perfectly," Sister Ann replied. The megaphone squealed again from feedback and she smacked it a second time. It would behave, or it would learn. "You think that because nobody's heard from the government in a year means you get to go and form a new government however you like. This great nation of ours does not work this way, Dale. Have you heard the news? The group known as Wolf Squadron is clearing boats at sea right now. There are reports of people being saved. We have a chance to do what is right. We still have a functional Constitution. This is still the Commonwealth of Virginia. You think our government is going to be okay with some tin-pot dictator less than four hours from our nation's capitol?"

"Bullshit!" he practically screamed. "The government died the day they released this poison onto the world! It's the government's fault everyone is dead!"

"Language, young man." Sister Ann frowned. I was a little confused. I didn't understand what he meant when he said the government released the flu. Though it was a long six months ago, that wasn't how I remembered it all going down. I specifically remember the words "Pacific Flu" being thrown around, and even rumors that it had been released by some random nutjob.

"Sorry for cussin'!" Dale looked down and kicked a stone into the swollen waters of the Jackson River. It left a few ripples that rapidly disappeared. His men milled around, looking at the girls. They didn't appear too comfortable. Either they had been hit by more shamblers than we had and were nervous, or they really didn't want to be here. "Sister, I have the canned goods, supplies, a tank, weapons, and manpower! What have you got?"

"Apparently the correct side of the river," she called back. Her tone remained merry. "And that is not a tank, young man, but the BearCat G3 SWAT armored vehicle you clearly stole from the Alleghany County Sheriff's Department, a highly customized one based off the Lenco BearCat model. It's supposed to be used for medical evacuations in a live-fire engagement area. BearCat, young man. Learn your equipment and do better research."

"Fine! My BearCat!"

"The sheriff's, actually. Not yours. Sir . . . go back to your home. Take care of one another. Leave us alone. Please. Our school is in the Commonwealth of Virginia still, which is a part of the United States of America and under the guidance of the Constitution. It will not, nor never will be, part of your so-called kingdom. Nothing you say will change that, Appalachia Rex."

"God damn it, quit calling me that!"

"Young man!" Sister Ann's voice was stern this time. Even I winced, because you knew you were in deep shit when Sister Ann used that tone. I heard one of the girls nearby—Kayla, I think—suck in her breath sharply and hiss "Oooh shit, he done fucked up now" to another.

Sister Ann continued, and boy was she hot. "You will not take the Lord's name in vain! He did not die for your sins to have you run His name through mud and filth in such a foul and disrespectful manner! This will be the last time I warn you. Do you understand me?"

The self-proclaimed King of Appalachia nodded, albeit reluctantly. This did not appease Sister Ann, however. We all knew it wouldn't, but it was pretty funny to see someone else suffer for a change. I would have been laughing my ass off except I knew better. The last thing I wanted now was for her basilisk gaze to turn on me.

"No, I can't hear you," she told him. "What do you say?"

"I promise!" he shouted.

"You promise what?"

Oh man, she is not letting him off easy, I thought and watched him struggle for words. Sister Ann never punished us, no. She gave us consequences that, in turn, were supposed to teach us. What we privately called it, though, was different.

King Dale was getting a lesson today. One all of us up on the hill had learned from day one: do *not* piss off a nun.

"I promise to not take the Lord's name in vain again!"

"Very good." She smiled, tone sweet and angelic once more. "Have a good afternoon, Appalachia Rex."

"Confound it, woman!"

Well, at least he was watching his language finally. St. Dominic's existed for a reason and had a pretty good track record, all things considered. One thing the school was noted for was instilling proper manners while still operating as a school. St. Dominic's didn't just teach us how to be independent women, but ladies as well.

Well-armed and self-sufficient ladies, that is. Nowhere in the Bible did it say meek meant unarmed.

She clicked off the megaphone and lowered it from her face. Turning away from the river, Sister Ann motioned for me to come closer. Once I was near, she started to speak in a low voice.

"They're going to find a way across that river eventually," Sister Ann said, eyeing the heavily modified AR-15 in my hands. She sighed and crossed herself before continuing, "Probably within a week or two. I wouldn't ask you to take a human life, Madison, but if it comes down to it, we can't let those vile creatures on the campus. We have young girls to protect and I can only imagine what he thinks he's going to find if he makes it onto campus. Even if he means well, there might be men in his group who have ulterior motives involving high school girls in uniforms."

"I have no problem with shooting that type of guy, Sister Ann," I told her. "I was the one who shot Sister Margaret when she turned into a shambler, remember?"

"I didn't forget, Maddie." Sister Ann offered me a reassuring smile. "But there is a cost to the soul when taking a life. I'm not sure if there's one for shooting the shamblers, but humans? Definitely a dark stain."

"No offense, Sister, but I'll let God judge me when I go to heaven,"

I told her, trying to sound casual about it all. Her words, though, were making me feel a little twitchy. I hated feeling like that. She had the uncanny ability to shift things around in my head. "The school's given me the ability to protect others in a way nobody ever protected me. I intend to use it."

Sister Ann rested a hand on my shoulder. Despite the dark green coat I could still feel the warmth and concern in the gesture. She bowed her head.

"Just . . . don't come to enjoy it," she told me. "It's addictive and becomes easier if you let it. I saw it many times in the past, in both Iraq and Afghanistan. You start seeing your fellow humans as nothing more than targets, and you lose a large part of yourself when that happens."

"Shamblers are one thing, Sister," I admitted, feeling slightly embarrassed. Once again Sister Ann saw through my mask and pointed out what I was truly feeling. I *had* been looking forward to hurting the men across the river. They probably wanted to do horrible things to the girls who were closer to me than my own family. I'd heard stories from other survivors via the shortwave radio. They alluded to a lot of abuse suffered before they were rescued. I wasn't about to let that happen, not to anyone at the school. It didn't matter if they were my worst enemy. They had a soul, and everything I'd learned while at St. Dominic's told me the soul was most precious indeed—including my own. "I know it'll be rough, ma'am. I'll be aiming at their legs to start with, if that helps ease the conscience a little."

"God always was a little fuzzy about kneecaps, wasn't He?" she asked, her expression bemused.

CHAPTER FIVE

Reminder to all university staff: the Violence in the Workplace annual training will be taking place next week. Please make sure to check your assigned days and times. If you're bringing your personal weapon to training, please arrive 30 minutes early to have it checked by instructors. Research staff, please remember to bring any PPE you wear for the additional required Violence in the Laboratory training session held afterward.

—Memo from the University of the South's
Human Resource and Training Department, 2049

There was something oddly satisfying about watching someone put a round through the head of a shambler on her very first try.

While King Dale was figuring out how to cross a river, I was busy teaching my young protégé how to shoot shamblers. Like Sister Ann had predicted, the girl was a natural. All of the training we'd done to this point was on the line. Could the eleven-year-old shoot and kill something that had once been a living, sentient being? Shooting targets were one thing. A man—one naked, covered in sores, and frothing at the mouth notwithstanding—was far different from a piece of paper.

"Breathe out, relax," I'd murmured in Ulla's ear moments before she took the shot. "That's not a person anymore. That's a thing that wants to eat us. It's not a real person, just a monster. We shoot monsters. You understand? Good. Now inhale—don't tighten your shoulders, okay?—and start your second slow exhale. In the middle somewhere, when you're starting to relax, just gently squeeze the trigger and—"

The sharp report of the rifle almost caught me off guard. The shambler dropped like a sack of potatoes. It twitched once and lay still. The .270 round, unlike the 5.56 fired out of Baby, accomplished the job with only a single shot. The birds in the forest around the clearing went silent as the gunshot echoed loudly. I carefully hid my smile and waited to see if the young girl remembered our lessons.

Ulla did not disappoint. She popped out the hearing protection and scanned our surroundings, keeping a careful eye out for any stray shamblers that might have been drawn to the rifle fire. We waited for two more minutes but there was no keening wail of a hunting shambler looking for its next meal. Not seeing any, Ulla carefully pulled the bolt action back, ejecting the spent shell. I snagged the hot shell in midair and juggled it between my hands, blowing on it. Yeah, it was pretty stupid, but I didn't want it dropping to the ground below and getting lost in all the dry leaves. Causing a fire because we weren't paying attention? No thanks. If we survived the subsequent forest fire, Sister Ann would kill us.

"Okay, so that was the only one we've seen so far this week," I told her. "What does that mean?"

Ulla shrugged and carefully set her rifle down. She began to slowly sign: *No more shamblers?*

I wish, I didn't say. No need to crush the girl's spirits just as she was starting to come out of her shell. The last sign was one we'd been forced to make up, since it took too long to spell it out and neither of the sign language books had the word *zombie* in it. Making a walking motion with two fingers, then curling it to a ball as it fell to the open palm is pretty self-explanatory, if you ask me. Signing was still the only way she would communicate. Which was a shame. She'd been a little chatterbox before her sister Celin had been killed.

On the positive side, my signing was improving by the day.

Since King Dale wasn't making a move toward the campus just yet, Sister Ann had declared it was perfectly fine for me to continue working with Ulla. I wasn't a pro, not by any stretch of the word, but I could help her with the basics. I was in dire need of someone else who was willing to shoot them when one wandered too close to the campus. Fortunately for my sanity, Ulla seemed perfectly happy shooting them. Or at least fine with it. Either way, it meant less work for me.

She nudged my ribs with an elbow and repeated her question. *It means no more shamblers. Right?*

"No more that we can see," I corrected her gently. "Remember there's those other kinds that like to hide. They usually run from the others but sometimes...you know how a cornered animal is dangerous? Just because they try to hide doesn't make them any less dangerous. You understand?"

Ulla nodded at this. Silent she might be, but the girl wasn't stupid. Not by a long shot. Another reason why she was the perfect choice to learn the nasty business of shambler eradication.

Sister Ann always seemed to be right.

"Okay, looks clear," I told her after another few minutes of relative quiet. The birds were singing again and the sun was just starting to dip behind the Blue Ridge Mountains. Sunset was about half an hour away, maybe less. With clouds spotting the horizon, it promised to be a beautiful one. I sighed. Back before the Fall had occurred, sunset was my favorite time of the day on the mountain. Sometimes, when the last rays of sunlight hit the trees just right, it made the entire mountain appear to be on fire. It was fleeting, but beautiful.

I shook off the memories. We didn't have time to dwell on beautiful things anymore. There was too much to do, and not enough time to do it in. The world had ended and here I was, wasting time. We needed to scoot. I didn't want to be in these woods after dark. Not because I was afraid of shamblers, no. Well, maybe a little concerned about them. I was more concerned with the growing number of bears I'd seen in recent weeks. They seemed to be growing bolder and angrier since the world had pretty much ended. Probably because shamblers attacked them on sight, and I was willing to bet bears held a grudge. *Humans are the dominant species, my ass*, I thought. "Let's get back up to the school."

Ulla nodded again and carefully slung the bolt action rifle we'd taken from Mr. Stitmer's gun safe across her chest. It was a little big for her, but she would grow into it. Plus, there was no way I was giving up Baby. Double-checking the strap to make sure it was secure, the skinny little blonde began to shimmy her way out of the hunter's blind to the ground below. I waited for her to get about halfway before I followed down the metal ladder.

Once down, I noticed Ulla was scanning our surroundings. *Good girl*, I thought. There were only three other trees nearby, but none of them were large enough to hide a person behind. This particular deer blind was out in the middle of a field near but not visible from the main road that ran past the Moose Lodge. I'd seen more shamblers down here than anywhere else—except for the day when all hell broke loose up on campus. For some reason the shamblers preferred the overgrown field near the Moose Lodge. I wasn't about to complain. As long as they stayed away from campus, I couldn't complain too much.

Thank God Mr. Stitmer had been an avid hunter with plenty of disposable income. The man had had one *hell* of a hunting addiction that we were benefiting from.

It was a bit of a hike back to school. If we took the main road, we could be there in less than thirty minutes. However, the main road was still dangerous, since it was also the easiest path through the mountain and out toward West Virginia. Since Covington was the largest town in almost all directions for at least forty miles, it made sense the shamblers would head for it.

For safety's sake, we followed the old railroad tracks that ran beside the creek to the back of the campus to the secret entrance. There was a narrow hiking trail up the sheer cliff face that was impossible to see until you stepped on it. Eventually the creek joined the Jackson River, which was just another reason for us to keep that entrance a secret. No need to give the self-proclaimed King of Appalachia another direction to come at us.

Assuming he ever figured out how to cross the Jackson, at least.

I would say that King Dale was quickly becoming the boogeyman, except for the fact there were still shamblers wandering around the wilderness and in Covington proper. Many of the girls were whispering about the nightmares they were having. Not me. Not because King Dale didn't bother me, but because I'd stopped having nightmares after I blew off Sister Margaret's head with a shotgun when she'd turned.

Ulla and I made great time thanks to the railroad tracks. It was easy to get lost in the woods behind the school if you didn't know where you were going. The tracks were washed out as well, but that was farther down the line where it used to cross the Jackson River and continue on into the town of Clifton Forge. I'd triple-checked them, just in case, because I didn't know if anyone would be able to cross there. One *could*, theoretically, but it was really dangerous. If I absolutely had to cross the river, I'd pick somewhere else to do it at.

Are you going to tell Sister Ann I didn't catch the empty cartridge? Ulla signed after waving her hand to get my attention. I shook my head.

"That's why we're a team," I replied as we left the tracks and began hiking up the narrow path. I'm pretty sure it was older than most of the buildings at the school and had once been a main path for the school. Nobody had ever tried to widen it to allow cars, even though it was the only route onto the campus that wasn't ever in danger of flooding.

Ulla smiled a little at my comment. It wasn't much but it was better than the emotionless robot who'd been following me around the past few weeks. She was coming out of her shell.

Thanks, Maddie, she signed. I gave her arm a quick squeeze.

"Anytime, kid."

When I'd first arrived at St. Dominic's, I'd hated all the other girls. Not that I liked them much better after the Fall, though. They were all so full of themselves, big-city girls in small-town Virginia. They acted like they were better than everyone else in town. Okay, once upon a time I had the same attitude. I mean, come on. I was from Cali. Orange County, to be more precise. My parents had annual passes to Disneyland *and* Knott's Berry Farm. This was rural—and when I mean rural, I mean "I hear banjo music, paddle faster" rural—Virginia. The land of DNA tests before you date anybody just to see if you were related.

I wish I were kidding.

The area eventually grew on me, though, like Sister Ann promised it would. Especially after Sister Ann took some of us new girls on a hard-core camping trip up to the top of our mountain. Suffice to say that, after the camping trip in the mountains with just Sister Ann, me, and three other girls, I came to a better appreciation of both the area and the school. It took a while but eventually I bought fully into what the school was trying to teach. More importantly, I started to *believe* I could do better. There was something more to life than simply coasting along.

As Sister Margaret had said: try your best, rise above the rest.

I really missed that old bird sometimes.

We saw two spotters up on top of the cafeteria and waved. They waved back and disappeared from view. Experience told me they were younger girls who were coming down to see just how well our shambler hunt had gone. The most recently dispatched shambler had been wandering around, clearly confused by the lack of food in the area. However, with Dunlap Creek being one of the cleanest creeks around, there was plenty of water to be had. Which was all that they seemed to need. Though we hadn't spotted a nest, it was clear that the shambler had started to settle in. Eventually it would have found the campus's main entrance and wandered up the road in search of a midmorning snack.

That would have been bad, so the decision was made to take it down before it could make it that far.

The two girls came out from the side entrance of the cafeteria. I recognized them immediately. On watch today were Lea and Melinda. They were clearly glad to see us back. Neither of the girls were armed with more than a radio but I knew from experience that someone else was watching their back from up on the rooftop. Probably Kayla, though Emily had recently started standing watch with one of the rifles we'd found. Considering the number of responsibilities Emily had around the school, though, I knew her watch-standing days would be few and far between. Still, she tried to help, so I would be forever grateful to our little wannabe engineer. Well, I also enjoyed showers, and since Emily was the one responsible for our well having electricity to draw water up out of...

Best. Person. Ever.

Even if the water was cold. It was clean. That was all that mattered to me.

"What's new?" I asked the two as we paused at the converted tennis courts. The raised planters within looked pretty dead, except for the last of the pumpkins. Kayla had been overjoyed when she found the seed packet and planted them. We hadn't expected anything but they'd grown. Though they were still on the small side, Kayla said that we could harvest them in a few more weeks when they'd be ripe.

"Rohena's sick," Melinda stated without preamble, brushing her long, raven-colored hair from her face. She was one of our Philadelphia girls who'd never get to go back home. Apparently, Philly had descended into anarchy and burned *before* the lights went out. Hooray for the City of Brotherly Love.

My hand tightened on the grip of Baby. *Not this crap again*, I thought. I wasn't particularly looking forward to shooting another turned student. "*Sick*-sick, or just sick?"

"Fever." Lea looked afraid. But then, Lea always looked like she was perpetually terrified of something. Shamblers? Terrified. Scraped knee? Frightened. Early dinner? Scared. I think it was just her natural default expression. Me? I've been told I have an excellent RBF. "Sister Ann thinks that it's some sort of spider-bite infection or something. There's a big red spot on her ankle."

Okay, so I wasn't going to have to shoot another one of the girls. To be fair, I didn't exactly *like* Rohena, but still . . . cleanup sucked. And it gave the younger girls nightmares. "Did she want to see me?"

"Yeah, she told us to tell you to go see her when you got back from bagging that shambler," Melinda said, nodding. "Did you get it?"

"Did you?" Lea asked as well.

"Ulla got him," I responded, jerking a thumb at my young protégé. Ulla blushed and looked away, embarrassed. "One shot. Right through the head. *Bam*. Beautiful. Shambler brains everywhere. I couldn't have done any better."

Instead of being impressed, though, the two girls exchanged wary glances. I realized just then I'd royally screwed up. Shame filled me, as well as embarrassment. Ulla, the girl who everyone already thought was weird because she stopped talking, was now like me in their eyes. A killer. Someone to be shunned and avoided. I knew the younger girls were afraid of me, and now? They'd fear Ulla the same way.

I glanced over at Ulla. There was a look on her face that suggested she might have realized what I'd just done as well. However, the flinty stare she gave the other two made me think she was tougher than I'd initially thought. Or maybe she just didn't give a crap about their opinions. Not just physically tough, but emotionally as well. Sure, she signed instead of talking, but Ulla still communicated with us. That had to count for something.

Right?

"Don't worry about them," I told her once we were out of earshot and continuing along the path to the dining hall. The two middle schoolers would call it a night before too long and join us. We wouldn't be undefended, though. The nice thing about living on a mountain in the middle of nowhere is that the dark is a natural defense as much as the creek and river were. So far as we knew, King Dale's crew didn't have any sort of night vision devices on them. Granted, we also hadn't known about the BearCat thing, but who figured he'd steal a police vehicle? Flashlights we would spot from a long distance, and we always had at least one person on duty throughout the night. Usually Rohena, since she was a night owl anyway.

If she had an infection and was sick, though... that meant someone else would have to stay up. I already knew who that would be. The only question was, who would Sister Ann foist on me for the night?

Stuck-up bitches, Ulla signed with a glance back toward the two girls on watch. I tittered and adjusted Baby on its oversized sling.

"Who taught you that word?" I asked, sling situated for the time being. Ulla stared ahead for a long while before she carefully replied in sign.

Snitches get stitches.

I cracked up. Ulla smiled. A cautious smile, sure, but it was progress. Sometimes, laughter was the best medicine of all.

Once Ulla cleaned her rifle and left it secured on the rifle rack in my room, she found her way to the common area in the bunker. A few of the other girls her age were quietly reading in the candlelight before bed. The bunker was naturally dark, thanks to the lack of windows, but with the candles it was bright enough to read. The twins, Finlay and Fiona, were both studying a chemistry book together and whispering. Part of me wanted to see what they were cooking up, while the other part wanted to run away in fear. I'm not ashamed to admit that the twins frightened me a little.

Ulla joined them and I wandered into the smaller room where the student council usually met. Since it wasn't our normal night, most of the council members were probably in their rooms. Lucia, however, was sitting at the head of the table, her feet propped up. She blinked and looked at me as she hid something under the table.

I looked at her suspiciously. "Whatcha got there?"

"*Nada*," she replied. She tried not to have a guilty look on her face. Fortunately, I was getting pretty good at reading facial expressions.

"Really, now."

"Okay, fine . . . promise not to tell Sister Ann?"

"I'm not gonna promise crap until you tell me what it is."

Lucia sighed and brought her hand up. She was holding a can of ginger ale. "So if I share this with you, is it considered cannibalism?" she asked as she took a sip from the can, her eyes locked on mine. "Or is this one of those ginger exceptions you get, like when you steal the souls of boyfriends who wronged you to add to your freckle collection?"

I was sensitive about my freckles, but not that sensitive. "Gimme."

Lucia smirked and passed it over. I took a long pull and nearly choked. The ginger ale was flat and tasted funny, but it had sugar. Oh my God did it have sugar. My head started buzzing immediately. I passed it back and emphatically smacked my lips at her. *"Ahhhh."*

"Nasty *puta*," she grumbled as she finished the rest of the ginger ale in one swallow.

"Hey, language," I said, looking around. Sister Ann wasn't in earshot but the nun had a scary tendency to simply *know* when we'd used foul language. She tolerated the signing, though, since it helped Ulla with her language skills. It's why we usually signed out our swear words. Ignorance was bliss.

"She's in the back," Lucia told me as she seemingly read my mind. "I found a whole shelf of those canned chickens upstairs in one of the staff apartments, and some of these. Grabbed a few cans for myself. Never was a fan of ginger ale but . . ."

"Wait, hold up," I stopped her. "You went in an apartment?"

Sister Ann had told me not to clear those yet, since we didn't know if anyone had died in them. The only thing we did know is that none of them had any shamblers in them. If they did, we'd have heard it by now. Sister Ann had instructed all of us to stay out of them, saying it wasn't the proper time yet. Too soon, I think, were her exact words.

"Just the end one. Ms. Whitney's room."

Oh, that one was probably safe then. Ms. Whitney, the middle school government and ethics teacher—don't laugh, St. Dominic's still took its education seriously, even if half the girls had bad reading scores before coming up the mountain—had been one of the first to die of the Pacific Flu at the hospital. She'd lived on campus but had no family. None of the sisters had gotten around to packing up her small studio apartment, since the flu then ripped through campus and started turning random people into shamblers. In hindsight, it was one of the apartments we should have cleared early on and would make an excellent place to live—once we were certain no shamblers could get up the stairs, at least. The apartment was next to a fire escape, which theoretically meant a shambler could climb in.

Maybe.

"What's up with Rohena?" I asked, changing the subject. The idea of going through a dead woman's stuff gave me mixed feelings. Then again, I hadn't even hesitated for a minute when we cracked open Mr. Stitmer's gun safe, so there was no need for me to be a hypocrite and say anything to her.

"Spider bite, looks like," Lucia said, frowning as she tossed the empty can into the trash. Sister Ann was very strict about keeping the living areas clean, even after the end of the world. "Might be a black widow. No idea."

"Damn," I whispered.

"*Language,*" Sister Ann said from right behind me. I didn't jump, though. After three years of this I'd grown accustomed to her simply appearing out of nowhere. However, instead of scolding me further, she moved around and wrapped an arm around Lucia's shoulders. She pulled her close. "I really didn't want those apartments rifled through yet, Lucia."

Somehow she knew. There was no way she could have heard us beforehand. Sister Ann was *terrifying* like that.

"There's no shamblers in there, ma'am," the slim Latina stated. Sister Ann shook her head slowly.

"I'm not worried about you finding shamblers in any of them," the nun corrected gently. "Some of the support staff who lived in those apartments had families. Tell me: did either one of you see the Yox family at all on the day of the Fall?"

I frowned, thinking back. It'd been pretty chaotic, and since I'd been forced to kill my best friend—and some nuns—my memory of that rainy spring day was a little blurry. However, I couldn't remember any member of the Yox family around the campus during those frantic few hours.

"I'm worried about the families you might find in those rooms," Sister Ann continued as a creeping realization came over me. "I'm worried what you might find will be something you can never forget."

"I watched Miss Badas—uh, Maddie brain our valedictorian with a freaking field hockey stick," Lucia stated boldly. I didn't say anything. Lucia didn't get it, not yet. I think I understood what Sister Ann was trying to say. "I'm not worried about seeing dead people."

"Dead people, no. We've unfortunately seen plenty of that since these trials of faith began," Sister Ann said, her tone soft. "But seeing a desiccated child corpse, not even five years old, who's never going to get to see the sun again, nor play out in the field, or celebrate his sixth birthday? Little Jacob was adorable and all the girls loved babysitting him. You watched him a few times, too, didn't you? How are you going to handle finding his body, dried out—or worse, rotted, damaged? Eaten? Can you remove him and bury him if this happens?"

Lucia opened her mouth, then shut it quickly. I could see her thinking long and hard about it. After a full minute her shoulders trembled. Tears formed in her eyes. She covered her face with her hands and shook her head. "No. I couldn't," she whispered.

"Nor should you have to," Sister Ann said, not unkindly. "I know it's difficult sometimes, and my methods don't always make sense, but there are still some things I can protect you from. That's one of them."

Always teaching. Once upon a time I'd looked up to my parents as role models. That changed when I grew up. As I got older and more rebellious, I'd stopped looking up to any adult as a positive role model. Until I met Sister Ann, at least.

"How did Ulla do today?" she asked, changing the subject. The point to Lucia had been made. There was no need to press the issue any further. Not now, at least. "Did she listen to you?"

"Yes, ma'am," I replied automatically. "No problem whatsoever."

"Did she take the shot?"

I nodded. "No issues."

"And after?"

"Uh . . . we walked back?"

"I meant, how did she react after shooting the shambler?" Sister Ann clarified for me.

"Oh. Uh, fine, I guess," I answered, shrugging. Ulla had actually done pretty well, all things considered. No tears, no shaking or anything like that. In fact, she'd done better than I had. "She's a tough kid."

"The odds are, it's going to affect her later," Sister Ann warned. "Be there for her."

"Of course."

"Meanwhile, we have a bigger problem on hand." Sister Ann ran an open palm across her face. "Rohena's spider bite is looking infected. I don't have any antibiotics here. I don't even know what type to get her, or what. I never wanted to ask either of you this, and I doubt you'll find any, but . . . I need you to go through the admin building and see if there is any penicillin in the nurse's office. Or any meds. Both of you."

Startled, I shared a look with Lucia. The admin building was still considered a no-go zone, especially after Tammy. Besides which, other than the reception area, we hadn't really gone deep inside. There were too many unknowns inside, with a dozen rooms and a basement that had probably flooded since the Fall—as it did every time it rained. Water and dark places usually meant shamblers. The two-story building was not something I was looking forward to exploring, and even Sister Ann had said to stay out of it.

Until now.

"Sister . . ." Pausing, I looked cautiously at Lucia. She had a frightened look on her face. It wasn't an unreasonable response, either. I'd killed shamblers before, and more than a few in front of her. How would she react if it all went to crap while inside and it was just the two of us? Would she panic and freeze up? Would she bail and leave me there, alone?

"I'm good," Lucia said. She must have read the look on my face perfectly. The girl was, like the rest of us, different from when she first arrived on campus. "We need those meds, right?"

"If they're even down there," Sister Ann reminded her. "I don't know. I know there was an inventory of what we had in there, but Sister Mary Theresa had it, and . . . we need to double-check."

"Too bad we don't have a nurse up here or something," I said. "Or a doctor."

"I pray every day we find someone who fits our needs," Sister Ann replied. I knew she meant it, too. One of the other girls once told me that the nuns at St. Dominic's used to pray for four to five hours a day. At that rate they could cover every person in Alleghany County in their prayers.

The nuns probably had prayed for them all, without hesitation. They were good like that.

"When do you want us to go?" I asked.

"Immediately," Sister Ann said. "Rohena is burning up and it's getting dark. Ibuprofen only goes so far. I need aspirin and, if we have any left down there, penicillin."

"I'll take a bag," Lucia said.

"I've got three spare mags for Baby," I added. "Should I take more?"

"Three should be enough. We're going to secure the bunker until you return," Sister Ann stated as she looked at the two of us. The concern was evident upon her face. Beneath it, I recognized her determination. As much as I enjoyed annoying the crap out of Rohena, I didn't want to see her get sicker. Or die. If there were meds down there in the admin building, we'd find them. "Please hurry, but be thorough. Meet me in your room in five minutes. And Maddie? Make certain you both use the restroom before you leave. Trust me."

The admin building was less than two hundred yards from the cafeteria, but felt like two hundred miles. With daylight fading, we had to hurry. The lower level of the building, according to Sister Ann, was very dark at night when there was no power. Any shamblers hiding there would be impossible to see until they were right on top of us—or if we were very, very lucky.

Considering how things had worked out in the past, I wasn't putting much faith in my luck quotient.

There was just a little bit of light remaining when we reached the front entrance. It looked like we had maybe another fifteen minutes, tops. Lucia had a backpack slung over her shoulder and a flashlight.

I had Baby, three spare magazines, and nothing else. The plan was for her to load up any meds we found while I provided site security. Quick and easy, get in, get out. Sister Ann had been adamant about that part.

Because we were in a hurry, we screwed up right out the gate. It was my fault. With the amount of experience I had killing the damned things, I should have known better. Or at least, remembered the stupid door.

"Quick, clean," I reminded Lucia in a low voice as we carefully walked up the concrete steps to the door. Though warm out, it wasn't nearly as hot as it'd been before the storm hit.

"Got it."

"If we find shamblers, stay calm. I'll shoot them."

"Yeah."

"Seriously. Try not to panic if something happens."

"I know."

She was clearly terrified. I couldn't blame her. It was starting to get to me as well. Normally by now we were locking down the cafeteria. Being out this late, when it was rapidly growing darker by the minute, was unnerving. Plus, we both had plenty of bad memories of this place after the Fall. Though we hadn't really gotten along, Tammy had been Lucia's friend. The shambler that had gotten her had come out of nowhere just as she stepped on the porch of the building.

I shoved the image away. We needed to focus. With a deep breath and silent prayer, I pushed on the partially open door and we slipped inside.

The interior was darker than outside. Though there were plenty of windows in the office area, they all faced east, so none of the setting sun helped light it up. Lucia gently closed the door quietly behind us. As it did, though, a bell jangled merrily from above. My eyes widened in surprise as she jerked her arm back. The ringing echoed throughout the old building.

"What the hell?"

"Crap." I'd completely forgotten about the bell attached to the doorframe. The last time I'd snuck in here I hadn't bothered closing the door.

A low, guttural moan responded to the bell from somewhere in the darkness. Lucia spun around, trying to locate the source. The flashlight seemed to light up random spots, creating a terrifying and surreal scene. For some reason a Latin phrase popped into my head.

Exultant lusibus clava immortui—the nightclub of shamblers. Or something like that. Latin was a weird language and my brain always got a little manic when terrifying things occurred around me.

Lucia somehow managed not to blind me when she turned back around a third time. She looked about as scared as I felt, and I was rarely afraid when fighting shamblers. A second moan responded to the first, which turned into the all-too familiar keening howl of a shambler on the hunt. Swallowing, I had Baby up and ready before I could blink. Neither of us could see them yet but they sounded close.

Real close.

"There! Shamblers!" Lucia screamed, shifting her flashlight toward the opposite side of the receptionist's desk. I pivoted, just as Sister Ann taught me, and raised Baby up as I identified the targets. Two shamblers were staggering out from behind the reception desk, their movements sluggish. I didn't recognize either of the emaciated figures immediately. It didn't matter.

I squeezed off three shots, centering the green dot on the lead shambler's chest. Each round impacted solidly and the shambler fell to the ground, moaning but struggling forward. The damned thing was determined. The other was getting closer. Shifting slightly, I fired off four more shots and the second one dropped as well. This one died immediately. The first continued to crawl across the floor, leaving a long, bloody smear on the tile. It continued to gasp and growl as it crawled closer, desperately trying to get to us.

"Stay back," I warned, my ears still ringing from the gunfire. As much as I'd wanted to put on my hearing protection, I knew that I'd want to hear any shamblers that might be hiding in the building. Keeping out of arm's reach, I carefully aimed and fired another shot into the top of the wounded-but-alive shambler's head. It finally stopped moving.

My heart hammered in my chest. I was breathing heavily and starting to sweat. I wiped my nose on my sleeve. That was the closest a shambler had gotten to me since Tammy had died. There was a reason I tried to find deer stands up in trees to shoot them from.

"What if there are more?" Lucia asked fearfully as my eyes drifted around the office area. Monsignor Dietrich's office door was open, and it was dark inside. The odds of another shambler hearing the gunfire and *not* coming to check it out were low, but not impossible. We needed to be in and out, quick, but watch our backs at the same time. Being trapped inside the admin building with shamblers popping out behind us was a recipe for dying messily.

"Just stick close to my back and keep an eye out for me," I told her as my heart rate began to slow down. I tried to ignore the quaver in my voice. Maybe Lucia hadn't noticed it. Once I had my breathing under control, we slowly walked toward the darkened office. Aiming Baby carefully, I entered and saw it was still neat and orderly, just how I remembered it being from my first few days during my intake process. Just to be thorough, I checked behind his desk as well. No signs of any shambler nest. Apparently the duo had been happy camping out behind the secretary's desk in the front office. Breathing a small sigh of relief, I checked the drawers for any extra bottles of aspirin or anything like it. There was a bottle of Benadryl but nothing else useful. Snagging it, I tossed it to Lucia, who caught it and quickly stashed the plastic bottle in her bag.

"What else is up here?" she asked. I tried to recall Sister Ann's directions for the first floor before answering.

"There's a bathroom down by the stairwell and a conference room. Nurse's office is downstairs."

"I know *that*," she hissed. "Do we need to check the other rooms up here before we go downstairs?"

"Yeah." For a quiet moment I lamented Monsignor Dietrich's death. He'd been a really nice guy and had been fair in the decision-making process. Plus, he'd decided to take a chance on the girl everyone back home had called "Mad Maddie." Though I doubted he could have seen this outcome, he must have seen *something* in me nobody else had. Not even me.

Poor old guy. *Requiescat in pace, Padre.*

"*Shit.*"

"Language," I murmured automatically, my eyes drifting up to the crucifix mounted on the wall behind the monsignor's desk. I could hear Sister Ann's voice in my head gently correcting Lucia. The woman was insidious like that. "Room's clear. Let's go."

After exiting the office, I closed the door to protect it from any potential future shamblers. It would make it easier to secure later if—

no, *when* we would come back. We carefully avoided the two dead shamblers I'd shot as we continued down the hall. They were dead but still bleeding, and the tile flooring was bound to be slick when wet. Idly, I wondered if I should find one of those yellow "Caution: Wet Floor" signs to prop up.

Fortunately for us, it didn't look like either the bathroom or conference room had been opened during the Fall and there might not be any rude surprises inside waiting for us. Still, we had to be careful. Shamblers had a nasty tendency to survive what would kill regular people.

With the hall secure and no sign of any other shambler responding to the sound of gunfire, we slowly moved toward the rear of the building and the stairwell. Since I was the one who was armed and more than willing to shoot a shambler in the face, I led the way. Honestly, I was just glad Lucia hadn't run away yet.

We hit the bathroom first. Thankfully, it was clear. I treated it the same as the office. It had one of those self-closing mechanisms on it so it couldn't stay open. Which was probably why it was clean and empty. Curious, I checked the water pressure. It was still good, which was odd. I hadn't known the well pump was connected to the admin building as well. I made a note to talk to Emily about it. If we were wasting electricity keeping the well pumping to all the buildings, maybe she could rewire everything so the hot water heater worked again.

Or did it run on gas? *Damn it.* I knew I should have paid more attention to Emily's talk on the stuff.

The conference room door was closed, too. Pushing it open slowly, I peeked inside. It smelled bad. Like, really bad. Someone had died in here, though not too recently. Keeping Baby at the ready, I slipped into the room and checked the near corner first. It was the only part of the room I couldn't see when opening the door. Sister Ann had told me that if I was ever clearing a room by myself, check the blind corner first. Lucia came in right behind me.

A naked, partially rotted corpse was propped up against the wall. Nearby, clothes had clearly been ripped off and piled up on the floor. Judging by the uniform on the ground it had once been a student at St. Dominic's, like me. Apparently she'd been in the conference room for some reason when she'd been turned into a shambler and hadn't been able to get out. I didn't recognize her, though. Not that I made much effort. It was pretty nasty. My main concern was that she didn't get up and try to eat us.

"Skylar," Lucia whispered, her eyes on the body. So much for that mystery. The brunette had been in my history class. Not in the same cottage, though. I knew her, but only in passing. She hadn't been into field hockey.

"Nobody else," I replied, checking under the large meeting table. It was clear. Skylar had been the only person trapped inside. Thank God. I didn't want to deal with any more bodies at the moment. I checked the conference door. It was covered in scratches. Deep gouges ran up and down the solid wooden door. Shambler-Skylar had tried real hard to get out. The sight was a sad one, but I'd grown used to these things over the past six months. Seeing things like this caused my heart to harden. It took a lot to rattle me these days. "Clear."

"No meds. Let's get out of here."

"No. We need to go downstairs, remember? Nurse's office."

"*Shit,*" she swore.

I didn't correct her language this time. We backed out and headed to the stairs. The lower level was a bit isolated from the rest of the building, thanks to the heavy cinder block and concrete structure. Sound was muffled and distorted, so the possibility of a shambler not hearing the gunshots were there. When they'd built this place way back in ancient times, the intention clearly had been for it to stick around longer than the builders. Plus, some mad genius had probably considered making it a bunker like the cafeteria before changing their mind.

How this building passed inspection by the fire marshal was beyond me. It had been a death trap *before* the Fall.

It was almost pitch black in the stairwell. Lucia shined her light down and we waited for a minute for a shambler to show up. To emphasize the point, I tapped the butt of Baby against the guardrail. The loud pinging sound echoed down into the lower level. Still nothing. We waited another full minute before I was convinced. If there was a shambler down there, it wasn't one of the fast, energetic ones. I motioned for Lucia to stay on my left before we started our descent.

Going down the stairs and keeping Baby ready was a small problem. Lucia kept jerking the light up and down with every step, not keeping it level anywhere. The random laminated signs on the walls—a notice about worker's compensation, FML something, and a large one talking about federal labor laws—kept reflecting Lucia's flashlight back into our eyes. I finally had to stop and wait for the purple blobs to fade away before we kept going.

"Sorry," she hissed.

"Keep it low, waist level," I told her. "If something moves, tilt the light up at its face."

"You think . . . you think there's a shambler down here?"

"Probably not. One would have come running already."

"But—"

"Hey, we're good," I tried to reassure her. "Let's grab any meds and get out of here." *And keep that damn light out of my eyes*, I didn't say.

The layout to the lower level was simple. There was a single long hallway that ran beneath the length of the building with rooms on both sides. The right side of the hall had two offices and a storage room, though Sister Ann hadn't been too certain *what* was stored in it. The other side had the nurse's office, two more offices, and the donations closet. I'd only been down here once before, when I'd gotten sick during the early days of the Pacific Flu and recovered quickly.

Lucky me.

The nurse's office door was partially shut, but there was one of those rectangular windows built into it, so I peeked inside. A small slit window near the ceiling allowed in fading daylight, so it wasn't as dark as the stairwell. It stank in here as well. There was a small cot, a desk, and a chair all next to a floor-to-ceiling cabinet, which looked locked. I couldn't see what was on the shelves but there definitely was something in the med cabinet. No signs of any shamblers, though there was another door in the room.

Thinking back, I vaguely remembered puking my guts out in a bathroom when I had the flu, and that I'd crawled from the cot to do it. The mysterious door probably led to it. Still, it was worth checking out after. I sniffed to confirm. The smell down here was just as bad as it'd been in the conference room. Could stink seep through concrete? Something to ask Sister Ann about.

Lucia wiggled the light to get my attention before shining it down the hall. We still had seven other rooms to clear, and time was of the essence. Neither one of us wanted to be down here when it got fully dark.

Three of the office doors were locked. I tapped on each one with a knuckle and listened, but there was no answering noise. Either it was empty or a shambler trapped inside had long since died. Since we didn't have keys there was no point in forcing the issue. It quickly became routine. Approach a door, test the handle. Locked, I would knock twice and listen. No response, move on.

The storage room was unlocked and chock full of goodies. There were bottles of bleach, ammonia, toilet cleaner, detergent, and other supplies we could use. Paper towels were stacked high on shelves, the top almost reaching the ceiling. I didn't know what we would do with it all at the moment, but eventually when we cleared and cleaned the cottages, the supplies would definitely come in handy.

The clothing closet/donations room was also unlocked and stuffed to the gills with clothes and personal supplies, like tampons and pads. I nearly squealed in delight. There were camo jackets and shirts neatly folded up in a pile, and multiple pairs of almost-new hiking boots laid out on another rack. It was like Christmas come early for me.

"Since we cleared it, you think we get first dibs?" Lucia asked.

"We better," I muttered, eyeballing a pair of hunting pants that looked like my size. They had pockets *everywhere*. There were also a pair of hiking boots that intrigued me. I did not know hunting camo and pink could work, yet here we were. "Maybe I can finally quit parading around like a dirty old man's wet dream."

"That's nasty."

"Yeah, well . . . not like anyone had a size zero pair of jeans just laying around."

"A zero . . . ? Bitch."

"I love you, too."

The final office wasn't locked, but it appeared as empty as the others. We checked the desk and the cabinet, but both were locked tightly up. Unlike Monsignor Dietrich, the sisters who'd worked down here with the admin people had followed the strict drug protocols they had here on campus and kept everything locked up either in their private rooms or the med cabinet in the nurse's office. Which was both smart and inconvenient. One day, though, we were going to have to clear the convent rooms behind the school.

I was dreading that day.

"You smell that?" Lucia asked, wrinkling her nose in disgust. I sniffed and shrugged.

"Might be another body down here somewhere," I murmured and closed the door. The admin building might be worth using in the future, once the shamblers stopped coming up to campus. The cleanup upstairs would be a pain, but no worse than some of the younger dorms were going to be. Easier, in fact. Other than the mess I'd caused in the reception area upstairs and the partially rotted body in the conference room, the building was remarkably clean.

Working our way back down the hall, I pushed open the nurse's office door. Earlier I noticed that the stench in here was pretty bad. Now that I was inside, it was arguably even worse than the conference room. The smell was an all-too familiar one. It was the smell of death and rot. Looking around, there was no sign of any other bodies. Whatever had died nearby had the decency to do it out of sight. Hopefully it was a possum or something in the air-conditioning vents.

The nurse's office was abandoned. Lucia flashed her light around and it reflected off shelves mounted on the old brick wall. The shelves—locked tight behind thick glass—were stocked full of goodies. I didn't know if any of them could help Rohena, but at least we found medicines. This trip had been extremely fruitful.

"There's a shit ton of meds down here!" Lucia exclaimed excitedly as she shined the flashlight around at the shelves. "I don't even know what half this stuff is! Oh, aspirin! Hey...I think I found it! Amoxicillin! That's like penicillin, right?"

"I guess? Hurry up. I want to get out of here," I told her as I kept an ear out for any other shamblers. So far, so good. Other than the two on the main floor, we appeared to be in the clear. Though the horrid smell was worse in here than the hall. Surprising, that. Though there was a steady buzzing sound nearby that tickled the edges of my memory. I looked around the nurse's office as Lucia began opening the drawers, looking for the keys. It was pretty much how I remembered it, except for the small puddle of water coming in from beneath the partially closed door to the bathroom.

"Where'd Sister Ann say the keys were kept?" Lucia asked me. I sighed dramatically.

"Right-hand middle drawer," I reminded her, my eyes on the door. There was a background noise coming from somewhere nearby. Also like an electrical buzzing, the same that the fluorescent lights used to make. It bugged me. Every instinct I had was screaming at me to run, to get out of there. My hand tightened on Baby's grip. There was an indescribable evil here. Thoughts of rehabbing the admin building for future use had gone out the window. I just wanted to get the hell out of there. "Hanging from the hook on the left. Pink tape on the key."

She began digging in the drawer. "How do you remember this stuff?"

"Because I paid attention." *And I had Sister Ann remind me again while you were in the bathroom*, I didn't say as I looked her way.

"Fou—"

"Sssh!" I hissed at her, holding up a hand. Lucia froze, the medicine cabinet keys in hand. Had I heard something? My eyes drifted back to the bathroom. The buzzing sound remained steady and constant. Had the noise come from in there? What was making the noise? The odds of a shambler hiding in there were slim, but not none. I brought Baby up and slowly crept to the partially closed door. My heart hammered heavily in my chest. The horrid stench grew worse. I knew what I was going to find, but at the same time I hoped I wouldn't. With the barrel of Baby, I pushed the door the rest of the way open.

On the tile floor in a large puddle of water lay the emaciated, half-eaten corpse of a child. Lying in the water, it had partially rotted, though the top half appeared to have mummified slightly. There was a swarm of flies near the feet. The stench was overpowering, and made me gag.

The impromptu inspection continued. It grew more horrifying with each passing moment. The child's short blond hair was partially ripped off, like something had been in the process of eating him before being interrupted. Lucia gasped and covered her mouth as she recognized the boy. I did, too. One mystery of that fateful spring day was solved. Little Jacob had hidden in the nurse's office, hoping that the scary monsters wouldn't find him.

They had.

"This is what Sister Ann was worried we'd find in the rooms," I whispered and gently closed the door. The buzzing sound ceased. Lucia was crying. It was hard for me not to as well.

One day we'd come back and give little Jacob a proper burial, but not today. We needed to focus on saving the living.

"Get the meds," I managed to choke out. My eyes burned and my throat felt dry, as if I hadn't had a drink of water in years. We needed to flee, burn the place down, and never come back. *Ever.* Fuck clearing the building. It should be burned to the ground. "All of them. Hurry."

Lucia nodded, her cheeks wet from tears, and unlocked the cabinet. She began dumping all of the meds into the bag, not even paying attention to what they were. Let Sister Ann figure it out. I didn't want to spend another minute in there. Neither did Lucia. We had what we came for.

Whispering a silent prayer for little Jacob, we headed back upstairs. Fortunately for the shamblers, none lingered where I could shoot them in their faces.

CHAPTER SIX

"This guy is nuts. He's, like, claiming to be the King of Miami and the ruler of the Kingdom of Florcubatamp, whatever the hell that is! He's absolutely crazy! Where's the military? How could they let this happen? How?"

From: *Collected Radio Transmissions of the Fall,* University of the South Press, 2053

The best way to forget something as traumatizing as finding little Jacob's remains was to focus on other things. Fortunately for me, we had plenty going on around our little mountain of fire.

As it turned out, Sister Anne had been a little too generous about the ingenuity of King Dale and his crew. It took them a full month before they figured out that the river was too deep and they would have to build a bridge to cross it. With autumn steadily dipping toward winter, their time was running out. They lost two men and almost a third before they figured out that the water was also too cold to swim across.

We celebrated Thanksgiving quietly. No turkey this year. While there were turkeys literally *everywhere* in the Alleghany Highlands, shooting the damn things was difficult. Camouflage really didn't work with them, and they would see you long before you saw them. Plus, they were pretty much invisible until they decided to move. This is why turkey farms were such a big deal, pre-Fall.

It was hard to find things to be thankful for. Spam and potatoes? No chocolate? Ugh. Still, Sister Ann did her best, and a lot of the younger girls were simply happy to be alive. For them, I pretended to be in a good mood, to show them that Maddie the Shambler Slayer wasn't someone to be afraid of. Lots of smiling and even a few hugs. I even read to the younger girls one night before bed.

Sister Ann said it worked, and they were starting to be a little more comfortable around me. I had my doubts.

With Rohena slowly on the mend thanks to the old penicillin we found in the admin building, and Ulla now on guard duty up on campus, I could keep an eye on King Dale's bridge-building progress. Or what could be called progress, at least. Apparently none of his men knew anything about how to construct a bridge. To be fair, though, I think the only person left in the county who *did* have any idea was Emily.

King Dale's makeshift construction project was slow going. First, they tried to simply throw some downed trees on the ruined bridge near where he and his crew first spotted us. That failed because, according to what Emily said after I reported in, it didn't have a strong enough anchor point on both sides of the river. They tried getting fancy and found some old steel plates to put on top of it for stability, but the weight caused it to sink to the bottom of the river. Eventually, the logs floated back to the surface, sans plates, and were washed away downstream.

In the end, they simply lashed a bunch of logs together and made a floating bridge of sorts. It worked well enough, but before they could test it properly it floated away like the first logs. Nobody had tied it off. Again. It would have been hilarious except I knew why they wanted to get across the river so much. To be fair, zombies can be very distracting. Especially when they show up in a horde and without much warning.

Up until then, I hadn't realized the city of Covington was still chock-full of aggressive types of zombies. Rex and his gang inadvertently brought down a mess of them when they started making all sorts of noise while building their bridge. Chain saws were noisy. Shamblers loved noise. It was a match made in heaven. The idiots thought that just because they didn't see any shamblers at first that meant they'd all left or died or something.

In reality, the shamblers had all been down by Interstate 64 because one of the buildings there was solar powered and featured a tall pole with a lantern and a sign on top. While not the brightest light in the world, it was still the only one around and the zombies were drawn to it. Since Rex and his group had come the most direct route from Lexington, which meant over the hill along I-64 until they exited at State Road 60, they'd unwittingly avoided the shamblers—until the chain saws started, at least.

It was stupid, really. If they'd gone down I-64 farther, they would have found the rear entrance to the school. It wasn't really that big a secret. Most local people knew about it. Or they could have even just waded across the river, maybe. Yeah, it wasn't shallow, but it was easier than trying to rebuild a bridge using logs from the nearby lumber company cut onsite. To be honest, it would have been even easier if they'd crossed over and raided the partially collapsed paper mill plant *right there next to the ruined bridge,* and done the repair work from the mill's side. Well, what was left of the paper mill, anyway. When the dam went, it had done a number on every building next to the river. Most of downtown Covington remained partially flooded, but still ... for a guy who was supposed to be king, he seemed pretty dumb and not the most creative thinker.

He must have really wanted to make his grand entrance to the school with his stolen SWAT vehicle. Otherwise, he could have just made a simple rope bridge and crossed that way. Or a fancy one with wood. One of those guys had to have been in the Boy Scouts, right?

I was perched high in the deer stand at the river bend, watching King Dale and his men work on their latest bridge attempt, when the first shambler arrived from downtown Covington. These were not the same as the early ones we dealt with up at the school, but skinnier, and slower. *Much* slower. They weren't the horror movie type of shamblers, though they were faster than what Lucia and I had dealt with in the admin building.

However, these ones were still moving fast enough to surprise Rex and his crew. It was interesting to watch precisely how they dealt with them—from a purely tactical point of view, I mean. I took mental notes because, well, I'd never seen anyone else handle shamblers before.

The first shambler hit the guy who was supposed to be on lookout but seemed far more interested in watching the bridge being built. He didn't even have time to scream before the shambler had latched onto his neck and started chewing away. Between the noise from the river, the loud arguing of Dale's men, and the one chain saw running there was almost zero chance they heard the poor guy get attacked.

Old King Dale must have sensed something, though, because he half-turned toward the lookout just as the man fell twitching on the ground, shambler latched onto his shoulder. He shouted an alarm as a large mass of shamblers appeared from behind the ruined old post office half a block away. The group turned and their weapons were up and ready—except for the dude with the chain saw—before the shamblers were too close.

I'll give credit where it's due: they knew what a proper firing line was. They were precise with every shot and didn't seem to waste any rounds. They might not be the brightest bunch for following the self-proclaimed King of Appalachia around, but they knew how to defend against an oncoming shambler horde. Shamblers dropped in rapid succession as the men fired. Still, his followers were kind of the enemy if they got their bridge built and made it up to campus.

King Dale did make one huge tactical error, though—he forgot to make sure both the lookout and shambler on the ground were dead and not just injured. Sister Ann told me to always double-check the body. Somebody should have told Dale. After shooting the shambler that attacked the lookout, they'd just forgotten about him to engage the approaching horde. It didn't take long for the lookout to turn, and even with the gaping neck wound the man was up and back on his feet in a matter of minutes. That was interesting. I hadn't known someone could turn so quickly. Maybe it was because he'd been bitten?

The newly created shambler almost made it to Rex before the so-called King of Appalachia pulled out what looked like one of those chrome-plated Desert Eagles from his hip holster and blew the guy's head off with a single shot.

With the new shambler down, Dale began barking orders to his men. I couldn't hear exactly what he was shouting over the gunfire, but eventually they began focusing on the shamblers in front of the crowd. Golden rule of the zombie apocalypse: If you can bring friends to a shoot-out, bring lots of guns, and even more ammo.

I looked around my side of the river to see if I was still safe. No sign of any shamblers, but that meant nothing. Sometimes you could almost step on one without waking them up if you were quiet enough. Other than Lucia, I was probably the sneakiest girl on campus. More than once I'd stumbled onto a shambler nest and had to get out of there without waking the creature up. Fortunately, they stayed away from the railroad tracks that led into town. Back before the world ended, it was also the best route for some of the girls to sneak out at night to meet up with townie boys.

Not that I've ever done anything like that. I've just heard what the other girls say and stuff. I swear.

Somebody shouted and pointed in another direction. Turning, I looked to see what the fuss was all about. He was pointing up toward U.S. 220, the only road you could take to get to Warm Springs. I blinked, surprised. An ungodly number of shamblers were coming down the road. They were quicker than the original group. These shamblers were clearly better fed and in a hurry. There was also a lot more of them. I'd never seen that many in person.

Where are they coming from? I thought as I looked across the river. Alleghany County had *maybe* ten thousand people in total before everything happened. A lot of them died during the original outbreak of the Pacific Flu. There were a couple hundred in the seething mass coming down the road. Something else to talk to Sister Ann about. Shaking my head, I climbed down from the hunter's blind, jumping the last few feet to save time. Landing on the loose gravel near the tracks, I crouched down and checked to make certain I hadn't damaged Baby any. After a quick inspection, I was satisfied. The AR-15 didn't even have a scratch.

It was time to leave. I didn't want to get tagged by a stray round or a ricochet, and since Rex's men were on a shooting rampage the odds were decent of that happening. Hightailing it along the tracks, I headed back toward campus. It was time to report in. Sister Ann was not going to be happy with the number of shamblers still in and around Covington.

I was right. She wasn't happy at all with the news.

"You saw *how* many?" Sister Ann asked, clearly bothered by what I had to say about the shamblers. She'd been planning exploratory scouting missions farther out from the school for a few days now, hoping the shambler population had died off some. This sudden arrival of more seemed to have everyone in a down mood.

"About two hundred at least, some more coming from Warm Springs," I supplied in a quiet voice. The younger girls were undoubtedly listening in from the other room, even though we'd told them to stay away. They were as starved for news as everyone else was. The twice-weekly Wolf Squadron reports were nice, but they were also depressing. News from something close by, that they could potentially see and hear, was far more exciting.

"That's not good," Sister Ann murmured and leaned back in the chair. She glanced at the student council members sitting with us around the table. The nun was not going to cut the council members out of this meeting. Decisions were ultimately made by her, but she was slowly teaching us to come to a consensus without our usual bickering. "Still, they're on the other side of the river with King Dale. We're okay for now. I still want to explore the option of sending out search teams to some of the stores. What are some of our options?" she asked us.

"We're good on supplies, though low on protein options," Lucia answered immediately. She was looking down at the notepad in front of her. A frown was on her dark face. "I'd like to find more canned chicken or Spam or something. The canned stuff will last longer, but I don't think the younger girls are going to like nothing but canned carrots and potatoes and protein shakes. The corn is a total loss, if I remember you saying correctly?"

"Yeah, it's all gone. Those weevils got them all. Beans, too," Kayla confirmed, Boston accent growing mildly thicker from the stress. "Bugs, I mean."

"Then we'll need more vitamin supplements." Sister Ann sighed.

"At least we have pads and tampons now. If we want to keep on top of vitamins, though, we need to go out and find some, and soon," Lucia said as she looked up from her notepad. "Sister? I think we should start hitting houses down by the Moose Lodge and take our chances that there might be shamblers inside them. The Moose Lodge had a good stockpile of canned goods the last time we volunteered down there. Plus, not a lot of houses down next to it. Maybe a half dozen. Those supplies still might be there."

"If we get spotted by King Dale and his group, they'll figure out there's a way across the river," Rohena pointed out. Though the spider bite had been over a month ago, she was still pale but looking loads better. I rolled my eyes but didn't argue, even though I wasn't too sure if her brain was back in it. She'd been pretty delirious. "If we head north, then circle back east and check the gas station up on top of the hill along State Road Sixty, we might get a few things if the zombies haven't destroyed the inside yet and Dale won't spot us. Even if those zombies came from Warm Springs."

"Girl . . . I'm telling you, that one cute cashier is either a zombie or dead," Kayla remarked with a smirk. "Even if he lived, there's no way he stayed around here."

"Talk all the crap you want, but they had a lot of canned stuff there," Rohena said with a disdainful sniff. "Water's probably gone, but they might have sodas. I know it's not water, but it'll add caloric intake a bit, right? Maybe some of those vitamin-laced smart waters? I don't know. Point being, unless shamblers figure out how to use complex locks, it should still have some stuff in back. They're only dangerous now if they horde up or get in too close."

The fever must have made Rohena smarter or something. Other than wandering around where King Dale and hundreds of shamblers could get to us, it was a solid idea. Sister Ann must have thought so, too.

"Lucia, draw up a plan for checking out the gas station," Sister Ann said. "It's a low priority, though. At a minimum, Maddie on security and two older girls with hiking backpacks."

"People gonna die," Lucia muttered under her breath as she continued taking notes. I almost laughed but managed to turn it into a cough at the last moment, and started twisting my hair.

"Speaking of water . . ." Sister Ann continued as she pretended not to hear Lucia's comment. "The well pump is still running decently?"

"Decently enough, Sister," Emily responded. Not for the first time did I find myself happy she'd made it into the cafeteria bunker. With the knowledge of power being diverted over to the admin building, she was now looking for ways to stop that and maybe instead have lights in the bunker. Like I said, freaking brilliant girl. "I know some of the girls want to use the solar panel to heat the showers, but without the power from the solar panel we don't have water for more than ten minutes. There's a reason we shower in the daytime. They can either have cold showers, or no water at all. They need to quit bit—uh, complaining about it."

"I'll mention it again at Devotionals tonight," Sister Ann promised. "What about hand pumps?"

"Yes, ma'am, sorry." Emily leaned back in her chair and closed her eyes. Her expression changed as she continued. "I understand the concept behind it, but finding water is actually harder than it sounds. Yeah, if we had a lot of back pressure, we could bring it up from Dunlap Creek. That'd be the easiest way but we would need mechanical pumps for that since the uphill incline is so steep. More electricity. I was reading about something interesting but we'd have to find a lot of pipes and a natural spring above us somewhere. Basically, water flows downhill, and we just build a gravity well with piping to direct it into the purifiers . . ."

"There isn't a natural spring above us that I'm aware of," Sister Ann pointed out.

"I figured you would have mentioned a natural spring flowing down the mountain if there was one," Emily stated. "No manual well pumps for now, sorry."

"How long do you think the well pump will last?" I asked, curious.

"Really hard to say," Emily replied as she looked at me. I could see the worry in her eyes. A seventeen-year-old girl shouldn't be under the stress she was. It was her responsibility to keep everything mechanical running. Then again, nobody should be doing what we had to in order to survive. I, for one, shouldn't be running site security on the campus. "They're built to last thirty years and this one was just installed five years ago. If the pipe doesn't freeze or rupture, then we're good for a long time. Last winter was mild. This year? I don't know. Those woolly worm predictions are garbage, by the way. No offense. But the weather . . . for next year? Again, no idea. February is always the worst around here. If it gets too cold and a pipe bursts . . ."

"We'll worry about that when the time comes, Emily," Sister Ann told us all in a gentle tone. She looked at all of us before continuing. "The time I've privately dreaded has come at last. I'd hope . . . prayed . . . done everything I could in order to keep everyone here as safe as I could. But . . . Maddie?"

"Their bridge is almost built, ma'am," I told everyone gathered around the table, twisting my hair tighter around my finger as I spoke. Everyone around the table stared at me, scared. We'd been talking about the possibility of the bridge being completed for days. Now that it was completed, though, it suddenly became terrifyingly real. "That shambler attack slowed it down, but they're pretty much done. Bet that they're going to cross first thing once it's finished fully. They're expecting us to fight up here, on the mountain."

"If they were smart they'd cross the bridge tonight and camp on our side of the river, establish a beachhead there," Sister Ann murmured as she closed her eyes. After a few moments of silent contemplation she continued to speak. "Maddie ... how determined did they look to cross?"

"Well..." I stopped and thought it over. I nodded slowly as the idea began to germinate in my brain. "He really wants to get up here with that BearCat thing, ma'am. Like, *really* wants this. Roll up on us like a boss and make us afraid. You once said fear is sometimes mistaken for respect. King Dale thinks making us afraid of him and his not-a-tank is a sign we respect his authori-*tayh*." My inflection on the word made a few of the others giggle. That was a good sign. "He's deluded."

"Agreed." Sister Ann smiled at me before looking around the table. "So how do we hurt him without a massive gunfight breaking out, putting us all in danger? Or actual *killing* of regular people?"

Silence. How did one beat a dirtbag hillbilly wannabe king? Especially when none of us actually wanted to shoot a real, living, breathing human being?

Shamblers didn't count in my book.

"Uh ... what about stealing his tank?" a small, timid voice asked from the end of the table. Everyone looked down to the far end of the table, where Finlay and Fiona had been sitting quietly together. Not sure which one spoke, I motioned for them to continue. The twins shared a look.

"Or blow it up." That was Finlay speaking. The small black mole on her cheek was distinguishing.

"*Stealing* it would be easier," Fiona countered. Apparently this was not a new discussion between the two. *When* they'd talked about it, though, would be news to me. Unless the twins really were psychics ...

"Well, hold on a second," Sister Ann held up both hands to forestall any argument between the siblings. "Forget blowing up the

BearCat for a second, girls. Keep that around as Plan C. No, D. Let's go back to the original idea, Plan A. Do either of you know how to steal a car?"

They looked at each other before Fiona answered. "Our mother's lawyer advised us to not answer any questions like that without him or our mother being present."

"Ha! I *knew* it!" Lucia laughed and clapped her hands together in delight. "Grand Theft Auto! My little *cholalitas* are criminals!"

"Okay, great, they *might* know how to steal a car," I said once the laughter died down. "What's stopping King Dale's dudes from shooting us when we're stealing it?"

"A distraction..." Sister Ann suddenly smiled. "A big one."

"What's a bigger distraction than stealing the man's tank?" I asked.

Sister Ann didn't reply. Instead, she looked back toward the twins. Her grin doubled in size.

It was ... *unnerving*.

CHAPTER SEVEN

"Hubris! Mankind's hubris is a sin in the eyes of the Lord! Damnation is at hand! Fire will cleanse the soul and purify the wicked! The end is nigh!"
From: *Collected Radio Transmissions of the Fall,*
University of the South Press, 2053

"We are *so* going to die," I murmured quietly as we crept through the darkness.

Of course, I volunteered for the most dangerous part of the mission Sister Ann had decided to call "Operation Not-A-Tank." I don't think anybody expected anything else. Not a single other girl on campus was capable of what I was going to do—with the exception of one other, who had the misfortune of being with me at the moment. With full hunting gear taken from the clothing closet and my red hair tucked safely away under a black beanie, I blended in better with the environment than usual.

The poor individual Sister Ann had sent with me was Lucia, dressed similarly but carrying a bag instead of my loadout. She was the only person both Sister Ann and I trusted to get past the bulk of King Dale's crew. The tiny Latina was not happy about it, though. She started to let me know about it from the moment we left campus and hadn't stopped complaining since.

"Of course we're going to die. This is stupid," she whispered for the umpteenth time as we made our way down the railroad tracks. We knew already where Appalachia Rex and his crew were holed up.

I'd been watching them for days, after all. The abandoned gas station turned liquor store near the ruined paper mill was a good place—close to the river, and with good lines of sight to their bridge. The building also had bars over the windows, which had helped protect it during the Fall. It'd been high on my list of buildings to potentially clear when Sister Ann gave the word.

Aware that the shambler population had grown a lot since this morning, I shushed her and made a walking motion with my two fingers. She sighed, held up the letter *B* in sign language to her chin, and jerked it down before giving me two quick waves of her hand. I giggled.

Bitch please, I mentally translated. Lucia had a point. We didn't need to be silent, merely quiet.

For the record, I was not one "those" girls who liked to traipse about in the darkness after sneaking out at night to meet townie boys, pre-Fall. Not my thing. The woods and mountain used to be terrifying to me when I first arrived. Back home, it was never really "night" in Orange County like it was out here. At night in Southern California there were always light in the background, and noise as well. It didn't matter how late the hour, there was always the persistent glow of the cities, from Santa Ana all the way up to the Anaheim Hills.

Out here, up in the Alleghany Highlands, the heart of the Blue Ridge Mountains? My first night during a camping trip with Sister Ann had been an experience, to say the least. None of us had ever slept out under the stars, and all of us all came from big cities. It was the first time I'd ever truly appreciated just how small I was compared to the rest of the universe.

The spot where we'd camped had overlooked an entire valley. The lights from Covington were blocked by the mountain. There was dark, and then there was that night during what Sister Ann called our "crucible." There was nothing but the small fire we'd built and the billions of stars in the sky above. It was the first time I really considered a future—not just mine, I mean, but the future of all those around me, and how our choices would affect not only ourselves, but those who cared for us. It'd been an uncomfortable experience for me.

The sky was mostly cloudy now, the moonlight sporadic. We moved like ghosts through the trees, confident in our knowledge of the game trails leading alongside the Jackson River. Lucia knew these paths almost as well as I did. It was still the best way to sneak down to the river without revealing the back entrance to anybody who might be watching. Plus, I hated using the main entrance and remembering the secret codes to avoid raising the alarm, so everybody was happy.

For now. If everything went according to plan, King Dale wasn't going to be too pleased. Not that I gave a crap about how he felt. Screw that guy.

Eventually we found where King Dale and his goons had tied up their mostly-completed bridge, which bobbed up and down gently as the river washed beneath it. I had no idea what sort of bridge it was, but it looked like the logs were thick enough to drive over. Watching them move with the current slightly, I began to have doubts. Cutting the lines would have been easier and probably safer, but unless those logs were destroyed King Dale could just fish it out and tie it back up. We'd delay them for a day, maybe two tops. What Sister Ann had in mind was a more permanent solution, and a slap in the face to his ego.

Sister Ann always preached about hubris and how it would lead to the downfall of mankind. I liked to think people weren't that bad, just . . . prone to bouts of the stupid. The *real* stupid.

After watching it for thirty minutes, we took a risk and crossed the makeshift floating bridge. Both Lucia and I kept watching the riverbanks, certain that we'd get spotted by a lookout or something. Surprisingly, he didn't have anybody out there to protect it. Considering they probably didn't have any way to see in the dark, it made sense the more I thought about it. It wasn't as though the shamblers would do anything to the bridge besides cross it, right? He had to be thinking something along these lines. Plus, a school filled with teenage girls protected by a single nun? How dangerous could we be to his plans in the middle of the night?

The poor man had no idea what nun he was messing with.

One thing Sister Ann had done before we departed campus was to pass out handheld radios. They were good ones, not the cheap sort you'd find at a discount store. They had to be to work in these mountains. Sister Ann had hoarded these radios, keeping them safe from harm and conserving all the batteries we could find. There was a surprising number of batteries in the bunker, actually, but since most of them were size *D* and didn't match up with the handhelds, we hadn't really used the radios all that much. There were plans to, whenever we started going farther out to scout for supplies. The *D* batteries we had in abundance were perfect for the shortwave radio, however. Emily thought we had enough to last the shortwave five more years at our current use. Though sometimes we really didn't want to use it. Other than reading and chess, which I hated, the shortwave was our only source of entertainment—as depressing as it was.

I turned my radio on and switched to the prearranged channel. We were risking a lot in using these radios. Anybody who happened to have the same channel we were using could potentially hear us. It was why Sister Ann told us not to talk, merely turn it on and hit the transmit key three times before shutting it back down. The signal was meant to tell her we were safely across the bridge. The next time we were supposed to use the radio was when we completed the second stage and found the stolen BearCat.

Staying in the shadows of the parking lot across the street from the mill, we snuck in closer. Still no signs of any lookouts. Hubris. I could almost hear Sister Ann's lecture in my brain. Ducking behind a particularly large pile of debris left over from the dam failure, I spotted the BearCat parked directly in front of the liquor store. The massive beast of a truck was partially blocking the front door. It was a smart idea, actually. It provided King Dale with added reinforcement to the station's main entrance while keeping their vehicle close. We peeked inside. I almost laughed. The problem with King Dale's brilliant plan, however, was that he had left the keys in the ignition and nobody outside to guard it. The doors were unlocked as well, and we didn't see anyone sleeping within.

Talk about a stroke of luck. God really was looking out for the juvenile delinquents of St. Dom's. It would make what we were about to do next that much simpler.

We quickly climbed inside. It smelled like ass but otherwise was in good shape. The quick lesson the twins gave us on how to "theoretically hot-wire a car" wouldn't be necessary. Locking the doors, Lucia slid into the back area to ensure it was secured as well. We did not want any unexpected passengers during our attempt at grand theft auto. Satisfied it was locked and there was no way, outside of a spare key, anyone else was getting in, I flipped the radio back on and clicked the transmit key three more times. Turning the radio off, I climbed behind the driver's seat and waited. My gaze drifted toward the makeshift floating bridge, which could just barely be seen down the block.

Shadows moved around the bridge. I prayed that it was only our girls and no shamblers. I doubted the twins would respond well to a couple of shamblers showing up while doing their thing.

It took a bit longer than expected. I chalked it up to the logs being wet from the rapidly flowing river. Or perhaps the coolness of the evening. But eventually the combined kerosene and Styrofoam packing peanut bags lit the logs on fire. Soon there was a bonfire any good ol' Southern boy would have been proud to call his own. If anyone had been outside on watch, that is.

Of course, the fire wouldn't burn the logs completely. The bridge could still be repaired. That was where the second part of the plan came into play.

I was growing irritated by the moment, though. Sister Ann and the girls had worked hard on making their makeshift napalm, and there was nobody from Rex's crew to witness it. For the first time, I was disappointed there was no lookout. I leaned forward and peered inside the gas station. There was absolute darkness inside. This was another smart move by the intrepid King Dale, since shamblers were drawn to light. I looked back down at the river. The flames were high in the air now, creating enough light to gain the attention of anyone within five hundred yards. The bridge was still holding fast. The wait was almost unbearable. I looked at the handheld in disgust. What was taking them so long? There was a lot of smoke rising into the air. I turned back to let Lucia know what was going on when disaster struck.

I slipped and my elbow slammed down hard on the steering wheel. The loud car horn of the BearCat echoed into the still night. I jerked away from the horn, horrified, and scrambled into the back with Lucia. She was staring at me, eyes wide.

"You think anyone heard?" she asked in a hushed whisper.

As if in response, a keening wail answered. Then another, and another. Dozens, if not hundreds, of angry shamblers howled somewhere out in the darkness in reply.

"Shit," I hissed, terrified. "Yeah, someone heard."

Men started running out of the darkened gas station. They were well-armed but clearly had not been expecting a truck horn to signal all of the shamblers to wake up. We ducked down and hoped we wouldn't be seen by Dale's men. Confused, a few tried the doors to the BearCat, only to find them locked. I could hear them arguing outside.

"Who locked the fucking keys in the tank?!" someone screamed. It sounded like Rex, though I couldn't be certain.

"Forget the keys!" another voice interjected. "The bridge is on fire!"

"How did the bridge catch on fire?" a third voice asked. "Quick, to the river!"

I risked a peek and I counted eight men, all armed with AR-15s similar to mine, running toward the fire. As they drew closer one of them raised his rifle and shot across the river. Someone was out in the open. It was either Finlay or Fiona. I winced, but the shot thankfully missed. She continued scrambling behind a small pile of rocks but there wasn't enough cover. As the shooter readied a second shot, a screech interrupted him. A shambler bodied him to the ground. Struggling, the man tried to turn the AR. The shambler was in too close, and the shooter started screaming as the shambler's teeth started gnawing on his face. A melee erupted as more shamblers poured into the men. Vengeance was no longer an option. Saving the bridge was secondary. They were fighting now purely to survive.

Then the bridge blew up and I finally understood why Sister Ann almost had a heart attack the first time the twins asked about using Tannerite to take care of shamblers.

As Finlay and Fiona had pointed out to us back up on campus and before we started this trek into town, Tannerite was not something that exploded when it caught on fire and I was worrying over nothing. Even something like a handgun round didn't always set it off. No, it needed something with a little more *oomph* behind it. A powerful impact worked the best. Since we were all out of blasting caps, though, someone needed to shoot the backpack filled with the stuff. And since the Tannerite wasn't about to shoot itself, my little shambler-killing protégé Ulla had been given the task of hitting the backpack filled with fifteen pounds of the stuff with her rifle from long range. And one thing I'd quickly learned about the tiny blond girl was that she never, ever missed.

The twins were wrong about one thing, though—I *definitely* would have been worried if I'd known about the size of the explosion beforehand.

The blast was felt by both of us, even through the heavy plating of the BearCat. For a moment, the sensation of my insides being squished sideways almost made me throw up. The vehicle rocked slightly from the explosion, the shocks absorbing most of it. A second later it began to rain logs. One particularly large chunk of wood crashed down on a shambler that was about to reach King Dale. The upper half of the shambler simply *disintegrated*. King Dale, who somehow made it through completely unscathed, was bathed in blood, guts, and who only knew what else. He looked surprised. Another splintered, smoldering log was driven *through* the engine block of an abandoned truck nearby. Not one of those small pickups, either. It would have made an awesome flagpole.

Considering how far away the truck was from the source of the explosion, though...

"Holy shit!" Lucia squeaked in a tiny voice. She looked terrified. I probably looked the same.

"Damn. I think it's time to go," I muttered and crawled back into the driver's seat. Once Baby was safely in the small, mounted rack, Lucia climbed into the passenger seat. Checking the dashboard, I was surprised to see the truck had similar controls to a regular car, just as Sister Ann had predicted. I softly cursed. "She was right. I owe her three packets of noodles."

"You bet against a nun? Stupid," Lucia grunted as I turned the key. The well-primed diesel engine coughed and roared to life. I flipped the switch for the lights, which drew the attention of all of the shamblers—as well as King Dale and his men.

I revved the engine once and shifted it into gear. If pressed, I will swear before a court of law that I'd never driven before I got behind the wheel of the BearCat. Between you and me? I'd "borrowed" my mom's car the first time when I was thirteen. Driving was easy. Passing the written test was a little more difficult.

The BearCat had a very powerful engine and it kicked up a lot of smoke and dirt as the wheels spun out a little before finding traction. The heavily armored vehicle slid sideways just a tad, then quickly straightened out as I barreled over a small group of shamblers that were late to the party. I barely registered their impacts. It was glorious. I preferred this method of killing shamblers over any other I'd tried so far. With gore sticking to the windshield and more shamblers trying to grab hold and overwhelm the truck, I decided it was time to get out of there. A tactical decision and all. However, I had one more pass to make.

Not only were we there to steal his not-a-tank, there was also a message that needed to be sent.

The look on King Dale's face when I shot him the bird as we drove past was one I'll cherish forever.

Sideswiping another shambler and running over two more, I pressed the gas pedal as far as it could go. The big diesel engine roared in response. I'm almost certain another shambler was killed by the exhaust plume alone. A large crowd of mindless hordes soon tried to follow us, but the armored BearCat was too fast and soon enough we left them behind. I guided the truck up State Road 60, cresting the large hill on the eastern half of the town. From what I could see behind us the shamblers were falling behind in their pursuit. I had no idea what happened to King Dale and his men but it seemed like pretty good odds they had bolted when the shamblers had all decided to chase after the BearCat.

"Well, Rohena isn't going to be happy," I commented and slowed down as we passed the gas station she had wanted us to explore. It had been burned to the ground at some point and now was nothing more than a charred husk of a building. The roof had collapsed in during the fire and the front was completely gone. I counted six bodies near the fuel pumps, all burnt to a crisp. There were signs they'd been gnawed on a little, but with that much fire damage there wasn't much left for a shambler to eat. "I seriously doubt there's any bottled water or supplies in there."

"*Ay, cabrón,*" Lucia added. "I hope none of them were that cute boy Rohena liked."

"Probably all shamblers now," I suggested and turned the BearCat onto I-64. From there we began to head west, the abandoned interstate only partially overgrown with kudzu in this part. Sticking toward the center of the freeway we passed over the Jackson River, the bridge well above where the mass surge of water had been when the dam gave way. It was still terrifying, though, since part of the opposite side of the road had fallen off sometime. One of the support beams must have failed on that side.

Once we were across the high bridge with no visible pursuit, we were home free. I knew the back way into the school was at Mile Marker 10, then we'd have to backtrack a bit to make it to the school. A rockslide blocked the eastbound side, but that wasn't a big problem. Before I could get off the freeway, though, Lucia had me stop.

"Just . . . wait a sec, okay? Stop the tank," she said. I obliged and parked the BearCat right there in the middle of the freeway. It wasn't like we were going to stop traffic or anything. Plus, something in the tone of her voice suggested that correcting her about it not being a tank would be a bad idea.

Looking over the fuel gauge, I was surprised to see it was at almost full. Rex had gotten gas somehow, somewhere. I made a quick mental note to ask Sister Ann about it. I had no idea how long fuel was good for before it went bad. She might, though. If not her, then definitely Emily. Still, there had to be diesel fuel *somewhere*.

"What's up?" I asked Lucia as I shut off the engine. No point in wasting gas. We were completely safe inside the armored vehicle and had time to spare. Sister Ann and the other girls wouldn't be able to return to the school for at least an hour. It wasn't the shortest hike, even following the railroad tracks.

"We could go home," Lucia whispered.

"We are," I said. "We get off at the next mile marker and head back to school. This way is safest, just like Sister Ann said."

"No," Lucia shook her head and pointed straight down the freeway ahead. At the dark and foreboding west. "I mean, *home* home."

"Oh." I understood. She meant California, where our families were from. Had been. Possibly still were, but that was unlikely. It was about twenty-five hundred miles away or so. There was no way we could make it, not on one tank of gas. It was impossible. And yet . . . the temptation was there. The idea of driving off, going home. Finding our families and discovering that they all somehow survived.

We could use the armored BearCat to go anywhere and not worry about the shamblers. Maybe head out to Utah? I'd always wanted to go to Utah and see the mountains there.

I sighed. In my heart I knew they were gone. Los Angeles had a massive breakout before the rest of the country had even been infected. It was a mess. The last thing we'd heard over the shortwave before Sister Ann had made us turn it off was that LA was half-burned. Fires had torn though Chavez Ravine. The San Gabriel and San Fernando valleys had been devastated by structural fires. Even Orange County, my home, was ruined. There would be no more trips to Knott's Berry Farm anytime soon.

"It's all gone," I reminded her. "Our families. Our old lives. Even if we could go back, what would we find? Nothing will ever return to normal. Not the way it was. I know, deep down, my family's gone. Yours? I don't know. But . . . why not build something here, for them to come to? Maybe . . . I mean, if we could get lucky heading west, maybe they'll head east, to us? Luck swings both ways, you know?"

"They wouldn't make it," Lucia said in a despondent voice. "My mama can't drive. *Mi padre* is a horrible driver on a good day, and *Tia* Juanita's car couldn't even get out to Riverside. No, they're stuck there, if they lived . . . which they probably didn't. I don't know, Maddie. I just want to go home."

"I know. It's a hard decision, but one we need to make. Tonight. So what's it gonna be, *chica*?" I asked Lucia. "Head west, possibly make it all the way there—doubtful, since fuel is scarce—and find out what happened to our families? Or stay here, be the protectors of the younger girls, and maybe build something better for ourselves here?"

"*Odio cuando tienes razón*," Lucia muttered in a quiet voice.

"*No habla*," I told her. "White girl from the O.C., remember?"

"I hate it when you're right," she translated for me and let out a weary sigh. "Let's get this tank back up to the school. I don't think we need to worry about King Dale tonight. Or anytime soon. Not as long as we have his tank, and the bridge is burned up."

"The BearCat, but yeah. Pretty sure it did. Plus, that was a lot of shamblers drawn to the bonfire. And that boom? *Epic*. As long as they're not on their way up to the school already, we should be okay. Maybe we got lucky and shamblers ate King Dale and all of his men?" I suggested as my mind drifted.

In my heart, I'd figured my family was dead months before, but I don't think I'd really accepted it until that moment. The weight of it felt crushing on my chest. It hurt. As annoying as my brothers were, they were still my brothers and I loved them. My parents, too, even if they'd shipped me off across the country to make sure I graduated high school. I wiped my eyes as they started to burn from tears and tried to comfort Lucia instead of focusing on my own pain. Home wasn't California anymore, not for either of us. "Besides, you know our families are probably... dead, right?"

"I know."

"This is the safest place to be. At the school, I mean."

"I know!"

"Hey, it'll get better. Maybe one day some hot, single marines will leave Wolf Squadron and come to rescue us." I tried, but Lucia still appeared upset. It was hard to cheer someone else up while I was on the verge of bawling my eyes out as well. Humor had always been my fallback position. I decided on my one remaining option. "So... you wanna drive the tank back to the school?"

Lucia looked at me, a frown upon her face. She'd stopped crying at least. This was good. "I don't have my driver's license."

"Neither do I. What, you worried about a ticket? Ha!"

Lucia was quiet, clearly intrigued by the idea. Her facial expressions ranged from curious to fearful, with a dash of excitement at the prospect of driving something like the BearCat. I couldn't blame her for any of it. The thing was pretty awesome, and helped quash some of my anxiety. I recognized her facial tics. They were probably the same ones I had on my face when Sister Ann first suggested we steal the armored vehicle. Finally, she nodded. It was only once, but there.

"You know what? Yeah, I want to drive the tank up back to the school."

"Attagirl!"

"Um... I've never driven before..."

"That's cool. This thing's armored like a boss. But... let's go *real* slow, okay? Just in case."

Part Two

ON A LONELY DARK PATH

I do not love the bright sword for its sharpness,
nor the arrow for its swiftness, nor the warrior for his glory. I love
only that which they defend.
—J.R.R. Tolkien, *The Two Towers*

CHAPTER EIGHT

"Just going out and abducting research subjects is not appropriate scientific conduct. First, you have to create and receive approval of your abduction plan, including methods, locations, and targeted demographics..."
—Lecture part of "Grad 725—Research Methods for the Infected" by Dr. Tedd Roberts, University of the South, 2047

Unfortunately, King Dale and most of his men survived the shamblers that night. However, his plan to conquer the school seemed to be on hold for the time being. On foot and looking worse for wear, we'd watched him limp back eastward with his surviving men. The direction they headed pretty much confirmed that they were either holed up in Clifton Forge or, less likely, the tiny town of Selma next to it.

Not that any of this mattered much. Without the BearCat and apparently lacking any other impressive armored vehicles, it didn't look like they had the capabilities to come at us anytime soon. Maybe ever, if we were lucky. King Dale didn't seem the type to quit so easily, though, so Ulla and I kept target practicing.

"Stay vigilant" became our new mantra. It was a good mantra to have, especially since we'd been living it since the day our world ended.

We celebrated Thanksgiving, giving thanks for our survival. We stayed quiet not because there were a lot of shamblers around campus, no. Any that made it up the mountain were taken care of, and quickly. Thanksgiving was a little muted thanks to the bears who were starting to come in closer to campus. They were growing bolder with every passing day. One of them—not the loyal Sir Chonk, slayer of shamblers, but a smaller one, probably a cub—even managed to climb the fence around our makeshift garden and destroy the last remnants of the crops. Which, unfortunately, included all of the pumpkins.

Still, the mood on campus was better than it'd been since the world around us ended. Lucia had managed to find paint in an old storeroom behind the gym and the younger girls began painting our newly acquired BearCat. The entire front end was quickly covered with stick figures, suns, flowers, and peace signs. Emily, always creative in her own ways, managed to rig up a brush guard on the BearCat that looked straight out of a *Mad Max* movie. It was an odd clash of styles: a rugged, deadly-looking armored vehicle with a smiling sun, rainbows, and flowers painted all over the front and side armored paneling.

St. Dom's . . . what can I say? We're an odd mixture of stability and insanity.

The best part? The elementary school girls nicknamed the heavy vehicle *Oso*, after Sir Chonk the Shambler Slayer, after talking to Lucia about what "bear" translated into Spanish was. I heartily approved, and even Ulla smiled a bit after.

Just before Christmas we had a new problem arise. Well, not so much a problem, but a situation that could potentially become one if not handled quickly. Since it fit into Sister Ann's vision of rebuilding society, it was a welcome situation. Just one without shamblers running around.

Dunlap Creek, at the bottom of the mountain, was still a hotspot for them. They were almost as bad as rats, and far more dangerous. Though not nearly as numerous as the summer, they were still a threat. The banks along the slow-moving creek seemed to be the perfect place for shamblers to build their little ratty, makeshift nests. The opposite side of the creek was a sheer cliff face—which turned into an interesting waterfall when it rained—that protected anyone down on our side of the creek from the elements. The Alleghany Highlands got some snow, sure, but what really made winters tough was the wind on a cold day. The weird cut in the base of the cliff created a little area protected from the wind.

Thanks to this, Ulla and I kept having to go down there at least twice a week to clear out shamblers. The worst part of it was that one of them kept running away the minute I got close. The spot was good for one or two of the crazy psycho ones charging me, so those were easy target practice. The other one always fled. Ulla, perched up in the same deer blind I'd watched Sir Chonk from months before, one time tracked the timid one all the way to the road. Without a clear shot, though, she followed instructions and didn't want to risk missing.

Wolf Squadron spoke about "betas." While I couldn't be certain this was what we were dealing with, it was clearly a different type of shambler. Since it didn't come up the mountain and always ran away, I decided it wasn't worth chasing down. The minute that it showed up someplace where it could cause harm, though?

Then it would be showtime.

No, the "not a problem but sort of is" arose on a sunny but cold Thursday afternoon. Apparently the BearCat rumbling along the back way onto campus alerted people that there were survivors up at St. Dominic's because two days before Christmas Eve, our first refugees showed up. Three of them, in fact: one old geezer and two young kids, probably his granddaughters. From the way they clung close to him and how he was constantly surveying the area, he'd been protecting them from the beginning of the Fall.

The man was clearly unnerved when they arrived at the front gate. The trio stopped at the bridge over Dunlap Creek, where two middle schoolers were on watch. Wendy, the younger of the two, had the radio while Julia held the rifle. The magazine was empty, but that was something no one in the small group needed to know. The real danger was me on Mr. Stitmer's four-wheeler not too far away. I was watching for any sudden movements by the man, not that I was expecting any trouble from him. Not with the two girls clinging to him and making movement difficult. Ulla was on shambler overwatch, just in case one of them showed up and wanted to get froggy.

"Is the Mother Superior still alive?" he asked without preamble. He had a small pistol on a hip holster but that was all. Brave man to wander around with nothing more. Or a desperate one. It was hard to say. The girls clung to his side, their eyes wide as they looked around. Those were the eyes of children who had gazed into the dark and not fully come back yet.

Judging by how pale their skin was, I was willing to bet the trio had holed up in a basement when the Fall started and only recently began venturing outdoors. They were a little on the skinny side but clean. Their clothes were in good shape and they were prepped for the cold. Another point in the man's favor. The old dude had a bushy beard that extended down to his chest, but he might have had that for a long time before the world ended. There was no way for me to tell. My beard growing experience was pretty nil.

He also sported a really impressive scar on the side of his head. There had to have been one hell of a story behind that.

"I radioed up," Wendy told them as Julie tried to look intimidating. She pulled off scared, which probably unnerved the man more. Scared teenager with a weapon? Yeah, I'd be terrified a bit, too. "Sister Ann said she is coming down to meet with you."

"The Marine nun?" He shook his head and smiled. "Thank God Almighty. The Lord works in mysterious ways, don't He? Ain't no coincidence that she survived."

"Who are you?" Julie asked, sounding curious. He knew us, and well apparently, but I had no idea who the man was. So far as I could tell, none of King Dale's men had known any of us by name. His knowledge of us was actually a point in his favor. If he'd been working with King Dale, then they would have known who all of us were from the start.

"Temple Kessinger," he said, looking at her. I swear he visibly relaxed when he noticed how she had her weapon slung. Not the usual reaction I was used to. He was either a vet, or an experienced hunter.

Staying out of sight, I breathed a small sigh of relief. He didn't appear to be dangerous and I didn't recognize him as being any of King Dale's men from the bridge. Plus, he was old. The two girls on guard duty could easily outrun him if he made a grab for them, though I doubted he would.

I watched Sister Ann come down the hill, her gaze sweeping over the situation. None of the others noticed her, so they missed the look of relief that crossed her face when she saw the man and children on the bridge.

"Temple Kessinger, as I live and breathe," Sister Ann said. I could hear the smile in her voice as she rounded the bend. Behind her, Lucia and Emily were right on her heels. "It's nice to see a friendly face. You're looking well."

"Well enough, Sister," Temple said. "It was a rough spell. Still is. I never did get to thank Monsignor Dietrich for his kindness, and your school's assistance during my recovery."

"The Church is part of the community, Temple. As are you."

"Still . . . thank you, Sister. My family appreciated your church helping out during that time."

"You are very welcome, Temple," Sister Ann said, nodding slightly. "We are all God's children."

"I ain't been to church in years, Sister," Temple admitted in a quiet tone. "Yet the monsignor . . ."

"Sir? I'm not comfortable sitting around in the open like this, even armed," I interrupted them, sliding out of the four-wheeler and emerging from the bushes. Temple started, while Sister Ann gave me a small smile. It was clear he hadn't even suspected I was there. Score one for the home team.

"I know you," he said, offering up a small smile. "Well, recognize you, at least. You played field hockey against Covington that one time."

"Played them a few times, actually," I corrected. Those were good days, smashing my opponents on the field and earning those yellow cards the proper way. Oh, I also scored a goal, but who cared about that? Field hockey gave me a way to embrace therapy through violence without worrying about going to juvie.

"Only one time I remember," he admitted with a shrug. The girls clung tighter to him. He gave the smaller one a comforting pat on the head before continuing. "I didn't get out much before the zombie apocalypse happened. Brain tumor . . . damn near killed me. Recovery went on for years. Survived all that, radiation, surgery, only to watch the world end once I was back on my feet. Talk about bad timing."

Internally I winced. That was pretty much the definition of bad timing. Also, it explained the scar on his head. Not as interesting of a story as I'd thought. Still, the old dude was a survivor. Had to give him credit for that.

"And who are you two?" I asked the girls clinging to him. The older one buried her face in his side but the smaller one offered me a shy smile.

"Rosalind."

"Nice to meet you, Rosalind," I said in a gentle voice. "Is this your grandpa?"

She nodded. "Daddy went to Heaven after Mommy ate him and ran away."

Holy shit. No wonder the older girl looked traumatized. "Um . . . and this is your sister?"

Another nod. "Her name's Charise. She doesn't like to talk anymore."

"Do too!" the older girl protested before burying her face in flannel once more.

"Sister Ann? Sir? Can we head up the mountain, where it's safer?"

"One moment, Maddie." Sister Ann held up a hand to forestall my coming protests. She knew me too well. It was frightening. "Temple, are you comfortable? I know you're on medication. Do you have enough?"

"Can we talk about that later, Sister?" he asked and looked down at his granddaughters. The oldest still had her face buried in Temple's flannel jacket, but the younger was staring at me. She had a confused expression on her face. I had no idea why. "There are some things I'd rather not talk about in front of certain people, if you get my meaning."

"I do," Sister Ann acknowledged with a sad smile. Something had passed between them in that moment, but I didn't know what.

"How'd you survive?" I butted in. Not my most subtle moment, true, but I'd been burning with curiosity the moment the radio call came up the mountain. One old man and two very young girls? There was no way they should have survived this long on their own. If Temple had managed to pull that off, he'd be one hell of an asset to have on campus.

Apparently Sister Ann felt the same, but had way more tact than I did. "I'm not going to make you or your girls dwell on the past. When you want to talk about it, Temple, I'll be more than willing to listen," Sister Ann said in as reassuring a tone as she could manage. The old man smiled and nodded.

"I appreciate you, Sister. All of you. If I can intrude on you a bit longer..."

"You need somewhere to go for the girls, and yourself," Sister Ann said knowingly. She began to nod. "Throughout history the Catholic Church has been there for the people, even in the darkest of hours. St. Dominic's was established to help wayward girls become ladies. We can find room up here for all of you."

"Even if we aren't Catholic?" Temple asked. I knew the answer to this one.

"I don't think God cares if you're Catholic or not, sir," I replied before Sister Ann could. "You need help, and the Church is here. I don't see any problems."

"It *is* as simple as that, Temple," Sister Ann said, giving me an approving nod before turning back to the old man. "What's the point of the Church being a beacon in the night if we turn away those seeking refuge?"

"Like I said before, the Church and I ain't been particularly close..."

"Yet you've found your way here," Sister Ann said before shrugging. "Come on up the mountain, Temple. Eat. Rest. We'll discuss the finer details on full bellies in front of the woodstove."

"You got a woodstove? I forgot y'all were set up to survive a nuclear holocaust up here," Temple muttered as he looked up the road. He shook his head. "Well, it ain't nuclear, but it's still the end of the world."

"We're still here, Temple. Not all of us, but enough of us to make a difference. Come. Let's get you warmed up. I have tea."

After I was relieved on watch, Rosalind and Charise were fed and taken upstairs to Mrs. Whitney's old apartment by the twins, and Temple joined the rest of the student council and Sister Ann in front of the small woodstove we'd "appropriated" from the Moose Lodge months before. Mysteriously, some of the canned goods we'd seen then had disappeared since our last visit. It'd been a dicey expedition, since the four-wheeler was not designed to haul a trailer loaded with that much weight, but we managed. Towing a trailer attached to a four-wheeler is not for the faint of heart.

Getting it down into the bunker had almost killed us all. The thing was *heavy.*

Dinner was plain, canned chicken and some potatoes, and some Tang to wash it all down with, which was better than plain, boring water. We didn't have much of it left, but this was considered a special occasion so Sister Ann broke it out. Temple attacked the protein like he hadn't seen any in weeks. Which, given how thin he was beneath the bulky layers of clothing, was probable. He'd been neglecting himself to take care of the kids. My esteem for the man went up a few notches.

Emily had somehow rigged the smokestack to go out an old vertical pipe she said had once been used as a vent for a long-replaced boiler, so it would be able to handle the heat and the smoke without too many problems. It also put out a crazy amount of heat with very little wood inside.

The girl was definitely my favorite person on campus.

The outside air was dropping below freezing but inside the bunker, with the cinder block, reinforced walls, it was downright cozy. If it'd had windows I would have asked if we could crack one open, it was so warm. A few candles were lit but no more. Sister Ann had decided too much light would draw the younger girls back after being sent to bed. Even Devotionals had been cut a little short tonight. The newcomers hadn't talked very much, though it was clear to me that Rosalind was going to easily adapt to living with the elementary kids. Eventually, I meant. Things were a little different up here. Charise, though, seemed to be a tougher nut to crack. Still, she was talking. It was better than silence.

Nothing against Ulla, of course. My little protégé was different.

"We knew it was coming," Temple said once everyone on the council was situated around the stove. "We saw it—that flu, I mean. On the news, spoke about it at the stores, listened to the radio." Temple paused and wiped his eyes. To hear him talk was heartbreaking, but necessary. Other than the Wolf Squadron updates, we'd heard almost nothing about the outside world. Temple might have been hidden away during the Fall, but he'd still know things we didn't. Have a point of view none of us could relate to. He coughed, muttered an apology into his beard, and continued. "My son called me up and asked if he could bring the family over. They lived down in Covington proper, near the high school, and wanted to get away from their neighbors before they got sick. Seemed like a right smart plan to me, so I invited them up. I had the space, a few months' worth of food, and a freezer full of deer meat. Had a generator and six gas cans sealed up, too. Probably should go and grab that eventually... Sorry. My train of thought derailed there for a moment. I thought we'd weather the storm and in a month, two max, we'd be good to go. Only..."

"Only one of them brought the flu with them, and it turned into something more than just a flu," Sister Ann said in the gentlest voice possible. Temple sniffled, wiped his face with his sleeve, and nodded.

"My son. Bless his soul. He got sick first, then the girls and me. It was the worst flu I'd ever had in my life. I thought I was going to die. Convinced of it. But no... apparently God wasn't done with me yet. I didn't understand why until... until *she* turned into... into a monster. It was in the middle of the afternoon when my daughter-in-law became a zombie. Bit my son. No, she ripped his throat out with nothing but her teeth. My only boy... I grabbed the girls and ran to the basement. She chased us. I got the door closed and locked from the inside—I had never understood why that door was like that, but I was mighty thankful—and we waited. For three days she howled above us, destroying everything looking for food. Testing the door. Trying to get to us, her girls. Her own babies...

"His body rotted up there, Sister. It turned ripe and stank. It was hot and muggy. She... did things to it. Ate it. Him. I tried not to dwell on what I heard up there. It was the stuff of nightmares. Plus, I had bigger worries.

"The girls were terrified and crying. None of us could sleep for days. Just kept waiting for her to bash the door in and finish us off. I was afraid for the girls... and I was angry, Sister. I felt an anger I'd never had before. It wasn't fair of me. I was mad—no, *furious*—at her for killing my boy. Right in front of her own children, she killed their father. My only boy. I grew angry at my son for bringing the sickness out to the farm with them in the first place. I was filled with anger at myself for not being able to do anything more. And I was angry at God, Sister. God help me, I was so mad. Rage makes a man blind to it all. If not for those two little girls, I would have grabbed my rifle and tracked that she-devil down and finished her off.

"But... they saved me. The girls. *His* children did for me what I couldn't do for him. Sister, they truly saved me. The girls needed me.

There was no way I was going to throw away their lives for the sake of my own revenge. Instead of tracking her and putting her down like a dog, I took care of her daughters. We lived, and with every passing day, Sister, my anger ebbed. Just a little, you understand. Just a little. But it was better than that all-consuming hate that had been fueling me for weeks on end.

"But I never did get to say goodbye to my son. I couldn't bury him. There was almost nothing... nothing left. She'd picked him clean, like a scavenger. My boy..."

Temple stopped talking as fresh tears flowed freely down his face, disappearing into his beard. He was clearly having trouble with what to say next. After being so forthcoming and spilling everything, he was on the verge of clamming up now. I understood completely. Everyone reacted to trauma their own way. I didn't know the family very well—truth be told, not at all—but I could see where he was coming from. It was a cultural thing.

As much as I make fun of the people in the area, they were serious about their families. Fights often broke out between townies and St. Dominic students over perceived insults about third or fourth cousins, and the family expectation to defend their honor. They were also big on passing down their memories, family lore, stuff like that. Just seemed to be their thing. Firstborn sons were, like the rest of the world, seen more like prizes than progeny. Okay, that might be a bit unfair, but it's close.

To watch this old man break down and cry because he couldn't even bury his own son broke my heart.

"I'm sorry you had to see that, sir," I told the sobbing man sincerely. I meant every word, too. The other girls on the council were silent, each either crying tears of their own or in silent contemplation. Even the twins, for once, didn't speak.

"Temple... on the walk up here, you mentioned the old Boyd farm next door to yours," Sister Ann said as she laid a hand lightly on his forearm. "Mrs. Boyd was the elderly woman who did all the canning for her neighbors, yes? And her late husband did deer processing?"

"That's right," Temple said, sniffling. He pinched his nose and wiped his eyes. The elderly man was clearly happy to talk about anything else at this point. "He had one of them old-fashioned hand-powered grinders to make ground meat. Usually did it for venison, but he could do it for hog. Also had a machine that could make cube steak, but that was powered."

"I remember, yes. Mr. Stitmer used to take his deer to be processed by them." Sister Ann nodded. "Temple, you and the girls are welcome to stay here as long as you like. I'm not going to lie and say our trials are over, though. If we're to rebuild society, then there are going to be challenges ahead."

"Rebuild, Sister?" Temple looked at her, confused. "You plan on rebuilding society? All of it? Even . . . ?"

"Yes, Temple. The bedrock of life has to be founded on something. We can't, in good faith, hide up here and simply wait to die."

"Never heard it put like that before," Temple admitted. He stifled a yawn with a closed fist. "Sorry. It's been a long day."

Sister Ann looked around the room before locking onto the person she was searching for. "Lucia? Will you join me in assisting Temple up to his apartment, please? Madison, you've got this?"

"Yes, ma'am," I replied immediately.

"My knees ain't that bad," Temple groused but allowed the two to help him to his feet. "I have to tell you something, Sister. You might have to take care of the girls without me in the near future."

"Why? You planning on dying?" I asked. Rohena coughed and looked away, while Kayla and Emily both blushed. After a moment it dawned on me that my words had been rather blunt. "Uh, sorry. That came out wrong. I meant—"

"I understand," Temple said, chuckling as he waved away my concerns. "Planning on dying? No. Expecting it? Yes. I've been slowly rationing my blood pressure medication for the past few months. My heart's not what it used to be, child. I have enough for two, maybe three more months. Four if I really like dancing with the devil— which I don't, I'll add. Never was one for rhythm. But most likely I'll run out of my pills at the end of March. So . . . when that day comes? I plan on my grandchildren not being anywhere around me. They don't need to see that. Not after what they've had to see in the past. You can make sure that happens, Sister?"

"I believe so," Sister Ann said as she led him to the stairs up to the cafeteria. Lucia was right behind them.

He paused at the base of the concrete stairs and looked back over his shoulder at us. There was a deep sadness in his eyes, something

I hadn't really noticed before. "Thank you again. Really. I don't know what I would have done..."

His voice trailed off as Sister Ann guided him to the stairs.

"That right there is some depressing...stuff," I muttered as they disappeared from view. Thanks to Lucia clearing it awhile back, Mrs. Whitney's old apartment was the best place to put Temple and the girls for a few nights until we finished with the rest of the apartments.

One of the things Sister Ann had been reluctant to do was going to happen whether we wanted it or not. Rebuilding society was not going to be an easy job, and apartments didn't magically clean themselves. We were going to have to clean them out if more survivors showed up. That, or dig into the cottages and try to repair the easiest ones first.

"It's so sad," Emily agreed. "I can't even imagine what that poor man's gone through."

I turned and looked at her, surprised. "Really? You can't?"

"It's different with us," she said, immediately picking up what I was alluding to. Even though we weren't necessarily besties, she and I clicked on some level. "We didn't see our families die, you know? Other than Ulla, I mean. Everything happened from a distance and it doesn't feel real yet. It will, one day—be real, I mean. For a lot of the girls, they're still in denial. They all think their family somehow survived the Fall. Temple? His girls? Ulla? They had to watch their families die."

I was silent for a moment as my thoughts drifted back to when Lucia and I stole the BearCat from King Dale. Sitting there, in the middle of I-64 after the successful heist, we'd contemplated risking the chance to drive cross-country, back to California and our families. I'd known then, deep down, that it was a waste of time, but it was still there. That fantasy, the idea of my dysfunctional family managing to pull together and surviving the apocalypse. Lucia had a similar moment, I'm sure.

It was a bitter comfort knowing I hadn't really dealt with the loss of my family.

"Hey," Emily said, nudging me with an elbow. "I'm on watch tonight. Want to hang out?"

"You're on watch?" I asked, somewhat surprised. Emily would pull a watch here and there but never an overnighter. "What about Rohena?"

"She traded me two packets of noodles to cover for her," she explained.

"I'm not even going to ask," I muttered, shaking my head. Rohena loved the overnight shift because it got her out of morning chores. The girl liked to sleep almost as much as I did. Thinking it over, I shrugged. "I need to get some sleep sometime, so I can't stay up all night. But I can hang for a few hours."

"If we talk, we need to keep it down," Emily said. I looked at her, confused, before I remembered: Temple and his granddaughters were in an apartment now and would probably be able to hear us.

"Right. Forgot."

"Don't forget to tell Ulla you'll be up late. She gets weird when you're not around."

"Okay, Mom."

She chuckled. "Ugh, no thanks. Don't want to be your mom. You're a river baby."

"Huh? A what?"

"A river baby. You know, when nature creates some kind of aberration, like a deformed pup, the mother of the animal will take it and drown it in a river. That's you. A river baby."

"What the ... ? Hey, wait a minute. That's bullsh—"

"Language," Emily cut me off, smiling. "Rooftop. Midnight."

"Not even a clue?"

"Nope."

"Dang it."

"A river baby?" I asked her two hours later, once we were up on the rooftop of the cafeteria. The air was cold but tolerable. Still, we'd grabbed our winter coats and a few extra blankets for just in case. Unnecessary, but one never knew.

It was a clear sky and, with the moon not even a sliver in the western sky, it was as dark as it could be. Above us, I could see the Milky Way and recognized a constellation or two. The Big Dipper was easy, but I was pretty sure I pegged the Little Dipper as well. My favorite constellation, Orion the Hunter, was low on the horizon to the east. It was surreal, and a sight I really hadn't had a chance to enjoy since before the Fall.

"That was unfair. Sorry. By the way, you missed a really cool meteor shower a week ago," Emily stated, settling down in a chair. Propping her feet up on the low wall of the rooftop, she leaned back and gazed upward into the sky. I sat down in the other chair and wrapped a blanket around my legs. It took me a minute to get comfortable. I wasn't used to pulling watches up here. The river and lowlands surrounding the mountain were more my speed. Observe, track, then kill the shamblers. Being on the aggressive side of things was preferable to sitting around and waiting for them to come to me. Usually. "The Geminids. They come from around the handle of the Big Dipper over there. I saw something like seventy or so in half an hour."

"You're forgiven. Meteors. Huh," I said, trying to sound interested. In reality I was tired and just wanted to enjoy the view. In silence, if it were at all possible. With Rohena it usually wasn't, but Emily . . . "It's pretty."

"Yeah," she said and yawned. There were a few minutes of silence between us before she spoke again. "I wanted to talk to you."

"I figured that part out when you asked me to come up here. What about?"

"Watch the sky," she told me. Turning my head, I gave her a look. "Humor me?"

"Fine," I grumbled and looked up at the night sky. It was pretty, with satellites flashing by every once in a while. One entire universe out there, filled with galaxies. The sight was awe inspiring. I hadn't seen it this clear in over a year. Without the background lights of the path around the central field and gymnasium, it was much easier to see the sky above. "Yeah . . . really pretty," I allowed.

Something hard and cold touched my arm. I jerked away instinctively. Glancing down, I saw Emily was holding a small device in her hand. She pressed it against me again.

"Check it out," she said. I grabbed it and, confused, stared at it for a moment before I realized what it was.

"Is this a cell phone?"

"No. Better. It's a GPS device."

"How is that better?" I asked, confused. I flipped it over and inspected it. The screen was dim but on, which amazed me. "How's the battery still working?"

"It runs on double *A*s," Emily answered. "We have tons of those and nothing to use them on. Except this. Go ahead, keep it. Figure it out. It's pretty easy. I thought you could use it when you start ranging out farther away from campus. You can add a pin on the digital map to help orient your way home, no matter where you are."

"Hey, the school is already marked on the map," I stated as I used a finger to drag the screen around. "Did you do that? Shows the creek, the river, and even where the James River forms down past Iron Gate. Cool!"

"Yeah, it is," she said. Something in her voice told me this wasn't what she really wanted to talk about, though. "It's cool enough."

"But...?"

"It got me thinking," she said, taking a deep breath in the cold mountain air. "I read the manual and a few other things involving GPS trackers like this. They run off of triangulated satellites, right? So you always know where you're at within seven meters. Maybe closer."

"Uh-huh..." I had no idea where she was going with this. Or even what she was talking about, to be honest.

"It's got a clock on it, too. But it needs an atomic clock to tell the time from somewhere else. So do the satellites," she explained in a hushed whisper, mindful of a possibly sleeping Temple being awakened. "An atomic clock here on the ground, in the U.S."

"Okay...?"

"That means somewhere there is a place where some branch of the military is holed up, safe, keeping time and waiting," she finished with a triumphant look on her face. "Those satellites up there are probably still communicating!"

"They need people to physically keep time for... satellites?" I was thoroughly confused now. "It's not all automated?"

"Someone's gotta make sure the computer systems are up and running. Which means power. Someone, somewhere, is hiding out and keeping the clocks on. Keeping the GPS signals running."

"But... why?" I asked when I was finally able to find my voice. "Why are they hiding?"

"I don't know," she admitted. "Maybe they're afraid of getting sick? You know, being locked up in some basement in the middle of Montana or something would—"

"Montana?" I interrupted. "Why would they be in Montana?"

"I don't know. Maybe because that's where our nuclear missiles are?"

"We have nuclear missiles in Montana?"

"Probably? I think so, maybe. I don't know."

"You say so."

"Look, it doesn't matter where they are." Emily was clearly growing exasperated. The poor girl was trying to share some potentially earth-shattering information with me and I was being a bit of a bitch. Instead of interrupting again, I let her speak. "The fact is, they're out there, making sure the GPS is still up and running. GPS that those people in Wolf Squadron need to sail across the Atlantic, and Caribbean, everywhere!"

She had a point. If anyone knew about this stuff, it would be Emily. But why the secrecy about it? I couldn't think of a good reason, so I asked. Her answer was immediate. I could tell she'd been preparing it.

"Because what if they want her back? To be a marine again, and leave us?"

"Wait . . . Sister Ann?" I asked.

"You know of any other marines around here?"

"She wouldn't leave us. She *can't* leave us." My tone was emphatic. I knew Sister Ann, and trusted her. She was the only person who could make sure St. Dominic's continued to function and protect all of us girls here as well. There was no way she would abandon us for some military person in Montana or wherever. My voice lowered to a whisper. "She can't, right? Don't her religious nun-vows mean she's here forever?"

"I don't know," Emily admitted, shrugging. "But the end of the world happened, Maddie. Rules change."

"Sister Ann doesn't." I paused and stared at the stars for another minute. Another satellite passed across the sky while I pondered what she'd said. "Why tell me all this?" I asked her.

"What do you mean?"

"This." I waved my hand toward the stars above. "The satellites. The government. Sister Ann. Everything. Why tell me all this?"

She stared at me for a moment like I was stupid before saying, "Because you're the one in charge. Duh."

"No I'm not."

"Uh, yes, dumbass. You are."

I scoffed at her and crossed my arms. "No. No way."

"Look," she said, shifting in her chair. "You've been running things for, like, months now. Ever since Sister Ann put you in charge of security you've been the boss. Sister Ann directs the meetings and stuff, but think about it: When did she push a plan on us that you didn't support or come up with?"

I started to protest but stopped. If I argued with her, she'd probably just find a way to prove me wrong. The nerd was definitely smarter than I was, and even before the Fall I'd never won an argument with her. Instead, I opted for silence. I hadn't come up here for a fight. No, I'd just wanted to hang out with someone for a change. Try to be friends with someone I actually tolerated. Being the ostracized—

"Is that why everyone avoids me?" I asked without thinking. "Because they think I'm in charge?"

"Never argue with the girl who kills the shamblers," Emily pointed out. "Or carries the gun and runs security."

Fair point. I'd never been one to shy away from *either* of those responsibilities. "Look ... I don't want to be in charge."

"Tough."

Emily was exasperating. Partly, because I had to admit that she was probably right. Sister Ann had been letting me call a lot of the shots lately. She'd been so sneaky about it that I hadn't even caught on. I shook off the thoughts. The time to dwell on that was later. Now? I just wanted to relax.

"Can't we just, I don't know, enjoy the stars? *Quietly?*" I asked.

"Up to you ..."

"Thanks."

"... *boss.*"

"Oh, come on!"

CHAPTER NINE

"Every time we go outside, they're around. Zombies. Everywhere. Shoot one, two more appear. It's better to hide. Always better. Safer. Safety is better than aggression. They don't hunt you if you stay quiet and hide."
From: *Collected Radio Transmissions of the Fall,*
University of the South Press, 2053

The next morning, I was up just after dawn. Sister Ann and a few of the younger girls were preparing breakfast. It wasn't much—grilled potatoes and some Spam—but I'd grown to like it over the past few months. I wolfed mine down quickly before heading out. Temple's farm, and his neighbor's, sounded like they were still well-stocked and I wanted to get out there and check them out.

Normally I would have brought Lucia with, but since I wasn't planning on grabbing anything just yet, I figured I would make it a solo trip. Plus, after how much Lucia had been doing around campus lately, a five-mile hike would wipe her out. If I found anything worthwhile, I'd bring her back with the four-wheeler and load up on stocks. Temple had already told us he didn't have much left at his farm. The shamblers had done a number on his pantry and kitchen. All that was left was what he'd already stored down in his basement.

His neighbor's farm, the Boyds', on the other hand, had remained abandoned the entire time. The old lady who'd lived there had died of the flu in the hospital and Temple had locked it up in anticipation of her son coming in to go through everything after the funeral.

Except . . . the world had ended, there'd been no funeral, and nobody had come to the farm since.

Temple, in a moment of brilliant foresight, had latched the storm shutters over the first-floor windows before the Fall had truly kicked off.

He hadn't been too interested in what was inside, though he did remember from the few times he'd gone over to check on her before she'd gotten sick that she had a massive canning addiction. Apparently the woman had canned everything from whole chickens to bread—and was good at it to boot, and had been doing it for longer than most of us have been alive.

The possibility of canning supplies alone would have made the trip worth it. Kayla was *pumped* about the prospect of having a magnetic lid lifter. Whatever that was.

The morning was cold. Last night, while out on the rooftop with Emily, it hadn't been too bad. Apparently I'd angered nature by commenting it'd been too nice out for this time of the year. Whatever cold that had been lacking previously was in full effect today. There was frost everywhere and every step made a soft crunching sound. On pavement it was going to be slick, which meant I'd have to be extra careful when crossing the tracks behind campus on my way out.

Testing out the new GPS device Emily had gifted me, it was pretty easy to locate Temple's farm. There weren't many houses up the road that way. I plugged the location into the map and then set the distance. On a straight path it was two miles. Since I wasn't stupid enough to stay on the road, though, it was probably going to be closer to four. This was going to be an all-day trip. Sighing, I pocketed the GPS and headed out.

Carefully navigating the path down, I noticed the morning was eerily quiet. Curious, I paused and waited. Usually I'd hear *something* out in the forest, even if it was only a few birds. This morning? Nothing.

That usually meant a shambler. Not always, though. Swallowing, I decided not to risk it. Slowly bringing Baby up into what Sister Ann called the low ready position, I began to scan my surroundings. Each part of the forest was quickly divvied up into quadrants as I searched for threats. I didn't see anything, but that didn't mean there weren't any shamblers around. The beta that had been hanging around down by the creek might have crept closer to campus.

Movement. Left, in the underbrush by the tracks. There was a cluster of trees right there. Turning, I started to back slowly up the way I'd come before stopping. I could see *something* behind one of the trees. The odds of it being an aggressive shambler were almost zero, but I hadn't survived this long being stupid. As cold as it was, if it was a shambler it could be nearly dead.

If it was the beta, though, this was the perfect time to take care of it.

Instead of hurrying back up the path to grab Ulla so we could hunt some shamblers, I moved sideways and slipped behind a large bush. The odds of it being here by the time I returned with her were slim and I didn't want to waste more time. Plus, I was tired of this thing lurking around. With the bush between me and the shambler, I was able to move quicker. The challenge was avoiding all the sticks and leaves on the ground as I moved. While doing this, I kept a close eye on where I'd seen the shambler at. The damn thing wasn't getting away this time.

There! A flash of tan to my left. Pivoting, I kept Baby up and ready. Considering how sneaky this little beta seemed to be, I didn't want to waste a shot and run the risk of others in the area coming to investigate.

My breath came out in short little puffs of steam. It felt as if the air temperature around me was dropping. Feeling dampness on the back of my neck, I realized I'd started to sweat. I mentally cursed. The last thing I needed was to be covered with sweat in below-freezing temperatures. Taking another cautious step to the right, I tried to get a better angle on the shambler. The damn thing continued to keep the tree between us, though.

Silently swearing, I moved behind a smaller tree closer to where the shambler was hiding.

The cold stung my eyes. My fingers began to ache from being in the same position for so long. Carefully flexing my left hand, I tried to get the blood circulating again. It was painful. I hadn't realized just how tight I was holding the grip.

The beta was still behind the tree. Something was odd, though. My instincts were screaming at me that this was different, but I didn't know what just yet. My eyes kept flickering around the forest, looking for any signs of additional threats. There were none that I could see or hear. While it was a little comforting, Sister Ann's lessons echoed in the back of my mind: Stay focused, and stay aware. Trust my instincts. Keep my booger hook off the bang switch.

Freaking Marine nun...

I was on its blind side now. The shot was still obscured, however, so I moved farther right and closer. Somehow the damned thing kept the tree between it and me, like it knew I was trying to sneak up on it for a better shot. Shamblers weren't normally this smart.

"Gotcha," I muttered.

The shambler screamed in fright, then tried to run away. It slipped on the icy ground and fell, tumbling through branches and leaves as it rolled down the hillside. Leaping around the tree, I took off in pursuit. It fell fast. I struggled to keep up. It finally came to a halt abruptly—by slamming into a downed tree. It let out a low groan and raised its hands in the air. I moved in closer, preparing to take the shot.

"Please...please don't shoot me!"

I stopped just before pulling the trigger. Squinting, I watched as a very sane-looking face looked up at me between the branches. What I'd thought was the beta shambler was something else entirely.

It was a boy.

The guy being clothed should have been my first clue that he wasn't a shambler. In my defense, the tan jacket and old, dirty khakis played tricks on my eyes. It being freezing cold didn't help my awareness, either. Plus, I was tired. I'd stayed up too late with Emily watching the stars.

He looked about my age, probably. It was hard to tell. He was skinny and dirty, as if he'd been on his own for a long time and hadn't been able to find a lot to eat, but enough to stay alive. A lot of the girls at school had that same look. The Fall, it seemed, had become the world's greatest—and by greatest, I mean worst—diet plan. Not that I'd needed it in the first place. My hardest problem was keeping weight on so the other girls would quit calling me anorexic.

"Uh...hi?" he said in a meek voice, holding his hands up in surrender. He was trying to be as nonthreatening as possible. His eyes kept flickering back and forth between the AR-15 and my face.

Keeping Baby pointed just off to the side, I just stared at him for a few moments before finding my voice.

"What are you doing up here?" I finally asked. It was a stupid question, sure. But I hadn't expected to find, well, a *real* person running around up here.

"Hiding from the zombies," he answered. "Please don't shoot me."

"Hiding from shamblers up here?" That seemed even stupider than my question. But then, lots of things had become stupid since the world ended. This was just another checkmark on the dumb-ideas list. "Why up here? How long have you been watching?"

"I saw lots of girls with guns running around," he replied after a moment. "Y'all were killing zombies left and right. I didn't want to get shot, so I stayed away from the campus. Lots of little cabins around here. Hunting cabins, you know? Some were trashed, but there's a ranger station not too far away that seemed safe. Been hitting some building near the river not far from here for food. It had a stove but then y'all took it."

So *that's* where all the canned food from the Moose Lodge went. One mystery was now solved, at least. I don't know about killing shamblers left and right, though. We hadn't shot one in days. "And?"

"And what?"

"And why are you out here? Hiding out? We've got survivors living with us." Kind of true, thanks to the arrival of Temple and the girls. I wasn't going to give this guy exact numbers, though. I had no idea who he was and didn't want to encourage him. I knew some of the local townies from before the Fall but he wasn't one of them. "You could've come down the main road and, I don't know, asked for help. Like any reasonable person would. Where you from?"

"Grew up in Lexington. Moved to Callaghan three years ago after my dad left us."

I kept my face calm, but my guts churned. Callaghan was farther west from Covington, and one of the last towns before West Virginia. Callaghan was also at Mile Marker 10, off the back road that led straight to campus—and the one way we didn't want King Dale coming from. Since the boy had been lurking on the mountain, he also probably knew about the secret path along the railroad tracks by now. He'd admitted that he'd been watching us, but hadn't said for how long. The idea of someone spying on us from up here made me shiver unexpectedly. It was suspicious as hell.

"Please don't tell anyone I'm up here," he begged. "Please? My mom turned into a zombie and . . . I had to . . . she . . . after, I ran. Can't go back. I'll go to jail. They'll put me in the chair or something." The last few words came out in a whisper.

Suddenly, his not showing up at the front entrance of the school made a lot of sense. His instincts had been to come down, but what he'd done stopped him. He'd had to kill his own mom after she turned, and then live with the guilt forever after. I understood completely, but I'd come to terms with shooting shamblers. As Sister Ann had put it, I'd made the mental disconnect between people and the shamblers. They weren't human anymore. Junior here hadn't managed to do that just yet. Depending on how long it'd been since he'd had to kill her, he might never.

"Look . . . you really should come over to the school and join us. No one's going to judge you. Besides, it's safer there."

"Can't." His voice was hoarse. He looked away and shook his head. "No. I can't."

"Okayyy." I let the word drag out slowly as I tried to think. "You said you found the ranger station here on the mountain?" He looked back up at me before nodding. He looked rather pathetic down there on the ground, and I felt sorry for him. "We'll work it out. You can stay there. How are you looking for food?"

"I've got some cans of those mini hotdogs left."

"Some?"

"I don't know. Three, four?"

The kid was going to starve if I left him to his own devices. But since he didn't want to come back to the school, it was going to be hard to keep him alive. He had to *want* to live. That was one of Sister Ann's points early on: give us something to work toward besides just surviving.

Plus, he was unarmed. If a shambler found him—or worse, one of King Dale's men—he wouldn't last long even with food. Starving, he wouldn't have the energy to run far. Only weapon I had besides Baby was a small pocket knife, so I wasn't about to give him either. Besides, Sister Ann would kill me if I gave a complete stranger a weapon, no matter how innocent they seemed.

"Come on, get up." I helped him to his feet. He brushed a few icy leaves from his pants and jacket. He wasn't even wearing any gloves, the idiot. "Look . . . just stay hidden for now. We'll . . . I don't know, we'll figure it out."

"What do you mean?" he asked, his tone suspicious.

"Sister Ann is going to have some ideas—"

"No!" he interrupted me, clearly terrified. "Please, no. Don't tell anyone, please?"

"Okay, fine! Sheesh." I paused and looked around. The coast was clear. No sign of a shambler anywhere. Or anyone else, for that matter. "Will you at least tell me your name?"

"Uh, yeah. Colton. Colton Raher."

"Nice to meet you, Colton. I'm Maddie." He nodded but didn't say anything more. After a few moments of awkward silence, I continued. "Look, I want to help you, but you can't stay up here forever. The shamblers are going to find you eventually." *Or King Dale*, I didn't say. If he didn't know about the wannabe ruler already, then I saw no reason to accidentally steer him that way and give the tinpot ruler a new potential ally who knew his way around the mountain. I pointed at his jacket. "That's looking kinda thin. You got anything else warmer?"

"No."

How the guy survived this long was beyond me.

"So you said you've been staying at the ranger station?"

"Once or twice," he said through chattering teeth. "It really gets dark up here at night."

"Yeah. That's a feature, not a bug."

"Is it always like this?"

"When it's cloudy, it's almost pitch black," I told him. He looked a little pale at that. Or it could have been the cold. He was shivering, which was a good sign. Hypothermia victims stopped shivering in the cold. Speaking of . . . "Look, you need to get out of the cold. Since you won't come up to campus, let's get you someplace warm. Ranger station?"

"Uh . . . okay?"

He wasn't thinking clearly, which was a potentially bad sign. "Come on, let's go."

"You know where it's at?" he asked.

"Duh. I've lived here for three years almost. I know this mountain better than anyone else." *Except for Mr. Stitmer, bless his soul,* I didn't add.

The way to the ranger station, in a straight line, was a little under a mile. However, we were in the mountains, so nothing was in a straight line. Also, it was on the far side of the campus, below and to the south. If I wanted to avoid prying eyes, we'd have to go the long way around—which meant crossing Dunlap Creek down toward the ruined paper mill. Not my favorite way to go but if I didn't want to be seen by whoever was on watch—or, more importantly, answer some awkward questions later—then it was the best way.

Looking across the mountainside, I wondered for a moment just *why* Colton was over here. It wasn't as if this was an easy route to take. There were other paths around the ranger station that were easier to navigate. The only plausible idea I could come up with was that he had been heading toward the Moose Lodge when I'd stumbled on him and started the chase. Since I am the opposite of shy and subtle, I asked directly.

"What were you doing over on this side of campus anyway? If you were creeping on us, I'll shoot you in the kneecap."

"What? No!" he protested. "I was, uh, heading to look at some of those houses by that lodge place. The elk? I think. I was hoping they'd have food or something."

As I'd suspected. "Okay, good. You were on the right path. Good thing you didn't try to cross the tracks. With the ice and how much you're shivering, you'd probably fall into the creek and freeze to death."

"What are *you* doing out here, anyway?" he asked me. "It's really cold out."

"I was on my way to scout out some locations when I thought I saw a shambler running around," I replied, jerking my chin in his direction. He chuckled softly.

"Oh."

"C'mon," I said, motioning for him to follow. "I still have stuff to do."

"Where are we going?" he asked, clearly nervous. I sighed and tried not to roll my eyes.

"The ranger station, remember? I need to get you somewhere safe for now, since you're afraid of coming to St. Dom's."

"I'm not afraid . . . I just don't want to go to jail."

"News flash: there are no police anymore. Just us."

"Still . . ."

"See? This is why I suggested the ranger station. Multiple times now," I said. Turning, I started walking the roundabout way to the station. After a few seconds I stopped and looked back. He hadn't moved. "I'm not carrying you. I don't think I can. Let's go."

I could have sworn he muttered something about crazy gingers under his breath but since I was in a somewhat forgiving mood—I remembered how shook up Temple and his girls were when he spoke about what had happened to his family—I ignored his comment. Instead, I focused on my footing as we trekked around campus, slowly making our way to Dunlap Creek. We'd have to cross it, then circle back and cross it again, but it was the only way I knew of to the station without Ulla spotting us.

The deer trail was narrow and slick. The freezing temps did nothing to make the going easier. Still, we made decent time to the creek. Only once did Colton slip and land on his butt. Fortunately, he didn't hurt anything other than his pride. I didn't even make fun of him once.

See? I can be mature.

Crossing the falls was another matter altogether.

Longtime residents of the area probably didn't even know this, but Dunlap Creek had a little waterfall area and a pond right before it fed into the Jackson River. There were some *massive* fish in the pond, too. I wasn't into fishing much, but if I were I'd be happy catching one of those. The pond and the waterfall were both still technically on St. Dominic's land, so nobody came down here.

Nobody, that was, except Sir Chonk, loyal slayer of shamblers and trash bins.

"Crap!" I hissed and froze as the massive black bear lumbered out of the pond. Everything I'd read about the bears in the area said they'd be hibernating for another month or two. Apparently nobody told the bear that he was supposed to be asleep. I don't know why, but I was absolutely certain this was the same bear who had inadvertently helped me out months before.

In his mouth was probably the biggest fish I'd ever seen caught around here. Mr. Stitmer would have cried jealous tears.

We watched and waited quietly as Sir Chonk slowly ambled on the opposite bank of the pond toward a small recess in the rocks next to the waterfall. The fat bear suddenly disappeared around the corner. I blinked, confused, before realizing it wasn't a regular recess back there but a cave.

"Well, that's convenient," I muttered quietly.

"Is it going to eat us?" Colton asked.

"No. Sir Chonk is a loyal shambler slayer."

"Huh?"

"Nothing. Come on."

"There are bears up here?" Colton asked in a low voice, clearly reluctant to move. I nodded.

"Three or four, I think. Besides Sir Chonk, that is. Okay, it's safe, probably. Come on," I whispered, and he followed. We continued along the path next to the pond. Every few steps I'd turn and look back to see if Sir Chonk was following us until we were past the pond and the falls. From the new angle I could see the cave better. I wondered for a moment how I'd missed it in the past before continuing.

The bear didn't follow us. Apparently the fish was more than enough for his midwinter snack. The idea of Colton and I trying to outrun an angry, incoherent, and probably hungry bear was a dumb one. It would have come down to my aim versus his hunger, and the odds were about even there.

Plus, I felt like I still owed Sir Chonk. I'd rather leave him be.

Eventually we came to the path which led back up to the ranger station. It was more washed out than I remember it being, something I blamed on the wet winter we'd had so far. The forest around us was quiet, which meant the birds knew we were there. I stopped for a second so Colton could catch his breath while I listened for any sound of shamblers.

Relieved, I leaned against a tree as Colton bent over at the waist. He was breathing heavily. A few moments passed before I asked him if he was okay.

"Yeah," he replied after a few seconds. It was clear he was struggling. "Just not used. To walking so much. At one time."

"Cardio is your friend," I told him. He cracked a smile at that.

"Cardio is the devil."

I snorted. The guy had a decent sense of humor, I'd give him that. "Come on. We're almost there."

It was another quarter of a mile on a steep incline before we reached the abandoned station. Though it was only slightly lower than St. Dominic's, elevation-wise, it felt like farther down the mountain due to the steep drop below. Colton sounded like he was dying the entire way up. Mentally I was dropping the odds of his survival with each passing step. He clearly was not cut out for any sort of long-distance hiking. Not yet at least. Maybe after he got some more food in him and built up his strength and endurance? I wasn't sure.

The ranger station was an old log cabin that actually had been upgraded a bit over the years. While it definitely lacked power, it at least had a relatively new roof and covered porch built on. The path to and from the front door was clear, though the back was partially blocked off by a cluster of blackberry bushes I hadn't even known were there before the Fall.

We picked that sucker clean the moment berries appeared. Lots of it was canned but for a week, all the surviving girls of St. Dominic's had blackberries for dessert. It was wonderful.

"Wow," Colton muttered once he got his breath back. "That's smaller than I thought it would be."

"I thought you said you slept here?" I asked, suddenly suspicious. He turned and nodded.

"It was dark. I was gone before sunrise. Didn't get a good look at the inside. Too dark."

Oh, that made sense. I knew how dark it got up on campus. Down here, without moonlight and in the shadows of the mountain and all its trees? Still, in the morning hours it got plenty of light. Once it changed into late afternoon, however, the building would be cast into darkness. Not enviable for the rangers who might have been stuck in here back in the day. I undogged the latch, pulled the heavy door open, and slipped inside. Colton followed closely behind.

Inside it was much warmer. I wouldn't have thought the station would be insulated but I've been wrong before. Either that or it had some sort of natural heat source I wasn't aware of. Perhaps the plywood-covered windows were better at keeping the heat than regular windows? It was worth investigating later, especially when we started using the cottage dorms again. This sort of insulation would make Emily cry happy tears.

There was a loft with a ladder on the far end of the single-room building. I remember Sister Margaret showing a few of us the station when I'd first arrived on campus. She'd told us the history of the building, its purpose, and how the forest service rangers used to sleep up there. There used to be a tower that rose about twenty feet into the air connecting to it but apparently it was removed some years ago when the forest service quit using it full-time. Sister Margaret had been saddened by the loss. Apparently it was one of the more unique features around St. Dominic's, and the nuns loved climbing it to gaze upon the wonders around them. Not quite a cloister but according to her, good enough.

Maybe that's what she meant when she'd said, "try your best, and rise above the rest"? Probably not. Rising above everyone else? That was more my speed.

Colton clambered up to the loft while I inspected the rest of the station. I hadn't been in here since we'd first been discovered by King Dale down by the river, and was surprised at how clean it still was.

He hadn't used the stove at all. For a guy who'd stayed in probably the safest place on the mountain not named St. Dominic's, he'd declined to take full advantage of the place. Or perhaps he didn't know how to use a woodstove? It was kind of absurd, but not everyone was a camper. Or understood that the body's core temperature couldn't get too low before hypothermia set in. The fact that he hadn't froze to death just yet was further proof that God loved children and fools.

The ranger station was safe for now. It was a good spot and, because they used boards over windows and locked everything up tight when it was not in use, the inside was in great shape. In the long term, I'd need to convince him to come up to campus where it was safer. For now, though, he was fine. Just needed to keep Ulla from accidentally shooting him. It would be bad if he died because she thought he was nothing more than a shambler.

"Try to keep away from shamblers," I told him as he moved around up on the loft. He disappeared for a moment. After a second his face reappeared. There was a huge smile plastered on his face. Seeing it made me grin as well.

"I can see everywhere from up here," he stated as he swung back down the ladder. The guy was surprisingly nimble. He landed next to me. His smile turned into a frown. "Well, I can't see the school."

That was by design, I didn't say. It would have been real creepy if a forest ranger had a clear view of the dorms at St. Dominic's. "We can find you a better place later ... maybe until you think it's okay to come up to the school?"

"They'll lock me up in jail and toss the key," he said in a mournful tone. I nodded and pretended to understand. I'd shot enough shamblers at this point that I'd stopped considering what they'd once been. I doubted there would be anyone stupid enough to arrest anyone for shambler killing these days.

"Okay, you can stay here until we find something better," I told him, looking around. It was dry and dusty, with no sign of leaks in the roof. Not that I knew what to look for. You'd think they'd be easy to spot, though. Large stain on the ceiling? Yeah, easy.

"What are you going to do?" he asked, fearful. Trying not to roll my eyes, I explained.

"I need to get back and tell Sister Ann—"

"But you said—"

"—and tell Sister Ann that there might be survivors out and about. Nothing about you or you being up here, okay? Relax. I'll then tell the others not to shoot someone on sight, just in case," I finished, barreling over his protests with the grace of a water buffalo. "We don't need anyone shooting you accidentally."

He swallowed, clearly wary. Good. His whining was starting to get on my nerves a little bit. "Okay."

"Only burn the woodstove at night," I warned him. "Cook for the entire day during then. Keep the windows closed. Light attracts shamblers, and smoke from a chimney attracts curiosity."

He nodded. "Okay."

"I'll get some food for you from our stash," I added and reached out to squeeze his arm comfortingly. Blinking, I let go quickly. The jacket hid a bit of muscle. Maybe he was eating better than I'd thought? "Just ... stay safe, okay? When you're ready, maybe I can convince you to come up to campus, where it'll be safer."

"Live at a school full of girls and nuns with guns? No, thanks," he chuckled darkly and pushed his lanky hair out of his face. His eyes met mine. They were a light blue, almost green like mine. "Uh . . . thank you for . . . all this."

"Don't thank me yet," I warned him. "There are still shamblers running around. You won't be safe until you're down at the school with us."

Plus, you still might freeze to death because you have no idea how to gather firewood, you cute idiot, I didn't say. I stopped and blushed. Fortunately, he wasn't looking my way. *What the hell, Maddie?*

What the hell?

CHAPTER TEN

"While the infected packs have been documented roaming and hunting together, when there is a decided lack of available food supplies they have been known to turn on one another. In an infected hunter pack, when food is scarce, it is truly the strongest and most aggressive that will survive."
—Lecture part of "Grad 725—Research Methods for the Infected" by Dr. Tedd Roberts, University of the South 2047

It was almost noon by the time I was back on the path toward the Boyd farm. The delay in dealing with Colton wasn't too long but my legs were already burning as I trudged along the railroad tracks past the Moose Lodge and farther up into the mountains. Even with the amount of cardio I do on a daily basis thanks to my patrols, hiking up and down the mountain had taken a lot out of me.

Eventually the tracks would take me to Humpback Bridge, where I'd then angle off and head on down to Temple's farm. Just a little farther, according to his directions, and I'd reach his neighbor's.

Part of me just wanted to call it a day right then and there. If I'd taken the main road, it would have been easier, sure. But it also would have meant more potential shamblers. Not that I was too concerned about them, but I was also aware of our ammo supply potentially running low in the future. We were safe for now, but what happened if someone got a little more aggressive? Someone like King Dale, for instance. Sister Ann wanted me to conserve as much ammo as possible, just in case.

Which meant I couldn't go traipsing down some random paved road like an idiot looking to shoot some shamblers.

Unfortunately.

Humpback Bridge is an old, covered bridge that, pre-Fall, had been a local tourist attraction. They sometimes had car shows there to raise money for local charities as well. There was an ancient, weathered plaque next to the bridge talking about all the interesting local historical stuff about it that bored me to tears. Pretty sure Emily or the twins would have found it fascinating. Or possibly Sister Ann, though I was sure she'd been up here multiple times in the past. It was off the only road that passed by the school, after all.

My thoughts drifted to Colton briefly. He would have had to come this way if he'd walked from Callaghan. Safely, too, which told me there weren't many shamblers around here. Or he was a very lucky guy. Considering he'd managed to get up the mountain without getting shot or eaten, someone was definitely looking out for him.

I spotted Temple's house first. It was in rough shape, with the windows busted out on the entire first floor and the front door smashed in. Since I knew Temple had already cleared out the easy access stuff, I didn't bother checking his place for anything. There was no need. Other than perhaps some extra women's clothing from his now-turned daughter-in-law, there was nothing of value left in there. It was just a house now, according to Temple—not even a home.

The Boyd farm was actually hidden from the road beyond Temple's, nestled in a wooded area. It wasn't much of a farm, if anyone had bothered to ask me. There was a small white shed that looked half-destroyed due to time and kudzu.

Kudzu was something I'd never dealt with before coming to St. Dominic's. Not directly. I'd heard of it but out on the West Coast, everything "not native" was either amazing and great or invasive and horrible. It was irritating because what a plant or animal was labeled depended on what day of the week it was.

Except for fruit flies. Those were always bad.

"Flamethrowers," I muttered as I eyed a nearby stand of trees that were being devoured by a clump of kudzu. Flamethrowers would take care of the kudzu problem. Probably not permanently, though. The plant was seriously difficult to get rid of.

I eyeballed the house from the dirt driveway, looking for any signs of shamblers. Just as Temple had told us, he'd shuttered the first-floor storm windows, and they looked like they were still intact. The porch, while shadowed, appeared empty. The front door was closed and, I presumed, secured. My hand drifted down to my pocket. Temple had given me the key so I wouldn't have to break in and risk exposing the inside to the elements. Or any shamblers that might happen on it.

The porch was old but in relatively decent shape, only creaking slightly as I walked up to the front door. Testing the door handle, it didn't budge. Still locked. Another good sign. Shifting Baby's sling, I dug the key out of my pocket and unlocked the door. It opened easily and quietly.

It was dark inside. There was an old musty smell, and an underlying scent of something vaguely familiar. It wasn't the nasty smell I'd come to associate with body decomposition, which was another positive sign. Still, whatever the other stench was, it made me uncomfortable. I stepped inside and left the door open. It was the only source of light in the entryway and I didn't want any surprises.

Temple had said he thought the canning supplies were in the kitchen but he hadn't been absolutely certain. If they weren't, then they were in the basement—somewhere I did not particularly want to go. I hated basements. We didn't really have them out in California. Basements and root cellars seemed to be a Southern thing. Plus, dark places where there would be little to no light? No, thank you.

Instead, I decided to check upstairs first. The stairs were shallow and narrow, but I managed to avoid knocking down pictures hung on the wall. At the top I looked both ways. There was a narrow bridge connecting two landings that seemed to run the entire length of the living room below. It was open on both sides, too, which allowed for a very surreal view down below. If I were afraid of heights, it might have gotten to me.

I checked the left rooms first. Both were closed but I entered them cautiously anyway. Temple had locked up the windows and I hadn't seen any broken, but none of us girls had survived this long by taking stupid risks. Every risk we took, according to Sister Ann, was a calculated one. Still risky, true. But not stupid.

The first room had nothing of value that I could see. It had a set of twin beds that looked like they were in reasonable shape. They both had plastic mattress protectors covering them, and neither had sheets or blankets. Clearly they were there simply in case relatives came to visit and not for anyone actually living there.

The other room had a sewing machine and plastic crates filled with scrap fabric. There were also bundles of fabric wrapped around long wooden sticks as well. If I had any interest in sewing, this might have been a great find. Since we didn't have power and the sewing machine needed it, it was a wash for now. Later, perhaps, if and when more survivors showed up, I could come back and grab more stuff.

Closing both doors, I made my way across the narrow bridge to the other side of the second floor. Though the downstairs window shutters kept it dark, there were two skylights above the bridge that let in some natural lighting. It was enough for me to see the living room below. It was a little messy, though the bridge did create an odd shadow running all the way toward where I surmised the kitchen to be. Two saloon-style swinging doors prohibited me from seeing farther. I shrugged. The kitchen would still be there after I finished checking the upstairs rooms.

Both doors on this end were open. Left or right? After a moment of debate, I chose right.

It was a bad call. There were floor-to-ceiling bookshelves along every wall in the room, with only one small window. That wasn't why I regretted my decision, though. No, on each bookshelf were numerous dolls: porcelain, rag doll, old ones, new ones, and the creepy "I'm straight out of a horror movie and I'm going to stab you in the heart" types. I'd never hated dolls growing up, or anything like that. Suddenly, though, I found myself really, *really* hating them and wanted nothing more than to get the hell out of there, fast.

Turning, I bumped into one of the shelves. A large vase, set precariously on the edge, was knocked off the ledge. Reaching out with my free hand to catch it, I fumbled it and just missed catching it. The vase fell to the floor, seemingly in slow motion. It shattered on impact, the noise seemingly louder than any gunshot in the small space. I stared at the damage for a moment before I swore. "Damn it!"

A low, keening moan erupted from across the narrow hallway in the other room. It quickly rose into a howl that nearly made me pee my pants. Turning, I barely managed to back away from the doorway as a filth-covered shambler stumbled into the room. Thin as a rail and tall, the creature had clearly seen better days. It fell to the floor, slipping on the shards of the broken vase. Its howls echoed in my ears as the shambler struggled to reach me.

Breathing heavily, I brought Baby up but jerked the trigger early. A round passed through the floor next to the shambler's arm. Swearing enough to give me demerits for a month, I moved to keep the distance between us and fired four more shots. The first struck the shoulder, but the next three went into the shambler's head. The howls abruptly ceased.

Panting heavily and my ears ringing, I almost didn't hear the responding howls coming from downstairs.

The action sounded like it was all downstairs. For now, at least. If there were many more, it wouldn't stay that way. I could hear footsteps and howls below me. There were definitely more. How did I miss them? Thinking back, the answer came to me fairly quickly— I hadn't checked the kitchen yet. Or the downstairs, really.

Which actually might have saved my life.

The shamblers below were clearly hunting, but they were staying downstairs for the time being. Shamblers were dangerous, but also dumb. No cunning ambushes and many lost track of their prey during a hunt. This gave me a little bit of time. I risked stepping into the hallway and looking back across the bridge toward the stairs. They hadn't even started to the stairwell yet, but they would soon enough. I needed to get the hell out of there.

How, though?

From what I could see at the base of the stairwell, the path to the front door was clear. However, with an unknown number of shamblers running around downstairs, I'd be in a footrace once outside. There were too many variables outdoors, things out of my control that would let them get me. The little bridge connecting the two halves of the second floor was a nice chokepoint and, from what I could see, was the only path to these two rooms on this side. I could make a stand here and hope for the best. Or I could go super aggressive.

I didn't have enough ammo for that option. Staying sneaky had to be the plan. Let them come to me.

The howling grew louder over the near-steady ringing in my ears. Risking another glance over the railing, I counted at least seven shamblers moving around in the living room area. They were clearly searching for me but from the looks of things, none had thought to look up just yet. I had time. Not much, but a little. It was better than none at all.

My hand was slick on the grip. Despite the cool temperature inside the house, I was sweating like crazy. The burning in my legs from the long hike was growing worse and my right calf felt like it was going to cramp up any second. The howls downstairs grew louder. They were getting frustrated. They'd come upstairs soon. Every single howl made my belly flip nervously.

I'd dealt with shamblers in the past, true. I'd killed a lot of them. But never while I was trapped in a house. Every time I'd gone shambler hunting they'd come into my zone, and I shot them on my terms. It wasn't a game of survival. This? Situations like this were what I'd worked so hard to avoid over the past nine months. Here I was not in my element, but in theirs.

It was a place I did not want to be.

A shambler—female from the looks of it—found the base of the stairs and started sniffing the air like a wild animal. She growled ferally and began to slowly ascend. Shakily, I exhaled and waited. I wanted her to get closer to the middle of the stairs before I did anything. Too high up and the others might climb over her. Too low, and they'd pull her out of the way. I needed my shambler roadblock at just the right—

I stroked the trigger twice. Both shots punched through the ribs of the skinny shambler. It howled in pain and slid down two steps. Not too far, though. Enough to make it difficult for any shambler to come up after.

The gunshots attracted more attention. The others came running for the stairs, their growls and howls setting my teeth on edge. A short fight broke out between two male shamblers, both of whom apparently really wanted to go first. The larger of the two shoved the smaller out of the way and started climbing the stairs.

Fortunately, my makeshift roadblock slowed him down. Taking careful aim, I put two shots into his side. Blood splashed on the pink-striped wallpaper behind him. Falling, the shambler began to howl in pain and anger. The stairs were becoming slick with blood. The other shambler tried to move past but the injured one grabbed its ankle. The larger one must have really wanted to go first. I rewarded him by putting another round through his head.

Lining up my shot on the smaller shambler, I squeezed the trigger two more times. The first shot went right into its chest but on the second, nothing happened. I fired again and nothing.

"Shit!" I screeched and ripped the magazine out, just as Sister Ann had taught me. Slapping the magazine against the wooden railing of the bridge, a stray round went flying from the magazine. The charge handle was next. I worked it quickly three times, just to make sure. The dim lighting made it difficult to see if the chamber was cleared, but I didn't notice any obstructions. I double-checked the magazine quickly and the next two rounds looked fine. I was almost tempted to toss it aside and grab one of my spares, but I still had over half the mag left and figured it would be enough.

Working quickly, I fed the magazine back into Baby and jerked back the charging handle one more time. The shambler I'd shot once was almost to the top of the stairs now. It was clearly having issues with the slick wooden staircase and my makeshift barricades. Who knew dead shamblers made terrific obstructions?

I'd never had a jam before, so I was keenly aware of lots of things that could go wrong on my next shot. Praying, I lined it up with the smaller male shambler's head and pulled the trigger.

It broke cleanly and the shambler dropped. Three down, four to go. Grinning, I strode out onto the bridge. My confidence was back with a vengeance. There was a new sheriff in Shambler Town. "Come and get some!"

They came. Or rather, tried. None of them made it up the stairs. Baby and I made certain of that. It took almost an entire magazine but eventually they all died. By that time, though, it felt like I'd been shooting for hours. I wanted to get the hell out of there. The canning supplies, if they were even really there, could wait.

Exhausted, I carefully navigated down the stairs and stumbled out into the front yard. I was alive and unharmed. Somehow.

"Sister Ann is going to kill me," I whispered as I checked my arms for any signs of scratches or cuts. I didn't see any. Looking back at the house, I glowered at it. If it wasn't for the canning materials somewhere inside—and a decided lack of matches and an accelerant—I'd burn the damn place to the ground.

Clearly I'd been spending too much of my free time around the twins.

There was no reason to tell Sister Ann what had gone down. It would save me from a very stern lecture about securing each and every room before turning my back on it. It was one of the first lessons she'd put me through when I told her I wanted to go out and kill shamblers. Check, then recheck. In my haste, I'd forgotten.

"Stupid, Maddie. Real stupid."

The aftereffects of the firefight began to take hold. My hands were shaking. After a few failed tries I managed to fish out the GPS and check the time. Blinking, I double-checked the numbers, thinking they were wrong. They weren't. I'd only been inside for twenty minutes, but it'd felt like five hours. There wasn't much else for me to do. Not now, at least. Eventually I'd need to bring someone up here to help find the canning supplies, and clear out the bodies. Definitely bringing the four-wheeler as well.

The adrenaline began to bleed off me. My hands were cramping thanks to how tight I was gripping Baby. I tried flexing my fingers but that only lessened the sensation. Shivering, I finally noticed something I should have when I'd first arrived. There was a side entryway on the right side of the house. I'd missed it before because I'd come in from the opposite angle. Now, though, it was easily seen. The screen door had been torn off its hinges. It didn't take a rocket scientist to figure out that was how the shamblers had gotten into the house. Temple might have done a fantastic job with the storm shutters but apparently he forgot to check the side door.

I couldn't blame him. Not really. This was on me. The number of times Sister Ann had told me to triple-check my surroundings was staggering, and yet here I was, covered in sweat and reeking of gun smoke, alive only because these particular shamblers had been really damn stupid.

There was no point in hiding any of this from her. Sister Ann would know just by the stench of gunpowder that clung to my clothes. She was practically psychic when it came to ferreting out information like this from the other girls. I was even easier to read. We all were an open book, she the librarian. It just wasn't fair.

As I started back toward campus, one thought resonated more than the rest: this lecture from Sister Ann was going to be a long one.

CHAPTER ELEVEN

"Juniper, PFC Castañeda... there's clearing, and then there's 'clearing,' sir. This isn't a one-person job... unless you're Shewolf, that is. And with all due respect, sir, I am not."
From: *Collected Radio Transmissions of the Fall,*
University of the South Press, 2053

We started to get more survivors up on the mountain after a muted Christmas celebration on the mountain. Not a lot of family members, though one elderly woman managed to keep all four of her young grandchildren alive by hiding in the stockroom of a feed store for three months. Unlike Temple, though, she'd had plenty of food and water. Most of her issues had been hiding from the random shambler that came close to the building occasionally, and keeping the rambunctious boys from making too much noise.

Those who weren't with families had to be vetted by Temple. This was Sister Ann's decision, and I supported it fully. For a man who'd survived brain cancer, he seemed to know just about everyone in and around Covington. His memory "might not be what it used to be" but it was good enough for him to know who we could trust, and the few who we'd keep an eye on. Not because they were criminals or anything, but because they weren't what he would call "hard workers."

One thing we quickly figured out about Temple was the old guy had a wicked sense of humor. Not inappropriate or anything like that, no. He just had a fun laugh and managed to find humor in just about every situation—as long as we didn't talk about what he'd lost. Sister Ann suggested that he and I, along with Ulla, make a journey up the mountain to the place where I'd passed the crucible. She told me that it would be a great chance to show him what we're trying to save. I thought that making him tour the campus and seeing the inside of the ruined cottages, as well as how much we've cleaned since the Fall, would be better.

But I'd learned long ago that it was a waste of time arguing with Sister Ann.

Temple, despite living almost his entire adult life in Alleghany County, had never been up to the peak of our mountain. Not that many people had, when you got right down to it. The school was secluded, and other than a narrow fire road, it was not a very easy hike up the rest of the way to the mountaintop. A large rut had formed over the years in the middle of the road and the Forest Service had never gotten around to filling it, which discouraged the random local from taking their vehicles up there.

When I'd done my crucible with the other girls and Sister Ann, we'd hiked it. With Temple's heart condition, though, Sister Ann suggested taking the four-wheeler.

"No point in putting me in the grave sooner than necessary, am I right?" Temple joked as he helped me with the ammo box. Ulla had her .270 and I had Baby, so security was set, but Sister Ann hadn't suggested we take more rifles.

"No, sir," I replied automatically. He snorted.

"You can call me Temple, you know."

"I know, sir. But Sister Ann told all the girls to either call you sir, or Mr. Kessinger," I told him as we got the ammo box situated in the back of the four-wheeler. Between the three of us and the ammo, the all-wheel drive was going to get a workout. Still, it'd managed to bring the woodstove from the Moose Lodge to campus, so we should be fine.

"And I'm telling you that you can call me Temple," he answered, nodding at Baby resting on the four-wheeler's gun rack. "You run security here. To me, that makes you the boss."

"Sister Ann's the boss," I reminded him. Ulla waved her hands to get my attention.

You're in charge after her, she argued.

"Just for security," I said, shrugging. "The student council is next in charge. Come on. It's a drive up to the peak, and daylight's burning."

"I don't see the fire," Temple said as he dramatically looked around. I groaned.

"Dad jokes? Really?"

"I have puns, too."

"No." I shook my head. "No, please. Dad jokes are fine."

"You sure? Puns are pretty lit these days."

I groaned. "Absolutely."

"Suit yourself. I used *lit* correctly, though, right?"

"Yep."

"Thought so."

The drive up was long. With the condition of the road being so poor, we had to go slow. There were some birds out, but no sign of any shamblers. Briefly, I spotted the Dunlap Creek when we rounded a turn, but thick pine trees cut off the view a few seconds later. It was early in the afternoon when we finally came to the point that Sister Ann had once called the crucible rock.

"This is it," I said as we pulled up. Making sure the parking brake was engaged—Rohena had forgotten once and had to chase it halfway down the road, much to our amusement—I hopped out and checked out the surroundings. The area around crucible rock was clear of leaves, which had probably been blown away during the winter storms. Keeping an eye out for any shamblers, I moved toward the rock.

It was flat and stuck out just a little over a steep drop to the valley below. If one sat on the edge, it felt as if there was nothing between you and the valley floor. From here one could see most of campus, the old ranger station, and even the Jackson River. While on the crucible with Sister Ann and the others, watching the sunrise from the peak was the most beautiful thing I'd ever seen in my life. It had also been a life-changing moment.

"This sure is something to behold," Temple said as he gazed out across the Blue Ridge Mountains. "I can see now why the school founders built up here."

"Yeah," I said, looking at Ulla. Her bright blue eyes were wide as she stared off into the distance. She'd never been up here, either.

While her sister Celin had done the crucible like I had, Ulla had been too young. If the world ever returned to normal, it would be another year or two before Sister Ann would let her.

But this little drive up to the peak wasn't about Ulla. Not today, at least.

"Why'd she choose you, anyway?" Temple asked as he stared off into the distance.

"What do you mean?" I asked, though I had a suspicion I knew what he was asking.

"The shooting of the zombies and security stuff... why you?"

I thought it over for a moment. It was something I hadn't really considered. The role of security had pretty much fallen on me in the early days of the Fall, when we still had quite a few shamblers running around campus. I'd definitely become more comfortable with the role when we found Mr. Stitmer's gun safe. Shooting shamblers from a distance felt a little more disconnected, like it wasn't really me doing it—unlike when I'd had to bash a few heads in with my field hockey stick.

"I don't know," I answered truthfully. "It just sort of fell on me. Nobody else was going to do it."

"You have a strong sense of duty or something, girl?" Temple asked. I shook my head.

"Nothing like that."

"Then why?"

"Did you know they used to call me Mad Maddie when I first came here?" I asked.

Temple snorted. "Yep. One of the girls mentioned it to Rosalind. Said something about you used to get a little crazy."

"Yeah, something like that," I admitted. "But yeah, I think Sister Ann remembered that when she put me in charge of security."

"I don't think it's that at all," Temple said. "I asked because I wanted to know what you think. I have a decent idea what Sister Ann thinks... which is to say, she saw you as a vengeful but protective girl who would do anything to keep the others safe. Which, to be fair, you come across as."

"Vengeful?"

"*Protective.*" He stressed the word as he turned to face me. "When you're out there servicing targets—and that's what you have to see them as, targets—you aren't thinking about anything other than making sure the zombies can't hurt the girls at the school. You get in a zone and your protective streak comes alive. It's one of those mixed-blessings kind of deal."

"Yeah?"

"Yeah. But that's just one old man's opinion," he muttered and sat on the fender of the four-wheeler. "I doubt I'll ever really understand a woman's thought process, though. Much less a nun's."

"Yeah." This sort of talk was the kind I tried to avoid. After a few moments of awkward silence, I looked at Temple. "So . . . got any good dad jokes?"

"Dad jokes? It's hard to make dad jokes when you're in the middle of a forest," he said, waving a hand around at the scattered trees. "Mountains are easy."

"Why?" I asked, suspicious.

"Well, because they're *hill areas.*"

I stared at him for a full minute until it clicked. "Really?" I managed to sputter at last.

"You asked for it. Besides, you can't ever take a mountain for *granite.*"

"Oh, come on!"

One of the worst parts about leaving campus and scavenging for more supplies wasn't the shamblers, but the dead. Specifically, the kids.

I considered myself pretty lucky in that regard. My brain would see the body and immediately forget it for some reason. As long as it wasn't moving, it was nothing but a corpse. Human remains. Gross, but nothing more. It was pretty easy for me to not dwell on what it had once been. Getting caught up in the gory details was not something I wanted to do, and my imagination complied.

Others, though, weren't so lucky.

It'd been two weeks since I stumbled upon Colton and had the mess at the Boyd farm go down, and a week after we'd gone up to crucible rock. Sister Ann had been upset with me for not paying attention at the Boyd farm. The lecture had been pretty epic, as predicted. I hadn't admitted *why* I'd been distracted, only that I had been. She put me through a few drills to keep my guard up and how to properly breach and clear a room. She'd shown me before but apparently felt the need to hammer the lesson home.

Colton and I got along well enough, considering it was the end of the world. The late January afternoon was a cold, wet one. I was returning back from another scavenging trip, though this time I hadn't gone alone. Colton had tagged along with me, which made it less work somehow. He still didn't want to come up to the campus, or let Sister Ann and the others know he was around, so we'd found an abandoned house not too far away near the Moose Lodge that was in great shape. The previous tenants hadn't fouled it up when they'd turned and nothing had been inside since. A quick search had turned up plenty of blankets, a working fireplace, and running water. How they had running water was beyond me. Another mystery I wanted to throw at Emily—except with Colton living there, I couldn't really bring her down and show her.

Besides, Colton liked the place. He said it reminded him of home. The boy also liked it because he said it was closer to me.

The feelings . . . were starting to be mutual. A little. Which was terrifying because of what had happened with my ex-boyfriend, and the path that particularly abusive relationship had led me down.

The climb up the path was a slippery one but I managed without killing myself. Deep down I was a little worried. I'd been using the back path so much that it was starting to grow more noticeable. I needed to take a break from walking up it for a few weeks once spring hit, to give the undergrowth a chance to hide it better once more.

Up on campus, Lucia was waiting for me outside the dining hall. Her expression was troubled. I couldn't tell if she'd been crying and only just stopped, or was just really cold. She wiped her face with a hand as I drew close.

"Hey, you okay?"

"Y-yeah." She sniffled. "Maybe."

"Bad find?" Definitely crying. Lucia hated the cold as much as I did. If not for the tears, she'd be in the bunker, where it was warm and dry. There wasn't much that made her cry these days.

After we'd stolen the BearCat from King Dale and had our heart-to-heart moment, she'd changed. The rough, abrasive girl who had enough of an edge around her that made the younger girls nervous

had chilled out a bit. Not a lot, of course. But enough that they talked
to her even when they didn't need anything.

Sometimes I was a little jealous. They were all still afraid of me,
and probably avoided me because of it. I didn't care what Emily said.

"Dead kids."

Ah. That would do it. "I'm sorry."

"I knew I'd see some more eventually," Lucia said in a quiet voice.
Finding Jacob in the nurse's office bathroom had shaken us both for
days. I didn't know what to tell her now, so I stayed silent. After a
moment she continued. "But these two managed to barricade their
room shut. Shamblers didn't get them. They stayed in there and
just . . . died."

"You didn't go in, right?" I asked, worried. Nobody had gotten
the flu since the initial outbreak, but after Rohena's infected spider
bite Sister Ann had told us to be more careful than before. We had no
idea what else could be lurking in the homes besides shamblers.
Copperheads were a problem up here, though the time of the year
was wrong for them.

"No. I checked out the rest of the house before I found their room.
It was barricaded from the inside. Went outside and looked in
through the window. It's up on the hill so the water didn't hit their
house. Once I saw them, lying on the floor holding hands, I left. They
were sisters. Young. I don't . . ."

"Damn," I whispered.

"Language," Sister Ann said from right behind me. I didn't jump,
though. After three years of this I'd grown accustomed to her simply
appearing out of nowhere. However, instead of scolding me further,
she wrapped an arm around Lucia's shoulders and pulled her close.
"I know what I say won't ease your pain this moment, but they're
both with our Lord in Heaven, together, just like they were in life.
Try to find some comfort in that."

"It doesn't make sense," Lucia mumbled. "Why let us live and
those girls die? God's not fair."

"It seems like that sometimes, but could you imagine if God was
fair in the way we view things?" Sister Ann asked as Lucia pressed her
head into the nun's shoulder. I perked up. I'd never really gotten one
of the deep philosophical lectures from Sister Ann. Before the Fall,
Sister Margaret had given me a few, but back then I'd still been Mad

Maddie (as my mom had put it before sticking me on a plane and flying me across the country). I hadn't been ready to listen. Not just yet. No, I hadn't wanted to hear what the nuns had to say either, at first. By the time I did, the lights had gone out and we were fighting for our survival.

Sister Ann sighed and gently stroked Lucia's head. "Back during the so-called Dark Ages, the Church was a beacon of light in a world of darkness, standing tall with faith as a shield. We weren't perfect, not by a long shot, but lots of friars, monks, and nuns did their best to bring hope and faith to the masses who were surrounded by death and despair. They, in turn, were hounded by enemies of God. But they all believed with every fiber of their beings that He was watching them, that His love would save them, if not on Earth then in Heaven.

"Things happen that are part of God's plan that we cannot begin to understand. Our minds aren't made to understand. We're simple beings, flesh made in His likeness. Since we can't even begin to imagine what God thinks, only His word through the Bible, we do our best to understand and obey. Or not. Humanity is a strange thing. We pray for fairness, then curse in anguish when we suffer. Our own wants and needs are not the same as someone else's, nor are they remotely in mind with what He intended for us. Do you know what He gave us that is the greatest gift of all?"

"Free will?" I answered for her. Sister Ann smiled but shook her head.

"While a gift, that is not what I had in mind. He gave us faith, girls. Faith and hope, so that even in the darkest of nights, we have a beacon to lead the way."

Lucia lifted her face from Sister Ann's hoodie. "Even when there's no beacons?"

"The beacons are lit. Gondor calls for aid," I muttered, only half sarcastic. Sister Ann had told me to read the books during my down time between leaving campus. Weirdest. Nun. Ever. Lucia giggled and even Sister Ann smiled a little at this.

"Almost. Why do you think our school is on top of a mountain, Lucia? Right now, we are the beacon. Remember that. Your faith, all of our faith, lights the way for those still surrounded by darkness. And in the dark of night, we will lead the way."

∽◌∾

After dinner and our daily Devotionals and all of the refugees had returned to their assigned cottages, Sister Ann gathered the student council down in the main bunker for a meeting. It promised to be an interesting one.

"All right, girls," Sister Ann murmured quietly, interrupting our conversations and effectively bringing the meeting to order. "Lucia brings news, and while I would normally make the decision here, this is something that the council must decide as a whole, since some of you are over eighteen and should be getting ready to graduate. Finlay, Fiona? Even your votes will count here."

That got everybody's attention.

It was weird. We all knew we could leave, since all of us seniors had turned eighteen months before—or in the case of Lucia, nineteen—but it was another thing entirely to hear Sister Ann say it. We all exchanged glances but said nothing. What could we say, anyway? It wasn't as if we were simply about to bail on the younger girls. Or Sister Ann, even though she was more than perfectly capable of taking care of herself.

Well, I couldn't speak for the others, but I knew I wasn't going anywhere. The rest of the world was gone. Sure, Wolf Squadron had actually made some sort of daring raid on London—details were sketchy over the radio about what had happened, but there was now a legitimate King of England, which was weird but cool at the same time—but they could only be in so many places. We were inland, over two hundred miles away from the closest naval base. Unless Wolf Squadron really wanted to tempt fate by trying to navigate the James River, we were still on our own with nowhere to go. If they even knew anyone this far inland was still alive. While we could receive on the radio, we still had no way to broadcast.

Plus, this was a home worth protecting. Leave? To where? No, I was good right where we were, and I was pretty certain that the others felt the same.

"Okay, so, you know that new *chica* who'd bought that house down near the transfer station back before the Fall?" Lucia started. Kayla rolled her eyes and grimaced.

"That narrows it down."

The transfer station had been down by the Jackson River before the flooding hit. It'd been the place where everyone could simply dump unwanted stuff off for free. Loads of the locals would bring their junk that they couldn't sell for scrap and dump it there. It would be weighed and measured, and the locals would drive off and the people working at the transfer station would take care of it by shipping it somewhere else, probably Roanoke. I'm not sure.

It was gone now, wiped out completely when the massive wave from the dam failure hit it. I'd made the trip down there and checked it out with Lucia two weeks ago, hoping to find anything worthwhile. There was nothing. Farther down the river we'd seen a new dam had formed, created by all the trash, logs, and debris from Covington. The Jackson River still managed to pass through, but at a much slower rate. The entire area was now a lake. That particular stretch of I-64 was almost fully beneath it, too. The new dam was also why downtown Covington was still flooded.

"The veterinarian, stupids," Lucia said, glaring. Kayla wisely shut up. You could take the girl out of the *barrio*, but ... "The one who set up back before ... ?"

I knew who she was talking about now. Dr. Brittany Jefferson was new to the area—or rather, had been new, moving here just before the Fall. Nobody knew why she'd chosen Covington of all places to set up a new vet practice, especially since there were already two in the area. Small town, no family ties anyone knew of ... rumors ranged from her being in witness protection to being a drug kingpin. Or queenpin, rather. Meth was pretty big in the area. Or rather, had been.

"Okay, what about her? She alive?" I asked, curious. Lucia nodded.

"Her office building's gone but she must have moved because I swear I saw her duck inside one of the houses over by where the bowling alley used to be," she replied. "The ones that didn't flood, I mean. You know, next to the candy shop?"

"Could it have been someone else?" Sister Ann asked.

"Unless some other *chica* had a pair of giant Great Danes around here that nobody's seen before, I doubt it."

"A veterinarian ..." Sister Ann's voice trailed off as she stared at the far wall of the bunker.

"Yeah?" I looked at the nun, confused. "What about it? We don't have pets up here."

"To be a veterinarian, they need to study biology, though," Sister Ann corrected me in a tone that told me she was thinking rapidly. "Anatomy as well. Sutures on small animals . . . Do you know what the difference between a veterinarian and a doctor is?"

"Uh . . . no? Wait—medical school?"

"No. Well, yes, but no. Veterinarians are used to their patients trying to bite them."

"Oh!" It suddenly dawned on me just where Sister Ann was going with this. "She could come up here and join us, be like a doctor!"

"I've got decent field medic training, but someone like Dr. Jefferson would be far more knowledgeable." Sister Ann confirmed my guess with a nod. "She would also be more likely to have a medical go bag for emergencies with her. She might not be a medical doctor but she can hum a bar or three. We should go and see if she would like to come up here. Kayla, can we handle that with food?"

"One more person isn't going to hurt," Kayla answered almost immediately. Since she was in charge of our makeshift garden, she would know what we could handle. Between that and her keeping track of what we had for canned goods with Lucia, Kayla had turned into our storekeeper. Of course, they didn't know about my pilfering to help keep Colton alive, so her numbers might have been off a little. Not a lot, though. Colton was starting to scavenge houses up past the Moose Lodge himself, and doing a decent job of it. "But you said something about dogs . . . ?"

"Yeah," Lucia said, nodding. "Great Danes. Big ones."

"Those eat more protein than we do, I think," Kayla pointed out, looking at Sister Ann for help. "Probably. I don't know for sure. Point is, we don't have any dog food up here. I didn't even think to check the cottages down low to see if they had any."

"Grab some of the girls to go and check them out," Sister Ann said. "We don't know if she'll agree or not, but most dog food has grain in it. Might make fertilizer? Something to look into. Remember, don't take any of the younger girls into the Johnsons' place. If you want, you can avoid it completely. They only had a small cat, if I remember right. No point in going through that again."

Kayla nodded. I grimaced. The Johnsons had been one of the families living on campus. They'd been in charge of a small herd of horses that were kept down on the farm for over twenty years, but by the time I arrived there had been only one horse still here, and it had died not long after. Still, nobody asked the Johnsons to leave, so they got to stay and live on campus. One of the Johnson kids had gotten infected during the first few days of the Pacific Flu and . . . it'd gotten ugly down there. Since the whole of campus had been on lockdown, nobody had managed to make it down there until two weeks ago. By the time I did look inside, it was a mess.

I'm glad I don't really dream anymore, because it'd been the stuff of nightmares.

"There's some bad news, too," Lucia added, looking around. Specifically, at me. "I spotted some of King Dale's guys sniffing around down by the old supermarket."

I'd been wondering when King Dale was going to rear his ugly head again. Ever since we'd stolen the BearCat he'd been staying on his side of the river. But there had been a huge population difference between the two areas before the Fall, and he had to be hurting for food by now. Both of the big grocery stores were in Covington—one near the bowling alley, and the other closer to where downtown had once been.

"That place is trashed," I muttered, thinking back to when the two of us had scouted it out. One half of the building had collapsed on itself after the flooding, which was the part where all of the canned goods had been stored. Unfortunately for us, anyway. There was almost too much debris to even make our way past the cashier registers.

"Well, they were poking around inside," Lucia said. "I don't think they had any luck, though. The water's mostly gone but there's too much debris in there to really get to the back. I checked."

"Did they see you?" Sister Ann asked. Lucia shook her head.

"No, not me," she replied, then paused. "They might have seen Dr. Jefferson, though."

"That's probably why you only caught a glimpse of her ducking into a building," I said under my breath. "She was trying to avoid *them*."

"Then we might have a bigger problem on our hands than we thought," Kayla stated, saying out loud what the rest of us were thinking. "You know that King Dale's probably gonna want to 'talk' to her, right? Have her go with him, like he wanted to with us."

"*Wants* us to go, not wanted." Lucia glowered. "*Hombre* isn't going to take being told 'no' well."

"I don't doubt it in the least," Sister Ann said as she folded her hands on her lap. Her gaze swept over us and for a brief moment I was under her intense scrutiny. Old me would have squirmed, but that girl is gone now. I've changed, and I met her eyes without a second thought. Apparently satisfied, she continued. "So we're going to ask her if she wants to come up while preparing for Appalachia Rex at the same time. We'll ask *nicely*, and if she declines, then so be it. St. Dominic's is, first and foremost, a sanctuary for young women, no matter what the faith."

"How're we going to convince her to come up while stopping King Dale without shooting anyone?" I asked. Sister Ann's smile was practically serene.

"With cat toys and a little bit of gumption."

The rest of the planning meeting with the student council wasn't worth paying attention to. The security situation—with the exception of King Dale and his goons—was better now than it'd been since before the Fall. Which meant less work for me. With so few shamblers roaming around these days, more and more girls were willing to stand watch at the bridge or even up on the rooftop. Of course they offered to work now. It was "safe." The heavy, nasty work of shooting the shamblers by the dozen had already been taken care of by yours truly.

Well, I mean, other than Ulla. She really seemed to enjoy shooting the shamblers and not just warning me about them. The other girls? Absolutely worthless when it came to shambler disposal.

Sister Ann liked to say that bitterness is a cavity on the soul. While I strive to be better, I'm also comfortable knowing I'm human, so being a petty bitch at times is perfectly fine by me.

After the meeting, I bailed fast. Night watch was set with Rohena up on the cafeteria's roof, so unless a shambler somehow found its way onto the main campus, I was free to do whatever I wanted—and what I wanted was to sleep. The sooner I went to bed, the earlier I could wake up and go see Colton before Sister Ann and the rest of us headed into town to try and recruit the veterinarian.

The boy had no idea what I was sacrificing to wake up early and bring him food. Other than shooting, sleeping was my most favorite thing in the whole wide world. Seriously. If it were an Olympic sport, I'd win a gold medal.

Assuming there'd ever be an Olympics again.

Using a candle to light my way down the hall, it was easy to traverse around the old boxes containing most of the canned goods we'd scavenged the past ten months. My bedroom—nothing more than a converted storeroom—had been designed to hold… something a long time ago, but in the years since the Cold War ended everything from extra toilet paper to school supplies had been stashed down here. Fortunately for me, it was closest to the shelter door at the foot of the stairs, which meant should an emergency happen, I could be out there first.

"Designated speed bump number one," I'd jokingly referred to my room's position when I'd chosen it back when we first hid down here. Sister Ann, surprisingly, hadn't corrected me. She'd known then what would need to happen for us all to survive. It was spooky how often she just seemed to know.

I set Baby on the gun rack, mindful of Sister Ann's strict lectures about safety and storage. Since I hadn't fired Baby today, there was no need for me to clean her. Still, just laying the rifle down on the floor felt like sacrilege, so I'd "borrowed" a gun rack from Mr. Stitmer's house. I don't think he would have minded. Before I'd "acquired" her, she'd been his little pet project.

Yeah, okay. Fine. I stole a heavily modified AR-15 from a dead man, then went back for a gun rack later. Also, I stole his four-wheeler. Sue me.

I changed into my nightwear and got ready for bed. Some of the girls liked actual pajamas but sweatpants and a hoodie were known to be superior. If something happened, I wouldn't be caught dead out in the open in pink fluffy-bunny pjs. Let the other girls be unprepared and look ridiculous to boot. Hoodies and sweats—comfy survival clothing for the modern postapocalyptic girl.

I heard footsteps coming down the hall. They stopped right outside my door. Half expecting the knock, I wasn't surprised when two gentle taps were made. After a moment's pause, the door cracked open and a very familiar face appeared. I smiled at Ulla as she pushed through the small opening and quickly closed the door behind her.

"Nightmares?" I asked her, already knowing the answer. It wasn't the first time, and everyone knew it wouldn't be the last. Ulla had been through too much. All of us had, really, but Ulla was one of the youngest. Plus, she was the only girl at school who'd been forced to watch their own sibling die. She nodded and began to sign at me.

Can I stay here with you tonight?

"Sure," I replied. She was a good kid, one nobody else seemed to fully understand. Kind of like me, but without the anger issues. I'd managed to wrangle a king-sized bed down into my room (Lucia, Emily, and Rohena had all helped—after complaining and a lot of bribes involving packets of ramen noodles) and there was more than enough room. Besides, if she started kicking in her sleep, I could always sleep on the floor. The bunker had a concrete floor, but pillows could work in a pinch to make it tolerable. Plus, as much as it bothered me to admit it, I liked the company. "Did you go to the bathroom already?"

She scowled, gave me a rude gesture, before signing again. *I haven't wet the bed since I was ten.*

"Just checking." I smirked. For a just-turned twelve-year-old, she had the sarcastic eyeroll down pat. I could take lessons. "Come on."

Once Ulla was settled in, I blew out the candle and crawled beneath the blankets. The bunker wasn't exactly cold, but it wasn't necessarily warm, either. In the winter it could get downright frigid. I had a mountain of blankets but I was not equipped for winter. Give me summer any day. It's one of the reasons I kept my door closed. It kept the heat in. That, and I liked the privacy.

Alone with my thoughts, they drifted to my mom and dad back home. What the house looked like. The neighborhood. My old school and friends. And my two younger brothers.

The sad thing was, I'd never really been close to either of them before being shipped off to St. Dominic's in a last-ditch effort to help me do something with my life. They'd been annoying little brats who could do no wrong while I was always blamed for not helping out enough, or not watching them so my parents could do their own thing for a few hours. Sure, it was selfish of me—something I realize now—but at the time, I was angry at them. All of them.

I'd give almost anything to have them now. But like the rest of Southern California, they were gone. My only hope was that they died quickly and hadn't been turned into shamblers.

Something moved across the blanket. I tensed before remembering where I was, and who was with me. Ulla clutched my hand in the dark. Her grip was tight but there were no trembles. No nightmares would come for her tonight. She was a good kid who deserved so much better than what life had given her. It didn't matter, though. She'd survived and, one day, would help rebuild. Ulla was tough. I smiled. Her breathing was steady, regular. Sleep comes easy when we feel safe. She might not be blood, but thanks to the Fall she was the closest thing I had to a sibling.

The idea of having a little sister was . . . nice.

CHAPTER TWELVE

"While there are many papers published on what the differences are, the cause of the difference still remains unknown, including whether it is due to mutations of the H7D3 virus. Our goals today are twofold: characterize disease progression for—as well as differences between—alphas and betas, then determine how H7D3 affects the central nervous system during disease progression."

—Lecture part of "Grad 725—Research Methods for the Infected" by Dr. Tedd Roberts, University of the South, 2047

The next morning I was up before dawn. Not wanting to disturb Ulla, I got ready for the day in absolute darkness before slipping out of the rooms. I caught sight of Sister Ann in the main room of the bunker, but she only waved at me as I went out the door. She knew today was potentially going to be a big one, and me getting out early to do a perimeter sweep was important. The last thing we needed was for some shambler to find its way up to campus while most of the girls were in town.

Before exiting, though, I snagged a few cans of baked beans and stuffed them in my jacket. Nobody really liked them, so they were sitting near the back of the inventory shelf. They were high in protein and had enough fiber to make poop levitate six inches above the water—or so I'd been told—so they were a healthy option for Colton.

It was a cold morning. Winter had definitely arrived, though we still hadn't gotten any snow yet. Frost, sure. That was an everyday occurrence now. The wind was cold and biting. Thankfully, we'd raided the donations room finally and cleaned it out. Maybe one day it would be filled with donations from locals again, but since Sister Ann didn't want to go back down there after we told her about little Jacob's body in the nurse's office bathroom, we'd cleared out everything of value we could find. We did have to remove the other three bodies Lucia and I had left in there, though, before we could hit the donations room. One of the prizes had been worth the work, though: a really nice winter coat that'd probably cost a small fortune when new, which I gave to Ulla since it was too small for me.

With Baby in its sling, I made a deliberate effort to let the lookout on the roof watch where I was heading. There was no reason to give whoever was up there—probably Emily, but maybe Kayla—any reason to wonder where I was going. Everyone knew by now that I took the same path down every time, unless there was an emergency. The back entrance of the school was simply expected. It would look suspicious if I went any other way.

Even if it was the opposite way to Colton's.

The trek around campus was slow going. Sticking to a well-worn deer trail, I moved through the brush with practiced ease. Having been down this trail at least one hundred times, I could have probably done it blindfolded. If not for the admittedly slim chance of running into a shambler, I might have tried.

It was quiet around me. My breath came out in little puffs of steam every time I exhaled. The cold stung my cheeks a little. It was a far cry from what I'd grown up with in Southern California. There I might need a hoodie on chilly mornings, maybe. Before coming to St. Dominic's I'd never experienced cold like this. Sure, I'd gone up to Big Bear a few times in the winter, but the air up there was dry. Even snowboarding up in Mammoth wasn't like it was here.

In the South, even the freezing cold was humid. There was almost never a reprieve from it.

There no shamblers out this morning. Nothing was out, actually. No birds, no wild animals running around. The air was cold but still. The patrol was quickly turning into nothing more than a calm, peaceful walk. Still, I needed to stay aware. Shamblers had a nasty tendency to simply *appear* as if by magic when you least expected them. It was really annoying.

It took awhile for me to make it to the small house where Colton was staying. While it definitely would have been a shorter trip if he'd stayed in the ranger's cabin, someone might have seen something eventually. The building wasn't easy to see from campus but if Rohena was actually paying attention during the midnight watch, there was always the chance she could have seen him. Down here, closer to the main entrance of the school and the Moose Lodge, was better in the long run.

There was a slight fog around Colton's place. It wasn't much, only coming up to the knees, but looked eerie in the early morning light. Keeping on eye on the two neighboring houses, I hurried up to the front door. I knocked twice, waited a moment, then knocked again. Colton answered almost immediately.

"I saw you coming," he said. Impressed, I smiled.

"Didn't even see the curtain move," I told him. Digging into my coat pockets, I pulled out the extra beans I'd pilfered from the pantry. "Brought you these."

"You're up early," he said as he accepted the cans of beans. He looked down at them and smiled. "Thanks."

"*De nada,*" I replied with a shrug. "They've got brown sugar in them, so not the healthiest."

"Heh." He snorted, clearly amused. "Like I'm worried about how healthy the food I eat is. As long as it keeps me alive, I'm not too picky."

"I've got plenty more of that," I told him. "None of the others like baked beans, so we've got tons." Looking around the small house, I was impressed by what I saw. There was a small pile of electronics and what looked like batteries. If society ever rebuilt he'd make a killing in the used electronics department. Near that pile were some canned goods he'd found somewhere. The boy had been busy since I last saw him. "Been out scavenging a bit, have we?"

"Oh, uh, yeah." He waved a hand at the pile of stuff in the corner. He set the cans of beans on the small kitchen table. "I hit a few houses down the road. I checked for zombies . . . uh, shamblers. Didn't see any so I checked the pantries. Found some stuff. Hope you don't mind."

"I don't think it matters," I admitted after giving it some thought. Sister Ann had mentioned sending a group with me that way to see what we could find. I guess we weren't going to find much now. "How far down the road did you go?"

"A mile or two," he said.

"Ah, yeah, toward the old golf course up there?"

"There's a golf course around here?"

"Used to be. There was talk about restoring it before the Fall." I guess he hadn't gone as far as he thought.

"Oh. I didn't see it."

There was an awkward pause. I wanted to talk to him, but I really didn't know what to say. Fortunately, he was one of those people who have a way with breaking any tension in a conversation.

"So what's got you up and out so early anyway?" Colton asked as he stuffed his hands into his pockets. He leaned back and looked at me suspiciously. "See a shambler or something?"

"No, haven't spotted one in days," I said. Which was true, actually. It'd been a minute since I'd seen one running around, and that one was the strange little beta who kept coming down to the creek. Neither Ulla nor I could get a good shot at it. The thing was starting to get on my nerves. "Got something exciting going on."

"Really? What's so important that's got you up before noon?" he asked. He knew about my love of sleeping. I rolled my eyes and snorted, amused.

"Ten. Noon is for lazy people. And we're going into Covington to try to recruit someone."

"Oooh, sounds like fun . . . not really. Lots of zom—shamblers, sorry, in town still. I saw a bunch when I was sneaking through . . . well, around, really."

Shrugging, I looked out the living room window. The sun was higher in the sky and it was easier to see everything. Not only had he snagged some electronics and batteries, he'd also found a bunch of clothes. He'd listened to me and focused on earth-tone colors, which were less likely to catch the eye of a roving shambler. I don't know why but I was surprised he listened. "Calling them zombies doesn't bother me."

"But you call them shamblers?"

"Because they're not zombies, not really," I answered, thinking back to what I'd heard on the shortwave. "They're not the walking dead or anything like that. They're living, breathing, and can be killed. They're just . . . not human anymore."

"So . . . like aliens?"

"Hah. You're funny."

"Thanks."

"I was being sarcastic."

"Oh. So . . . who's in town that's got your nun so interested? You find some doctors still alive or something?"

"Did you see any?" I asked. He shook his head. "Well, then . . . no." Colton made a face and I immediately felt bad. Blame it on the early hour, but I was being unnecessarily cruel to the boy. I'd come to see him, after all. No need for me to be a bitch about things. "Sorry."

"No, it's okay. I shouldn't have asked. You guys do your thing up there. I shouldn't pry."

Now I felt worse. "You should know anyway. Might convince you to come up to campus. You know, where it's safe? We think we found a veterinarian."

He looked doubtful. "And?"

"And what?"

"What's so special about a veterinarian?"

"Are you crazy? They know *loads* of biology, and pretty much know everything a doctor knows. Kind of." I rubbed my face and tried not to sigh. "The point is, they had to pass biology and stuff like that. They know how to make splints and . . . I don't know, do surgery? Plus, all their patients are bitey. Shamblers are bitey. She's probably dealt with a few, you know?"

"Oh! I didn't know veterinarians could do all that."

"I didn't either until Sister Ann told me," I said, feeling a little better now that he was smiling again. "Animal doctors have to go through a lot of similar courses that human doctors do, according to Sister Ann. Give the doc a book and she'll know just about everything!"

"Oh, nice," he said, smiling again. "I hope she joins you . . . Well, uh . . . good luck?"

And then he reached out and hugged me. Instead of pushing him away, though, I carefully wrapped my arms around his torso in reply. We stayed that way for almost a full minute.

The act might not have been earth-shattering to most. For me and all my trust issues with boys? It was a first step in the right direction.

Even if I was being a bitch, he was trying. Had to give him points for trying.

No. No, I didn't, I reminded myself as the image of my ex-boyfriend flashed through my mind.

It was midafternoon by the time we had the BearCat fully loaded down and were ready to roll out. Sister Ann wanted us to be prepared for anything that might happen, so I had Ulla kitted up with a loaded rifle. I had Baby, and there were a few others who were carrying—though their weapons were unloaded. None of them looked really comfortable with their guns, but lessons from Sister Ann had them at least not pointing them at one another.

"Treat every firearm as if it's loaded, even if you know it's not," Sister Ann had warned the younger girls repeatedly. And will wonders ever cease, they actually listened. Even the twins paid attention.

Given their penchant for things that went boom, though, I shouldn't have been too surprised.

On our way down the mountain we rolled past Colton's place. I tried not to be too obvious that I was looking at the house as the BearCat rumbled past. Though I was pretty certain he wouldn't step outside to wave, it wasn't absolute. Plus, what if one of the other girls spotted him if he peeked out a window? Sister Ann would not hesitate to pull the BearCat over. It was in her nature to protect people and Colton, alone in the wild, was one of those people.

Stupid boy.

I smiled anyway. While he didn't seem the type to shoot any shamblers, him living on campus would be helpful for Kayla. She'd been doing most of the grunt labor and heavy lifting of things since the Fall. The girl was getting super jacked but a second person who could actually lift more than fifty pounds would be nice. As a side benefit, I could quit sneaking down the mountain to bring him extra food.

The drive into town took what felt like forever. Sister Ann, always a cautious driver, wouldn't get the vehicle up above forty. Not couldn't, but wouldn't. I didn't ask why though I really, really wanted to. Sister Ann probably would have gone on about how patience was a virtue, and things happen not in our time but on God's, which more than likely would have devolved into a lecture on the sins of haste or something. To save everyone else in back the hassle, I kept my mouth shut.

See? Total team player.

Once we exited I-64 and were in the town proper, it didn't take us long to find the house where Dr. Jefferson was staying. There weren't many houses in the area that looked like they could be lived in, and she'd picked the one that was in the best shape. Plus, the candy shop had been a distinctive piece of architecture, built in the shape of a teepee. Half of it had collapsed in on itself but it was still there, still somehow standing.

The story of us, really.

Though the BearCat had plenty of diesel fuel left, Sister Ann was quick to point out that we were going to be pushing our stolen armored vehicle soon unless we could track down more fuel. There were underground tanks around town but since the entire area flooded they were probably all contaminated with water. We hadn't found any place yet where diesel was stored above the flood zone. There was some hope of a gas station up past the Moose Lodge but since a mudslide had half-buried the road beyond, those hopes weren't high.

Dr. Jefferson's place was cute, a squat, short house that looked like it'd been built out of nothing but brick. I got out first and looked around, but there was not a shambler in sight. Ulla was up top in the turret. It was arguably the safest place for her to be with the rifle.

Dr. Jefferson had two massive dogs flanking her as she sat on her front porch. She was fanning herself and looked quite comfortable. The veterinarian's expression changed when Sister Ann exited the BearCat, but that was to be expected. Armed Catholic schoolgirls, led by a nun, in what appeared to be a tank, rolling up on her in the middle of a zombie apocalypse? Yeah, things post-Fall were weird. It would make even the most welcoming of persons a little nervous.

She was a nice enough lady, I guess. Her dogs seemed friendly as well, though they were alert and watching us as Sister Ann approached the house. Someone once said that's how you can judge a person, but dogs had loved Hitler, so who knows? First thing I noticed about the doctor was that she had a strange accent. Like she was from New York or something. Jersey maybe? Considering she and Lucia could have passed for sisters, it made me wonder which one of her parents had been named Jefferson. Pretty certain the other one was from Puerto Rico or something.

Sister Ann stopped at the edge of the lawn and waved. Dr. Jefferson waved back and invited her up to the porch. I couldn't hear much at first, but the initial introductions and pleasantries seemed to go well. Instead of paying attention to their discussion, I kept an eye out for any signs of a shambler. Covington, from everything we'd seen up to this point, still had some. Even with it being as cold as it was.

A problem quickly arose in the middle of their conversation—Dr. Jefferson didn't want to come up to the school with us. She was perfectly fine where she was, thank you very much.

"Look, I appreciate you wanting me up at your school," the short, dark-haired woman said as her dogs carefully sniffed each and every one of us—including Sister Ann, who the two giant Great Danes clearly were intimidated by. I couldn't blame them, really. She had that effect on all of us. "But as long as this King Dale leaves me alone, I'm happy down here."

"Why?" I asked, genuinely curious. It wasn't like there was anything left of the area. The massive tidal wave from the dam failing had hit this part of Covington especially hard. These particular homes were only standing because of the bend in the river, and how high these homes were above it. Even then, it was clear the candy shop had been tagged by debris. With the partially collapsed wall, it looked like a giant cave.

A cave maybe filled with candy? My stomach rumbled at the thought of all that abandoned sugar sitting in the dark, lonely.

She shrugged before answering. "Not to be rude, but a Catholic school and me aren't going to get along."

"You Mormon or something?" I pressed. She shook her head.

"No. I'm an atheist."

"Why does that matter?" I glanced over at Sister Ann. For some reason she seemed content to let me run this part of the conversation. She remained off to the side, dealing with the younger girls who'd come along to act as a security contingent. The only thing was, they were all for show. None of their weapons were loaded, save for Ulla's—which was my doing. There was no way I was going to have the only other shooter at the school unarmed. The girls up on campus were locked down in the bunker, watched over by Emily and Rohena, waiting for us to return. It was a risk, but gaining the services of the veterinarian was important enough, according to Sister Ann.

"Why does that . . . ? What sort of Catholic are you?" Dr. Jefferson asked.

"I don't know," I admitted with a shrug. "The good kind?"

"You seem like a good enough kid, but I'm okay for now."

"I'm not a kid," I protested. It might have sounded a little too argumentative, but I'd legally been an adult for months now. "I'm eighteen!"

"Sorry," she apologized as she motioned toward her cheekbones. "It's your freckles. They make you look very young."

Sister Ann rode in to save the day before I ruined everything with my anger. "You would be more than welcome up at the school."

"You are the oddest nun I've ever met," Dr. Jefferson muttered. Sister Ann beamed at that.

"Thank you."

A piercing whistle interrupted the conversation. Glancing around, I spotted Lucia in the distance waving her arms and pointing toward I-64. We knew what that meant—King Dale and his posse were on their way.

"Maddie?" Sister Ann asked in a quiet tone.

"BearCat should be hidden from his approach," I responded quickly, thinking over the different routes Dale could take to our location. If he were smart he'd split his men into two groups and come in from two different angles. Then again, he had no idea we were here. Plus, debris blocked the easy route in through town. He'd come en masse, thinking to impress the veterinarian with his numbers, probably. No, he'd stick to a group approach. Which meant . . . he'd come down Carpenter Drive. Yeah, the BearCat would definitely not be seen if he came from that way. I made my decision quickly. "Those two groves over there and there"—I pointed out to everyone else what I was referring to—"should be able to provide a good hiding spot for our, uh, snipers. Where do you want me?"

"We're all going to be out of sight," Sister Ann instructed. "You need to be closest to the building here should things go sideways. I'll have Ulla backing you up?"

"You sure?" I asked.

"Snipers?" Dr. Jefferson interrupted, confused. One of the Danes growled warningly. Faintly, voices could be heard in the distance. King Dale and company were coming. "Really, what kind of Catholics *are* you?"

"The choice is yours, Doctor," Sister Ann said, ignoring the shock in the other woman's tone. "If you don't mind, though, we would like to stick around and see how you handle Appalachia Rex."

"Appa—*who*?"

Sister Ann sighed dramatically. "The public education system has failed us in too many ways."

"I did quite well in school, thank you very much. And I can take care of myself," the doctor said as she reached behind her back and pulled out probably the biggest hand cannon I'd ever seen in my life. It was the sort of thing you'd see in an action movie or something. Images of Keanu Reeves came to mind. The dogs began wagging their tails excitedly. Clearly they'd seen the weapon before and associated it with something positive. What that could be, though, I'll never know. Or wanted to ask, really.

"Is that a Smith and Wesson Twenty-nine revolver chambered in a forty-four caliber? The 'Dirty Harry' special edition magnum?" Sister Ann asked before smiling and nodding in approval. "Quality choice. That's a very reliable piece. How's the trigger action?"

"What the *fuck* kind of nun *are* you?" Dr. Jefferson asked in exasperation. Sister Ann clucked her tongue, displeased.

"Language, young lady. Maddie? Girls? Time to scoot," Sister Ann ordered. We sprang into action. The dogs immediately went on alert as we pulled back, away from Dr. Jefferson's building and across the street. There were a few places we could hide and not expose ourselves as we moved around. However, if we wanted to be able to help Dr. Jefferson should things go to Hell in a hurry, I'd also need to be able to move quickly and quietly—which meant behind the cars across the street from the ruined candy shop.

"What I would do for a candy bar right now . . ." I muttered quietly as Kayla joined me behind the cars. Leaning against one of the ruined cars pushed partway onto the sidewalk, I risked a glance at the old candy store. The temptation was strong. Chocolate has a long shelf life, right? "You think . . . ?"

"Sister Ann would whup you," Kayla said before I could even finish the question. "She'd whup you good."

"Fine," I grumbled. I'd have to figure out a way to get a candy bar later. Maybe after King Dale gave up and went home? I would do horrible things for chocolate right now. Shooting King Dale in the kneecap was right up there at the top. Hell, I'd do it for free if Sister Ann asked. But still . . . chocolate. Less than twenty feet away, maybe. The temptation was all too real.

"How do you think this is gonna go?" Kayla asked as I watched Ulla settle nearby with Lea and Melinda. Some of the others were with them. As far as I could tell, they would be out of sight when King Dale arrived.

"Depends on when Sister Ann reveals that we're here," I replied after thinking it over for a second.

"A lady reveals nothing," Sister Ann interrupted our musings. Somewhere along the way she'd snagged the bullhorn from the BearCat—more likely, one of the girls had been carrying it for her and I hadn't noticed. Her voice was positively serene as she crouched down next to us. Kayla coughed, clearly embarrassed, and looked at me. It was always easy to forget just how good her hearing was.

"Good thing she's the only lady around here," I whispered. Kayla giggled and shushed me. We turned our attention back on Sister Ann.

"I am not the only lady here. Don't forget, girls," the nun added, somehow overhearing our whispered conversation, "St. Dominic's isn't here just to help you graduate high school or make you strong, independent women, but to guide you in becoming ladies as well."

"I don't think the average lady carries an AR-15, Sister," I pointed out. She just smiled slightly before forming a reply.

"What in the world makes you think any of you are average ladies? As if I would settle for any of you just being average. As you are wont to say: girlfriend, puh-*lease*."

She had a point. Sister Ann wouldn't rest until we all had reached our full potential. She was annoying like that. Endearing, but frustrating. It was hard living up to someone else's expectations all of the time. Sometimes a girl just needed a break and to coast. Sister Ann—all of the nuns, really—demanded more of us. Like we deserved to try harder than we had been. You know what? It'd worked.

That was, of course, before the Pacific Flu came along and ruined everything.

Shoving the thought from my mind, I hunkered down and waited. It didn't take long. King Dale might not be the sharpest tool in the shed, but he was a punctual man. The time it took him to appear until he was just about threatening the poor veterinarian was probably less than three minutes.

Punctual, and predictable.

"Good morning, Dr. Jefferson! You're in the Kingdom of Appalachia, which is mine by rule of law!" King Dale's voice echoed through the neighborhood. Meanwhile, the dozen or so men who followed him had spread out behind him. Most were carrying weapons, but nobody was pointing them toward the house, or Dr. Jefferson hiding inside. Instead, they were looking for shamblers over their shoulders. Had they run into some unpleasantness on their way into town? It was something to keep in mind.

Looking around, I could see two clusters of trees flanking where Dr. Jefferson was holed up. Sister Ann had pointed them out to us earlier. It was shady within them but I couldn't see any of Appalachia Rex's men near. Nudging Sister Ann with my elbow, I jerked my chin toward the trees. I followed it up with a pointed look at the girls who she'd designated the "Kitty Squad": Melinda, Ulla, and Lea, who were hiding behind a flipped pickup truck nearby. She immediately caught my meaning and began conferring with the younger girls in a quiet voice.

Meanwhile, King Dale seemed to be enjoying his little spiel. "That means you are under my protection, as well as my rule. Come back to my camp and you will be richly rewarded, and protected as well. It's dangerous for a woman, alone in this shattered, broken world. I have use for a doctor who is self-sufficient and skilled at her job."

"If you're a real king, then I'm the Duchess of Elenna-nórë, you illiterate halfwit!" the doctor shouted. I snorted.

"Did she just use Tolkien as an insult to counter during an argument?" Sister Ann asked quietly. Everyone looked at her, confused. I hadn't read that far in the series yet, so I had no idea. For a brief instant a spike of terror hit me in the stomach. What if Sister Ann wanted me to write a book report on them? However, she sounded more amazed than anything else. "I love this woman. She's going to be a wonderful fit up on campus. What a glorious day."

"Why do the bad guys always monologue?" I asked instead, not wanting to admit I wasn't caught up on my reading. Lucia tittered and slapped a hand over her mouth. Sister Ann shot us a look and we quieted down.

"I don't know what the fuck you're talking about, Doctor, but my kingdom is huge. It goes almost all the way up to Warm Springs. Hell, if I had more men, I could probably take Roanoke. I might even go to Lexington!"

I doubted he'd get past the tiny town of Iron Gate but I bit my tongue. We hadn't seen yet what the tidal wave from Lake Moomaw had done to Clifton Forge or to Iron Gate but, since both were on the Jackson River and in the direct path of everything headed downstream, I doubted King Dale would make it that far.

Apparently the doctor thought so, too. "You couldn't even take this house. Leave me alone or my dogs are gonna eat you alive!"

"I don't want to hurt your dogs, little miss," King Dale replied. He sounded sure of himself. "But I won't hesitate to put them down if need be. Might as well come with us. Nobody's coming to help you. Ain't nobody around who can stand up to me or my army."

"A straighter line from a fool has never been so smartly given," Sister Ann murmured as she took the megaphone from Kayla's hands. She nodded at her. "Take Kitty Squad. Split them into two groups and hide in those trees. Wait for my cue. You remember it, right?"

"Yes, ma'am," Kayla answered immediately. She sounded excited. Sister Ann smiled at her.

"Okay. Be safe. And make certain you stay out of sight."

Kayla took the younger girls with her. I watched them duck behind a large hedge of overgrown bushes and lost track of them. Unlike the last time we ran into King Dale's men, all of the girls were dressed in hunting gear we'd scavenged from the clothing closet and some of the abandoned homes in the area we'd only recently started to search. We weren't standing out in the woods again in pleated skirts and white blouses, I can promise you that.

Sister Ann smacked the side of the bullhorn against her palm before lifting it to her face. The megaphone projected her already loud voice to Biblical proportions. "Good morning, Appalachia Rex! How are you doing on this fine autumn day?"

King Dale's face contorted into a weird combination of fear, loathing, and uncertainty all bundled up beneath his beard. He spat out a mouthful of what I assumed were curses, though not loud enough for me to really hear anything specific. Sister Ann must have supernatural hearing, though, because she immediately admonished him.

"Language, Appalachia Rex."

"Damn it!" he fairly screamed as he ducked behind an old, abandoned car. His head began swiveling around in every direction, looking for . . . what, I wasn't sure. More infected? A pissed-off teenaged girl with a rifle? Considering the last time we'd run into one another like this, I couldn't really blame him. Those shamblers had nearly done a number on his groupies. Plus, we stole his not-a-tank. That probably stung worse than losing any of his men. "Why the hell do you gotta turn up in the middle of delicate negotiations?"

"Again with the language." Sister Ann clucked her tongue and sighed dramatically. "I thought you would remember. Some lessons you are slow to learn, it appears. Nevertheless, I must admit I am a bit surprised to see you in some sort of standoff with a woman who clearly doesn't want to join your 'noble' endeavor. What are you trying to accomplish here? You're projecting insecurities here by making demands. What is it that you're hiding? Is it shame? Fear?"

"You're the one who's hiding, Sister," he snapped loudly. "Hiding behind the cloth, that river over there, on top of y'all's mountain!"

"You're the one engaging in kidnapping," Sister Ann fired back. "Well, attempting to. Not a good look for you, really. What happens when you grow tired of hearing 'no,' Appalachia Rex? What sort of man are you when the chips are down?"

"You're still hiding!"

"It's not hiding. It's called prudence."

"You're a woman of the cloth! You say your faith can't be doubted. If your faith is so strong, then why don't you step out into the open and face us!"

"My faith in God is absolute and can't be questioned by the likes of you," Sister Ann called back in a loud voice. Her tone then dropped low enough so only us girls who were near could hear. "Nowhere does He demand His followers be stupid in the face of the enemy, either. Chesty Puller and Jesus definitely agree on that one."

I tittered at that. I had no idea who Chesty Puller was but she sounded awesome—although that was one unfortunate nickname.

"I'm not about to let you kidnap some poor woman who clearly doesn't want your help," Sister Ann continued. "I've got six rifles all aimed on you. Your men should be fine, but you will have a very bad day if you keep this up."

"What about 'Thou Shalt Not Kill,' Sister?" Rex shouted back.

"Who said anything about killing?" Sister Ann looked toward the two clusters of trees and nodded. "Show him."

None of the rifles we had were equipped with those old-fashioned laser sights you used to see in the movies. Thanks to the deceased Mr. Stitmer and his gun safe, we had plenty of the green-dot variety, but those you didn't really see if they were being pointed at you. However, he also loved his cats and had the little red laser pointers scattered throughout his house. The cats had run off during the early days of the Fall, hopefully were surviving in the wild.

Good old Appalachia Rex over there didn't know about our cat laser toys, though. Laser pointers were cheap, their batteries lasted forever, and they made great psychological weapons in a standoff.

They were especially effective when the dust from their own moving around allowed for the red laser beams to show up rather nicely. It looked even more impressive when there were six coming in from multiple angles and aimed at unexpected areas. Instead of being aimed at his head or chest, the other girls had pointed their lasers at, well, his junk. For some reason guys would rather have their head blown apart than risk injuring their manhood. Stupid, right? It was very stupid, but also effective.

Cat toys for the win.

King Dale looked down and I swear his face turned a new shade of white.

"I don't know about you, but it appears that you should survive a shot there." Sister Ann's voice was as sweet as honey. I shivered. Sister Ann terrified me, even while earning my respect and love.

"Why do you torment me so, woman?!" Dale fairly screamed as he tried to brush away the laser dots. His reaction was predictable and also hilarious. If not for the standoff, I would have died laughing my ass off right there. "Lawlessness is something God hates! Says so right in the scripture! I'm bringing order to a chaotic land! To my people in my land!"

"By trying to take young women and girls away from my care to serve in your totty harem?" Sister Ann replied hotly. Something about what he said had royally ticked the nun off. Not for the first time I wondered about what had happened to her before she'd left the Marines and joined the Dominican Order. Being a Dominican nun was not something any woman went about casually—at least, that's what Sister Ann always said. Something had to have happened when she was a marine and it had left a mark on her. I noticed that one of her hands was trembling slightly as she raised the bullhorn back to her mouth and continued.

"Kidnapping a young woman, taking her against her will?" I wouldn't say she was yelling, because Sister Ann only speaks in a voice that everyone could hear. If it were any of us girls, though, it might be called yelling. Through a bullhorn. With the volume set to MAXIMUM. "It's clear she does not want to go with you. You claim to be a good king, yet you do villainous things! Or try, which is worse! You think your men—who were good men before our tests and tribulations began, no doubt—want to watch you take young girls into your bed? You think the bad men who follow you won't get jealous and want something similar? Or to take more later? How many of your men are fathers, or were? How many do you think will stand by and idly watch as you crown yourself some hillbilly despot? You are a nuisance, but you haven't descended yet to filth. Yet. You can still change, Brother Dale. You can do better. You should be better than this."

I twitched at that. It was the first time I'd ever heard Sister Ann call the so-called King of Appalachia by his given name.

"I'm tired of this game, Sister!" he screamed back. He couldn't see us but he had to know roughly where we were at. The laser pointers showed him roughly where they were originating from. "Either shoot me, or leave me be. Dr. Jefferson is coming with me and my men!"

"I told you I wasn't going," the doctor yelled from within the dilapidated house. "I'd rather go with the nun than you creeps!"

Well, that was one way to recruit.

The men who'd been standing not too far behind Dale had backed away at the sight of the lasers shining in the dust. He continuously made a swiping motion near his junk, trying to get rid of the lasers. Failing, as well. The pure absurdity of the situation was something I would never have believed if not for the fact I was watching it with my own eyes.

Fortunately, none of King Dale's guys looked like they were ready to shoot at us just yet. A few of them even appeared amused by it all. Not many, of course. But they were there. Watching the self-proclaimed king. *Judging.*

They were the cracks in King Dale's armor, I suddenly realized. A sword smashed against a shield just made a loud noise, and sometimes broke the sword. Just like we were threatening to do now. But a dagger in between the ribs while the shield is elsewhere? Clarity struck me.

Sister Ann's words about trying to kidnap or coerce the veterinarian against her will hadn't been for King Dale, no. They were for the men who followed him. The fathers whose children died during the Fall. The grandfathers who'd seen their grandbabies die. The men whose wives had turned into mindless raging things and they could do little to save them.

I looked at her in a new light. Sister Ann was way more devious than I ever would have given her credit for.

Freaking nuns, dude.

King Dale's men started to drift away. Slowly, but it was there. They weren't looking for a fight with us. Most of them, anyway. I could see one or two of them with looks on their faces that suggested bad things could come if they had the chance. We could worry about them later, though. First things first.

King Dale must have sensed the change of mood with his men because he started backing away. He raised his hands and shook his head.

"There's a reckoning coming, Sister!" he shouted one final time at us. None of his men could be seen. He was almost out of sight as well. We'd won without a single shot being fired and nobody dying. Progress. "The King of Appalachia doesn't take kindly to this!"

"Run, inbred hick! Run your dumb ass home!" I crowed as he disappeared around the bend in the road. A soft cough interrupted my triumph.

"Madison?"

Aw, damn it. I should have known better.

"There is no need to mock him," she admonished. "And watch your language. You owe me demerits."

"Yes, ma'am," I said, chagrined. Of course I'd be the first one to get demerits since the Fall. Lea and Melinda came around a big tree just then, their unloaded rifles slung over their shoulders. Both girls looked immensely pleased with themselves as they pocketed their lasers. Not that I could blame either of them. Their timing with the laser pointers had been perfect. Ulla trailed only slightly behind them. She carried the loaded rifle and had been ready, just in case King Dale got a little froggy. Fortunately, the wannabe King of Appalachia had decided discretion was the better part of valor and had moved far enough away that he was no longer in clear sight. The road had a slight jog to it so it would give us time to get out of there. Or "egress" as Sister Ann would call it. It felt like there was little chance of him coming back to try again. We'd managed, once more, to avoid a direct fight with the man. "Good job, you three."

"You are definitely better at this than old Dale over there," Dr. Jefferson said as she exited her house. With experienced hands she guided her two Great Danes toward the BearCat. The black one turned and stared at me while the brindle-colored monster easily hopped into the back of the vehicle. Dr. Jefferson climbed in. The smaller brindle followed Dr. Jefferson inside. The doctor stuck her head back outside. "I'll try my luck with you lot, if you don't mind. I can't believe you went out and stole a tank!"

"It's not . . ." My voice trailed off as she disappeared within once more. Yeah, she was a veterinarian, but the woman seemed to have the attention span of someone half her age. Still, she would be invaluable up at the campus. While Sister Ann seemed to be a font of information, the only type of medicine she was used to dealing with were battlefield dressings and first aid. Dr. Jefferson? Probably much more. I sighed. The doctor was going to be as bad as Rohena.

"It's not a tank," I murmured in a quiet voice.

Lea and Melinda were already in the BearCat with the dogs and I could hear them *ooh*ing and *ahh*ing over the Danes. Okay, yeah. For dogs the size of horses, they were cute. I guess. I don't know. The only dog my family ever had was one of those demonic Chihuahuas who seemed to have it out for everyone but my mom. Besides, nobody ever looked at six pounds of hate and rage and said, "Oh, how precious."

Nobody sane, at least.

In hindsight, that explained a lot about my mom . . .

Ulla's sudden scream shook me to my core. I'd let my guard down and something had attacked. My head whipped around, looking for any sign of the shamblers. Instead of a shambler I spotted a large man struggling to hold Ulla's arm while covering her mouth. She was fighting ferociously against him and he couldn't get a good hold. It took less than a second for me to realize what had happened.

Someone had snuck around behind us when we were distracted by Dale and waited to make a move. If Ulla hadn't managed an incoherent scream he might have snagged her without anyone noticing. He was clearly with King Dale's men. I'd seen him before. There was no way of knowing if he'd been a good one, or bad, before the Fall. Nobody could know. The Fall changed us all, one way or the other.

None of that mattered now. He was trying to take Ulla. My innate protectiveness kicked into full gear in a heartbeat.

"Let her go!" I shouted and brought Baby up. Just like Sister Ann had taught me, I aimed with the green dot while keeping my finger resting on the trigger guard. Relaxed but ready. My heart was hammering in my chest, unlike the drills she'd put me through before. My attention was focused purely on the guy grabbing Ulla's arm. She was clear and not in the way, but Sister Ann had drilled it into me that things could change in a hurry.

Ulla shrieked again and tried to jerk her arm away. The big man had a firm grip and jerked her farther away. Melinda tried to grab her but slipped and fell. I could hear confused shouting from the other girls but in my head it was just a jumbled mess. Lea was screaming. None of the words made any sense. All I could see was the camouflage hunting jacket, the gray undershirt peeking out at the collar, and the green dot.

"Let her go, damn it!" I yelled. Despite the cool air, sweat stung my eyes. My mouth was dry and my throat hoarse. Had I been screaming? Blinking to get the stinging under control, I tried to control my breathing. In my chest my heart was hammering. Everything around me smelled funny.

More incoherent background noise. I could see Dr. Jefferson out of the corner of my eye. Her two giant dogs were pulling hard at the leash. She was hanging onto the back handle of the BearCat with her other hand, but it was a near thing. It was clear both dogs wanted to get in on the action. Somebody else was screaming. Probably Kayla.

Melinda was crying. In the sea of anarchy, I only heard one calm, collected voice in my ear.

"Take the shot. Protect the innocent."

It was Sister Ann, and yet it wasn't. The voice with which she spoke was born not in the studious halls of St. Dominic's but on the fields of some war-torn foreign land in the midst of battle. Calm, firm, decisive. She understood what was at stake, more than anyone else. Not just the life of a little girl or of a violent man, but the soul of a young woman.

I've never been one to express my feelings well. It was why I'd taken the role of security at the school. Shooting the shamblers was far easier than dwelling on those we'd lost. But at the moment I understood what love truly was. Unabashed love. My soul was only in danger from myself. If I hesitated, the dark spiral into depression would be fast, especially if something happened to Ulla because of my inaction. Sister Ann knew me, knew all of us. Understood what made us tick. If I allowed Ulla to be taken, or hurt?

Worse still, if I could have prevented it?

Green dot, center mass. Big center, too. It was almost point-blank range. There was no way I could miss. I'd done this enough times with the shamblers now that it was almost second nature. But this wasn't a shambler, wasn't one of the rabid creatures who'd once been a person. This was a person. A human being with a soul. I hesitated. Ulla shrieked wordlessly again. Sister Ann's calm, quiet words were still ringing in my ears.

The man's free hand dropped to his hip. The holster was as clear as day. His fingertips brushed the handle of the gun. He was going to kill someone. The decision was easy now. The danger was clear and evident. Every lesson drilled into me was shoved to the side by a single thought.

God, please forgive me.

I squeezed Baby's trigger. The shot was high, clipping him in the right shoulder. He shrieked in pain but didn't let go of Ulla. The man grabbed his gun and tried to bring it up but quickly realized his arm wasn't really working anymore. Shoving Ulla away, he tried to switch the revolver from his right hand to his left. His eyes burned with anger and intent. There was no saving him, but I could still protect Ulla and the girls.

At what cost?

Didn't matter. *Protect them.*

I'd pay it. The girls of St. Dominic's were all I had left in this world. *Please . . . please forgive me, Lord.*

I pulled the trigger two more times. The first shot punched him in the gut, low and near the hip. It was a painful wound, one that would have led to a slow, agonizing death. I'd seen it before with the shamblers. They didn't feel pain like we did, but they could still die after being shot like that. Eventually. The second round hit his chest, three inches to the left of center.

Groaning, the man dropped his weapon and slowly stumbled back. He didn't fall dead immediately, though. Baby's rounds were too small for that, as Sister Ann had repeatedly drilled into my head. They were lethal but unless it was a head shot, it wasn't an immediate death. Instead, he dropped to a knee. His left hand was clutching the belly wound I'd given him. His brain must not have begun to process the chest shot yet.

I kept Baby's barrel trained on him but it was clear he was no longer a threat. His eyes were glazed, unfocused. I tried not to meet them, instead staring at the blood seeping out of the hole in his hunter's coat. Coughing, he began to tilt to and fell onto the ground. His breaths came in heavy wheezes now as he struggled to breathe. One breath, then another. Each exhale came slower and slower until . . .

. . . they stopped.

He stopped breathing. Only the dead did that after being shot. Right?

Right?

"Holy shit," I whispered. My hands ached and I didn't know why. Everything was doubled. Baby felt like she weighed fifty pounds. The world was starting to spin. I really wanted to throw up. "Holy shit, holy shit, holy shit . . ."

"Language, Maddie," Sister Ann's quiet murmur cut through my litany of swearing. Blinking, I turned and stared at her. She pushed Baby's barrel down and away. Looking down stupidly, I realized I'd trained the AR toward her. My hands let go and the safety harness let the weapon hang free. Sister Ann gently took the rifle from me and safed it after clearing the chamber.

Lucia turned to stare at me. I couldn't meet her gaze. Her eyes drifted over to Sister Ann.

"Back to the school, Lùcia. Now, girls," Sister Ann instructed as she sat next to me. She draped an arm over my shoulders and pulled me closer. I buried my face in the coarse fabric of her sweater. Nothing made sense. She should hate me for killing a living, breathing, noninfected human being. I didn't get it. I didn't understand. "It's okay, Maddie. It's okay."

But it wasn't. Or at least, I wasn't. Not even close.

Nobody from Dale's group pursued us. They'd probably heard the shots and decided not to come back, thinking there might be shamblers running around. Even if they had, they couldn't have kept up with the BearCat anyway. With Lucia at the wheel of the lumbering armored vehicle, we practically flew down what remained of I-64 to Mile Marker 10, then backtracked up to St. Dominic's. It was the safest and best way to the school and, without any vehicles that we'd seen, there was no way Appalachia Rex was ever going to get there. Not unless he really wanted to hike up a massive mountain or four.

I wasn't really aware of anything specific going on around me during this time. Oddly enough, I was also hyperaware of everything. Every single bump in the road seemed to jolt my nerves, but the words of the other girls around me were muffled and incomprehensible. The only thing I was really aware of when it came to the others was Ulla clinging tightly to me, her skinny arms wrapped around my waist. I knew I was soaked in sweat but for some reason couldn't figure out why. It was the strangest thing.

Eventually we made it up to the school. Dr. Jefferson and her dogs were shown to the bunker while Sister Ann took control of the security contingent. Peripherally, I was aware of everything going on. This was my job. I wasn't doing it. I'd failed. Or I'd wildly succeeded. Depends on who you asked. Security was supposed to be my responsibility. Yet I stood by and let the sister do her work.

Somehow I made it up to the roof of the cafeteria. I don't remember climbing the ladder, or even why I chose it as my destination. Maybe it was the views it offered? Before the Fall, the top of the building had been one of the more popular places for girls to sneak up to if they wanted out of their cottages without leaving campus. It was the unofficial "cool" zone. Since none of the girls smoked up there, most of the sisters had let it slide. Even Sister Ann, and she was a stickler for the rules.

I was seated cross-legged on the ledge facing the mountains when I finally realized where I was. Blinking, I glanced around. There were people standing around but nobody was too close. A good thing, too. I didn't want anyone to be close. Not at the moment.

They didn't seem to want to talk, though. Sister Ann, Ulla, and Emily. That was nice of them. My eyes traced back to the outline of the tallest mountain in the distance. I wondered if it even had a name. Probably did. The people in this area named everything. They even had names for certain parts of Dunlap Creek.

Taking a deep breath, I tried to let it out slowly. Instead, all that came out was a choked sigh.

I killed someone. I'm a killer. My brain was a jumbled mess.

This was not how I'd envisioned my day ending.

"How do you feel?" Sister Ann asked as she sat down next to me. Clearly she'd been waiting for me to come out of whatever trance I'd been in. Taking my eyes off the dark mountaintop in the distance, I sighed. My heart hurt. Or was that my soul? I couldn't tell. Talking might help. Or not. There was only one way to find out.

"I don't know," I answered truthfully. "It feels weird, you know? Like, one second I'm okay, then *bam!* I feel like a horrible person and I'm going to Hell. Then it turns right around and I think it's fine because he was trying to hurt Ulla."

"Did you recognize him?" Sister Ann gently probed.

"No, I don't think so." Shaking my head, I stared back out into the distance. "I mean, I've seen him with Dale before, but that's it. Does that make it easier?"

"I don't know." There was an honesty in her tone I found comforting. Sister Ann had never lied to me before. It was comforting to know she wasn't going to start now just to ease my own inner turmoil.

We sat in silence for more minutes than I cared to count before I felt comfortable speaking again. "Am I going to Hell, Sister?"

"God's forgiveness is expansive and great," Sister Ann responded neutrally.

"That's not a 'no,'" I pointed out.

"Why did you shoot him? Other than me telling you to, I mean."

"He was trying to hurt Ulla. Or kidnap her. I don't know. It all happened so fast..."

"An unknown man was trying to hurt one of the girls you are responsible for," Sister Ann mulled it over, almost speaking to herself. "On one hand, 'Thou Shalt Not Kill' is pretty definitive. But there are always justifications. The defense of the innocent is something God takes very seriously. So no, Maddie. My gut tells me you are not destined for Hell because of this. Repentance... yeah. It's not an easy feat. As much as this might haunt you, you did the right thing. Thank you for protecting Ulla when I couldn't."

Deep down, I knew I had. I think that's what hurt worse than anything else. Knowing I'd "done the right thing" by killing a human being. It made me feel cold and empty inside. Shivering, I pulled my knees up to my chest. A breeze blew across the rooftop, leaves dancing on the wind as they flew by. It was warm, but beneath it I knew what was to come. There was a deep chill in the air. Was it going to snow again? Sure felt like it.

Would King Dale attack us during snowstorm? I wanted to say no, but truth be told I had no idea. Not anymore.

None of his men had ever done anything so brazen before. Sure, he'd made threats and even tried to build a bridge to come get us. After what had just gone down, though, I was having second thoughts. What if there were girls back at wherever he was holed up? What if they'd been kidnapped? What could we do if there were? How would we stop it?

How would we stop *him*?

My gut told me that it was only going to get worse from here. More and more people who'd survived would be looking to either help, or harm. The shamblers were a menace, true, but the survivors could be even scarier. My hands started to tremble. It was getting harder to breathe. Was I going to have to kill them all? How could I repent for being such a monster? Was I to be nothing more than the school's killer? What sort of person was I? How could I even be a person?

"Take a minute, Maddie." Sister Ann interrupted my thoughts with a gentle nudge to my ribs. A strong, calloused hand grasped mine. She gave it a reassuring squeeze. The trembling stopped. When did it start? My ribs were hurting. Had I been hyperventilating? Jeez. How bad was I? She pulled me to my feet. "Just breathe easily for a minute. Don't worry about tomorrow, or next week. Focus on the now. Everyone here is safe. All the girls in our care—no, *your* care—are safe and preparing for dinner. They'll do Devotionals tonight before bed, then we'll say a prayer for the souls of those who've died. *All* of them. Even *him*. Names don't matter. God will know. Then the girls will go to sleep, comfortable knowing that anyone who would try to hurt them would have to go through both of us first. Some of the other girls might have feared what you do before, but after today? They'll know you'll always be the one to protect them. You are there for them, and they find comfort knowing this. Some might hide behind their own insecurities and be cruel now, but at the end of the day, when the barbarians are at the gate? It'll be you they look to. You'll stand and fight for them. They trust you."

They shouldn't have, but her words made me feel better. I felt the guilt slowly drift away, leaving me feeling drained but . . . okay. Not the best word, sure, but I'd be lying if I said everything was great. Of course, I couldn't say everything was horrible at the same time. Yeah, "okay" worked fine for now. Later?

Sister Ann was right. I could deal with that later. Now? I just needed to breathe. Small steps.

Breathe in, relax, exhale.

Time passed. The sun drifted lower in the sky. Ulla silently joined us. She pushed her hip against mine and clasped my hand with both of hers. It felt okay, like the way my younger brothers used to back when we got along, before I'd become a total bitch to them. Ulla trusted me to keep her safe. The way they had, once. It was a nice feeling. It was humanizing.

The mountains grew darker still as the light made one last, desperate attempt to fight against the encroaching blackness. For a brief moment the sun created a wall of flame behind the changing leaves of the tree atop the mountain as light filtered through them. This was one of the rare instances when nothing on earth should be allowed to be so beautiful. The view was stunning. It was fleeting, sure, but the moment was there. A beacon of light, hope. Slowly I began to understand. I did not choose to kill someone. I chose to protect another. Was I ready to accept it, though? No, I wasn't quite ready for that yet.

There was no light anywhere on the campus visible from where I sat, but for a moment I could almost imagine how it'd been before the Fall. It cheered me up a little more. As much as I'd hated it when I first arrived, St. Dominic's really was the sort of place for a girl like me. I was not a monster, no. Protector was a better word.

I could deal with that, too. But later. Right now? I just needed a moment of stillness.

Breathe. Release.

Good girl.

Ulla rested her head on my shoulder another moment before quietly leaving. She'd been through a lot already, and today had almost broken her. Almost, but not quite. One of the youngest surviving girls of the school, she was made of stern stuff. We all were. Sister Ann had been absolutely right about another thing when it came to us girls: Why settle for average when you could be extraordinary?

None of us were average. Not after this.

"Sister?" I asked, my eyes on the setting sun as the sky began to change to reds, purples, and blues. It was a beauty I'd missed in the mad scramble to survive, and one I hadn't paid attention to in months. Not since before Thanksgiving, at least. For the first time in what seemed like forever, I felt okay. Not only with myself, but with those of us who'd survived. However, something else had been weighing on my mind and I needed to know. It would help distract me from . . . other stuff. Things that I might actually dream about later. Questions are good. Seeking knowledge is never bad. Sister Ann believed that there really wasn't a stupid question, merely an uninformed one. "Can I ask you something?"

"Of course you can."

"Umm, you know how you talked about your friend Chesty? Uh . . . how big were they?"

"What do you mean, Maddie?"

"Her, uh, breasts."

"What?" Sister Ann stared at me now. She was clearly confused. This conversation was not going how she'd expected it to. "What are you talking about? *Who* are you talking about?"

"You know," I said, shrugging. It was a little embarrassing. Embarrassing was better than the empty feeling I'd had earlier. It let me forget what I'd done, even if it were just for a minute. "Your friend, Chesty Puller? Your marine buddy? I mean, with that nickname, I can only imagine how big her boobs were. So, like, how big were they?"

Once she was able to form coherent words again, Sister Ann informed me that Chesty Puller was actually a dude. She told me his entire story, trying to distract me from my own thoughts. It was a good attempt. He'd been a badass marine from a long time ago and done lots of stuff, and saved many marines. But, still a dude. What sort of guy runs around being called "Chesty," anyway? It was weird.

It was also distracting . . . which was good enough, for now.

I think.

CHAPTER THIRTEEN

"A noble man compares and estimates himself by an idea which is higher than himself; and a mean man, by one lower than himself. The one produces aspiration; the other ambition, which is the way in which a vulgar man aspires."
—Marcus Aurelius

"Maddie? Can we talk?" Sister Ann asked quietly as she poked her head in my room. I was up but I wouldn't call it awake just yet. My jumbled, half-asleep brain had started braiding Ulla's hair about ten minutes before I'd crawled out of bed and gotten dressed. The kid had climbed into my bed again sometime in the night, long after I'd passed out from sheer exhaustion. Her nightmares had probably come back with a vengeance after what happened yesterday.

Not that I could blame her. I was still reeling emotionally from everything.

Since I was out of bed and already dressed, it was pretty easy to slip out of the room without waking Ulla. She'd gone through a lot yesterday. There was no need to wake her up just yet.

You went through a lot as well, a silent voice reminded me as I followed Sister Ann out into the main room. None of the other girls were up yet, which was strange. I glanced around as my brain finally began to register that it was early in the morning.

"What time is it?" I asked.

"A little after five," she replied instantly. She handed me a cup of warm water. It smelled odd. Sniffing, I realized she'd used one of her precious few remaining tea packets to give me a little boost of caffeine. Raspberry oolong tea, if I wasn't mistaken. I looked at her, suddenly suspicious. Was she concerned about how I'd slept? Short answer: I hadn't, really. But I was not going to admit that. Not to anyone.

"This is serious," I muttered but sipped the warm beverage anyway. It was bliss. One thing I missed more than anything else was caffeine. We had some, sure, but it was carefully hoarded stuff, like Sister Ann's tea. Eventually we would run out. That would be a sad day for everyone. There might even be tears.

Humor is what kept me going most of the time. Dark humor. *Very dark.*

"How's our security situation?" she asked after I'd lowered the cup from my face.

A jolt of nervous energy ripped through my chest. Did she know about Colton? I'd planned on going to see him today, to tell him what had happened. He'd understand, I think. Swallowing, I paused for a moment, giving my heart a chance to calm down before I replied.

"Decent, I think. Not a lot of shamblers running around on our side of the river. If they ever learn to swim—or remember, whatever—then we might have some problems."

Ah. I knew where this was going now. She was trying to keep my mind focused on tasks instead of the man I'd killed. Part of me wondered if she had any idea how much I appreciated her efforts.

"Not what I was thinking," she said, her eyes locked on my face. "We might have a bigger problem."

Does she know? I couldn't say. Not wanting to volunteer any information, I stayed quiet. Instead of speaking, I took another sip. Speaking when not asked a direct question was just one of the insidious ways Sister Ann managed to get the truth out of other girls. A student of her game, I knew it was in my best interest to let her ask a direct question before answering.

"I'm thinking King Dale showing up at Dr. Jefferson's around the same time we did was a very odd coincidence, don't you?"

I swallowed the tea, feeling a little better. This wasn't about Colton but something else. "You think he's watching the entrance somehow?"

"We know he's got horses, and there have to be other cars he's acquired, but who knows what else he has? We have radios that work up in the mountains. Who can say he doesn't as well? Someone watching the front entrance or the main road and reporting in when we move."

That made a certain amount of sense. It also kept the lingering thought of what had happened the day before from breaching the mental defenses I'd thrown up. "What do you want me to do?"

"Just be wary out there," she told me. "After yesterday, they might try and snatch one of the girls. I never thought King Dale would do anything so drastic, but..."

"He's been trying to get up here for months," I pointed out, ignoring the hurt in my heart. The sick feeling wasn't as bad as it'd been the night before, but it was still there. So much for my defenses. "What do you mean, you didn't think he would do something like that?"

"It's all psychological for him, Maddie," Sister Ann explained as Lucia stumbled into the room. She looked at the two of us, shook her head, muttered something under her breath in Spanish, and staggered back the way she came. Sister Ann waited another few seconds before continuing in a lower voice. "The BearCat, the bridge, everything. He wants to be seen as the conquering hero, not simply the conqueror. If he really, truly wanted to take control of the school, he would simply swarm us with guns and men. They *do* outgun us, and there are more of them then there are of us. His mentality is that he's *saving* us from the dangerous world. To protect us. On the surface, it's a noble gesture and idea. You said it not too long ago yourself. The problem is when someone rejects his saving them, like we are. He can't comprehend why we refuse to be saved. In his eyes, I'm being selfish by keeping all you girls locked away up here when he thinks you would be safer with him. Get it?"

I thought so. He really thought of himself as a good guy. I *had* said something along those lines back before we stole the BearCat, but nobody ever listened to me. "So he wants to roll up on us like the big hero and be cheered on, like some sort of Johnny Football?"

"Precisely. And that makes him dangerous."

"Huh?" Unsure where she was going with this, I motioned for her to continue.

"There is nothing more dangerous than a noble villain who is convinced that he is in the right."

She had a point there. "So keep an eye out for anyone who might try to snatch one of the girls, or me. Got it."

"And shamblers."

"Naturally."

"And Madison?"

"Yes, ma'am?"

"While I can't hear your Confession, you can always talk to me about *anything*. You know this, right?"

I took a final sip of the tea and nodded. She was right. I *could* talk to her. What happened the day before, for instance. I could talk. The question was, would she understand? The answer was *probably*. I couldn't be certain, though. She'd never told any of us why she chose to become a nun so late in her life.

Sister Ann always listened, though, and accepted without interrupting—unless we were lying and she knew it. But even then, she oftentimes just let us talk it through. It was one of the many things I loved about her.

But some things I just preferred to keep to myself. Things like what was going on in my head, and Colton.

Who, as it turned out, didn't even have the courtesy of being home when I got there.

After waiting on the front porch for a few minutes, I wandered around to the back. There was a privacy fence that wrapped around the entire backyard—stupid, since the closest neighbor was about two hundred yards away or so. However, one thing we did figure out early on was that the tall privacy fence had kept out any shamblers from having easy access to the backyard.

Another added benefit was that the backyard got a lot of sunlight. Someday, someone might be able to start a garden back there.

Looking around, I could see he'd made some improvements. One of them included a strange-looking device that sort of reminded me of a solar panel. Only this had a weird bend to its shape, instead of being flat like I'd seen in the past. He had even run some wires through the former owners' doggy door inside. Curious, I went in to investigate.

Once my eyes adjusted to the darkness, I could see the boy had a future running an electronics store. He continued to grab any and all electrical devices apparently while I had been up on the mountain.

Not that anybody really cared since every house we'd found along this way had been abandoned, but it still felt a little weird seeing him hoard a bunch of dead people's stuff.

"What are you up to?" I muttered as I continued to look around. He really hadn't added much to his food stocks, despite my advice. Other than some canned Vienna sausage and some mysterious unlabeled soup cans, he didn't look like he had much food left. I frowned. The last time I had been by he had had about the same amount. It was like he wasn't even trying to prepare for the future, only thinking of staying alive in the moment.

Except... there was all the electronic equipment. Mentally, I shrugged. He was a weird boy.

He did have some new clothes neatly folded and piled to the side. Well, new-ish. At least he wasn't running around the mountainside in nothing but a cheap jacket and torn jeans anymore. This was progress. Honestly, he probably would've frozen to death by now if not for me. It was a good thought, me being responsible for his surviving.

Sister Ann was right—again. I really did like keeping people safe and protecting them. Now here was something I never thought would happen. I was responsible for other people. My parents would have fainted if they'd ever found out. Or rather, they would have fainted if they had been around to see this.

Stupid zombie apocalypse...

I decided to be nosy and check out what else he'd done around the place. He'd made some changes since the last time I'd been inside. What had been the dining room before was now his bedroom. It made sense, really. There was a window, but it was high off the ground and too thin to climb through. It was also on the south side of the house, so it probably was warmer. While the living room had the fireplace, this room was more secure.

I guess my lectures had stuck.

For some reason I felt like I was intruding in somebody else's personal space. Which was stupid. We found this place together. Okay, sure, we had found it for him, but it wasn't like it was his place to start with. The sensation was persistent, though. Like a nagging voice in the back of my mind. I needed to leave. Or at least, be somewhere else.

Which sucked, too. Colton would've understood. He was a lot

easier and less judging to talk to than the girls back on campus. Well, except Ulla. But then again, it wasn't like she argued with anybody.

I went out the same way I'd come in, being very careful to shut the door behind me. The hinges squeaked a little as it closed. Listening, I could hear a few birds somewhere in the distance making noise. Even in the dead of winter, life went on. The birds didn't seem to care whether it was freezing or not outside. They were made to sing, and sing they did.

Adjusting Baby slightly on its sling, I walked back around the side of the house to the front. Still no sign of Colton. Frowning, I started walking up the road toward the Moose Lodge. There was a slim possibility he'd gone there. What for, I didn't know. Maybe he'd seen something there he wanted that we'd overlooked? It was hard to tell with the kid sometimes.

Movement to my right. A keening howl pierced my ears. Stumbling, I managed to narrowly dodge a shambler as it came out of the shadows. I don't know how I missed it. I started to bring Baby up, but stopped as the shambler turned around and I got a good look at it.

The shambler was a dead ringer for the man I'd killed: beard, roughly the same height, and even looked the same in the face. Or did he? Were my eyes playing tricks on me? The only difference that I could see was that there were no bullet holes from where I'd shot him. Had I missed? No, I'd watched him die. So had the others. Sister Ann had even seen it happen. Yet here a shambler was, uninjured except for a festering, oozing wound on his thigh.

No. It couldn't be him. There was no way.

My trigger finger froze. I was shaking. Nothing wanted to move. It was like my spirit was outside of my body, looking down at the girl shaking in her boots. My brain was a jumbled mess. The shambler let out another angry howl. That keening cry seemed to pierce my soul. I couldn't shoot it. Taking a step back, I tried to warn it off with a shout, a cry. Something. Only nothing came out of my mouth. My heart was hammering in my chest. I couldn't breathe.

There was no way this was the same guy. Shamblers aren't zombies. They are not the walking dead.

Instead of shooting it, I turned like a coward and ran away. The shambler howled and pursued.

I don't remember much of the run back to the mountain. The

only thing I was really aware of was the sound of the shambler's bare feet slapping on the road as it ran behind me. My lungs burned and everything was blurry. Tears. I was crying. Why? It was just a shambler. What was going on with me? Was I broken?

Branches bereft of leaves slammed me in my face as I ran. Thorny bushes snagged my jacket sleeve. Plants seemed to be reaching out from the underbrush to grab at my ankles, trying to slow me down. I could feel the panic rising further in my chest. This was not how I thought I'd die.

Something cracked in the air. It sounded like thunder. I could swear I felt something brush past my hair. There was so much going on in my head that I didn't make the immediate connection. I heard something wet slap behind me. The shambler stumbled to the ground. Panting, I stopped to look back. Half of the damn thing's head was gone. For a moment I was confused. What had happened? Then I remembered.

Ulla. I don't know how I forgot about my protégé. In the heat of the moment, I suppose anything was possible. Of course she would be up on the rooftop standing watch while I was out. The girl was deadly with her rifle, and had been looking out for me. She was helping me do my job—just as I taught her. Why was I surprised?

Why was I so confused about everything at the moment? It was like my brain wasn't working at all.

The shambler was clearly dead. Nothing could survive having half their head shot off. My girl hadn't missed. It was one hell of a shot from that distance. She was already a better shooter than I was. Thank God for that. Hurrying up the mountain along the secret path, I couldn't help but keep looking back over my shoulder at the dead shambler. It didn't get up. It didn't stagger to its feet to come and eat me like I was half expecting it to. No, it stayed dead. Zombies weren't real. Shamblers were something completely different. I knew this. We all knew this.

Why was nothing making sense at the moment?

My hands continued to shake. What was wrong with me? My stomach roiled and I felt queasy. Everything that I had done the day before came back to my mind. The smell of gunpowder, the stench of blood. Ulla screaming for help. The bearded man trying to take the little girl away.

I had to stop. I almost dropped Baby, which would have been a cardinal sin. Turning, I heaved my guts out onto the dirt trail. What little I'd had for breakfast went everywhere. Even precious tea. Or at least, I hoped it was the tea. Stomach acid burned when it came up.

The taste was foul but it didn't burn. Spitting once, twice, I tried my best to get the aftertaste out. It was no use. The nasty combination of vomit and breakfast was going to stick with me until I could brush my teeth. Thank God we found the toothbrushes and toothpaste in the donations closet. For a moment I wondered if I should change boots. I'd been dying to try those new ones out.

Why was that on my mind? My thoughts were nothing but a jumbled mess. The only thing I knew for certain was that there was a dead shambler behind me, courtesy of Ulla. My lungs hurt from the cold air, and the run. My calves were cramping. How far had I gone? Colton's house was almost a mile from campus. Had I run the entire thing? I couldn't remember. Judging by the burning in my thighs, though, I would say I had. No wonder I felt wiped out. I hadn't had to run that far in months, possibly before the Fall even.

Crossing behind the cafeteria, I passed by one of the younger girls. I thought it was Wendy but I wasn't sure. Faces were a blur at this point. I wasn't really paying attention to anything anymore. There was only one thing I wanted, and that was to get inside, get situated, and then . . .

Then what? I had no idea. Maybe sleep. Yeah. Sleep sounded good. I could crawl into bed, bury myself beneath the blankets, and ignore the rest of the world for as long as I lived. That sounded like one heck of a plan.

Only I knew I couldn't.

Sister Ann greeted me at the back door. The concern was evident on her face. I don't know how she knew, but she did. Or at least, she knew enough. That much was evident.

"Maddie?" she asked. There were so many questions in the way she said my name. It was weird. In that single breath she asked if I was okay, what had happened, and if anybody else was in danger. The weight of the world was on her shoulders, and she was more concerned about me than anything else. I don't know why. I didn't deserve it.

Shivering uncontrollably, I collapsed into Sister Ann's arms. "I'm sorry. I'm sorry. I tried. I couldn't. I tried. I'm so sorry!"

She held me tightly and stroked my hair. I don't know how long I cried for.

It was after midnight when I dared come out of my room again. Ulla was sound asleep, having somehow snuck into my room during one of my crying spells. She'd snuggled up against my back so gently I hadn't even noticed she was there until her snoring kicked in. For some reason it made me feel a little better. Not much, but it was there.

I padded silently into the main room. The stove was still radiating plenty of heat, which told me someone was up and tending it. There were faint voices in the stairwell just outside the bunker door. I recognized Sister Ann's immediately, but not the other. Curious, I crept closer until I figured out who it was.

Dr. Brittany and Sister Ann were locked in a heated discussion about . . . something. Listening in, it didn't take long for me to realize what they were discussing. More accurately, who.

"She's just a kid," Dr. Brittany said hotly, though she managed to keep her voice down. "She's a kid who thinks she has to protect everyone."

"She's capable of so much more—"

"That's your problem! You think everyone can be great because you think God put them here for a reason," Dr. Brittany said, cutting her off. "This is why I'm atheist, you know. There is *no* greater purpose for her! We're in a screwed-up world trying to do the best we can."

". . . in the eyes of God," Sister Ann added calmly. "Believing everything that has happened up to this point, including us surviving, was because of pure chance and not divine inspiration is far-fetched, even for someone who claims to believe in nothing."

"Chance? Luck? Ever hear of those things?" Dr. Brittany asked. "I got lucky. *You* got lucky!"

"Perhaps," Sister Ann said. "Or perhaps it was the Almighty, guiding us to be where we needed to be. There were many instances that occurred throughout my life that could have taken me down a different path. Would I have I been called to the cloth if I had joined the Army instead of the Marine Corps? Would I have even joined the military at all, if not for an ex-boyfriend? While we make the choices, it is God who lays down the path. Every single action in my life, every decision, every choice, has led me to this moment. A former marine turned Sister of Notre Dame de Namur, a Catholic convert who was raised Protestant, the only survivor at a school filled with at-risk teenage girls in the middle of what many could argue are the end times.

"I cannot believe for an instant that every single happenstance and coincidence lined up perfectly in this world to allow me to be here, where I would be needed the most. All your decisions in your life, Doctor, led you to choosing Covington instead of, say, Roanoke. Is that luck? Happenstance? Or maybe you are part of God's plan as well?"

"I'm not."

"You can't say that unless you have belief in God, Doctor. I believe you are to play an integral part here. God led us to you for a reason," Sister Ann told her. "As for Madison . . . she will do her part as she sees fit. I will never ask her to do anything I believe she is unfit for. Right now, the best thing I can ask her to do is rest. She's been through a lot, and she's vulnerable. She will decide what she wants to do next."

I crept back to my room, mind whirling. The thought that I was vulnerable was absurd. Sister Ann knew me, and knew I was past things like that. To suggest I was a broken little girl was almost insulting.

How was Sister Ann so calm and reasonable with someone who only believed in coincidence and luck?

Conversely, how was Sister Ann's faith so unflagging after all that she'd seen, experienced, and suffered through?

I didn't know.

I doubted I would ever know.

Either way, I slept on the floor that night. I didn't want to disturb Ulla, or the two Great Danes who'd somehow taken over my bed.

CHAPTER FOURTEEN

"You readin' this, Pecos? Those boys from Van Horn came for us at sunrise. Not zombies, but people like you and me. Regular folk from the next town over. We thought they were here for trade. They were here for something else. We hurt 'em, bad, but they killed Fred. Stole some horses, too. It truly is the end-times when a neighbor can so easily turn on someone, and for what? A couple of horses?"

From: *Collected Radio Transmissions of the Fall,*
University of the South Press, 2053

Shame. It was a sensation I wasn't used to dealing with. Not since I'd come to St. Dominic's, at least.

Because of the incident with the shambler, Sister Ann gave me a break from patrol duties. She told me it was to rest, but she had no way of knowing I'd heard her argument with Dr. Brittany. Temple and Ulla teamed up to fill in for me while I was more or less out of commission, while Finlay and Fiona started pulling more watches up top to cover for Ulla. The twins weren't quite ready to start shooting shamblers left and right just yet, but they were game to at least *try.* Worst case, they got to blow more stuff up. Sister Ann was teaching them the finer points of explosive ordnance—something I never thought I'd see happening, ever.

For me, it was embarrassing that a couple of preteens were doing my job. It was also necessary. I was an emotional wreck and in no shape to do much of anything.

Perhaps Sister Ann was right about the vulnerability thing?

This was far different from what had happened while I was at the Boyd farm. There I'd been in control, easily handling shamblers while keeping them at a distance. Sure, it'd been a lot closer than I would have liked, but after the first one I'd never really felt I was in much danger.

Of course, that had been before I'd murdered someone. A real person, not a shambler. One survivor of the Fall, a living, breathing human being, snuffed out because of me.

A few more survivors straggled in, and we found space for them, just like the others. Not many. Not nearly enough for what Sister Ann wanted. They were from Moss Run, which was sort of like Callaghan only more up in the mountains. They were backwoods, but they knew gardening. Kayla was glad to have them. When the planting season came, they'd be invaluable and very helpful. In the meantime, though, we had to find more space. Which meant cleaning and rebuilding... and when you're missing a lot of tools, it means risky scavenging.

Temple led a small group back out to the Moose Lodge. I knew from past scavenging hunts there probably wouldn't be much of anything to be found, but it helped some of the new arrivals get their feet under them. According to Sister Ann, those who want to help do so because they have an innate sense of responsibility. Those who follow through with their offer, though, have a work ethic.

"And work ethic, Madison, will rebuild this country. Come on. Help me bring in more firewood."

I still had no answers for the reason I panicked when dealing with the shambler. Every single one before then I'd had no problems about giving them a quick demise. But now? I wasn't what you could call "gun shy," but I was definitely having issues dealing with shooting a shambler.

Deer, on the other hand? Deer were easy. Bucks were fair game now that the rut was over and they'd done their deed, so Ulla and I bagged six in as many afternoons. The meat was gamey and tougher than a doe's, but it was protein—something we were starting to run low on thanks to the new arrivals.

Fortunately for me, I wasn't allowed to stay in a funk for long.

It was later than usual and Sister Ann and I were up listening to the shortwave. The past few weeks the updates were getting increasingly bizarre, and Sister Ann was concerned. She'd stopped letting the younger girls listen in at night. Not all of the new arrivals knew about the radio, either. Which was important for reasons I didn't fully understand. But one thing I'd learned during my time at St. Dominic's was that if Sister Ann thought it was important, then it was. Arguing over it was a simple waste of time.

The radio was droning on, spewing out needless info that contained a lot of words but said absolutely nothing. It was as though they were being deliberately obtuse, something I pointed out to Sister Ann when there was a break between shows. Devil Dog Radio was usually way more informative—and, truth be told, more interesting—than what we were getting. It felt censored, which was stupid. Who in their right mind would try to censor a marine?

Frustrated, I flipped frequencies. We had all of the ones worth keeping track of preprogrammed, but sometimes the time zone differences and clocks being off meant we were often early or late. This time, once we found Armed Forces Radio, we were late, joining in the middle of an important announcement.

"...for the immediate cessation of hostilities toward those afflicted with the H7D3. They are human beings like us, and deserve respect. As acting President of the United States of America, I, Elizabeth Sovrain, Secretary of Education, am issuing Executive Order 14221: Any citizen who commits wanton slaughter of infected persons shall be immediately arrested and tried on a minimum of charges stemming from second degree murder and upward. This genocide will not be tolerated by this administration..."

"Wait, what?" I stared stupidly at the shortwave for a full minute, listening to the clearly unhinged individual play the cruelest practical joke in history on us. "I thought we were in February still? Is it April Fools' Day or something?"

Sister Ann didn't say anything. Turning, I looked at her. She was chewing her bottom lip, clearly lost in thought. I'd seen her like this a few times before. It usually meant she was mulling over something very important. Every time it had led to a decision that changed the path I'd believed St. Dominic's to be on.

"Sister?"

The clearly crazy person on the shortwave droned on. "...furthermore, any and all previously retired or discharged military personnel are recalled to their former ranks, effective immediately, and are to report to the closest National Guard duty station that is still functioning. There you will assist the infected individuals with housing, the feeding and care of, and assisting in fulfilling their humanitarian needs in accordance to Executive Order 14222—"

Sister Ann flipped the radio off with such abruptness that the silence was almost startling. I waited for a long time to speak, not sure what I could say. Fortunately, I didn't have to think of anything.

"Follow *orders*?" Sister's Ann's flat, cold tone was . . . *terrifying*. I swallowed nervously. She'd never spoken in *that* voice before. All of us were very familiar with her mannerisms and how she addressed us when we screwed up by now. This? This was something else.

"Does that mean . . . Is that real?" I asked carefully and started thinking about what Colton had said when I first met him. He'd been terrified that they would throw him in jail for killing his mother after she'd turned into a shambler. The acting president had confirmed this. Would they come for me after? Ulla? "They can do that?"

"Yes. I think so. Since we're in a State of National Emergency, and have been for over eight months now, I believe they can legally do it."

"Well, good thing you're a marine—"

"Do I *look* like a marine to you?" Sister Ann asked me in a cold, quiet voice. "I. Am. Not. A. Marine! Not anymore. I gave that up for a higher calling, and I was promised this would be honored. The woman who was the marine is gone. Gone! She will *not* return! That . . . deranged individual on the radio can . . . can . . . go find Christ!"

There were plenty of things I could have said to her at that moment. However, I'm not dumb or suicidal. Instead, I replied as meekly as I possibly could. "No, ma'am. Not a marine."

She inhaled deeply, then slowly exhaled. It was possibly the angriest I'd ever seen her, hands down. If I hadn't just witnessed it firsthand, I wouldn't have believed her capable. It wasn't irrational anger, though. This was deeper, more primal. It was pure, unadulterated rage.

"I'm sorry, Madison. There was no need for me to be abrupt with you. That was uncalled for."

"The fu—uh, heck you say!" I caught myself just in time. That had been close. "That was totally called for! Shamblers are dangerous and not people anymore! Is that bit—uh, person on crack?"

Sister Ann actually chuckled at that. "I can't say to her state of mind, but her judgment is unsound."

"Did they really... They're pressing charges against anyone who continues to shoot shamblers?"

"So they say."

"So that's it?" I asked, dumbfounded. "We can't shoot shamblers even when they try to come up here and eat us? We have to babysit them or something? You're just going to leave us here and go be a Marine again to babysit *shamblers*?"

She snorted. "I swore an oath to protect and defend the Constitution from all enemies, both foreign and domestic. But... I also swore an oath to you girls, to protect you from harm, and help guide you to become the brilliant young women God intended you to be. Every single one of you has tried their best. What sort of mentor... what sort of *human being* would I be if I left you now?"

I smiled. "Not a good one."

"Besides..." She paused and scratched her chin thoughtfully. "I don't think an acting president has the power to issue sweeping executive orders like that. Granted, my civics knowledge is admittedly a little rusty, but until she's sworn in, I do believe that she is outside my chain of command."

"Too bad we can't find the President. It'd be crazy if he was at the Greenbrier or something."

"That would be something," she agreed. "In the meantime, let's put this lull to good use. The twins are getting a little too comfortable with explosive ordnance for my taste. I want you to take them, Ulla, and... Charise and Rosalind down to the ranger station. Take some of the camping gear with you."

"Ma'am?" I asked, surprised. My heart began to hammer in my chest. Did she know about Colton? No, there was no way. I hadn't been down to see him since my little breakdown after the shambler. Panic started to make my chest tight. Had she seen him lurking around? Had the stupid boy come up to campus trying to look for me?

"Rosalind and Charise need to bond with someone close to their age," Sister Ann explained, her voice calm and peaceful. It was a far cry from the vengeful one I'd experienced not too long ago. "The twins need an outlet other than blowing things up and working on the education track—especially since we have one other senior citizen here now who can assist me with that—and Ulla won't sleep if you're not here in the bunker."

All valid ideas and points. Still... "Is it... safe?"

"There's a slight risk," she acknowledged with a simple nod. "But be honest. How likely is it that there is a shambler running around out there right now? With the cold as it is, and how well you and Ulla have thinned their numbers out."

"Not very."

"And since the ranger station can be locked from the inside, and barricaded, and we've cleared it multiple times now, it should be safe."

"Wait, hold up. Are you telling me to have a girls' night—a *sleepover*?—with a bunch of preteens in the middle of the zombie apocalypse?"

"Not zombies, but yes. Yes, I am."

"Oh, come on!" I protested. "I mean, Ulla and the twins, sure. That makes sense. But the other two? They're so *young!*"

"And they lost their parents. All they have is Temple, who is not going to see many more months. His medication is almost out. They need to bond with a group here, and someone older who they can look up to."

"And you think *I* can give them that?"

"You, and Ulla. And the twins. Yes."

"I..." Pausing, I let out a slow, exhausted breath. There was no point in arguing. She would win. Arguing with a nun was like demanding the tide quit rolling in. Pointless. "Tomorrow?"

"I'd like that." She nodded. "Pack up the four-wheeler with sleeping bags and enough food for dinner and breakfast the following morning. Talk to them. More importantly, *listen* to them. It helps make them feel appreciated and part of the group. If all you do is listen to reply, then you never hear anything. It's hard to converse when you don't hear their words."

"Yes, ma'am."

"Are you saying that because you agree, or because you want me to shut up and leave you alone?"

I chuckled softly. The woman really knew teenage girls. "Because I agree, ma'am. Honest."

"I hope so. Maybe you'll figure some things out for yourself as well."

"Ma'am?"

"Don't worry about it," she said and straightened my hair. Even in the winter there was enough humidity in the air to make it frizzy. "Oh! Don't let the twins bring any of the Tannerite with them, okay? Search them thoroughly before you head out. *Thoroughly*, Madison. They are too sneaky for their own good."

I inwardly sighed. Not having explosives was going to tick the twins off. It promised to be a long and argumentative night.

It wasn't my first time spending the night outside the bunker since the Fall occurred. I'd slept in a tree blind once or twice back in September when Sister Ann wanted me to start scouting and exploring our perimeter. With someone else, though? Practically camping in an unsecured building with four hyper preteen girls? Well, that was something I thought would never happen in my lifetime.

And that's not even adding the end of the world into the mix.

Though I brought Baby and three magazines with me, I made Ulla leave her rifle up in my room, locked up and secured. Temple had picked up an old Garand that he seemed happy with, and if anything happened the old guy seemed more than a little eager to shoot some shamblers. However, since Sister Ann was locking down the bunker completely while we were gone, it probably wouldn't matter. Still, Ulla had been upset at first until she found out the twins had to leave the Tannerite behind.

I *still* didn't know where they kept finding the stuff. After blowing up the bridge, I'd thought they'd used it all. Apparently I was mistaken.

Though the original plan had us coming down and cooking dinner, Sister Ann had forgotten that all of us either sucked at cooking or were too young to have ever been taught how. So instead of heading down in the middle of the afternoon, we made our way to the ranger station just before sunset. The woods between the bunker and the station were dark but, thanks to the lack of leaves, not blocking off all light. Still, thick branches did blot out the sky just enough to cast the path in dark shadows.

Charise seemed to be the only one nervous. Her sister was hanging close to Ulla, clearly looking up to her and taking her lead on a lot of things. Both younger girls had already started to learn how to sign so they could talk to Ulla, though Rosalind was picking it up faster. Still, both were making excellent progress.

The distance between the station and the bunker wasn't too far, just enough to make me glad I'd come down earlier with all the sleeping bags on the four-wheeler. If we'd had to carry all the stuff down, I was pretty sure everyone would have been in a bad mood by the time we reached the ranger station. As it was, nobody seemed too put out by the time I unlatched the door into the building. I motioned for them to wait outside and held a finger up to my lips.

They understood the drill. It was unlikely that any shambler had managed to get inside, but there was no reason to draw the attention of any who might be lurking about. Poking my head in, I gave it the smell check. As stupid as it sounds, in a place like this the unwashed body of a shambler is a dead giveaway—something I should have noticed immediately back at the Boyd farm.

You learn from what doesn't eat your face off, I suppose.

Confirming that there were no shamblers inside went quickly. Since it was simply a large room with a loft that used to lead up to the observation tower, there really wasn't anywhere for a shambler to hide. No running water—there was an outhouse not too far away and downhill of the ranger station—and always being secured meant there was nothing inside that might attract a shambler. Of course, it'd served Colton's needs in a pinch early on.

The girls wasted no time in following my directions to set up our little slumber party on the loft. Fiona had wisely brought one of the few flashlights we had that took C batteries and used it so they could see what they were doing up there. It was a positive sign that the younger girls were planning ahead.

While they were doing this, I secured the front door from the inside with an old wood beam. Nothing under three hundred pounds throwing itself against the door was getting in without permission now. Not that I expected any issues.

Getting the old Franklin stove lit was easy. Once it was filled with wood and going, the residual heat from the metal stove would warm up the interior of the building nicely. It wouldn't stay burning all night but it would stay warm enough for us to make it through the morning, and then some.

Once I made it up to the loft, I pulled the ladder up behind me. The girls looked at me with funny faces as I hitched the collapsible ladder up on the ledge. I waited to see if they would ask me what I was doing but surprisingly, none did. Instead, they all started spreading out the sleeping bags and settling in. Rosalind had even tried to help me get mine unrolled.

"Thanks," I told her and finished setting it up. Kicking my boots off, I climbed into the bag and lay down. "Fiona? Light?"

"Gotta conserve batteries, I know," she replied and flipped the light off. The interior of the building was plunged into darkness and silence, with the only sound the wood burning in the Franklin stove below. This time of year there were very few noises up on the mountain. Far off in the distance, a hoot owl cried out.

"This is nice," either Finlay or Fiona said. Rolling on my side, I peered into the darkness. While it was almost pitch black, there was just enough light coming from somewhere that I could make out their faces. Glancing up, I realized I'd forgotten the small skylight in the ceiling of the station.

The moon wasn't full, but it was close enough for light to come in through the tinted skylight. For a moment I wondered whose bright idea it had been. They were long dead now, more than likely. Or perhaps not. People around here seemed to either die young or live forever.

Well, before the Fall, at least.

I could hear whispered voices in the darkness. The twins were talking again in their mystery language. Near my feet, I could sense that Charise was moving closer. Ulla was actually close to the twins instead of me for a change. While it was nice having some of my personal space back, I had to admit I was a teensy bit jealous that the girl I'd pretty much adopted as my little sister didn't need me at the moment.

Wow, I thought. Sister Ann was right. I really did want to be a big sister after all. Mentally, I laughed at myself. Sister Ann was always right.

"What are you two talking about?" I asked, sitting back up. If this was going to be a slumber party, might as well try to do the gossipy girl stuff I was never really good at.

"The Reynolds have a boy around our age," they said in unison. I sighed and shook my head. Of course. We had refugees up on the mountain and naturally the only one the younger girls noticed was the boy their age.

"Their dad is a mechanic, you know," I reminded all of them. "He's helping Emily figure out how to set it up so that we can have hot showers again."

"Yeah, but . . . a boy?" That was definitely Fiona.

"Boys are gross," Charise said as she made a face. Rosalind giggle-snorted and covered her mouth, which caused the twins to laugh. Ulla looked at them for a moment before signing something. In the dim lighting it took me a minute to decipher it.

"No, Ulla's right," I said after she repeated herself for my benefit. "Not all boys are gross. One day you'll learn this. Or understand it, at least. Not everyone wants to hurt us. Your grandpa wouldn't hurt us."

"He's not a boy!"

"Um . . . he's a very old man," I told them. "All men were boys, once."

"I heard one of the other girls say that's why King Dale wants to come up to the school," Finlay muttered darkly. I could see her twisting her fingers on her lap. Whatever she'd been told clearly bothered her. "The men, I mean. He wants to hurt us."

"Who said that?" I asked, feeling a small spark of anger flare up inside. It was one thing to talk about it with the older girls. To make the younger girls afraid about something like that? "Was it Kayla?"

"Kayla? No."

"Rohena?" Silence. Finlay wouldn't look at me. I had my answer, and made a mental note to rabbit-punch the petty little bitch in her kidney the next time I saw her. "Yeah, I figured. Look . . ." I paused for a moment, gathering my thoughts. Sister Ann had just explained this to me. Putting it into words where a kid could understand it, even if they were as smart as the twins, was a challenge. "King Dale thinks he's trying to help us. Well, he did, once upon a time. Now? I'm not so sure. But that's beside the point. It's not what I'm trying to say. There are good people with good intentions, and bad people with bad intentions. You understand the difference, right?"

All the girls nodded, even Rosalind, though I wasn't sure she did. Still, four out of five wasn't bad.

"Well, sometimes those good intentions are for the wrong reason. That can be used to describe King Dale, understand? He thinks he's going to rescue us because it's a dangerous new world, and strength will win in the end. He has strength, and he thinks we don't have any. Usually he'd be right, but"—I reached over and patted Baby on the stock—"this helps make the playing field a little more level. We're safe for now on campus. Eventually they—the *real* government or the military, I mean—will send someone our way. No, I don't know when. You heard the radio updates the same as me. But when that day happens, King Dale will have two choices: quit being a king, or fight to stay one. Sister Ann thinks he'll quit. I'm not sure."

"But Sister Ann is always right!" Charise squeaked in a tiny voice. I grinned. She might be young, but she was quick.

"That she is."

"But you think she's wrong?" she pressed.

I shrugged. "I *hope* she's right. But Sister Ann . . . tends to look at people more positively than I do. She hopes for their best. Expects it, really. Me? I'm a pessimist."

"What's that?" Rosalind asked.

"It means I expect the worst to happen."

Ulla waved to get my attention before asking, *Is that why we're sleeping up on the loft with the ladder pulled up?*

"Yep. I don't care how secure that door is, or how strong those storm covers on the windows are," I told them. "If a shambler got in here, and we were down there, we'd be toast. So, we sleep up here. It's warm, we've got a lot of sleeping bags, and the stove down below should keep everything cozy until the morning."

Rosalind yawned and leaned against her sister. She pulled one of the pillows to her chest. "I don't care what Rohena says. This isn't so bad. I like this. This is nice."

"Better than being in the bunker all the time," Fiona added. Ulla nodded in agreement.

"Do you think Sister Ann will let us do this again?" Finlay asked as she lay down in her sleeping bag.

"I don't see why not," I answered honestly, a little surprised at myself for wanting it to happen. Though I'd been against the idea originally, once again Sister Ann was showing just how well she knew me, and seemed to know precisely what I needed. These girls were the future of St. Dominic's, like me. If I was going to be the one to protect them, I needed to find the value in it. Being afraid was not something I could afford to be, not when kids like Rosalind and Charise needed someone like me to keep them safe. The twins and Ulla, being older, needed someone to look up to and show them how to become young women.

I smiled for their benefit. "This is kind of fun, you know?"

"But only us," Fiona stated. "This is our camping club. The other girls can find their own."

"Especially Rohena," Finlay chimed in.

"Oh, come on, she's not that bad," I argued, though my heart wasn't really in it.

"Yeah, she is!"

"Okay, okay. I'm not going to argue with you. Look . . . I'll talk to her. Let her know that she needs to . . . I don't know, chill out toward you?" I suggested. Finlay shook her head.

"She picks on the younger girls and makes us do her chores!"

"Did you talk to Sister Ann?" I asked. All three older girls shook their heads. "Well, how is she supposed to fix the problem if she doesn't know about it? You can't go through this life terrified of what might happen. Rohena backs down when you stand up to her. Ask me how I know. She's bigger and stronger than I am, but there's no way she wants to fight me again."

Ulla curled up in her sleeping bag. Sometime during our talk Rosalind had conked out and was snoring softly. Charise looked as though she was about to pass out as well.

"That's because you carry the gun," Finlay muttered quietly.

"We have the explosives, though," Fiona reminded her sister.

"Oh, yeah." Finlay sounded suspiciously happier now.

"And no using explosives to hurt other students or people on campus, you two. I don't want to be the one that has to explain that to Sister Ann." They all laughed at this. Ulla smiled, which was good enough for me. I yawned theatrically and stretched. "Let's call it a night, okay?" I told them. Though they sounded serious enough about it, I was pretty sure they weren't about to run around blowing up other students—no matter how annoying they were.

I hoped.

Charise nodded and moved her sleeping bag closer to her sister.

The twins could probably talk all night if I let them. I wasn't even sure if they actually slept or not. Looking at them, I realized that I had told them precisely what Sister Ann would have told me if I'd continued to run from whatever was scaring me about the shamblers, and killing that man to protect Ulla. I wasn't afraid of being a monster, but that everyone would think I was one. This little camping trip let the girls see me as a person and not some emotionless shambler killing machine.

I lay down and folded my hands behind my head. I wasn't alone, not anymore. The only way I could consider myself an outcast now was if I did it to myself. These girls weren't about to let me, either. Our families were lost to the end of the world. From its ashes, I found a new one. One I actually gave a damn about protecting, and finding worth in.

"Sister Ann, you are way too devious sometimes," I whispered as I drifted off to sleep. For the first time in weeks, that protective streak in me was back.

And it felt amazing.

CHAPTER FIFTEEN

"The cars'll run as long as we got gas . . . the problem we're running into right now is that the cities are packed with broken-down cars. No easy way to move 'em. Even with fuel additives the gas in ground storage tanks will be contaminated with water in ten months at the latest. Then what? Then all we have are fancy roadblocks. Granted, it helps keep the zombies in the cities, but then what?"

From: *Collected Radio Transmissions of the Fall,*
University of the South Press, 2053

A strange yet familiar sound woke me just after dawn.

The air around me in the ranger station was chilly. Sometime during the early morning hours, the woodstove ran out of fuel and was only providing faint, residual heat. I pulled the sleeping bag up and wondered why I was even awake. I was not an early morning girl if I could help it. In the distance, I heard what sounded like a car engine. Muttering under my breath, I rolled over and began drifting off to sleep.

Then it hit me and I sat up in the sleeping bag, confused. The noise was jarring for a moment because I felt as if I'd just woke up pre-Fall in preparation for a normal day at St. Dominic's. A full minute passed by before my half-asleep brain remembered that the end of the world had pretty much gone down and I was in a ranger station with a bunch of young kids . . . and there should have been no way for me to hear any sort of engine running.

I was on my feet and pulling my boots on before my conscious brain had time to even realize what I was going to check. None of the other girls were awake or stirring. Pausing, I waited. Had I imagined the sound? A second later it returned—the telltale growl of a motorcycle engine of some kind. Close, but not too close. Baby was propped against a nearby wall. I grabbed it and slung it across my back after making sure I didn't have a round in the chamber. I'd checked it the night before but Sister Ann was adamant about double-checking things like that.

Lowering the ladder quickly, I clambered down and hurried to the barricaded door. Leaning against it, I listened for any sound outside. Nothing but the continued faint noise of a high-pitched engine. The engine sounded almost exactly like the four-wheeler.

For a moment I almost panicked. Had someone stolen the four-wheeler I'd used to bring the stuff down to the station? I lifted the barricade and popped the door open. Not sure what to expect, I slowly peeked outside.

The four-wheeler was still there, untouched. The motorcycle engine was louder, but in the distance. With the valley around the southern side of the school and Dunlap Creek below, it was difficult to make out precisely what direction it was coming from.

"Wazzat?" a voice asked sleepily from inside. I looked back and spotted Charise standing at the edge of the loft. She was rubbing her eyes.

"Some kind of engine," I told her. "Wake up the others."

"We're up," one of the twins replied loudly. "Is that a car engine?"

"Sounds more like the quad," the other answered.

"Finlay, Fiona. I need you two to pack everything up. Leave it up on the loft and out of sight," I instructed as the engine revved in the distance. It was a little louder now. There was only one person who might have access to a dirt bike around here, and the idea of King Dale's men being on our side of the river was terrifying. "Once everything is put away, all five of you need to head straight up to campus and get in the bunker. Ulla, get up on the rooftop of the cafeteria once you're back. Take Mr. Kessenger with you. If anyone but me comes up the mountain, give them a few warning shots. I need the rest of you to tell Sister Ann that I'm going to check it out. I have a radio, channel five."

"Whoa." Finlay appeared at the edge of the loft next to Charise, Fiona right behind. "This is serious."

"Finlay, what channel will I be on?"

"Uh . . . five."

"Fiona?"

"You said channel five."

"Good. Hurry," I told them. The trio disappeared quickly and the sounds of the girls quickly cleaning up could be heard. Turning, I looked back out the door.

It was just above freezing outside. There was a little bit of fog clinging to the ground near the creek, but nothing up here. Glancing up the hill, I could faintly make out a thin trail of smoke coming up from the same area the cafeteria was at. Somebody was already awake up there, which meant Sister Ann probably already knew about the engine noise. More than likely she was anticipating me going to check it out. Still, assuming anything was a bad idea.

"We're set," Fiona announced. Turning, I spotted all five girls carrying nothing but their coats. Finlay handed me mine. It took me a moment to unsling Baby, then maneuver the heavy hunting jacket around and on. The extra padding the heavy coat offered was a nice change of pace from the normal pain the AR's sling caused on my shoulder.

"No delays, right?" They all nodded simultaneously. Even Rosalind, though younger than the rest by a bunch, understood just how serious this was. None of them looked afraid, though. Nervous, yes. But not scared. This was good. "What channel?"

"Five," Finlay, Fiona, *and* Charise responded all together. I nodded.

"Good. Go."

The five headed off up the hill. I watched them for a minute to make sure they weren't stopping before I walked over to the four-wheeler. Checking the girls' progress again, they were halfway up the trail and nearly to the chapel. There were no signs of a shambler anywhere. It was probably too cold for them. One could hope.

Quickly priming the engine, the four-wheeler started up fairly quickly. The tank had been filled up the day before, and nobody had ridden it except me, so I wasn't worried about running out of gas. Carefully shifting into gear, I rolled down toward Dunlap Creek to search for whatever—or more accurately, whoever—was riding around campus.

Two hours later and . . . nothing.

I'd slowly circled the very edges of campus twice, keeping an eye out for anyone riding around on a dirt bike. Once in a while I'd even turn off the four-wheeler's engine and wait to see if I could spot them. Whoever was around, they were doing a very good job staying out of my sight. Once or twice I heard the bike engine not too far away. Every time I headed toward it, though, it would vanish. It felt as if someone was taunting me.

Worst part about it, though, is I could *see* the dirt bike tracks in a few muddy places. They weren't regular, but in obvious places where somebody was sticking to the outskirts of campus and not coming up the mountain. This was both irritating and nerve-racking. They had to know what they were doing. My problem? Figuring out if this was someone scouting us out, an impending attack, or something else entirely.

Frowning, I pulled out the small radio and switched over to channel five. "Base, this is Mads."

"Go ahead." Sister Ann's voice was clearly recognizable, even over the radio.

"Tracks spotted but that's all. Someone's messing with us, ma'am." I clicked off the radio and looked around. I could hear the engine again but this time it was farther off in the distance. "Not sure what's going on."

"Check the river."

Of course. If King Dale—or anyone else, really—was going to come at us, they'd need to cross the river first. Which meant that there was somewhere along the banks of the Jackson River that they'd gained access. I didn't know dirt bikes very well, but it was hard to imagine one crossing the river easily. Unless, of course, someone managed to make a tiny bridge.

But where would they do that? I racked my brain trying to think of a good location. The main road down by the ruined hotel was out. Plus, there might still be shamblers running around down there. No, he probably wouldn't try that again.

There was a place up by the Falling Springs waterfall they could cross, but it was so far out of the way I doubted they'd explored that far to find out. Plus, they'd have to go all the way back up. Mile Marker 10 and the back road was also a possibility, but again, that would waste a lot of gas. Grinding my teeth in frustration, I restarted the engine and turned the four-wheeler around. I was missing something obvious.

Following the path alongside the river, I came to the junction where the old paper mill sat on the other side of the water. Before the Gathright Dam had failed and sent pretty much all of Lake Moomaw down to flood Covington—and the paper mill with it— there'd been a series of small ponds next to the mill. When the dam had let loose, though, they'd been completely filled with debris.

Or had been. Looking across the river, I could see someone had cleared away the debris and piled it next to one of the small storage sheds that had only been partially demolished. There hadn't been a lot of rain since the storms back in November, so I doubted it was there due to natural causes. Sister Ann had said in the past that beavers were pretty common around these parts, though I'd never seen anything that looked like the beaver dams in books.

Plus, I seriously doubted beavers were that organized.

"Weird," I muttered and shut down the engine. The water rushing along made enough noise that, since the engine was off, I couldn't really hear anything else. Down near the river the air was cooler. Not by much, but enough to be noticeable. There were also faint traces of ice along the riverbed—and dirt bike tracks here as well.

My eyes followed the tracks, which disappeared from sight near some rocks about forty feet ahead. My gaze drifted back across the river to where the debris-filled ponds had been. In the back of my head I could still feel that instinctual warning buzz but for the life of me, I couldn't see what the big deal was. Other than cleaning out the ponds and stacking the debris neatly against one of the destroyed buildings near the edge of the river, everything looked fine.

Muttering under my breath, I hopped off the four-wheeler and slowly made my way over to the pile of rocks where the tracks ended. It was clear that *someone* had ridden a dirt bike here recently. Had they ridden through the river somehow? Looking around, I spotted a tree branch that'd broken off from a nearby elm and grabbed it. It was long and skinny, probably about six feet total. Balancing carefully on the rocks, I poked it into the river.

The water came more than halfway up over the stick. Was that too high for a dirt bike to cross? Considering how close to the shore I was, the probability of it being even deeper toward the middle was pretty good. There was no way anyone could even wade across it. Swim, maybe. If they were willing to risk the currents.

Turning, I saw what looked like a softball lying on the ground beneath a tree. It was bright yellow, like the kind high school softball teams used to play with. I'd never seen it before, and I'd come down here a few times—though not since before Christmas. Had it been washed downstream sometime? It was possible. Walking over, I knelt down and picked it up. It was definitely a softball, all right. Someone had drilled or cut a hole straight through it and tied a smaller piece of rope through the opening.

"What the...?"

I jerked my hand back as I spotted what appeared to be a snake coiled up beneath some leaves next to the tree where the softball had been. Scrambling back, it took me a moment to realize it hadn't moved at all when I'd come close to it. Around here, copperheads and rattlesnakes were usually hibernating this time of the year. It was strange to see one out in the open on a cold day like this. Cautiously, I moved back toward it. Still nothing.

Using my stick, I prodded it. It refused to move. Either it was dead, or what I was looking at was not a snake. Kneeling in the leaves, I leaned in for a closer look.

It was not a snake. Instead, what I was looking at was nothing more than coiled rope. It was in good shape, so it obviously hadn't been lying here long, and someone had deliberately covered it with leaves so nobody would spot it. If not for the softball I doubted I would have seen the rope at all.

I looked at the softball, then back at the rope. Suddenly everything clicked into place and I knew what the softball was for.

Throwing rope is hard. I'd done it once when my family had gone to the Los Angeles County Fair and there'd been a rodeo exhibition. The cowboys had asked for volunteers to try and lasso one of those fake metal bulls. I tried my best but the weighted rope wasn't easy to throw more than a few feet. The cowboys explained that even they could maybe throw it up to fifteen, twenty feet accurately.

But tie a softball on the rope and you sure could *swing* it pretty far.

Probably even across this narrower part of the river. I looked back at the neatly stacked debris and noticed, for the first time, the long planks partially buried beneath the mess.

Had they built a bridge somehow? It was hard to make out details. Still, if they had a bridge, what did they need the rope and softball for? None of it was making any sense. Grumbling under my breath, I started walking around the river bank, trying to get a better look at the strange planks. They were darker than the average wood, and looked like they'd been dragged through a lot of mud and muck.

"Oh no . . ." Those weren't wooden planks. They were railroad ties. Specifically, railroad ties that were on the backside of the school—and that helped me get to the back entrance without being seen.

I sprinted back to the four-wheeler and turned it on. Making the tight turn on the path, I rode it as fast as I dared back up to campus, hoping against hope that my suspicions were wrong.

They weren't.

Standing at the bottom of the hill and looking up at the path I used to take on a daily basis, the acid in my stomach churned madly. I wanted to puke. While we'd been out camping, King Dale's men had ripped up all the railroad ties that helped create the path up to the back entrance of campus. Somehow they'd found it and made short work of the construction. With the railroad ties no longer supporting the steps for the steep climb up the hill, it was impossible to come this way. There was now only one way up to campus—the main road.

How? How had he known how to destroy the back entrance to pin us up here on the mountain? How had he known where it was at in the first place? I'd done everything possible to keep it hidden. So had the others. In fact, there wasn't anyone not on campus who even knew about it. And the only person who wasn't on campus who knew about it—

And then I had my answer. There *was* a person who knew about the back entrance and wasn't on campus. It was obvious in hindsight, so painfully obvious that even I should have seen it. In charge of campus security? Ha! I was the sorriest excuse, not even good enough to be a mall cop. King Dale had known about it because of me. I pretty much told him. Inadvertently, but it was my sharing that had led them here.

He wouldn't be making any attempts at the school now. There was no need. He'd already secured all the food in town and destroyed the best way off the mountain. We were now relegated to using the main road, where we could be easily seen—and reported on. And only one person had both the access and the knowledge of everything because we'd have to drive by the very house that I'd helped him find.

"Colton..." I hissed, anger bubbling up from the core of my being. Normally I would bottle that rage, keeping a lid on it and blowing off steam later. Not now. There was a time and place for self-control, and this was not it. "You rat mother*fucker*."

The ride to his house was a blur. I vaguely remember branches from trees whipping across my jacket, and almost flipping the four-wheeler at one point when I hit a sharp rock at the school entrance. Mostly I was focused on the absolute and utter betrayal of a boy I'd thought was my friend...and one I'd just started developing some conflicting feelings for.

How had I missed the signs? Maybe I hadn't wanted to see them at all.

Colton was sitting on the front porch when I slid to a halt in the gravel driveway. While his face was calm his body language screamed "terrified" to me. Good. He should be afraid. Lifting his head, he watched me closely as I hopped off the four-wheeler and stormed over to the porch. Pulling himself to his feet, he stuck out both hands toward me.

"I wanted to explain—"

"No." My voice was colder than the weather around us. There was nothing I wanted to do more than punch a hole through his smug little face. Of course, he had height and weight on me, but the desire was still there. "You don't get to explain."

"But—"

"No!" This time I practically screamed it. I'd been betrayed in the past before, but not like this. Never like this. "Was everything a lie?"

He reached out to me, stepping close. I stepped back. He moved another foot closer. "I just—"

I pushed him away, hard. There was no need to give him any chance to "explain." "How? How could you?"

"I did what I thought was right," he argued, shoving lanky brown hair up and out of his eyes. He was afraid, but also growing angry.

The fear I understood. He should be. I had the gun. None of King Dale's other lackeys were anywhere nearby to save him from me. Angry, though? The only person he had a right to be angry at was himself. "He's trying to bring stability to the area. Too much lawlessness leads to anarchy! He told me himself! He has a plan!"

"You've been spying for him. On us. On *me*. How long?"

"I..."

"How *long*?"

"Since we met. You caught me scouting out that back way up and I had to make up something so you wouldn't shoot me."

That was a punch in the gut. I'd done everything I could to keep him alive, keep him safe. Fed him, clothed him, even helped find him a home. I'd trusted him and, in return, he'd sold me out. Sold out the school, the girls I was supposed to keep safe, all the refugees who'd showed up since. Everyone. He lied to me from day one, and for what?

Because Appalachia Rex claimed he had a *plan*?

Something primal inside me snapped. I don't remember punching him. It wasn't much, but it was enough to make my fist hurt. Colton was slightly bigger than me, and I wasn't known for brawling. But the blow must have caught him off-balance because he tripped and fell to the ground. His eyes flashed angrily and for a moment I thought he was going to pop right back up and start swinging back. Instead, he stayed on the ground. His hand went to his mouth and came away a little bloody. I'd busted his lip open.

Good.

"Go," I croaked, my voice hoarse. "Leave. Just ... leave. I'm going to walk away now. When I come back, you need to be somewhere else."

"Or ...?"

"I'm going to put a round into you."

Without another word, I turned and walked away.

I hadn't realized how far up the road I walked before my brain was beyond the incoherent rage I was feeling and into the rough neighborhood of critical thought once more until I spotted Humpback Bridge. I stopped at the more modern bridge over Dunlap Creek and stared at the old wooden structure as the clear water slowly made its way beneath it. Watching it gave me time to think, to wonder, as I leaned on the metal barrier.

Colton. Of course. I should have figured. The timing had been too perfect. Why hadn't I seen it?

If I'd have actually looked, I would have. The moment Sister Ann pointed out that King Dale and his men had showed up to Dr. Brittany's at the same time we had should have tipped me off. She'd even suggested that someone was spying on us, and I'd agreed. Only . . . I hadn't even considered Colton at all.

You should have, that annoying little voice in the back of my head whispered. It wasn't wrong. The timing was too coincidental for him arriving. So soon after we stole the BearCat from King Dale? I should have suspected something. If I'd been honest with Sister Ann, she might have pointed it out as well.

Especially since he hadn't wanted to live up on campus in the first place.

Balling my hands tightly into fists, I screamed into the cold morning air and slammed a fist down on the metal barrier. Pain flared up my arm. Not a lot, but enough to let me know it'd been a solid shot. It felt good, purging all that rage and anger out. Still, it wasn't enough. I'd screwed up, badly. My stupidity could hurt the school, the refugees who are up there. The girls. Sister Ann. Ulla.

Somewhere in the distance, an all-too-familiar cry responded.

For some reason I felt immediately better upon hearing the hunting call of a shambler. More echoed nearby. There were a few, and they were coming in hot. Carefully unslinging Baby from my shoulder, I looked around. The bridge was two lanes wide and over water, so there were only two directions they could hit me from. The keening, haunting cries sounded off again. They were much closer now.

Though I preferred to shoot shamblers from up in a tree, like a deer blind or turkey stand, it looked like today I wasn't going to benefit from that advantage. Shamblers might be fast when well fed, but they absolutely sucked at figuring out latches on descending ladders. Plus, I'd stupidly left the four-wheeler behind when I'd stormed off from Colton's place. If it was still there when I got back, I'd be shocked.

Seven of them came loping into view from the west. They were tightly packed together while they jogged. The one in the lead—a very emaciated male from the looks of things—spotted me and howled. Its jogging turned into a full-on sprint. The others took up the lead shambler's cue and increased their speeds as well. They weren't Olympic sprinters, but they were running far faster than the usual shambler. This group must have been eating very well.

Unlike the last time I ran into a shambler while out, there was no hesitation now. Anger had replaced hesitation. I aimed at the center mass of the lead shambler and gently stroked the trigger twice. Without hearing protection, the two shots were loud and hurt my ears. Still, the ringing in my ears didn't affect my shooting at all. Both rounds went straight into the chest of the shambler and it tumbled to the ground in a bloody heap.

The others apparently didn't notice. They were clustered enough together that it would be hard to miss from this range. I began squeezing the trigger as fast as I could and still remain accurate. While much better than when I'd first started shooting lessons with Sister Ann, it was still a far cry from what she'd stated was basic qualifications for a marine.

Still, I did my best to keep the shots as close together on the shamblers as I could. Two shots each, then slightly pivot, and two more. One by one they fell while continuing their manic dash toward me. Forty yards. Two more shots.

Thirty. Two more shots, another shambler.

Twenty. Four shots in rapid succession, with only three hitting. I started walking backward to give myself more space.

Ten yards. One shambler left. A girl from the looks of things, possibly around my age. I didn't recognize her, but being out in the sun and exposed to the freezing elements did not do anything for skin care. Her shrill hunting scream almost drowned out the ringing the gunfire caused in my ears.

Two more shots just as she got within five yards. She was down, but not out just yet. For a moment I was tempted to just leave her there to bleed out, but then I remembered that while I had no compunction about killing a shambler, they'd been human once, too. Maybe that was why Sister Ann couldn't shoot them?

Not that it mattered. I was in charge of security—for good or ill, the jury was still out—and it was my job to make sure that the shamblers died. I aimed the green dot at the back of her head and delivered the *plaga mortifera*—the final blow—to the shambler.

None of the other shamblers were moving. Keeping a good grip on Baby with my right hand, I tried digging in my ear with the other hand to see if I could lessen the high-pitched ringing sound. Not that it helped, but at least it made me feel like I was doing something positive.

The adrenaline surge wore off quickly. I'd had a rough day, so it wasn't entirely unexpected. The shakes started soon after. I changed out the mostly empty magazine for a fresh one, stuffing the old one in my jacket pocket next to the other spare. Sore, exhausted, and still feeling utterly miserable, I headed back to Colton's house, praying the entire time that he wouldn't be there when I returned.

Thankfully, Colton was gone . . . just like I'd strongly *suggested*. I was glad. It still hurt, though. Nothing was going to make it better anytime soon, either. Though him leaving behind Mr. Stitmer's four-wheeler had been nice.

"Stupid boy," I said, and wiped my nose on the sleeve of the hoodie. The cold wind was biting but it was better than the nothingness in my mind. Leaning back against the vehicle, I slid slowly to the ground. As angry as I was at Colton, I was madder at myself. "Stupid Maddie."

It was so obvious in hindsight. I should have seen it. The boy had been unprepared to live up here in the mountains. How had he lived alone for so long? He hadn't. He'd had a lot of help and had gotten lucky with me finding him, and not one of the others. Was everything else about him a lie? I didn't know. Colton had fed me line after line, and I'd bought them all. Of *course* he hadn't want to come up to the campus. The more people he interacted with, the likelier he was to be recognized, or have holes poked in his story. Was any of what he said true? Had he really killed his mother after she turned? Was his name even Colton?

Stupid, Maddie. Real stupid. You'd think you would have learned after the last boy who showed interest.

A rustling sound near the side of the house made me look around. Everything was blurry. There was a large black blob standing in front of me, not too far away. Stupid tears. They were going to get me eaten by either a shambler or a large bear. Not that it mattered. I deserved it. I'd murdered a human being, and betrayed everyone I was supposed to protect, and failed at the one job I had.

Angrily, I wiped them away as I heard a whining sound. It wasn't the keening howl of a shambler, or the strange grunting sound that Sir Chonk had made when he'd killed that shambler months ago. The shape moved closer. A tail wagged. No, definitely not a shambler or a bear. It was one of Dr. Brittany's Great Danes.

How had it gotten down here? It took me a second to realize that it must have heard the gunshots and trotted down to investigate. The dog whined again and lowered its head until it rested against mine. It was Xander, the larger of the two. He normally wasn't as friendly as Willow. At least, not with me. Today, though, it was as if he could feel I needed someone. Even if he couldn't talk back. Dogs are great that way.

I was going to have to tell Sister Ann about Colton. The entire truth of it, including how I'd taken from our supplies and given to him so he would be able to stay alive. There was no telling how Sister Ann was going to react. On one hand, I could see her being upset at me because I'd taken the supplies without telling her. I'd also compromised our security situation here. King Dale had crossed the river undetected and destroyed the back path, all without any of us— more importantly, *me*—noticing.

The risk of helping Colton had always been there. It was stupid of me to be so trusting. On the other hand, Sister Ann wanted to rebuild society. Not to just live, but to thrive. Time and time again she'd harped on this. She might have been happy with Colton hiding out up here, but the odds of her holding it against me were slim. Trust would be needed to rebuild the world. High-trust societies always did better than low-trust ones. Of course, given who he was working with, and how distrustful *they* were . . .

No, I decided as Xander lay on the ground next to me. She would have insisted we forgive him and take him in. Sister Ann was a much better person than any of us. Better than me, that's for sure. She wouldn't have hesitated to shoot a shambler when she'd been a marine, though now she couldn't due to her vows. Or something. I never really did ask why she couldn't shoot a shambler. It wasn't like they were human anymore.

The Great Dane shoved his face into my stomach and whined. Looking down, I stared into those big brown eyes. It was hard to stay sad when a dog was trying to make you feel better. Just one of those things. I scratched his ears and smiled at him. Sure, the massive dogs ate a lot of food, but they also were good therapists. They listened and didn't judge at all. Both of them also liked snuggles when it got cold in the bunker, and brought calm to a lot of the younger girls who still had nightmares. Plus, they usually heard or smelled a shambler coming long before we saw them. Having Dr. Brittany on campus was nice, but the dogs were better. I chuckled softly and continued the pettings. Xander flopped down on his side and begged for belly rubs. I acquiesced.

For the first time in what felt like forever, there was hope in my heart.

Admittedly it was only a little, but it was definitely there.

Boys were stupid anyway. Colton more than most. Sighing, I climbed to my feet. Xander followed me up in an instant. His tail was wagging. It was time to face the music.

I was so *screwed*.

Part Three

TO RULE AN EMPIRE OF ASHES

I met a traveller from an antique land
Who said: "Two vast and trunkless legs of stone
Stand in the desert. Near them, on the sand,
Half sunk, a shattered visage lies, whose frown,
And wrinkled lip, and sneer of cold command,
Tell that its sculptor well those passions read
Which yet survive, stamped on these lifeless things,
The hand that mocked them and the heart that fed:
And on the pedestal, these words appear:
'My name is Ozymandias, King of Kings:
Look on my works, ye Mighty, and despair!'
Nothing beside remains. Round the decay
Of that colossal wreck, boundless and bare
The lone and level sands stretch far away."
              —Percy Bysshe Shelley, "Ozymandias"

CHAPTER SIXTEEN

"The weak can never forgive. Forgiveness is the attribute of the strong." —Mahatma Gandhi

Sister Ann had been upset by my revelation, but not terribly so. She was more irritated at the secrecy and less about the supplies I'd stolen to keep the lying jerk alive. We had a lot going on, and King Dale was still out there, waiting. Watching. Still, it was a lesson learned. Not just by me, but by everyone on campus. Staying watchful and vigilant while keeping an eye out for survivors. There weren't many— the school could easily house five hundred students and half as many staff—but some new arrivals brought the total up to fifty souls who now called St. Dominic's home.

Winter slowly began to fade. The one-year anniversary of the Pacific Flu destroying the world hit us before we even knew it. On the shortwave, we listened in on the various stations as Wolf Squadron started taking different small areas of the mainland. Sister Ann was particularly happy about some place called Blount Island being cleared but she didn't explain why. I guessed it was one of the places she'd been stationed at in her past life.

More good news appeared. Apparently the nutjob who'd proclaimed that anyone shooting shamblers would be tried in a court of law was given something the announcer on Devil Dog Radio called an "I love me" jacket after the *real* president had been found. Well, the Vice President, but once she was sworn in, everything was back to shambler clearance with a smile and a nine.

With spring fully in the air, we were starting to feel a little more alive. Winter had been cold but, with the exception of a massive late January storm that dumped about a foot of snow on us, it'd been pretty calm.

We went to Temple's place and cleaned out his stuff. The sealed gas cans, it turned out, were still good, so we had extra fuel now. Finlay and Fiona said they knew how to siphon gas out of a vehicle but Sister Ann didn't want them doing that just yet. We weren't desperate enough, I guess.

The number of shamblers we were spotting was down to almost none. If we spotted a shambler, either Ulla, Temple, or I would shoot it. Since they were few and far between now—apparently shamblers hated the cold about as much as I did—we were doing great by conserving our ammo. Still, there'd been a lot more of them when King Dale was first trying to build his bridge and cross the Jackson River. So we all found ourselves asking the same question: Where'd they all go?

My emotions were still in turmoil after Colton's betrayal, but obsessing over how he'd lied to me was a welcome distraction from the conflicting emotions I'd been having after killing King Dale's man. Sister Ann's suggestion of the "camping trip" to the ranger station had been a surprisingly effective balm to the pain and hurt I was dealing with.

There'd been no sign of Colton by the ranger station or down by the house he'd been staying at. He must have scurried back home to King Dale. Probably a good thing. He hadn't shown his face anywhere near campus, either, after I'd threatened to shoot him. Apparently, he believed that I would, in fact, put a bullet in him. Who knew I could be as intimidating as Sister Ann?

More survivors turned up. Small groups, no more than two or three at a time. After they were thoroughly vetted (Sister Ann called it that), they were set up in the least-damaged cottages. Since each of the senior cottages was supposed to be able to comfortably house forty teenage girls, there was little difficulty finding enough room for those who arrived. They were in charge of cleaning it up, not us. Most had no issues with it. One or two complained once to Sister Ann. I don't know what she told them, but they never complained again.

That nun was *terrifying*.

A few were good with tools and were able to help rebuild, repair. Doors were fixed and cottages were cleaned. Lots of ruined carpet was dug up and thrown away. We discovered that the hardwood flooring beneath was in remarkably good shape. Sometime in the '80s someone decided it was a good idea to cover the wood with carpet. That person should have been brought up on criminal charges. However, they cleaned up well enough. If we ever got a power sander working again, the bloodstains would probably come right out.

Things were beginning to look up. More new arrivals had brought more canned goods The school could hold over six hundred people comfortably, so we weren't worried about space yet. Food concerns? Definitely. Our stock supplies were going up, though. Deer were everywhere, and there wasn't a game warden around to yell at us for shooting bucks out of season. I tried not to shoot any does, though. Sister Ann reminded me constantly that they were next year's food supply. There were plenty of fish in Dunlap Creek and the Jackson River. King Dale and his cronies were no longer coming into Covington, so we were actually able to explore a little more while looking for any supplies that hadn't been ruined by the flooding. Unfortunately, it appeared that Dale's men had been thorough and got everything of value out before shutting down our access by blocking the freeway.

Boundaries, Sister Ann had told us, were set. He'd blocked our access points down I-64, sure, but was avoiding direct confrontation. Meanwhile, we had everything on our side of the river—and also Covington. That was fine by me. Some of the younger girls—and a few on the council—were starting to talk about the worst of it being over.

Like spring, hope was in the air. The garden was expanded. There were plans to start clearing out the chapel next. It was more symbolic than functional, true. But Sister Ann had a valid point: Goals give people purpose. Without purpose, we are lost in the middle of an unending ocean, rudderless, subject to the waves of chance to take us in whatever direction. With purpose we could start to truly rebuild society. It'd been a pretty powerful speech. I remembered most of it.

Of course, the cold water of reality dashed away that hope the moment we found the two men walking up the road toward campus. Well, one was walking, barely. The other was being dragged behind in what appeared to be a makeshift gurney.

Dee was the one who spotted the duo as they reached the base of the mountain. Kayla, who had taken the middle schooler under her wing the same way I had with Ulla, was on duty with her and had the radio. They called it in to Sister Ann and me before bolting up the hill and to safety. Thanks to King Dale, we'd had to change how our guard duty worked. He knew about the back entrance now, courtesy of Colton, so we had to double the watch. Fortunately, we had enough new people who were willing to work to cover this.

Since I was mostly over my issues about shooting shamblers, I was able to slip into the role of the intimidator. Well, okay. Maybe a little intimidating. Just enough to let them know that I meant business. I was a little jealous, though. Sister Ann could do it with just a look.

"Stop at the bridge!" I shouted as soon as they started to make their way up the road. After a few moments I realized that the gurney was one of those garden wagons my mom had used back in California, though this one was black and not green like ours had been.

The man obeyed, stopping just at the start of the bridge over Dunlap Creek. He was looking up into the tree line just at the curve in the road, clearly expecting someone to be there. It made sense that this would be a perfect spot to hide in. There were bushes and the wide branches of the pine tree created quite a bit of shade.

What he hadn't been expecting was a redheaded girl in camo who was skinny enough to hide behind the lone tree on the other side of the road.

"Whoa," he said, raising a single hand slowly as I leaned around the tree, the AR pointed in his direction. I had it aimed behind him, since I didn't think I was going to need to shoot him. He didn't need to know this, though. "I've got a wounded man here!"

"Good afternoon," Sister Ann called out. She *was* hiding in the tree line where he'd first guessed someone to be. "What can we do for you?"

"My friend's been shot!"

Upon hearing this, Sister Ann stepped into view. I followed her lead, though I did not lower my guard much. There've been enough movies where they used a supposedly "injured" comrade to ambush the good guys. I was thinking that a lot more now, thanks to Colton. "How hurt is he?"

"I don't know, ma'am," the guy answered. He sounded honest. "Took a round in his leg. I got the bleeding slowed down but I didn't want to put a tourniquet on if I didn't have to."

That was smart of him. Tourniquets sometimes can do more harm than good. Especially when there was no need for one.

Sister Ann apparently thought the same thing. "Is he still breathing?"

The man half turned and looked at his companion. While he was distracted, I approached closer and moved more to my right. This would give me a better look at the wounded man while keeping Sister Ann out of my potential line of fire.

"Yes, ma'am. He's still breathing."

"Bring him across the bridge," she instructed him. "Once across, you will get down on your knees and face away from us with your hands behind your head, fingers interlaced."

"I know the drill, ma'am," he said and began to pull the wagon across the bridge. That was interesting. What drill was he talking about? Had this guy been a marine like Sister Ann? Or was he still one? There was always the possibility that he was some sort of hardened criminal who'd broken out of prison when the Fall had occurred—though it seemed pretty farfetched even to me.

Once across the bridge, he complied with her directions after ensuring the wagon couldn't roll down into the creek or back the way he'd come. Sister Ann motioned for me to keep an eye on him as she went to check on the wounded in the wagon.

This seemed to surprise the uninjured man. "Not worried about me carrying a weapon, ma'am?"

"I'd be more worried if you weren't," she replied and quickly lifted a bloodied jacket from the wounded man's body. She grimaced. "Come on. Hand your weapon over to Madison and help me get your friend up the mountain. We have someone qualified to help fix him . . . maybe."

"You have a doctor?" he asked, sounding hopeful for the first time.

"Better. A veterinarian."

౧౧౧

An hour later, we were gathered in what once had been the prep area of the cafeteria. It was the only place where Dr. Brittany felt comfortable enough to potentially operate without making a mess down in the bunker and also still had running water. Granted, she made her newfound assistant, Rohena, boil the water first. It was also the only place where we could keep prying eyes away.

The girl who I'd thought would end up being dead weight was actually turning into a decent medical assistant under Dr. Brittany's careful tutelage. Plus, she was no longer picking on the younger girls or trying to make them do her chores. This was a different Rohena . . . which everyone else was eternally grateful to know existed.

"Upper thigh wound, looks like a bullet hole," Dr. Brittany murmured as she finished stitching the back of the injured man's leg. He'd lost a lot of blood, and there was nothing we could do about that, but Dr. Brittany didn't sound too discouraged. Apparently she was satisfied with his blood pressure and mentioned this to Sister Ann before glancing over at the uninjured man, who was seated not too far away. "This is the exit wound, so he was shot from behind. You were running away?"

"How . . . ? Yes, Doctor. Dragged him across the river, sort of."

Sister Ann looked at him, surprised. "You dragged him across the river?" When she said it that way, it did sound a little incredulous. I wasn't sure if she thought he was full of it, or simply delusional. "In a wagon?"

"No, ma'am. Found the wagon on this side of the river at a house about a mile down the road. Brought it back and loaded him up. He wasn't going to be able to walk much farther after the river."

"And how'd you get across the river?"

"Rope bridge, ma'am."

"A rope . . . bridge? With a wounded man?"

"It wasn't easy, ma'am, but if you know what you're doing it's possible," he explained. "Not going to lie, it was a lot easier to help him across while he was conscious. One-legged and everything. If he'd been passed out? I wouldn't have been able to do it."

"Then what?"

"Once I found the wagon, I got him loaded up and stopped the bleeding. Then I just started walking, ma'am," the man said. I snorted. Sister Ann looked at me and gave me a slight nod.

"You just *happened* to find the one road that led up to the school?" I asked.

"Uh... Well, I didn't know for sure—"

"You crossed King Dale's barrier while being chased, then a river with a wounded man, and then you kept hiking up this road... on a whim?" I continued to press. Since Sister Ann wasn't stopping me, I figured she had the same thoughts I was having. "You knew we were up here. You had to have. Why else did you want to cross the river so much?"

"I... didn't know... pure luck...?"

"Maddie?" Sister Ann gave me a serene look. "Shoot his kneecap. His holster is on his right hip, so make it the left one."

Kneecaps. I could probably do kneecaps. It was definitely better than killing an actual human. Maiming meant he could potentially heal one day. Granted, I really didn't even want to kneecap the guy, but before I even moved Baby the guy was holding up his hands in surrender.

"Wait! Wait! Fuck, lady. What sort of nun are you?" he stammered.

"The sort that does not approve of foul language." Sister Ann's eyes narrowed dangerously. "I also do not tolerate liars."

"Maddie really likes those knees," Rohena muttered as she handed Dr. Brittany another one of the precious sterile bandage packs the veterinarian had brought up with her. There was a strange expression on Rohena's face. "Something about a shepherd? I don't know, I never pay attention to her until she's ready to shoot something."

The man was looking around the room. "What the f—uh, heck?"

"Quit stalling," I said. "How did you know we were here?"

"You... Fine." The man let out a heavy, defeated sigh. "The governor. She sent us here to scout things out."

"The governor... of Virginia?" Sister Ann asked.

"The governor's *alive*?" I asked, not able to keep the disbelief out of my voice. "How? Richmond was burning before anywhere else! I think it went up before the rest of the state. Wait... it was on the news! They said she died!"

"The lieutenant governor got the virus, that's true, and was... pacified after turning. Richmond *was* complete and utter chaos. We barely managed to get out and down I-81 before it all went to shi— uh, crap. With the breakdown of social services, and some of the local feds... None of that matters now. Point is, it was safer to let people think the governor had died. There were... *people*... certain elements looking for her that we did not want tracking her down."

Sister Ann made a soft noise, one I knew well. She didn't believe the man, not fully. There was a certainty in his voice, though, that suggested there might be more truth in there than we wanted to admit. However, the nun had always been a little more trusting than me in the past. It was one of her good qualities, I guess. While she was at least willing to listen to the man, however, I was quietly thinking of ways to shoot his knee without interrupting Dr. Brittany's stitching.

Or I could simply find a way to chase them off the hill. Dogs. *Big* dogs. The guy with the bullet in his leg might be slower than his buddy—assuming he woke up, I mean—so him I'd give a slight head start. Then again, if they *both* were suffering from a gunshot to the leg, it might be a little more fair. Would Xander or Willow chase them, though? I wasn't sure, but I was willing to bet Dr. Brittany might be willing to put it to the test for me.

"What's your name?" Sister Ann asked.

"Uh... Atkins, ma'am. Scott Atkins, Virginia State Police."

"Does that mean I can't shoot him now that we know him?" I looked around at the others. Rohena shrugged, but Dr. Brittany gave me an exasperated sigh and went back to work on the injured man.

"Ma'am, really..." Atkins eyeballed Baby before looking up at me. I just stared at him. Well, more like *through* him. It was a trick I'd learned from the twins. He swallowed and glanced away. "Is she really going to *shoot* me?"

"I don't think she is planning on shooting you at *this* moment," Sister Ann muttered as she stared off into the distance. Inwardly, I chuckled. There was no way I would really shoot him... I think. She was clearly considering what he'd said. Her normally calm expression was gone, replaced by a troubled one. My hand tightened on Baby's grip. I didn't really want to shoot anyone but if Sister Ann told me to, I would. The odds of her giving the order, though? Low. Probably. Sister Ann sighed before continuing. "How many?"

"Ma'am?"

"How many does the colonel have with her? Her children? Security?"

"Who, the governor? Ma'am, I can't—"

"No." Sister Ann cut him off with a simple hand gesture. "Trust goes two ways up here. We try not to keep any secrets because this isn't the world we left behind. This is more than survival. This is about rebuilding. *Thriving.* You've seen what we have set up here. Our location up here is safer than what the colonel has at her home. We need to know just how many we've got coming up here."

"Colonel? You mean Governor Lenity-Jones? Coming up . . . here? I don't think the governor is going to relocate up—"

"She will." Sister Ann was on a roll today. She almost never interrupted anyone. "She's already making plans for it, I bet. Notice they've gotten reticent lately on long-term planning? Her, and whoever is with her. Not sharing as much as they used to? Her position is untenable. She knows this. That's why you're up here, whether you know it or not. The only question is who attacks the compound first—the shamblers, some unknown enemy, or Appalachia Rex."

"Appalachia who?"

"The leader of the men who were shooting at you," Sister Ann clarified. She pointed at his wounded companion. "Shot."

"A real kingly jerkface," I added helpfully.

"Huh?"

"Officer Atkins . . . when you were coming in, you were shot at as you moved through Clifton Forge, yes?" Sister Ann rubbed her face. Normally, the nun was always bright and alert. Right now, though, she looked tired. It was a little worrying. She noticed me looking and offered a gentle, reassuring smile before focusing back on the newcomer. "That's where your partner was shot. Your words. Why did they shoot at you and not try to recruit you?"

"Scott, ma'am. Please."

"Very well then, Scott. Humor me. Why didn't King Dale try and recruit you?"

"Well, he did say I should join him," Scott said, running his fingers through his hair. "Both of us, actually. But after I saw those pits I knew I couldn't. So we ran."

"Pits?" I asked. "What pits?" Sister Ann shushed me.

"You didn't run back to Deer Creek?" she asked. Or declared. It was hard to say. The man looked at her.

"How'd you know about Deer Creek?"

"I've known about Deer Creek for years," she clarified. "The colonel always spoke of her husband's ancestral home. Back to the topic at hand. Maddie asked a good question. What are these pits you were talking about?"

"The pits . . . Ma'am, I'm sorry, but this is all too much. Why do you keep calling the governor 'colonel'?"

His buddy groaned and shifted on the steel countertop, briefly interrupting our quasi-interrogation. I glanced over. Dr. Brittany was working on the other side of his leg now, muttering under her breath the entire time. It was clear she wasn't happy with the wound. We watched in silence as she continued to stitch it closed. Done, she stepped back and sighed.

"I think he'll be okay, but I need to watch for infection," Dr. Brittany said as she leaned away from the table. She removed her gloves and tossed them in the trash can. Rohena began to wrap a bandage around the leg. "Pressure is down but survivable. I think. I've operated on a dog with a gunshot wound before, so it was kinda similar. Lucky it was a through-and-through. We don't have pain meds, and digging out a fragmented bullet is not something I'm sure I can do."

"He'll be okay?" Scott asked. Dr. Brittany nodded.

"I think so."

"Pits," Sister Ann said quietly once Dr. Brittany backed away. She would keep a close eye on her patient, but knew when Sister Ann wanted space. "Talk to me about these pits."

"Not really pits, but that was my first impression. They're holding pens filled with zombies," Scott replied in a quiet voice. "Dozens, maybe even a hundred in the one I saw. Keep 'em penned up like cattle. They got one down by this outdoor amphitheater place, and another somewhere else. Some place called the armory? When I saw the zombies trapped inside the fenced area, I figured out what they were doing. I told David here what was going on and we split. They chased us all the way until we hit this barricade down on the interstate, where the mill exit was. Governor Lenity-Jones had told us to scout around up here originally and see if anybody survived. We weren't expecting Clifton Forge to be a fortress. Apparently your school is listed over in Richmond as Location Redoubt?"

Sister Ann snorted at that. "Sixty years ago, maybe. We've become too reliant on Covington now for that."

"You ran that far?" I asked. "From Clifton Forge to Covington?" Scott shook his head.

"No. We had a vehicle. Had to leave it at that funky barricade on I-64," he answered. "That was when David got shot, when we were bailing out of the car. It was weird, though. Once we were across the barricade, they stopped chasing. Didn't even shoot at us. It was like they didn't care anymore."

"That narrow pass is the only easy way into Covington from the east," Sister Ann pointed out. "They built the barrier to keep us isolated. Or keep us from coming at them that way, I'm not certain. It most definitely is a boundary, though. To them, a very real one. You escaped from the self-proclaimed Kingdom of Appalachia. Welcome back to Virginia, Officer."

Officer Atkins blinked. "What the hell has been happening up here?"

It took a while, but Sister Ann brought him up to speed. Afterward, he needed a minute or two to regain his composure. It was a lot to absorb. They hadn't had access to a shortwave radio like we did. However, down at this Deer Creek place they'd apparently not dealt with shamblers or King Dale much.

Lucky bastards.

Of course, the reason the governor had sent him to find out if our mountain was a tenable solution made our day worse.

"One of the governor's kids got sick," he began in a quiet voice. His face was drawn, haggard. "The well pump doesn't work all that well anymore and we can't fix it. Draws less than a gallon a minute. Plus, it's contaminated or something. There's a weird smell to the water. We were coming up with ideas when one of the governor's daughters started drinking from the river. She thought she was being helpful, but... she's nine, you know? Doesn't really understand why drinking water straight from the river without boiling it or anything can be bad. Only... nobody noticed at first. Not until the bloody diarrhea began."

"Giardiasis, amoebiasis, TD... could be a lot of things, none of them good," Dr. Brittany muttered. "All easily treatable, pre-Fall. I don't have a lab to do all the necessary bloodwork to determine precisely what we're dealing with, but amoxicillin should take care of it. She's not allergic to penicillin, is she?"

"No, not at all. We just didn't have any."

"And the mystery as to why the colonel wanted to move now makes sense," Sister Ann said. She looked at Dr. Brittany. "Maybe now you understand why you're the most popular woman on campus."

Once the wounded state police officer—his name was Officer David Pew, according to a seemingly smitten Rohena—was put in the empty apartment next to Temple upstairs, we called a meeting for all the survivors to let them know the good news—and share some potential bad. Sister Ann had a policy of complete honesty with the refugees who'd found their way to St. Dominic's. For better or worse, she was forcing them to trust her . . . and each other.

It turned out that Officer Atkins had never even been to this part of Virginia before. Not even driven through it on his way out of state. His assignments had always kept him in either the Richmond or Tidewater areas. A bummer, that. He missed out on the dying railroad towns, the meth problem, and luxury vacation spots like Lake Moomaw. Some people just had all the luck.

"We thought there'd be more survivors," Officer Atkins said as he looked at the gathered groups in the cafeteria. Most people were standing around in clusters based on what cottage they were staying in. Which, amusingly, was the same way we'd done it before the Fall. Tribal instinct was an odd thing. "Less than a hundred. The Covington–Clifton Forge area had about seven thousand people, maybe eight. Counting the surrounding area, ten thousand. Is this . . . all we have left to rebuild society?"

"We have our faith," Sister Ann stated firmly. "We have our faith in God, and in our neighbors. We've already survived, Officer. Everybody in here is a survivor. Now? It's time to rebuild, to thrive. Hiding is no longer an option. Not anymore. The governor is a legally elected official, and in the Commonwealth of Virginia that counts for a lot. We can elect a county commission and go from there."

"Even with guys like that nutjob over in Clifton Forge running around?"

"*Especially* with people like King Dale running around," Sister Ann confirmed, smiling. Some of the newer arrivals were watching the state police officer warily. It made me wonder just how many had warrants, pre-Fall. "You've met the survivors, Officer. Now come meet the student council. The girls who are *really* in charge of St. Dominic's."

We went downstairs into the bunker. Though the survivors were sleeping in the cottages now, Sister Ann had decided to keep the girls of St. Dominic's in the bunker. None of them complained. Lucia had started to make some noise about moving back into her old room and cottage. The problem there was that the dorm room was now being used by a handful of young boys, none older than seven, and their one surviving grandmother. Lucia would have to kick them all out. As much as she liked to portray herself as a hard-core girl from the *barrio*, she really was a decent human being. Neither Sister Ann nor I thought she'd follow through with the threat. Besides, she seemed to really enjoy having Kayla as a roommate in the bunker, and Kayla was not moving out anytime soon.

It amused me a bit just how quickly we could adapt and go back to worrying about minor things like moving around to the other cottages once the threat of the shamblers was gone. Humans are simply resilient beings.

And it's better than dwelling on other things, like the end of the world, for instance.

"Attention, please!" Sister Ann called out to everyone gathered in the dining hall. The mutters and whispers abruptly ceased. I really wanted to know where she learned how to do this. "For those of you who don't know, two members of the Virginia State Police found their way to our campus earlier today. There is good news, and there is bad news.

"First, the bad. Officer Atkins's partner, Officer Pew, was wounded by gunfire on their way here. I know we've asked before, but if anyone here has any sort of nursing experience, Dr. Jefferson would greatly appreciate any help. If you have this training, please see Dr. Jefferson after this meeting but before dinner. Her time is going to be occupied for the next few days treating her patient, so we need to know sooner rather than later if you can help.

"Now, the good news. The governor of Virginia is alive and well, and not too far away." This caused more commotion than the news of Officer Pew being shot. Sister Ann waited for them to quiet down before continuing. "I know the governor personally from my time in the Marine Corps before taking my vows, and I can attest that she is an honorable and just person. However, between her and us is the self-proclaimed King of Appalachia. If he learns how close to his domain she is, I believe the man would not hesitate to go after her. Though she has not let anyone know of her plans just yet, I believe I understand her intent, and we can guess her needs. However, in the meantime, we must discuss the reestablishment of a governing body for Alleghany County. A simple three-person commission will suffice for now. Once we have the state government back on track, as well as an honest-to-goodness functioning federal one, we'll start to explore our options from there. We'll be accepting candidates next Monday, and elections will be the following Friday.

"From there, we'll start to explore options of where the commission should be based. There are locations on our side of the river but within Covington city limits that would suffice. No, the commission cannot be housed here. This school is a refuge, and will remain so. I know it's not a lot of time, but this is something we should handle sooner rather than later.

"Does anyone have any questions about this? If not, then I thank you for your time."

Sister Ann turned and looked our way. The student council had formed a little cluster near the back of the dining hall. It was early, but from the direction she was walking we could tell she wanted to have an emergency meeting down in the bunker. Well, at least, I could tell. The others stood around stupidly as I headed for the stairwell. Pausing at the doorway, I turned back and motioned for them to follow.

It was much quieter down in the bunker. The younger girls were upstairs, which gave us the space needed for the meeting. Once Sister Ann brought things to order, she wasted absolutely no time.

Sister Ann waited until everyone was seated around the conference table. Once we were settled in, she began. "There has been a general recall for any and all active duty, active reserves, and inactive reserve personnel. I have yet to determine if it is legitimate or not."

The younger girls jerked in surprise. I'd heard the news when Sister Ann had, and Emily must have spoken about her fears and suspicions about her satellite clock theory with a few of the other girls on the student council because none of them seemed too surprised. Hurt and afraid, though? Definitely.

"When . . . are you leaving?" Kayla asked in a quiet voice, as though concerned anything louder might frighten Sister Ann away sooner.

"Still waiting to see if they are legitimate orders," Sister Ann said in a calm voice. "God will determine my path, as always. Have faith, girls. The nearest guard installation is at Fort Pickett, which is not very accessible to us at the moment. I'm willing to bet that it's a complete mess down there. It wasn't great even before the Fall. It's a shame we can't broadcast yet and find out. Emily?"

"Ma'am?"

"You've worked with some of the new arrivals on the radio a bit. How far out are we from rigging up something that would allow us to broadcast?"

"It's not the radio that's the issue. One of the guys said that it's about wattage, and we simply don't generate enough up here to broadcast anything. Even if I could pilfer every single solar panel in Covington—and there aren't many—it wouldn't be enough power to broadcast outside the area," Emily replied immediately.

"So that's settled, then," Sister Ann said as she leaned back in her chair and folded her hands upon her lap. "There's no way just yet to tell anyone what we're about to do. A shame, really. I would have really liked to hear Devil Dog Radio's response."

"What *are* we going to do?" Kayla asked, mystified. "Go to Fort Pickett?"

"Oh, no. Nothing that drastic. We're just going to go and rescue the governor of Virginia."

"*What?*" everyone in the room almost shouted as one. I kept my mouth shut. I'd suspected this was coming the moment the two state police showed up and told Sister Ann about the governor, and her daughter being ill. It didn't take a degree in rocket science to figure it out. Sister Ann's protective nature was second to none. The only surprising part of it all was that none of the other girls had seen it coming.

"If we don't pull the governor out of Deer Creek, King Dale is going to eventually figure out someone is there. Especially if he's looking to expand his power base." She paused, looking around the table. She lingered on me for a second before continuing. "Plus, with her daughter sick, she might not be thinking clearly. So we come up with a plan. Well, *you* come up with one. Me? After I meet with the governor, I need to determine if the order that came over the radio is legitimate or not. We can go from there."

"Us?" Rohena squeaked. "Plan?"

"I don't know . . ." Emily sounded nervous.

"Who do you mean? We plan? How?" Kayla asked, looking around the room. Her dark face was pale. She was clearly frightened. All of them were. Even the Great Danes standing next to Kayla looked worried, though I'd like to think it was because of the general mood in the room. Then every face in the room turned and looked not at Sister Ann, but me.

I blinked stupidly. "What?" I looked at them all before jerking a thumb at Sister Ann. "She's in charge."

"No, Maddie." Sister Ann shook her head slowly. "This school is under your care, with the assistance of the council, since they elected you president."

"The *fuck*?" I blurted out. When had that happened? No. No way. I didn't want to be in charge. My entire time at the school I'd avoided leadership responsibilities. I'd turned down being the proctor of my dorm, hadn't accepted the offer to be cocaptain of the field hockey team, and had initially said no to Sister Ann when approached to be on the student council in the early days after the Fall. There was absolutely zero chance of me leading them now.

"Language."

"Sor—no, no wait. No, I'm not *sorry*," I growled. I looked around at everyone in the room. The girls all flinched. Only Sister Ann remained unperturbed. "There's no way. You can't do this. There are rules and crap!"

"We had the election two days ago," Lucia offered in a tiny voice. "It was unanimous."

"*Et tu, Brute?*" I slapped my palm hard on the flat surface of the table. A resounding *crack!* echoed throughout the room. She looked away. "That's bull. No way. I didn't get to vote. I can't do it. No, I *won't*. There's better people than me—"

"Name one," Sister Ann challenged. I opened my mouth to name one of the girls in the room. My mind blanked as I tried to form an argument explaining why they were wrong.

"But—"

"But what, Madison?" Sister Ann asked in a quiet voice. "You've been doing the job in all but name for months now. I'm helping where I can, but I foresee problems down the road, problems that my being in charge of things will only complicate. For us up here on the mountain, you are the duly elected leader. There's a reason I'm having everyone else—those who are already thinking of leaving and setting up a new community down in Covington—nominate and elect their own leaders. But here? You are the best and easiest choice. Tell me: On which girl would you dump all the responsibility you've already shouldered?"

I wanted to argue, but I couldn't do that to any of them. Even though they were all standing around the table, and their faces were clear as day, I couldn't say any one of the names. Kayla, Lucia, Rohena, Emily... none of them could do what I did. Wanted to, or even had the capabilities. But no, the responsibility of others had been sneakily placed upon my shoulders by a nun who I was now convinced had been planning for this moment since Sister Mary's face had been eaten off by Chelsea the year before. She was conniving in ways no mortal being should ever be. My mouth closed and I sighed heavily.

Deep down I knew... Sister Ann was never wrong. I was the right choice and, if I had to be perfectly honest with myself, I was the *only* choice.

Damn it.

"Okay... but I'll need help."

Sister Ann's smile was serene. "That's what the council's here for. It's designed to help the elected president."

Tricksy hobbit. She'd been planning this for *much* longer than I'd been led to believe.

CHAPTER SEVENTEEN

"Multiple behavioral studies indicate the alphas will remain highly aggressive despite any alternate treatment methods. As it was with primate test subjects in the past who exhibited similar behavior and mannerisms, the most humane treatment we can offer at this point is euthanasia and postmortem study."
—Lecture part of "Grad 725—Research Methods for the Infected" by Dr. Tedd Roberts, University of the South, 2047

The first thing we had to plan out was the logistics of rescuing the governor. Basically, how we were going to move almost a dozen people up onto the mountain without getting spotted by King Dale.

The BearCat had plenty of fuel left, thanks to some of the survivors bringing in cans of fuel they'd salvaged from various buildings. Surprisingly, very little of it was contaminated with water. There were one or two cans that would have been better qualified as sludge than gasoline, but there was enough to top the beast off. It would make the run to where the governor was and back with plenty to spare.

Since we had Temple's sealed cans of gas as well, Sister Ann decided to bring them along for the ride. Not for the BearCat, though. The cans would be for any vehicles the governor might have.

"There's no way we're getting that many people in the BearCat, not with those gas cans and ammo," Sister Ann explained as we planned what she had dubbed "Operation Thunder Run." She looked at all of us gathered around the table. "They're going to have vehicles of their own. They get to use them. We're the tip of the spear, and they follow us."

"So we're the tip, and they're the shaft?" Rohena asked coquettishly. Sister Ann raised a single eyebrow precisely one centimeter in response. Rohena shut up so fast I could have sworn I heard her jaw click. The twins giggled at the joke. Sister Ann's ire turned on them almost as fast.

"Neither of you should be able to understand that reference."

"Wasn't me," I declared immediately, not wanting to get blamed for this. A chorus of denials from everyone else followed. Apparently the twins had simply been born with the knowledge of dirty in-jokes and references, because by the end of it not a single person in the room admitted to jack squat. Sister Ann sighed in defeat, a rare victory for us.

Teamwork makes the dream work.

Following Sister Ann's advice, I let Lucia load us up for supplies. Officer Atkins had said that everyone at Deer Creek was in relative good health, but they'd left a week ago and things could change. Their food situation was also worse than ours, so we packed any extra protein we could spare. She also grabbed some of the precious ginger ale from Temple's room, a sugary pick-me-up for added boost. It wasn't much, but better than nothing.

Plus, if they hadn't been eating much, the ginger ale would be easier on their systems.

Next, it was up to me to decide who was going. After discussing this with Sister Ann, I realized they needed to come from the student council. If the other girls were going to be advisors and stuff like that for me, then they needed to have skin in the game as well. This meant going down the mountain and, potentially, into danger.

Lucia was a given, and the most obvious choice. Besides Sister Ann and me, she was the only other one who had experience driving the BearCat. She also wanted to go, an added benefit. Since she'd done so well when we'd stolen the BearCat together months ago, and had been there when we recruited Dr. Brittany, she knew what to expect should we run into King Dale again.

Which meant nothing when Sister Ann decided she needed to stay behind. There was no way we could afford to put our logistics person out into danger. Plus, Lucia was the next choice to run the campus if I didn't come back. Ulla listened to her, which was a nice bonus. Emily was also out. She was the only person on campus who knew how everything mechanical worked. There was a new, older man on campus who'd survived with his son, both of whom knew car engines. However, they were still reading up on how Emily had rigged everything to work and trying to figure it out. We couldn't risk losing her just yet—ever, if I was being honest.

Finlay and Fiona were out for multiple reasons. The most obvious one was that they had only just recently turned twelve and were definitely too young for this. Finlay complained more about that than Fiona, but neither of them was happy about being left behind. While I valued their minds and skill sets, there was no way I was going to put girls that young into harm's way. To assuage their hurt feelings, I let them know privately that I had a different job for them.

"You still have some of that Tannerite, right?" I asked them when we had a moment of quiet together. Their eyes widened in surprise. And *maybe* an uncomfortable amount of excitement. There was no way for me to be certain but at least I had an answer to my question. "How much?"

"A lot," Finlay replied.

"Two hundred pounds," Fiona added.

I blinked. That was *way* more than I'd thought possible. "Where the heck did you find all that?"

The twins shared a look before shrugging simultaneously. "Around," they both said.

It wasn't worth the effort to question them further. "Screw it. I don't want to know. Do you think it would be enough to clear a path?"

"You want us to walk down to where King Dale built that barricade?" Fiona asked, surprised. I nodded.

"Not necessarily walk, but yes. Lucia can drive you both down in the four-wheeler. *Carefully.*"

"It would take half of what we have to blow up that barricade," Finlay said as she scratched at her tiny mole. I could tell she was already planning, the wheels in her mind turning rapidly. My stomach flip-flopped uneasily. I kept having to remind myself that they were on our side to keep from breaking into a cold sweat. "That's a really big truck, and loads of pallets and stuff."

"But you can do it?" I pressed.

"Uh…" They quickly started whispering to one another, using their made-up language. It was like watching two mad scientists decide if they were cooking up alchemy first, or building Frankenstein's monster. Rather fascinating, and simultaneously terrifying. After a few moments they stopped talking. Both were… I wouldn't call it smiling, not really. Well, if you could say a shark smiles, then yes, they were actually smiling.

Completely unnerving. The sweat started anyway, in spite of my mental reinforcements. There was just something about the way their minds worked that freaked me out.

"Yeah, we can do it," Fiona stated, sounding rather confident.

"Just don't blame us if the road isn't as smooth after," Finlay added.

I gave them the radio code words that we'd use if everything went smoothly. "Once you hear that, blow it and get out of there. Don't wait around. Even if the path isn't perfect, it just needs to be cleared."

"Will King Dale have guards at the barricade?" Finlay asked.

"He didn't the last two times I was down there," I told them, thinking back. I hadn't seen anybody there, but that didn't mean there weren't. "So unlikely. But if you see someone, just pick up the radio and say something about the color red—cardinals in the bush, cherries on a tree, whatever. After you blow it up, call in something about the color green. 'Frogs are hopping,' I don't care."

"Oooh, we're like spies now!" Fiona clapped her hands, clearly excited. I tried not to roll my eyes.

"You're like demolition experts stuck behind enemy lines," I corrected. "The French Resistance in World War Two. King Dale's men, if they're there, will try to stop you, or take you away. So don't get caught."

That sobered them right up. They remembered the man who'd tried to grab Ulla. "We won't," Fiona said.

"All right. I'm trusting you, so don't let me down, okay?"

"Okay," they agreed.

It came down to whether it would be Kayla or Rohena going with us. I wanted to pick Rohena, but Sister Ann changed my mind after she pointed out something I hadn't thought of.

"Bring Kayla," she told me after I explained who my picks were going to be. Seeing the look on my face, she explained. "The colonel is from Saint Martin island, in the Caribbean. French West Indies. Her family emigrated here when she was eight. Seeing Kayla would make her a little more trustworthy of our intentions. Even if she does recognize me."

"But why...?" I paused before it clicked. "You want Kayla because she's *black*?"

"To put it bluntly." Sister Ann nodded. "Look around us, Maddie. You see many African-Americans around here? Before the Fall, maybe ten percent of the population up here would qualify as such. I only saw two black men with King Dale during our little standoff. The colonel will see a friendly face in Kayla, and this will set her at ease enough to let me get close enough so she'll recognize me. Unless she's already recognized me, even after all these years. Kayla also knows seeds and plants. If the colonel has anything worth taking, she'd recognize them."

"That's..." I paused before shaking my head. "That's messed up, ma'am. With that mindset, it's either Kayla, Dr. Brittany, or Dee. Dr. Brittany won't go, and I would rather keep her up here anyway. And I'm *not* bringing Dee. She's, like, twelve."

"Thirteen, but I agree. So bring Kayla."

"You know she's more valuable to us than Rohena is, right?" I whispered, looking around. I didn't want anyone else to hear. "Kayla actually does a good job with the garden, and studies to get better at it. Rohena is...less...I don't know what the right word is."

"Rohena has less 'communal worth' is what you're trying to say," Sister Ann said in a gentle voice. "'Lazy butt,' the less kind would state. But she might have found her way with Dr. Jefferson. Don't forget what we're trying to build up here, Maddie. Communal worth only carries so much weight. Rohena is physically strong and capable for a girl her age. She'll find her niche. Just be patient with her. That spark in her will catch, if it hasn't already. I know it. In the meantime, Kayla comes with."

"Yes, ma'am."

There was one final task I needed to prepare for before we set out. Unfortunately, it was going to piss someone off—big time. I needed to make sure the campus was protected while we were gone. This meant leaving my most reliable person behind with our only medical person—which really upset Ulla.

I want to come with you, Ulla signed at me after I'd told her the news. Dr. Brittany had no issues with remaining behind, though she did point out that King Dale could attack the school while we were out. However, since he'd made no move after Colton was chased off, the odds of him choosing the exact moment we were out was not high. Still, the possibility was there, so Lucia would block the small bridge leading up the road to the mountaintop with one of the spare cars left over on campus. It wasn't one that ran, so gravity and coasting it down the hill would be the most dangerous part. Still, once it was at the bridge, the plan was to slash the tires and it would block the path. Good luck getting something past that.

None of this calmed Ulla down, though. It was plain to see how upset she was. Not that I blamed her in the least. She was far and away a better shot than me. Except...

"I need you to stay here and keep everyone safe," I told her, placing a hand gently on her shoulder. There was no way I was going to place her in any sort of danger. I tried to think of something Sister Ann might say in a situation like this. "You're the only person I trust with protecting all the others while I'm gone. You can do it."

But what if I can't? she signed hesitantly.

"I know you can," I told her. "You were the only one Sister Ann suggested to help me out. Did I ever tell you that?"

She shook her head.

"Out of all the girls on campus, Sister Ann said you were the best to help me shoot the shamblers," I told her, surprised that I hadn't said anything about my conversation with Sister Ann before. For some reason it'd just slipped my mind. "You saved my life, too. Remember? You killed that shambler that was trying to eat me?"

Are you going to be able to shoot without me? she asked, deflecting the praise.

I nodded. "I have to. If the governor is safe and alive like Officer Atkins says, then I'll have to protect her until we get back to campus. If that means shooting shamblers, then I'll have to."

I can shoot them, too. Her signing was growing more emphatic by the moment. Ulla was *pissed* about not going with us, and was doing a poor job of hiding it. Or maybe that was the point?

"I know. Which is why I'm trusting you to stay here and shoot any who might come up the mountain while we're gone."

You'll come back, right?

"I promise," I told her. "You'll keep them safe for me, yeah?"

I'll try, Ulla signed, uncertainty on her young face. It took me aback a little. Sometimes I forgot just how young we seniors really were, and how much younger girls like the twins and Ulla were.

"I know you will. Just try your best. Don't worry about failing, or dwell on it. Just keep going if you do," I told her. The second the words were out of my mouth, it hit me. Sister Margaret's words: *Try your best, and rise above the rest.* Of course. Rise above the fear of failure, not rise above other people and be better than them. Deep down, she'd been trying to tell me to not let my fear of failure prevent me from trusting someone explicitly again.

She'd known my past better than any of the other nuns at St. Dominic's, even better than Sister Ann. Sister Margaret had known a lot of my fears stemmed from being viewed as a failure, of what had happened to me with my ex-boyfriend. She'd seen, before anyone else, that I could do better. Time and time again she'd just tell me to try my best and rise above the rest. I'd completely misunderstood her and, because I'd been afraid of looking stupid in front of the others, I'd never asked for an explanation.

Deep down, I'd been afraid. Of course it took a zombie apocalypse to shove my fear of failure down and rise up to be the woman everyone else said I could be, and to open myself up again to really trust someone without reservations.

I trusted Ulla, and she trusted me. She was my sister, not by blood but by choice. All the girls up here were. This was my family now.

I would try my best to be the sister they needed.

I chuckled, then hugged Ulla tightly. "Be safe, kid. We'll be back. Just keep everyone safe until then, okay? You can do this. I have faith in you."

She only squeezed me tighter. That was enough.

Rich Patch Road was a long and winding path through the mountains toward Eagle Rock. It wasn't really anything special, but it did allow us to sneak around Clifton Forge to get to Deer Creek, where the governor was holed up. It was also free from any parked or ruined cars, and shamblers, but because it was a county road almost all the way, it was in rough shape. It was also a long trip and caused us to burn through almost half of the diesel in the tank. So overall, I'd call it a mixed bag.

We left just before dawn, which meant the sun would just be rising by the time we came out of Rich Patch. After passing Eagle Rock and turning north on U.S. 220, there was only a single bridge we had to cross before it turned into a straight shot to Deer Creek. I hadn't known about the bridge—it's not like I ever came down this way—but Temple knew the way and warned us ahead of time that it might be washed out. However, we were lucky. The wave that had nearly drowned Covington and probably Clifton Forge with it hadn't taken it out.

220 wasn't as long of a journey as Rich Patch Road had been, but it was challenging. Lots of cars were dotted along the roadside, with plenty of corpses spread around. Once we spotted a hunter pack of shamblers, but they were too weak and slow to keep up with the BearCat and we left them in the dust. I wanted to shoot them but Sister Ann stopped me. There was no need to waste ammo. There was a bigger threat ahead.

I let Temple ride up front with Sister Ann. He knew the way so it made sense for him to be up there. Kayla and I were crammed in the back with all the supplies, which included some of the precious penicillin with instructions from Dr. Brittany on how much to give the governor's sick daughter.

To get on to the road for Deer Creek, we had to turn off 220 right before the head of the James River. It was a dark, winding road that was almost as terrifying as the drive through Rich Patch had been. There was something about rural western Virginia that reminded me of old horror movies—only with more meth and trailer parks.

The morning was bright and cheerful when we finally found the proper driveway. The house was well hidden and off the road by a mile. Sister Ann took the turn slowly, driving up the steep, winding driveway with the lights on. While I understood her reasoning, I disagreed with it. Anyone in the house on the lookout—and I knew there would be, because we had lookouts back on campus—would spot us long before we got too close, and probably shoot at us. Sister Ann, though, seemed rather calm.

"They going to shoot us?" I asked as I leaned over the center console from the back. I noticed Temple was gripping the handle of the door tightly, and he was starting to sweat a little. "You okay, Temple?"

"I . . . think so?"

It did not sound like the voice of a confident man speaking. This did absolutely nothing to calm my nerves. I coughed and glanced at Sister Ann. "Sister?"

"Hmm . . . yes, I think this spot will do nicely," she said and brought the BearCat to a halt. The engine idled for a moment before she killed it. Without the familiar rumble of the engine it was eerily silent.

"Why this spot?" I asked her, swallowing nervously. My mouth had been dry before but now it felt like my entire throat was ready to close. "This seems like a very bad spot. Out in the open, no trees we can hide behind if we get shot at . . ."

"That's *precisely* why it's a good spot," she countered cheerily. "It shows them that we're not a threat to them. Plus, Officer Atkins gave me their security protocol. Parking in this spot, according to him, is the first step to the process."

"It also could be showing them that we're really, really stupid," I muttered.

"Nonsense. Kayla? Madison? Are you girls ready?"

"I don't know why I agreed to this," Kayla muttered as she crawled forward. "Or why we have to wear this stupid outfit again."

"The uniforms are a sort of armor. We're wearing them to keep us alive," Sister Ann reiterated for the fifth time since we left the campus. I scratched at the shirt—I hadn't worn the uniform since that fateful day down by the river when we first discovered the existence of King Dale—and wondered why it was tighter than I remembered. Then again, I'd been wearing loose, baggy shirts for the past six months, so going back to the more form-fitting dress shirt was an abrupt change.

Sister Ann, meanwhile, was wearing her full habit. She looked positively regal in the driver's seat, with her hair hidden away. It wasn't what I would have worn going into a potentially hostile environment. Then again, I wouldn't have brought two recent high school graduates in their school uniforms to meet the governor of Virginia.

"You'd think a nun wearing her full habit would be enough," Kayla continued to complain as she reached my seat. She looked at me and made a face. "Your shirt is almost out of uniform."

"I think it shrunk or something," I replied and shrugged. It was definitely tighter in the shoulders than I remembered. "Come on. Ready to get shot at?"

"Not funny!" Kayla snapped.

"Madison!" Sister Ann turned in her seat and glared at me. Even in the dark I could see just how irritated she was. Her frown created a crease in her forehead. "That was uncalled for."

"I'm sorry."

"Kayla? Relax. If you go out there a bundle of nerves, someone is going to think you're here against your will."

"But I am!"

"No, you're not," I argued. "Well, not exactly."

"Girls," Temple rumbled from the front seat. "I'm old, I'm sore, and this was not a gentle ride for these old bones. Quit bickering and let them know we're not here for a fight so I can stretch out and then die in peace."

"You didn't give me a choice," Kayla hissed angrily at me.

"Yeah, I did. You just didn't like the other option."

"I was *not* about to go supervise the twins while they blew something up!"

"Whine, whine . . . would it make you feel better if I went first?" I offered as a gesture of peace. She glowered for a moment.

"Yes."

"Okay."

"Welcoming party," Temple warned, jerking a chin toward the large house. Sister Ann followed his gesture and spotted the guards immediately. She slowly nodded and rolled down her window.

"Keys are being tossed out the window," she announced loudly and proceeded to do just that. She stuck her left hand out. "I'm using my right hand to open the door. I am a friend of your Uncle Morris. Once I exit the vehicle, I will turn and walk backward ten steps from it with my hands raised above my head. Just like Aunt Judy did. I will then stop and interlace my fingers behind my head. Unfortunately, I will not be kneeling in this mud, which is what Cousin Tanya did. You will then speak with Temple Kessenger, a local man, and you will ascertain that we come in peace, and to help. In the back are two teenage girls and supplies. Tell the governor that help has arrived."

Kayla and I shared a look.

"Sounds like you've done this before," Temple muttered quietly.

"Al Asad," she explained without explaining. "We had to practice a lot there. I'm a bit rusty, though. Did I get the order correct?"

"Close enough to get the message across," he said, nodding as Sister Ann slowly opened the door. "Protocols sounded just like what Officer Atkins told us they would be."

"Girls? Wait until they either accept the passcode, or they tell us to leave and never come back."

I swallowed nervously. My fingers tightened on Baby's grip. Was that a possibility? Officer Atkins had told us before leaving campus that these men protecting the governor had walked through a war zone before getting to their extraction vehicles. There was no telling what they were thinking, looking at an armored vehicle with a nun behind the wheel.

"My name is Temple Kessenger," he called out from the passenger seat, both his hands out the window as well. "Officer Scott Atkins of the Virginia State Police told me to relay that the redoubt is green, Rafe, but the overall situation is yellow, bordering on red. Password is the Crawfords of Pittsburgh."

"How ... Where's Scott and David?" a voice called out from nearby. Without windows in the back of the BearCat, I really couldn't see much except for what was directly in front of us.

Sister Ann and Temple both exited the vehicle slowly, exactly as they said they would.

"Officer Pew was wounded," Temple called out as he proceeded to walk around the front of the BearCat, his hands in the air. "Both of them found us up on the mountain. Officer Atkins remained behind with his injured companion." He turned around and proceeded to slowly walk backward until he was beside Sister Ann.

"Governor Lenity-Jones? Colonel? Ma'am? My name is Sister Ann Constance," she announced loud enough to be easily heard by those in the house. "You might remember me as—"

"Wait. I would never forget that voice. Gunny Towers? TNT?" a woman's voice called from inside the front door. Next to me, Sister Ann sighed. I gave her a quizzical look. She ignored me, so I leaned back. More than likely she'd fill me in later. Maybe.

"I go by Sister Ann Constance. I am a member of the Sisters of Notre Dame de Namur now, ma'am," she replied calmly, though there was something off in her voice. Something about being called gunny had set Sister Ann on edge. "But before my vows, yes. Gunnery Sergeant Tabitha N. Towers, Colonel, reporting as ordered."

"I can't believe it. Holy sh—uh, wow. You survived! Stand down! Rafe, Sammie, they're friendlies!" The woman's tone was commanding, clearly used to both giving orders and receiving them.

"But Madame Governor . . ."

"No buts, Rafe. Friendlies."

Two armed men appeared from the edges of the house. A third came out from a cluster of trees directly in front of us. Even out in the open, his hunting gear continued to help him blend in to the backdrop. Immense jealousy washed over me. There would be no way a shambler could spot me if I was wearing something that nice.

I looked over at Kalya and adjusted Baby's sling across my back. This was far more comfortable than in the ready position. "I think that's our cue."

"Wait. I think—" Kayla started to protest, but I was already opening the back door of the BearCat and climbing down . . .

. . . and I was almost shot for my troubles as a *fourth* person I hadn't even suspected was behind us had a handgun pointed directly at my face.

"Gun! Gun!" she screamed.

Two things saved my life in that moment. The first was the fact that even though her firearm was aimed directly at my nose, the woman was staring at my school uniform in utter confusion. The second was that Baby was slung across my back and not in any ready position whatsoever.

"Friendly!" I shrieked and held my hands up. There might have been a little pee involved as well. "I'm with the nun!"

"Drop your weapon!"

"I *can't*! It's on my back!"

"Drop your weapon or I will fire!"

"I *can't*!"

"*Stand down!*" Sister Ann's voice cracked like a whip through the air. It was a tone I'd never heard her use before, and I hoped to God I would never hear again.

Everyone froze. The woman with the gun in my face must have had the same reaction I did because she immediately lowered the handgun and directed the barrel away from me. I stayed in place, hands in the air. Kayla, who apparently had been right behind me, slowly climbed out as well.

"Can I put my arms down?" I asked. The woman with the gun not *quite* pointed directly at me gave the slightest of nods.

"Uh..." The security woman looked at me. Or, more accurately, at Baby. "You mind putting your weapon in the corner over there?"

"Baby? My AR? Nobody puts Baby in a corner."

The woman actually laughed. It was definitely better than being shot by an overzealous security agent. "How long you been waiting to use that line?" she asked.

"Line?" I asked, confused. I had no idea what she was talking about. The woman's face softened.

"Oh, my God... Child, how old *are* you?"

"Madison? Kayla?" Sister Ann called out. "Everything okay?"

"Yes, ma'am," I responded immediately. Looking at the other woman, I cocked my head questioningly.

"Yeah, we're good. Sorry about... you know," she said, as she holstered her weapon. There was an awkward pause as Kayla and I both eyed her a little suspiciously. Sticking out her hand, she introduced herself. "I'm Violet Flores, Virginia State Police... uh, cadet."

"Cadet?" I asked, surprised. She looked much older than me.

"Yeah. I'd just started when the flu hit," she answered with a shrug. She sounded a little embarrassed about this for some reason. "I was the only one in my class who didn't turn. That was... ugly. Got picked up by the governor when they were on their way out and... well, this is much better than being stuck in Richmond."

"I bet," I said, remembering the chaotic day when the campus had been almost completely overrun by the dozens of recently turned shamblers. It'd been far worse in the bigger cities like Richmond and Charlottesville.

"Yeah. Seriously, sorry about reacting like that," she repeated. "It's just... you're the first vehicle we'd seen in months."

"I get it. I run security up at St. Dominic's, so every new thing might be a threat."

"You? Security?"

"I'm older than I look," I told her.

"Girls," Sister Ann called out again.

"Time to go meet the governor," I muttered. Kayla shot me a nervous grin.

"She's really nice," Violet said as she led us around the BearCat and toward Sister Ann and Temple. Violet looked at Temple for a moment before turning back to me. "Your grandpa?"

"Ah . . . no. He knew the back roads to get here."

In front of the large house, Sister Ann was hugging a tall woman wearing some sort of uniform. It took me a moment to realize it was a mashup of various hunting camouflages and not a uniform at all.

"It's good to see that you're in charge of things still, Gunny," the woman—the governor of Virginia, presumably—said as we approached. Clearly they knew each other well, but other than telling us she'd served with the governor once upon a time, I hadn't known precisely how well. The governor glanced at me before continuing to speak. "It gives me hope that things might actually work out."

"Oh, I'm not in charge here," Sister Ann chuckled as the governor released her. Stepping back, Sister Ann motioned for me to come closer. I approached carefully. Her security team clearly did not like the idea of anyone with a weapon near their governor. Fortunately, they either decided I knew how to handle my weapon and were calmed, or fully believed they could take me out before I could swing the AR off my back and lift the barrel more than a few inches. "This is Madison Coryell. She's the president of the student council at St. Dominic's Preparatory School for Girls. She calls the shots on campus now. She's done an amazing job at keeping the infected away from campus."

"You always did like finding promising young officers and making their careers flourish. You did that for me, and dozens of others," the other woman said as she stuck her hand out to me. Cautiously, and uncertain about protocol, I accepted and shook hands. "Madison, huh? Named after the president?"

"I, uh, don't know, ma'am."

The governor turned and winked at Sister Ann. "You're too good at this, Gunny. Honest *and* respectful. She's, what, fifteen? Sixteen?"

"Eighteen, ma'am," I answered, looking down at my feet. Suddenly I was feeling very self-conscious for some reason. "Being short and skinny confuses people."

"Hate it now, Ms. Coryell. Love it when you reach your forties."

I had nothing for that. Sister Ann smiled at the governor.

"Colonel, if you don't mind . . . can we talk more inside? The security situation around here isn't the best," she suggested. After a moment it was clear that the governor was used to hearing her "suggestions" because she immediately nodded.

"Of course, Gunny. Let's get you and your group inside and figure things out."

"Figure things out, ma'am?" I scoffed, feeling a little more like myself now that nobody was sticking a gun in my face. "I don't think we have enough time in the world for that."

CHAPTER EIGHTEEN

"We're gonna make a break for it, Pecos. We gotta. Them zombies are almost all gone now. We ain't got any water left. Filter's busted. Food's gone. Mary's got some infection in her foot. It's now or never. If this works, we'll see you in about a week. If them boys from Van Horn try to stop us, well, God will surely know who is on the side of right here. If not? Well, He can figure it out after we stack them fuckers like cordwood."
From: *Collected Radio Transmissions of the Fall,*
University of the South Press, 2053

Governor Grace Lenity-Jones clearly cared for her people. It didn't matter if they were her actual family or the few remaining security personnel who had made it to Deer Creek with her. After a year together, if they weren't family by blood, they were by choice. At least, in her eyes.

The security people were an odd collection of individuals. Violet, who kept apologizing for shoving a gun in my face after hearing from Sister Ann and Kayla about what I'd done up on campus, was a thirtysomething recruit who had been a janitor before trying to become a state trooper. The decision had undoubtedly proven to be the right one, since she was still alive and not some shambler wandering around carrying a mop or something ridiculous.

Besides the governor's children—all vaccinated and brought to Deer Creek weeks before the Fall of Richmond happened with her husband—two other men had joined her security team during those hectic first few days.

Raphael "Call me Rafe" Morozov was a retired Army guy who had helped drive one of the big SUVs that got the governor out of Richmond. The big, lumbering vehicle had been swarmed by a massive crowd of shamblers when they hit one of the freeways leaving town. Apparently it'd gotten pretty dicey and they had a long-running shootout with shamblers and "someone else" while escaping. They somehow made it onto I-81, ditched their noninfected pursuers, and managed to get to Lexington before things . . . became complicated. Rafe didn't go into many details, but I was able to figure out that someone had turned in the middle of the drive. Rafe had taken care of the issue and got them to Deer Creek, where he pretty much became my counterpart for the governor, teaching Sammie Rameau everything he could about how to protect the governor.

Once upon a time, Sammie Rameau had been a lowly mail clerk interning in the governor's mansion. A sophomore from the Virginia Commonwealth University who'd originally called the rough neighborhood of Oak Grove home, he'd managed to escape a traumatic upbringing and make it to college. Then the Fall happened, the world ended, and Sammie had found himself pressed into duty to protect the governor as they tried to escape the Executive Mansion on the day he'd almost called out sick due to the rioting. Of the fourteen people who'd joined the group and become part of this impromptu security detail, only Sammie and the governor had miraculously survived their escape from the grounds. If he'd found a girl and saved the day, it would have been something out of an action adventure novel . . . or a B-movie plot out of Hollywood.

So *naturally* Kayla instantly gravitated to him and was instantly smitten . . .

Sometimes life is nothing but a self-fulfilling prophecy for the girls of St. Dominic's Prep.

It turned out that both Officer Atkins and Officer Pew had come down with the governor's husband and children when the flu had first cropped up. Fortuitous, and lucky for us. They'd provided on-site security until Rafe had arrived with the few survivors and gotten everything more or less organized. He was now more concerned about getting the governor's daughter under Dr. Brittany's care, and ensuring everyone made it up the mountain and to the relative safety our school provided.

The trip to the mountain, after a brief inspection of the vehicles and Rafe walking us through the damage report, was not looking so hot.

"These do not look like they're in good shape," Sister Ann stated as Rafe and the governor walked us into the garage where two massive, armored black SUVs were parked. Both were dotted with bullet holes and splattered in mud and blood, telling a violent tale of their wild escape from Richmond—an escape I really wanted to hear more about. Not because of the excitement factor, no. I wanted to know how the heck they'd pulled it off with only four people, and who was trying to get them—*besides* the shamblers, I mean.

"They're not, actually." The governor paused and shrugged her shoulders. She was taller than Sister Ann by almost a head, and positively towered over me. At the moment, though, she looked worn down and exhausted. The expected rescue party was not what she'd thought it would be, and the news about King Dale and what was going on in Clifton Forge put a damper on her spirits.

"The big one has a round through the tank and only fills up a quarter of the way. We got lucky there," Rafe said as he patted his side. He smiled ruefully. "Another round caught my spare mag on my hip: five five six, thank God. If it'd been a seven six two I'd probably be limping around with a round still in me. Or bled out somewhere on the side of the road. Smaller SUV has a dead alternator. We don't have the tools to swap them out."

"Even with the extra gas we brought, there's no way to get both your Suburbans through Rich Patch," Sister Ann murmured as she eyed the bullet-riddled vehicles. She pointed at the farthest one in the garage. "That other one's got a flat as well. You have any way to fill it up?"

"No, ma'am," Rafe responded as he scratched his beard. "Air compressor ran off gas, and we ran out of fuel months ago. Tried to keep the generator going longer than we should have."

"That's my fault," Governor Lenity-Jones admitted from the doorway, chuckling dryly. "I was hoping I could keep the power on the radio long enough to hear something . . . anything. All I got was a few stations going off the air, and lunatics declaring this is the Second Coming of Christ. If this were the Second Coming, I don't think it would start off as a zombie apocalypse."

"No solar?" Sister Ann asked, confused. "Officer Atkins mentioned something about having issues with your well?"

"Been using the Cowpasture River to force water up through the pipes," Rafe said and jerked his head somewhere to the west. "Wasn't easy to get it up that hill, let me tell you. Siphoning just about made me pass out, and that was with us all taking turns. Then it took us a few weeks getting used to the unpurified water ... even boiling it first only got it mostly clean. Lots of pine around here, though, so we could boil the water outside and then store it inside. Thankfully, the Cowpasture River is the cleanest in Virginia. But ..."

"But that was before the zombie apocalypse," the governor added in a quiet voice. I shivered at the thought of corpses floating in the river. In Covington, the Jackson had washed most of the bodies and debris downriver. There'd been some still in town but most of them had ended up near the transfer station. "I told the girls not to drink the river water, but Laveda thought she was helping ... She's sick, I don't know how bad, and I need to get her to a doctor ASAP."

"If it's bacterial, Dr. Brittany said the penicillin should start to help," I said, remembering the instructions our veterinarian had given me before we left campus. "But with bodies in the river ..."

"At least the bass are eating well," she added with a helpless shrug. The poor woman sounded on the verge of tears.

"No power, potential long-term water issues, immediate emergency with your daughter being sick, and an untenable security situation with your neighbors once they start looking this way," Sister Ann murmured and tapped her lips with her forefinger. "No wonder you had Officers Atkins and Pew scouting a route to the campus. How long have you been planning your breakout, Col—I mean, Governor?"

"Three months," Governor Lenity-Jones replied after a moment of contemplation. She coughed before continuing. "I was waiting to see if there would be any surprise flooding this season. Usually the rains flood everything out in March and April ..."

"And this was a mild spring following a mild winter," Sister Ann finished for her. "Then your child became sick, and you couldn't wait any longer. Breakout time."

"Breakout time, TNT. Give me the abbreviated rundown of Clifton Forge. How bad is it, really? Don't hold back. I need to know what my constituents have been up to."

"There's a nutcase who took over the entire town and says he's the King of Appalachia, ma'am," I interjected, feeling a little left out. "They came for us a few times, the last not too long ago. It was kind of a standoff situation until it ... turned into something more."

"How many died?" the governor asked me after a long pause. Her insight was surprising.

"One man was killed."

"Oh." She walked over to me and cupped my face gently in her hands. Her warm brown eyes stared into mine for what felt like an eternity before she pulled me into a hug. Confused, I hugged her back. "Oh you poor, sweet child. I'm so sorry you had to do that."

"How...?"

"I could see it in your eyes," she replied and released me from the embrace. "It leaves a mark. I'd seen it with many soldiers in Afghanistan. Young men, barely adults, having to take another human's life... they come back different. I'm sorry you have to go through all this. You didn't sign up for this pain."

"I volunteered to protect everyone," I told her, my voice quiet but firm. This was a demon I'd fought once already. Yes, I might have barely beaten it, but defeat it I did. Once exorcised, it wasn't welcome back. There was no way I would let it. "All the people up on campus and our mountain. He tried to hurt one of the girls, tried to take her away. I couldn't let him. I *wouldn't* let him, ma'am. I swore to Ulla she would be safe, and I keep my promises."

"How?" The governor stepped back and looked at Sister Ann. Her expression was a strange mixture of wonder and fear. "How do you find them... us... Gunny, how do you do it?"

Sister Ann shrugged her shoulders. "Everyone has the potential to be great. They just need to find a way to unlock it. I merely help as best as I can."

"Still..." Governor Lenity-Jones shook her head and stepped back. "The odds, Gunny? Low. Miniscule. Maybe you taking your vows and becoming a nun was the best thing after all."

"I ended up where I was needed most," Sister Ann said, her voice calm and sure as always. "God works through us all, whether we're ready for it or not."

I couldn't argue with that. Heck, nobody could. Sister Ann was never wrong.

It was late afternoon when we finally addressed the big, looming problem at hand.

"I'm sorry, ma'am, but there's no way either of your trucks can make it up Rich Patch," Sister Ann said after everyone sat down for lunch. The extra foodstuffs we'd brought along had been gratefully received by all, especially the kids. The governor and the first husband, or whatever he called himself, had been neglecting their own calorie intake on behalf of the kids. A noble gesture, but stupid. If the heavy lifting can't be done because of a lack of strength, then everyone suffers and dies. Those not working going lean was a far better alternative.

On a fundamental level, though, I understood her reasoning, and even agreed with it a little. There'd been quite a few meals when I'd skipped my share so one of the younger girls could have a little more. It'd left me wiped out the next day, and sometimes even affected how my brain worked when I was out on patrol. But it'd felt like the right thing to do. Sister Ann had put an end to it when she'd found out. Her insistence that I keep my strength up to protect everyone else was why I'd been forced to eat extra Spam for weeks after.

"We could try the freeway," I suggested as I looked at the large state map of Virginia that Rafe had pulled down from the wall. "I-64 is clear until you hit the first Covington exit...and that *will* be cleared by the time we get there."

"Is there another way out of this valley?" Sister Ann asked as her finger traced a line to Covington. She backtracked along the route and stopped at a juncture just south of Clifton Forge. "Looks like this road avoids Clifton Forge...Temple, that looks like 220."

"Yep," he replied, scratching at his beard. "We came up from the south on it. Continues north right through Iron Gate and splits, with one part going into town while 220 proper angles away from Clifton Forge, then meets up with I-64 about a mile up the road and you can go westbound on it, and eventually to reach Covington. If King Dale was smart, though, he'd have 220 blocked in Iron Gate... although...Governor? Doesn't McKinney Hollow Road dump out onto Longdale Furnace Road on the other side of the river?"

"If the bridge over the Cowpasture was still standing, yes it would," Rafe answered instead. His face was dark. "Didn't know if we were still being followed or not after Lexington, so a few days after we arrived, Sammie and I blew up the bridge."

"You blew up a bridge?" I asked. "How...?"

"Materials on hand," he answered in a decidedly calm voice. "It's amazing what household cleaning supplies can do, with just the proper application."

I shivered at the thought of what he could teach Finlay and Fiona. He would have to take a vow to never, *ever* show them how to blow up a bridge with household cleaning supplies before I let this maniac up on campus.

"So cutting through this little pass is out," Sister Ann said after looking at me. I must have been making a face. "Which means pushing through Iron Gate."

"Which is blocked as well," Violet added. "Spotted it about a week ago. Just after town, where the road gets twisty and narrow, and there's this rocky outlook thing? Someone set up a roadblock. It's not much, just a few barricades and a car, but it's there."

"That would be Appalachia Rex and his men." Sister Ann nodded. "As expected. He's like a tenacious dog."

"Who?" Violet asked. The governor snorted, amused, and answered.

"It's Latin, dear. It's means 'King of Appalachia.' It's probably what the sister here has been calling King Dale."

"He got *soooo* mad when he thought Sister Ann was making fun of him," I said, chuckling softly at the memory. "That was right before we stole his BearCat!"

"The armored vehicle," Sister Ann said for their benefit, though she did it with a smile.

"I was wondering how you'd grabbed one of those," Rafe muttered. "I'm a bit jealous, to be honest."

"I had help," I admitted.

"Still impressive."

"So how do we get through his roadblock, past the *other* roadblock you mentioned, and back to campus?" the governor asked, getting the conversation back on track. "We can't all fit in the back of your BearCat and go back through Rich Patch, correct?"

"Unfortunately, no," Sister Ann answered. "It's designed for six people in back. We can squeeze in ten, total. Maybe."

"Even sitting on top of each other, we couldn't all fit," I pointed out. "We've got, what, thirteen people, counting the kids?"

"Correct."

I walked away from the table, thinking. Timing was key. We didn't know yet just how sick the governor's daughter was, only that her stomach was hurting and she was having bloody diarrhea. We couldn't spend the time making two trips. Using the SUVs was definitely out of the question. As knowledgeable as Rafe was, if he knew how to swap out an alternator or replace a gas tank, he probably would have already. He seemed like the sort who didn't leave jobs lying around waiting to be completed.

We had the gas, though. Probably. The two five-gallon cans had enough fuel to get one of the SUVs through Rich Patch. The problem wasn't the fuel, but how much the damaged SUV could carry.

The one with the bad alternator was out of the question. According to Temple, cars and trucks were so electronically reliant these days that a single damaged computer chip could prevent a car from driving forever. These were government cars, part of the protective detail the governor used on a daily basis, so they were probably filled with random electronics.

Cutting through Clifton Forge was an idea, but a bad one. King Dale would be on us like a rabid dog, and if he had control of the governor? I shuddered at the thought. He could force her to proclaim him to be the legal King of Appalachia or something. Until the marines under Wolf Squadron arrived, he'd be the power in the region. And since they had no idea when they would start clearing anything remotely close to us, King Dale could potentially have years to establish a power base with the authority of the last governor of Virginia.

Walking was out. It would take us two or three days to make the hike, and none of the adults—other than Rafe—could probably make the trip with as skinny as they were.

"How much gas can the damaged SUV hold?" I asked, interrupting the group's muted conversation. They stopped and stared at me, each and every one of them confused... except Sister Ann. She had a knowing look in her eye.

"Maybe two gallons now," Rafe finally answered. "We stopped twice from Lexington to fill it up with the spare cans we had. That thing gets less than ten miles to the gallon."

"...a tenacious dog..." I muttered, thinking back to Sister Ann's earlier comment about King Dale. He'd risked everything for his stupid bridge, and it'd cost him his BearCat—and some of his men.

He did not like to have things flaunted in his face. Leave him alone, and he left us alone. But poke him in the eye . . .

I looked out the front door at the BearCat, then back at Sister Ann. An idea began to form in the back of my mind. It was a stupid idea, which meant it was brilliant. Or just really stupid. Really, *really* stupid. It was hard to say. These were strange days, after all.

No. It was *definitely* stupid. But just because it was stupid didn't mean it wouldn't work.

"Miss? Madame Governor, I mean?" I pointed at the speakers mounted on the wall surrounding the large TV. They were *nice*, and probably had cost a small fortune before the Fall. None of them had wires running out of them. *Bluetooth*, I figured. They were definitely high end. Perks of the job, I guess. But I was willing to bet they made a *lot* of noise. "What're you doing with those, ma'am?"

"They're dead," the governor said and shrugged. "No batteries. So . . . nothing. Why?"

"Oh, we've got batteries, ma'am. We brought *plenty*. I . . . wonder if I can use them?" I couldn't believe Sister Ann telling me to pack C batteries was going to pan out. It was like someone was whispering directions to her sometimes. Well, of *course* someone was. Life simply wasn't fair.

"For . . . ?" Sister Ann asked, one eyebrow quirked upward. I'd seen that look before—half curiosity, and half terror. She knew me too well. Or she'd dealt with the twins enough to know that I was planning on something both brilliant and simultaneously idiotic.

I grinned as the idea blossomed further. It *could* work, but we would have to sell the crap out of it. "A distraction, ma'am. No, *the* distraction."

CHAPTER NINETEEN

"Humanity's lost and in the dark. The deepest black. That dark, lonely road to survival is scary, but we're not giving up. No, sir. That's not how we do things down here. We're Texans, by God, and we're going to survive. Nobody ever accused a Texan of running away from a fight. You know what? That still rings true today."

From: *Collected Radio Transmissions of the Fall,*
University of the South Press, 2053

It took me three hours to secure the speakers to the BearCat. Sister Ann, sensing I was suffering from doubt, had left me alone for this endeavor. Kayla helped some, but she kept being distracted by Sammie, so after a while I told her to go and talk to him. She was happy for the dismissal and didn't even argue much before disappearing inside the house with the rest of the group.

Alone with my thoughts, I was able to actually think things through. Self-doubt can be a crippling monster sometimes.

It was a stupid plan, but it was better than nothing. Still, it put myself and Sister Ann in a lot of danger. There was no way to know if it would even work. But without us, then there was no easy way to get the governor up on the mountain to safety. Plus, the clock was ticking for her daughter. We had to get them to campus, and quickly.

Lost in thought, I failed to notice Sister Ann approach me from behind.

"Madison..." Her hand was warm and gentle on my shoulder. I

didn't turn around. Not yet. I wasn't ready to deal with the "what ifs" of this stupid plan. We both knew my idea was insane. She also understood this was the only way we could get the governor out of the house and to relative safety up on campus. There was a President of the United States again, sworn in, legal, and everything. America was not dead. Hurt, yes. In ruin, of course. We'd seen it, firsthand, in Covington. Cities around our country were probably worse off. Lots of places would never have someone live in them during my lifetime, or even my theoretical children's. But one day?

Maybe.

No girl from St. Dominic's would ever be accused of dying meekly, either. Not even the youngest under Sister Ann's care. She'd done too good of a job helping us become more than simple societal failures. We were girls becoming young women, and in this society rising from the ashes of the old, we'd be *legends*.

If I could pull this off.

"It's a risk, ma'am," I said, not turning around. "It's a risk we should take. The governor has...what did you call it? Legal authority? That will make King Dale sit down and shut up. We can hold out long enough for the marines to come, ma'am. With her governing from up on the mountain, though. Not Richmond. Here, where it's almost safe."

"Legal governing authority in her jurisdiction, courtesy of the state of emergency declared by both the state and federal governments," Sister Ann corrected me in a soft voice. "This is going to be dangerous."

"Life is dangerous, ma'am."

"You're starting to sound suspiciously familiar."

"Well...I do have a good role model in my life I quote on a regular basis."

Sister Ann smiled. "I know when you're trying to butter me up for something, Madison."

"Is it working?"

She sighed and nodded. "God help me, it is."

"This is the best way, ma'am," I repeated. "Like you said, the governor is the key. If she connects to that place you were talking about back on campus—"

"The Hole."

"Yeah, that place. We have a president again, ma'am. You heard the radio. In your own words, you said the Commonwealth needs a governor. We've got her. She has to be kept safe until she can contact the Hole, and be connected with the President. You said that, ma'am. Remember?"

She quirked an eyebrow at me and was silent for a long moment. "Since when did you start listening to me?"

"Since the end of the world began."

"Fair enough," she murmured as she gently squeezed my shoulder. "With the grace of God we will face the darkness. Together."

"Yes, ma'am," I agreed.

"You've got something else in mind, though," she said quietly, tilting her head to the left. I silently cursed. She knew me too well.

"Those pens that Officer Atkins talked about..."

"I was wondering if you were going to mention them to the governor."

"If I had, she probably would have wanted to make sure they were destroyed before she got up on the mountain," I said, looking away. "That would have probably meant the end of Maddie's Stupid Plan before it even began."

"You want to do something about them, don't you?"

"The idea's crossed my mind once or twice. I have ... another bad idea."

"It's the theme of the day, it seems. But whatever you decide, I'll support it."

"And I'm comin' with y'all," a gravelly voice said from behind. Turning, I saw Temple standing there. His expression was somber. "Gotta. This is how I want it to happen. I run out of blood pressure pills next week. Probably gonna die right after. Ain't gonna be a burden like that on y'all. You said when it was time, I wouldn't have to do it in front of my grandbabies. Your words, Sister. This is as good a chance as any. Let me get some back, for my son. Please?"

"I..." Turning, I looked to Sister Ann for help. She simply shrugged her shoulders before turning to go speak with the governor. Of course. It was my call. This crazy idea was mine, after all. Since I was running this, it would be my decision to make. Being a responsible adult *sucked*. "Temple ... be honest, sir. Can you handle the physicality of all this? It's going to be rough."

"Ain't got a machine gun up there that I can see," he said, confused. "Just that silly old blast shield. Stupid design if you ask me."

"Not answering my question."

"Just give me a rifle and all of the magazines you can spare and I'll be fine."

"Um...okay."

There was no point in arguing with him. The old guy was determined and, at this point, it probably made more sense for me to keep him as a top gunner than trying to send him along with the governor. Besides, there would be spots I couldn't hit a shambler from while riding inside in the BearCat. Up top, he would be able to at least let me know where they were coming from, if nothing else.

Best case? He got some measure of justice out of this. Somehow.

"I brought a Remington and one of those ancient Garand rifles that Mr. Stitmer had in his safe," I replied, thinking of the loadout in the back of the BearCat. "The ammo clips work for both because he did something to the Remington. It made Sister Ann cross herself, so I never touched the thing. Probably cursed by the Devil or something, I don't know. Which one do you want?"

"You got an honest-to-God *Garand*? I didn't even know you had it! How many ammo clips you bring?"

Well, that answered that.

Everything was set. The governor reluctantly agreed with my stupid plan after consulting with Rafe, who didn't think it was as stupid as I thought. Still, nobody had a better idea, so Maddie's Really Stupid Plan was a go.

Timing everything was the key for the plan to work. To do that, I had to part with one of the three spare two-way radios remaining. Kayla promised to take care of it and give it back to us once we were on campus again, but it still felt *wrong* to leave it—and her.

While the governor had a map that showed the front road into the school, Kayla knew more about the Mile Marker 10 exit and would guide them past that point. The big SUV, with two full cans of gas, *should* be able to make it. If not, there weren't many large communities back there, and the shamblers that had been surviving around Humpback Bridge were all dead now. The governor's group would be armed and probably able to protect themselves if they had to go the rest of the way on foot—at least, if they made it to the exit.

There wasn't much I could do about it but pray that they would make it. That part of the plan was completely out of my hands.

With Temple situated in the back and the BearCat's engine rumbling in the cool afternoon sunlight, Sister Ann drove us to where Violet had spotted the roadblock that King Dale—we assumed it was him—had set up near Rainbow Gap along 220.

Iron Gate was trashed. The town hadn't been much to begin with, according to Temple, but the subsequent shambler rampage and fires from old oil heaters going left most of the town a charred ruin. If the homes had been closer together, there'd be nothing left. Luckily—or perhaps not—there were still a few buildings here and there that had only been slightly singed by their neighbor's fires.

It was sad and depressing. It was also part of our new reality.

"God help us . . . the entire country's like this."

I hadn't meant to say it out loud. Sure, the thought had been on my mind ever since I first laid eyes on the ruins of Covington after the dam collapsed. That had been a weird fluke, though. Not every city was downriver of a dam on the verge of failing. Hearing about Richmond hadn't felt *real* to me. It was a distant thought, almost abstract. I don't know why, but I somehow imagined the rest of the country to be overrun with shamblers but more or less in one piece, ready for those of us uninfected to reclaim and simply move back in.

Iron Gate ruined that hope for me.

"What can burn can be rebuilt," Sister Ann intoned solemnly. "Don't lose faith, Madison. We survived. Next, we thrive."

The mantra had gotten us this far. No point in questioning it now.

"Yes, ma'am," I said resolutely, chewing on the ends of my hair as we exited Iron Gate and entered the Rainbow Gap.

They knew we were coming. The BearCat's engine was *loud*. We knew they were going to be there, hearing us, wondering. It still didn't make the meeting any less awkward.

Sister Ann stopped well clear of the orange plastic barriers that were set up on 220, effectively blocking the way. I knew that the giant BearCat could make short work of them, but the entire point of this was to get all of their attention. Simply ramming through them would only enrage King Dale, causing him to probably chase us. But it wouldn't do anything for the second part of my plan, which only the three of us knew about. If the governor had even suspected what we were going to try to accomplish, there was no way she'd ever let us try it.

It's much easier to beg forgiveness than to ask permission sometimes. Sister Ann told me that was the motto of the E-4 Mafia— whoever they were.

While the BearCat wasn't in gear, Sister Ann let the engine idle. We had plenty of fuel, though I knew there was no way to replace what we had once it was gone. Still, it was better than shutting the engine off. We had no idea just how King Dale was going to react. An unprepared target was a dead target.

"Only three of them," I pointed out as the men guarding the barricades stared at us. They were clearly confused. One of them even raised a hand in greeting. I bounced excitedly in my seat and looked at Sister Ann. "Can I?"

"You *may*," she corrected after an overly dramatic sigh. I rolled down my window and waved back.

"Hi!" I shouted at them cheerfully. "We *really* want to go through. Can you move?"

They gathered together and started talking to one another. I don't know what they'd been expecting when their BearCat—adorned with stick figures, flowers, and a giant sun painted on the side panels— pulled up to their little bloackade, but what they were getting was far different. Chuckling, I glanced over at Sister Ann.

"I think I broke them."

"We'd like to pass, if you will," Sister Ann hollered, leaning out the driver's side window while doing so. If I'd broken them, the presence of the nun reformed their mindsets. *Her* they knew, and recognized. The two older men standing next to the orange safety barriers fingered their rifles and looked at one another. One of the younger men quickly ran to a dirt bike stashed alongside the road and kicked it started. It took a few tries before the engine caught and sputtered to life.

"Look," I whispered and nodded toward the dirt bike. The rider was hightailing it out of here in a hurry, heading back toward Clifton Forge. "I guess they don't have radios?"

"I noticed that as well," Sister Ann replied as she gripped the steering wheel tighter. While the two guards manning the roadblock weren't quite aiming at us yet, I could tell they were ready to. "They might have some, but be out of batteries. Can't say for certain. Be ready. When King Dale arrives, these guards are going to become a little more nervous. They're already nervous. He's going to put them on edge, and that could equal disaster."

"Nervous men with guns and a high-strung hillbilly dictator," I quipped. "What could go wrong?"

"I've never told you how much I've appreciated your humor this past year," Sister Ann said, turning slightly in her seat to look at me. "You really are a good leader, Madison. Not by telling people what to do or bossing them around, but by showing them how to do things, and leading by example. You might not want the responsibility, but you never shirk it. That is a trait I admire."

"Uh..."

For once I was at a loss for words. Sister Ann didn't hesitate to shower people with compliments, but this felt different somehow. More sincere. Almost like it was something she'd been holding back from me, which was odd. She'd complimented me many times in the past. One of my favorite things about her was that she always made sure to let us know how much she appreciated each girl up on campus. Even when we screwed up.

No, *especially* when we screwed up.

"That was fast," Sister Ann murmured ten minutes later as three trucks came speeding along toward the roadblock. They stopped a respectable distance away from the orange barriers, parking alongside the narrow shoulder. A dozen men piled out of the trucks, each and every one of them armed with a rifle of some kind—except King Dale. His hands were free for the moment, though I could see that massive hand cannon holstered on his hip.

"You!" he thundered loud enough to be heard over our engine, his face turning a decidedly ugly shade of red and purple as he spotted his stolen BearCat. He pointed a finger at us and strode closer. He stopped when he was only ten feet away from our makeshift, rusted brush guard. None of his men followed past the barriers. "Give me back my tank!"

"He sounds angry," I muttered. Sister Ann nodded gravely.

"That he does. At least he isn't swearing. You see, Madison? Some lessons stick."

"Y'all give me back my tank!" King Dale screamed at us. "I ain't letting you past otherwise! Give me back my tank and git on back to your campus! Hell, we'll even drive you! You've got nowhere else to go! Roanoke is burned to the ground!"

"Appalachia Rex, this is the last time I will correct you on this. This vehicle, which you errantly regard as a 'tank,' is a BearCat G3," Sister Ann hollered back, revving the engine once to emphasize her point. "Know the machinery, respect it, and people will take your claims more seriously."

"I will take back what is rightfully mine!"

"Take back? I got something you can take back, all right. Preferably where the sun doesn't shine," I murmured as I triple-checked the safety on Baby. I really didn't want to shoot Dale or any of his cohorts. More importantly, the desire to not put a round through the floor of the BearCat was a strong one.

"Madison . . . let me handle this."

"Yes, ma'am. Sorry, ma'am." Even in the face of death, Sister Ann was always teaching. She never let up. It was like she was hardwired to make sure I was the best person I could be. Even when I didn't want to be.

Especially when I didn't want to be.

Meanwhile, King Dale's ranting was slowly devolving into . . . something *weird*. "That is my chariot you done stole! A king needs his chariot! This is my kingdom, and there can only be one king! And I want my chariot back!"

The dude was seriously unhinged. Before, when we'd dealt with him, he'd seemed a bit pompous but sane. Now? He was coming off more like a crazy person than any kind of king.

"Oh, you can be king of this dung heap, hillbilly!" I shouted out the window. Sister Ann looked at me.

"I thought I asked you to let me handle this?"

"You did."

"And?"

A pause. "I was getting bored."

"Madison . . ."

"Okay, okay," I said and most definitely did *not* roll my eyes at her. That would have been beneath me. Sister Ann told me this dozens of times before. "Sorry, ma'am."

"You really need to rein in your temper sometimes."

"A heart filled with anger is not the way to go through life, young lady," Temple added from the rear passenger area, his voice audible over the steady rumble of the big engine.

"Seriously? You too?"

"If this were a movie, Madison, then your words of pithy rancor would be quite fitting," Sister Ann admonished me in a low and gentle voice. "But this is the real world. Pithy last words don't exist here. Antagonizing the man is not going to settle things. If anything, it could make it worse. Remember, we're not just here to destroy a tinpot ruler's power base. Eventually we have to be their neighbors again after this. Society *is* going to rebuild. Love thy neighbor...even if he's a petty tyrant. Remember that."

She had a point. It was really a bad idea to argue with a nun.

"Yes, ma'am. This isn't a movie."

"But quoting Aragorn in times like this is not completely unheard of."

"Now you're sending me mixed signals..."

"You need to give me back my ta—BearCat!" King Dale's voice was growing shriller with every passing moment. Around him, I could see the men were getting antsy and anxious, their eyes darting between one another but not speaking. It was growing obvious to us that they were losing their nerve by the moment. These were men who did not want to be there. It made me wonder just what had drawn them in to King Dale's orbit in the first place. There had to be more to it than promises of ruling Appalachia, or simply having a "plan" like Colton had claimed.

"Why do they follow him?" I asked Sister Ann as the yelling and screaming continued. He hadn't quite slipped into full-on cursing yet, but he was getting close enough. Creatively speaking, they weren't quite there yet. "Those men...they don't look happy to be here, you know? So why stay? Why help him?"

"This is their home," Sister Ann said. "Clifton Forge, Selma, Iron Gate, even some from Covington...I'm willing to bet that all of them are from this area. He gave them their homes back after the flu and the shamblers ruined it all. It's the idea that he can give them back what they once had that allows them to forget that things can never go back to the way they were."

"They're also scared, Maddie," Temple added from the back. "I know I sure was. Still am. I don't like it, no sir, not one bit. Those boys out there? They're just like me."

"They're nothing like you," I argued with a derisive snort.

"They're *exactly* like me," he repeated. "The only difference is, most of them don't have someone to protect anymore. Ain't like they all still have their families or nothing, you know? They got a mind to protect their families, but they failed. Dale offers 'em something to protect again. I know you ladies probably hate hearing this, but it's a guy thing."

"If you say so . . ."

"He's not wrong, Madison."

The radio suddenly crackled to life. A very young voice came over air. "*Uhh . . . green frogs sitting in a pine tree? Yeah, I know, I'm holding the stupid button. It clicked, see? Shut up! What? No! I got this! Oh, fine. Here. Green frogs in a pine tree? There . . . happy now?*"

The radio went silent once more. I barely stifled a laugh. That was the twins' code, albeit with a lot of added side commentary. I-64 was open. The twins and Lucia had managed to clear the road without any sign of King Dale's men, as well as doing it without killing themselves or anyone within a half mile.

Probably.

One of the trickier parts of this potential mess was taken care of. In the back of my mind, I really wanted to ask the twins just how big the explosion had been. However, Sister Ann was being a stickler about what she called "comms security." Asking for details would be a waste of time since they'd probably already turned it off and were headed back to campus.

"That's the call. I think we've given them enough time to get everyone ready for Operation Maddie Has A Stupid Plan. What do you think, ma'am?" I asked. Sister Ann sighed heavily.

"Yes. Plenty of time." She leaned forward and turned on the radio. She gave me a look, her figure hovering just over the PLAY button. "This is going to be very dangerous, Maddie. Appalachia Rex could shoot us both. No, he's definitely going to try and shoot us. The armor on this thing is good, Madison, but not infallible."

"Getting shot? Ma'am, that's, like, only the fourth thing on my list of worries right now."

"Only fourth?"

"Number one? I really don't want to be a shambler, ma'am."

"Okay, that's a good reason."

"And I *really* don't want to be caught by King Dale over there. That's, like, two and three."

"Fair enough. Let us go with the grace of God."

"And Axl Rose. Push play and crank it up!"

"Oh, I love this band," Temple said as the opening notes of Guns N' Roses' "Welcome to the Jungle" threatened to blow out the governor's really nice speakers. He reached up and grasped the "ready" handle on the roof. "Well, my son loved them. I'm more of a 'Freebird' type of guy. Whooo! Just let me know when I need to pop the turret hatch and head on up."

"I feel way less confident about this than I did an hour ago," I muttered under my breath. Sister Ann must have heard me. She snorted trying to hold in her laughter.

"If you were feeling confident right now I'd definitely be worried," she said.

"What I would give for a fog machine," I said wistfully as the screaming on the speakers began. "Having the BearCat come out of the fog would have looked pretty epic."

"You missed your calling in theater," Sister Ann replied. After a moment, she pursed her lips in a thoughtful manner. "Well, you could still be Air Force. You'd fit in well with them."

I sputtered, knowing an insult when I heard one. "How dare you! You take that back!"

"Ladies," Temple interrupted us from the rear. He'd crouched down so he could be heard better. Even over the BearCat's engine and the guitar intro I swear I heard both his arthritic knees pop. "As much as fun as we're having in here, it's getting a tad hairy out there. I'm almost certain that King Dale character is about to start shooting at us."

Glancing out the front window, I could see that Temple was right. It was time. Looking at Sister Ann, I nodded.

"Let's do this."

"God be with us," Sister Ann whispered as she pressed down on the gas pedal. Engine roaring, Sister Ann slammed the vehicle into gear. Tires squealed loudly and the BearCat lurched forward—directly toward the makeshift barrier cones erected by King Dale and his cohorts. Fortunately for King Dale, and unfortunately for us, he saw our intent and quickly jumped out of the way.

The indecision was clear on the rest of their faces as the BearCat gathered more speed. None of them wanted to shoot at us. The realization, though, when they saw we weren't about to slow down for their barricade was almost comical to watch. Yet they still didn't shoot at us.

At that moment I knew they weren't really our enemies. The words to explain just *how* I knew, though, would not come.

They had only a moment to react before the heavily armored front end of the BearCat, powered by a massive V8, filled with vehicular rage and accompanied by the opening riffs of the greatest rock song of the '80s, made short work of the orange barriers. The men outside had scant seconds to get out of the way—though I'm almost certain Sister Ann slowed down to give them a half second more. As the barriers shattered to pieces from the weight of our vehicle, I noticed peripherally that every single one of King Dale's men managed to avoid getting run over.

Even in the midst of chaos she remained a better person than I could ever be.

"We're taking the hobbits to Iseng*aaaaard*!" I shouted gleefully—and maybe, *just* maybe, a little maniacally—out the window as the BearCat roared up U.S. 220 toward Clifton Forge, King Dale and his men in hot pursuit, with the screaming vocals of Axl Rose leading the way.

CHAPTER TWENTY

"Forward, the Light Brigade!
Charge for the guns!" he said.
Into the valley of Death
Rode the six hundred.
—"The Charge of the Light Brigade,"
Alfred, Lord Tennyson

We barreled into Clifton Forge like a trio of teenagers hitting our first club armed with fake IDs and loaded up on White Claws.

It would have been glorious in any other situation.

Right past Rainbow Gap U.S. 220 split, just like it showed on the map. If we took the road to the right and followed it, we would have eventually linked up with I-64 and headed back toward campus, none the wiser. However, the goal wasn't for us to get safely back to campus just yet. No, we needed to distract Dale and his men by any means necessary because the only way the oversized Suburban filled with the governor, her kids and husband, the security contingent, and Kayla were making it to the mountain was via I-64. Which meant we couldn't go that way at all, and draw King Dale and his guards into town. Getting the governor away safely was the main goal here. That, and staying alive.

So instead we followed a narrow two-lane road along on the left. Sister Ann clearly did not know the road well because we suddenly made a sharp right turn, wheels squealing as she stomped on the brakes. Temple let out a series of muffled curses as he flew across the back of the BearCat.

"Sorry!" Sister Ann shouted as we drove slowly over a bridge.

Below I could see the twisted remains of railroad tracks half-submerged beneath the river.

"My fault. Forgot to remind you about that turn," Temple said as he extricated himself out of toppled ammo boxes. I almost said something about them going off before remembering that it would *probably* take more than the boxes falling over to start making rounds go off accidentally.

"Officer Atkins said one of those pits was located at the outdoor amphitheater, yes?" Sister Ann confirmed as the song continued to blast out from the speakers. No shamblers came running toward us, though. I had to give King Dale credit. He'd done an admirable job cleaning up the shambler problem in Clifton Forge.

He's keeping them penned up and using them to sentence people to death, a tiny voice in the back of my head reminded me. My admiration died as quickly as it arrived.

"Yeah. He said the outdoor one, not the big one," I called out loudly. "Whatever that means."

"Keep going down Main and then angle right," Temple shouted from the rear. "Look for Garlynda's Dance Studio. After that, turn right once past the post office. It'll be on the right side. It's on the backside of the Masonic Theatre."

"Why not turn early?" I asked, half-turning in my seat. Temple's face looked a little gray in the dim lighting.

"Right turns are easier than left."

"That makes no sense at all."

"Trust me, girl. Been driving these roads since before Sister Ann was born."

"All right. You heard the man, Sister."

"How many vehicles followed us, Madison?" Sister Ann asked as she accelerated down Main Street. I lowered the window and leaned out to get a better look.

"Looks like all three of them, ma'am."

"Send the message. Tell them the way is clear, and to get up to the campus as fast as possible."

"No, ma'am, not yet," I told her. She looked at me sideways.

"Not yet?"

"Too early. We need more chaos and mass confusion in town before we release the turtles, ma'am. Uh, with all due respect."

She nodded once, slowly. "I believe you are correct. Are you prepared?"

"I've made my peace with God, Sister, no doubt about it," Temple declared. "Now I'm just out to exact a little vengeance."

"Not the healthiest response I've ever heard," she said before shrugging slightly. "I've heard worse, though."

We turned right at a partially burned-out building that I assumed had once been a dance studio, judging by the sign hanging precariously above the front door. All the glass windows had been broken out. It was a sad sight, but one we didn't have time to dwell on as Sister Ann suddenly slammed on the brakes. The BearCat slid a second time in almost as many minutes, only now we came to a full and complete stop.

"There," Sister Ann said in a quiet voice. I turned and saw the reason why she'd stopped the vehicle so abruptly.

Between the burned ruins of Garlynda's and another brick building were two chain-link fences coupled together to block an alleyway. They'd somehow jimmied two additional fences to stand on top of the others, making the barrier over a dozen feet high. Inside the fence dozens, if not a hundred, shamblers were pushing against it. With the heavy concrete barriers blocking the lower edges of the fence, though, it wasn't budging at all.

"That's . . ." My voice trailed off as the shamblers began to turn on one another. I had no problems with killing shamblers, or someone else doing it. Or even letting a bear kill one for me. This, though? The sight was something else entirely. Before I even knew what I was saying, I gave the order. "We wanted chaos? Break it down."

"No arguments from back here," Temple said as the song came to an end. Since I'd set it up on a loop, the guitar riff kicked on again as Sister Ann revved the big engine. She slammed it in gear and the BearCat lurched into the chain-link fence. It bowed but did not break. The shamblers that had been pressing against the fence were thrown backward. One didn't get back up, though the others did.

Sister Ann backed up a little farther this time and repeated the process. This time the fence came tumbling down. More shamblers went flying, and even more came boiling out from the outdoor amphitheater beyond. Reversing the BearCat, Sister Ann dragged part of the fence stuck to the makeshift grill back with us. It caught on a fire hydrant and came unstuck, thankfully. I wasn't about to get out and wrestle it off with shamblers swarming around like they were.

"They're here!" Temple said as he popped open the turret hatch and stood upright with the Garand. He popped off eight shots in rapid succession before a loud *ping!* echoed in the back. Ducking back down, he grabbed another one of his strange clips. "Got one of their engines!"

Sister Ann slammed the gear into drive and floored it. The big block engine roared and the BearCat lurched forward, barreling through the growing crowd of shamblers that were free now. The small pickup truck Temple had taken out of commission had two men in back, both armed with shotguns. Fortunately for us, they were too busy trying to hold back the swarm of shamblers that had parted around us and fixated on the smaller target they could see in the open.

The other two trucks that had chased us from Rainbow Gap tried to pin us between them, but the BearCat was simply too heavy for them to do anything but scratch our paint job—which ticked me off a little. The elementary school kids had spent a lot of time drawing on the BearCat.

"Hey!" I shouted as the bigger truck on our left slammed into us a second time.

"Trying a pit maneuver on something this big moving this slowly? Amateurs," Sister Ann muttered as she turned the corner, passing what appeared to be a burned-out post office. The smaller truck on our left misjudged the turn and jumped the curb, nearly taking out a streetlight in the process. The bigger truck backed off when we made the turn, giving us a little breathing room. It didn't last because accelerating uphill was not something the BearCat was designed to do.

In a park a little lower than the road I spotted what looked like an outdoor theater stage. Surrounding it was tall fencing reinforced with those concrete roadblocks that prevented shamblers from knocking them down. Mounted on top was some really nasty-looking razor wire, with a rotted shambler body stuck in one spot. At the base were more dead shamblers, a few of which looked as though they'd been partially eaten. Revulsion welled up inside me.

"This is the kingdom that Appalachia Rex promises," Sister Ann commented, somehow reading my thoughts. "This is what we're trying to stop by getting the governor back up to campus."

Instead of responding, I cranked up the stereo louder. I didn't think it could go higher but somehow the wireless speakers managed. Slash started in on his mid-song guitar solo as the smaller pickup truck tried to sideswipe us again. Instead of continuing straight ahead at a steady speed, though, Sister Ann stomped on the brakes and jerked the wheel to the left. The front end of the BearCat slid on the street, following Sister Ann's guidance. The smaller pickup didn't stand a chance as the much heavier SWAT vehicle pushed it into the large front windows of a building.

"Shamblers are catching up!" Temple hollered down into the cabin. He continued to use the Garand with surprising accuracy. Shamblers were dropping everywhere. The old dude could *shoot*.

"So is King Dale!" I replied loudly over the stereo as I spotted the self-proclaimed King of Appalachia riding in the larger pickup truck. He had a massive revolver out but fortunately wasn't shooting at us quite yet. Like us, he seemed more preoccupied with keeping the shamblers at bay than trying to shoot actual humans.

For now.

Quickly rolling down my window, I started helping Temple out as best as I could. Two were beneath his line of fire, so I put three rounds into both of them as the BearCat bounced on a piece of broken sidewalk.

"This is starting to get a little exciting!" Sister Ann hollered as Slash continued his wicked guitar solo. We swerved around the downed tree on the sidewalk and smacked into a shambler that had wandered into our path. Sister Ann slowed, then backed up as another shambler ran toward the BearCat, howling the entire way. I waited until it was closer before putting three into its chest. It dropped with the grace of a sack of potatoes.

"Yes, ma'am!" I shouted back and fired at another shambler that stumbled into view. The howling was growing louder by the second. So was the guitar riff. The governor's speakers were freaking *awesome*. I really needed to find out where she got them. There had to be someone around who had a set and didn't need them anymore. "You know what the difference between a villain and a supervillain is? It's all about presentation!"

"I should *never* have let you watch that movie!"

"It's animated *and* rated PG!"

"Still..."

"It's so *quotable*, though!"

"Incoming! Right turn! Hang on, Temple!"

I jerked as Sister Ann threw the wheel hard. The BearCat sideswiped a small truck parked next to what used to be the Clifton Forge Public Library. For a brief instant I thought we'd turned too sharply as the BearCat started to tilt before it settled back down on all four wheels. I exhaled as Sister Ann stomped on the gas. The engine roared in response and a plume of black smoke erupted behind us. Any shamblers back there probably just sucked down twenty pounds of exhaust and would maybe die from carbon monoxide poisoning. Probably not, though. Still, the thick cloud of black smoke was glorious. I shot another shambler nearby just for good measure and switched out the now-empty magazine for a fresh one. The BearCat lurched forward. Sister Ann turned the wheel hard and barely missed another ruined car. She slammed on the brakes, nearly throwing us into a slide as nine tons of carefully constructed and heavily armored Hell on Wheels tried to stop before plowing into a *third* vehicle.

Apparently, Clifton Forge was where every car in Alleghany County had come to die. The Catholic Church was simply ensuring the vehicles stayed dead.

"Careful!" Sister Ann barked at me as I leaned back out the window for a better angle. Two quick shots dropped another shambler that had begun gnawing on one of its dead compatriots. Or doing something else. I didn't want to dwell on the difference for too long.

"I am being careful!"

"You are *not* being careful!"

"Oh-em-gee! You sound like the first boy I snuck into my house when I was fourteen!"

"Madison Coryell!"

"What?"

Sister Ann pinched the bridge of her nose. It took her a few seconds to regain control of her breathing. "Holy Father, I beg of you. Grant me the patience—"

"More shamblers incoming!" Temple shouted, interrupting her prayers. Some of them from the holding pit back at the theater had managed to follow us and were trying to climb into the BearCat. Fortunately, all the doors were locked and secured. The ballistic glass was holding so far, even with the heavy impacts it'd taken since we started this merry little joyride. One or two figured out the steps, but they were rewarded with headshots whenever I had a good angle. Up top, I could hear Temple shooting at shamblers unseen.

"Oof! That hand cannon Dale's got is a beast!" Temple added as an enormous *boom* echoed along the narrow street. Apparently King Dale was joining in on the fun.

Sister Ann's gaze drifted toward me. "If we survive this, Maddie, we need to have a little chat about honesty during discussion hour with the Sisters of Notre Dame de Namur."

Ah, damn it, I thought. *That's going to take a week, at least.*

Shifting the BearCat into reverse, she drove back over a few of the shamblers we'd already run over once. The ones that had made it on top of the engine hood slid off, howling with rage the entire way down. Checking my area, I spotted one I hadn't shot yet. I was going to put a few rounds into it before noticing that its legs had been crushed by the heavy armored vehicle. Even if the shambler survived the damage, it wasn't going to get far.

I shot it twice anyway. It was time for a reload and I figured a fresh magazine would be fitting for the next wave of shamblers.

"Smaller truck's gettin' swarmed by them zombies!" Temple yelled down at us. "Engine's dead. Poor bastards!"

Sister Ann's face was pinched. "Madison..."

"Got it," I said, swallowing nervously. This was something I'd been afraid of. Sister Ann was having an easier time dealing with the shamblers than I'd thought. She still held life precious, though, and the idea of uninfected men and women being turned was not something she could handle. Which meant we needed to save our enemies. Even if they were doing their best to capture us and ... *stuff.*

Some things were best not to be dwelt upon. Grabbing the door handle, I waited until she suddenly slammed on the brakes. One shambler that'd stuck in the brush guard went flying backward, tumbling five feet away before finally stopping. It tried to get up but it was clearly too injured. Popping the handle, I slid out the door and immediately put a round into the shambler's head. It stopped moving immediately. Turning, I swept to the rear of the BearCat and began looking for targets.

"Girl, are you crazy? Get back inside!" Temple yelled at me before firing from the other side. The Garand made its distinctive *ping* and the shooting abruptly stopped. "Damn it! Reloading!"

"Gotta save as many as we can, sir," I shouted, and began to shoot every shambler I could lay eyes on.

It was as though a weird calm came over me. I'd only felt like this once before, and it'd been on the field during a heated game against Greenbrier East. During the game, I just felt completely unstoppable after Sister Narcisa had inserted me in at center. The other team had no answer for anything we did, and I had scored with ease, dominating the center and keeping the ball in our possession for almost the entire game. It'd been a bloodbath, and field hockey at the high school level really doesn't have a mercy rule. All of us had been in the zone, and poor Greenbrier had been left picking their teeth up off the field after.

The same feeling washed over me now: absolute calm with a healthy dash of confidence. From this range I'd have to try in order to miss a shot. I *knew* the shamblers swarming the truck were going to die by my hand and, God willing, every one of King Dale's men would have the chance to run away. The only question that remained was which would happen first.

The nearest shambler had two broken legs but was still doing its best to crawl toward me. One shot and it twitched, then stopped moving. Stepping around it, I focused on the four trying to pull the hapless men in the rear bed of the truck down.

Pop! Pop! Pop! Pop!

Four shots, four dead shamblers. The men in the back were scrambling away from the edge, looking at me with bloodshot eyes. None of them appeared to be wounded, and none were aiming their weapons at me. This was a positive sign.

"Go home and take care of each other! Stay safe! And quit trying to chase us!" I ordered as I turned Baby's barrel toward the front of the truck. A shambler had managed to shatter the passenger-side window and was grabbing the screaming man inside. A single shot to the head took care of that infected. The man inside was sobbing and screaming. There was blood splashed across the front window—probably his. Unfortunately there was nothing I could do for him. More than likely he was infected, but I didn't have time to do anything for him. He'd change eventually, and then maybe he'd become my problem—if he didn't bleed out before then.

More shamblers appeared from back near the amphitheater. This town was too small to stay ahead of the shamblers for long.

"Run!" I yelled at the driver of the truck, who was desperately trying to shove his door open. Dead shamblers were piled up next to it and he was having a heck of a time getting out. Finally he crawled out the window and tumbled messily to the ground, somehow rolling to his feet without accidentally shooting himself. His trigger discipline *sucked*. Needing no further encouragement, he bailed on his buddies and hightailed it up the street. They weren't too far behind him.

Shots rang out behind me. Temple was back in action, and dropping shamblers as fast as he could shoot. Backing away from the truck, I watched as the passenger of the truck stopped screaming and slumped over. Promising to say a quick prayer for the dead later, I turned and hurried back to the BearCat.

Ping!

Temple was out of ammo again. The Garand was surprisingly efficient when it came to letting the person shooting it know that it was empty. He ducked down out of sight just as I came alongside the armored vehicle.

"Couldn't save them all," I told Sister Ann. "Saved most, though."

She bowed her head. "Even though their intentions weren't pure, we will pray for their immortal souls."

"Maybe later?" I suggested as *another* group of shamblers came staggering up the street. These ones looked to be in rougher shape and clearly weren't the dominants of the pack trapped in the amphitheater. I leaned out the window and took a shot at the lead. I missed, but hit the one next to her. Mentally shrugging, I refocused and tagged the lead in the leg. It howled in rage and pain, dropping to the street. The followers descended on her without mercy. "Ugh. Gross."

"There's always time to pray for someone, Madison."

"Even in the middle of a zombie apocalypse?"

"*Especially* then."

I sighed and shot another shambler in the chest. This one dropped and didn't move. "It takes a special kind of lady to do that."

"You're on your way to becoming a great lady."

I snorted derisively. "I'm no lady."

"You are a *lady* and you will show some class!"

"But—"

"I will hear no argument from you! Say it!"

"Right *now*?"

"Yes! You are a classy lady."

"But I'm—"

"Say it and *believe* it!"

"I'm a lady...?"

"That sounded more like a question than a statement, Madison Coryell," Sister Ann admonished as I spotted a shambler who'd noticed the idling BearCat and began heading toward it with decent speed. I waited until I had a clear shot before putting two rounds into it. They did the trick and there was one less shambler in the world.

"I'm a lady."

"Now say it with pizzaz! Convince me!"

"I am a classy lady!" I shot another shambler. Its head snapped back as the round impacted right above the bridge of its nose. Talk about a quality shot. "Classy is, like, my middle name! I'm a classy *freaking* lady!"

"And don't you forget it!" Sister Ann said and accelerated the BearCat down the street, leaving the swarm of shamblers in our exhaust.

"*Verpiss dich und stirb,* shambler!" I screamed as we turned a stray shambler to mulch on the rusted brush guard. Sister Ann didn't say anything about that one. Either her German was rusty or she didn't speak it at all. Or maybe it didn't count because it wasn't in English? Hard to say. It wasn't something I had the time to dwell on at the moment.

"Another shambler! Two o'clock!"

These things were like freaking cockroaches. I tagged it in the shoulder with my first shot as we closed the distance. It spun around, making me miss the next two shots. No matter. After a deep breath, I squeezed off a fourth. This one felled the shambler just as we passed by.

"Hahaha! Got you, you bastard!" I shouted gleefully as *another* shambler was crushed beneath the heavy front end of the BearCat. How had some many managed to get ahead of us? Just how many shamblers were lurking in the town?

"Language!"

"Sorry, ma'am!"

"You didn't sound sorry!"

"I kinda am!"

"You're impossible sometimes, Madison."

"Okay. I really am sorry."

"I hope so. Watch it! Right! Right!"

"I see—Oops, totally did not mean to shoot that one in the crotch!"

"Oh, I wasn't talking about that. Just stop trying to—"

Thumpthump!

"Sister Ann! Quit trying to run over everything!" I told her, half serious.

"I'm not trying to! They keep running out in front of me!" she protested loudly. Slowing the BearCat down, we took the turn onto another side street. In front of us was the main street we'd come in on originally. Other than the railroad tracks directly ahead, Main Street was the only way out of town. King Dale was probably certain that he knew what we were up to by now—destroying the fighting pits. There was no way he could possibly imagine what our real plan was. We'd caused too much chaos for him to be worried about anything other than shambler control, and stopping us.

"More incoming!" Temple shouted from above. He ducked down inside and looked at us. "That . . . is a lot of zombies."

"I think it's time, Sister Ann," I murmured as the batteries on the speakers finally died. Governor Lenity-Jones had warned me that full power would drain the batteries quickly. I just hadn't thought they would go *that* fast.

She glanced over at me and nodded. "On your call, Maddie. It's your plan."

By now, it was a safe bet that every single shambler roaming around in the town of Clifton Forge was on our tail. King Dale and a few of his most loyal followers were staying nearby, trying to stop us while avoiding the shamblers at the same time. We had everyone's full and undivided attention.

All according to my makeshift and totally *not* bonkers plan. I took a deep breath and slowly exhaled. I clicked the radio on. It was already on the prearranged channel. Phase Two of Maddie's Really Stupid Plan was a go.

"Let's do it. It's time to release the turtles."

CHAPTER TWENTY-ONE

"We've been looking for the enemy for some time now. We've finally found him. We're surrounded. That simplifies things."
—Lieutenant General Lewis Burwell
"Chesty" Puller, USMC

The trick to any plan where there are multiple fail points is to make sure there are plans in place for when, not if, said plan goes sideways. My idiotic and stupid plan? Ride through Clifton Forge, shooting shamblers and trying not to get caught by King Dale or his men, and cause as much chaos as humanly possible. Lots of fail points, true. But with plenty of ammunition and a pissed-off old man doing his best to become a rotating turret up top, the BearCat acted as a mobile fail-safe against those points.

Fortunately, what I'd thought would be the hardest part was quickly turning into the easiest. While we were dashing about the small town like a trio of lunatics, Kayla was helping the governor, her husband and children, and the surviving makeshift security team sneak north on U.S. 220 to take the right split before Clifton Forge, so they could link up with I-64. If it all went to plan. It might be argued the crazy chase around downtown Clifton Forge was a waste of fuel, true, but we needed to get the sick child up on the mountain as soon as possible.

With us causing chaos in town, we hoped that not a single person remained behind at the small roadblock King Dale had built at the Rainbow Gap. If they'd all left, then it would be cake. If not, Rafe had said he would "handle it." Which was more terrifying than watching a chonky bear crush a shambler.

Plus, Sister Ann had sort of destroyed the roadblock when we'd plowed through. With what looked like all of King Dale's men trying to stop us, the route to I-64 should be clear. The SUV should be making quick use of it. Granted, they'd have to deal with the remains of the second makeshift barricades King Dale had managed to create when they got closer to Covington, but if the twins had done their job right like they said—and I doubted they'd let me down, since they had permission to use as much Tannerite as needed to blow something up—then there was a path wide enough to drive through by now.

Hopefully the crater wasn't too deep. I shoved the thought from my mind. *One problem at a time, Maddie.*

"Turtle One, this is Rabbit, copy. Coast is clear. Move it, over." Sister Ann said after picking up the radio.

"Turtles are through the snare. Heading home now," Kayla's voice came back quickly. Sister Ann nodded approvingly. Kayla had been watching us from nearby when we first broke through the barrier.

"Copy, Turtles. Rabbit is . . . en route. See you at home, girls. Rabbit out." She set the radio back before half-turning in her seat. "Temple? You okay back there?"

During our stop, Temple stopped firing and had slumped down into the back. Either the shamblers were running around chasing someone else for a change, or they simply were all dead. I was willing to bet on the former. There was no way, given how packed that first holding pen had been, that we'd got them all. We weren't carrying that much ammo.

Nobody was carrying that much ammo.

"I'm good," he said in a strained voice as he bent over and tried to reload another fresh clip into the Garand. His skin had a faint gray tint to it and his face was pained. His free hand was rubbing his left shoulder a bit in between shaky breaths. It was clear the old guy was struggling. However, there was some satisfaction in his eye. "Feels good, you know? Shooting them. Like I'm getting a little bit of my son back."

"I understand," I told him. Sister Ann pursed her lips but didn't say anything. I understood what the look was for, but Temple didn't. Or perhaps he hadn't noticed. He hadn't spent nearly as much time with Sister Ann as we had. Since I'd been elected leader of this crazy expedition, I continued. "The point isn't to enjoy killing the shamblers, as tempting as it is. It's to not feel bad about it after."

"That's mighty philosophical of you, young lady," Temple wheezed as he continued to rub his shoulder. It was not the one he'd been shooting with. "Don't enjoy the killing, but don't feel bad about it. Kind of like hunting deer, I guess. I enjoy the hunt, but the actual killing? It's just shooting a deer. I can appreciate a good shot, but nobody enjoys the gutting and cleaning. But it must be done. Treat it like it's just a job, though. Nothing else."

It sounded about like what I had been trying to say. At least, judging by Sister Ann's expression, it was enough. She gave me an encouraging nod.

"You know... Officer Atkins said there were two holding pens, right?" I asked, looking back at Temple. He gave me a funny look before nodding once. "We only knocked down the gate at the amphitheater. Where's the other one? The armory?"

"That is a very good question," Sister Ann said. She motioned toward my window. "Shambler, three o'clock."

Pivoting in my seat, I leaned back and gave myself enough room to swing the AR up and out. The shambler was thin as a rail and moving very, very slowly. Lining up the green dot, I took aim and put a single round into its head.

"Temple?" Sister Ann asked calmly as I dispatched the shambler. "You seem to know Clifton Forge fairly well. Do you know where the armory is at?"

"Not too far from here," he responded without hesitation. "Head up the road a bit, hang a right at the school of the arts. It's next to Smith Creek and has the old Clifton Forge High School right there. It'll be on the right-hand side. Can't miss it."

"High school?" I asked, confused. "I thought everyone in town went to Alleghany?"

"Back in my day, Covington–Clifton Forge was the football rivalry," Temple explained. "It was closed down because they didn't have enough students. Alleghany was built instead, for all the county kids. Covington kids stayed at Covington."

"But is it a good place to build a pen, like the one at the amphitheater?" Sister Ann asked. Temple nodded slowly.

"Easy to block in, isolated, has access to water ... yeah, if someone wanted to keep their zombies penned up, that'd be a decent enough place." Temple's voice was wavering just a bit. He was looking a little worse for wear. "Makes more sense than the amphitheater, at least."

"That means we have to turn around," Sister Ann said. "Back past the library and into the maelstrom."

There was almost no hesitation in my voice. "Then back into the maelstrom it is. Those pens shouldn't exist. It's not right to force people to go into them and fight shamblers. Or to torture the shamblers like that. Kill them, and move on with your life."

"I agree with the little lady," Temple wheezed. He continued to rub his shoulder. His forehead was covered in sweat. "It ain't right."

"Are you okay?" I asked him. He nodded.

"Little too much excitement. Hard to breathe when I shoot too much."

"Okayyy," I dragged the last syllable out before mentally shrugging. Screw it. He was still down to fight. There was no way I was going to tell this man he couldn't help anymore. He was willing to give his all, and for what? A hope and a prayer? No, there had to be more than simple vengeance here. A random thought came to mind and I was talking before I even knew the words were coming out. "Into the maelstrom once more, dear friend. Not for gold, vengeance, or glory, but for those helpless few who need us the most."

"Gambling may be a sin, but Sister Margaret owes me twenty bucks when we meet up in Heaven," Sister Ann muttered. I shot her a confused look. "She said you'd turn into a mathematician, if given the right motivation. I bet you would become a voracious reader and read just about anything for fun. Maybe even become a writer one day."

"She bet ... wait ... math? I freaking *hate* math!"

"It must have seemed a reasonable bet at the time, all things considered. You hated reading, too."

"Is that why you had me chronicling the early days of the Fall?" I asked, half-turning in my seat to glare at her. "Because you thought I'd be a *writer*? What kind of career prospect is that?"

"Well, most writers are either dead or a shambler now, so ..." she said, her voice trailing off.

"Yeah, but ... okay." She had a valid point. If not for Sister Ann pushing *The Hobbit* on me when I'd first arrived, I probably would have never read for fun. And the likelihood of writers surviving the zombie apocalypse was pretty slim. "Wait . . . you gave me your copy of *The Hobbit* on a bet? And practically *forced* me to read *The Silmarillion*? Dang it. By the way, I'm not quoting Aragorn before we ride into battle."

"Théoden would have been more fitting for you . . ." Sister Ann mused.

"Ladies? I hate to interrupt your discussion on the finer points of classic literature versus mathematics, but I think I see some more of them zombies coming our way." Temple coughed before pointing back into town. "A whole passel of them."

"Can't believe Sister Margaret thought I'd be a math nerd," I muttered as Sister Ann shifted the massive BearCat into reverse. She pushed down hard on the gas pedal and the tires squealed just a bit before grabbing the road. The vehicle lurched backward, then gained speed. She quickly pulled the wheel left while smoothly shifting gears and hitting the brakes, executing a perfect J-turn.

"Temple? Up top, if you will. Once more unto the breach, dear friends," Sister Ann said as the BearCat lumbered forward. The shamblers swarmed, so Sister Ann did her best to keep from running them over. Temple popped back up into the turret but didn't start shooting. The shamblers must have been too close now, below his line of fire. "Madison?"

"On it," I called out and leaned partly out the window. Two shamblers had grabbed onto the side of the BearCat at the rear and were making decent progress trying to climb on board. We couldn't have that. Taking careful aim, I shot the first one right between the eyes. It tumbled off the moving vehicle. The second howled when it saw me and tried to figure out a way to get up where we were at. It would have been hilarious if not for the fact that the shambler was most definitely trying to eat my face off. Two quick shots and the shambler was gone, no longer a problem.

Pulling myself back inside, I glanced over at Sister Ann. She was concentrating on the upcoming turn, passing the truck we'd run off the road previously. None of King Dale's men had remained. There weren't any shamblers alive here, either.

"Most of them on your side?" I asked her, leaning across the center console.

"Four, maybe five," she replied.

I grunted. "Temple? Targets left. You got eyes on them?"

Nothing. Muttering under my breath, I climbed across the console and practically ended up in Sister Ann's lap. The interior of the BearCat wasn't that big, and if I hadn't been so small to begin with there would have been no way for me to pull this off.

"Don't get your brass on me," Sister Ann warned as I sprawled out across her.

"Like I can prevent that, ma'am," I told her as I spotted a tight cluster of shamblers fifteen yards away and moving toward us with purpose. Temple should have had an angle on them. Why wasn't he firing? It didn't matter. They were my responsibility now. "Ears."

"Hold on," Sister Ann and brought the BearCat to a stop. She leaned back as far as she could and covered her ears with her hands. "Okay, go."

Why shamblers liked to bunch together when approaching a potentially hostile metal monster—probably what the BearCat looked like to their rabid minds—was something scientists would probably want to look into later once the last of the shamblers had been killed off. In the meantime, it made shooting them much easier.

On a basic level, they had to know they were being shot at. However, they didn't seem to care. Those that didn't die immediately charged us, howling in that horrid pitch while bleeding everywhere from their wounds. These aggressive types all wanted one thing: to kill the big metal thing hurting them. With their speed and in my prone position, it wasn't the easiest to shoot with accuracy. More than a few rounds missed, but fortunately I had enough to spare. Changing out a magazine in this position would have been next to impossible.

"Clear left!" I called out and Sister Ann removed her fingers from her ears. Mine were ringing but the hearing protection was dampening most of the gunshots. Thankfully. Otherwise, I would probably be deaf by the time I turned twenty.

"Eject your mag, then clear your chamber. Roll up the passenger window, then see what's wrong with Temple," Sister Ann told me as I pulled myself off her lap. I followed the instructions and was surprised to see that I only had one round left. How had I lost count? One of the first lessons Sister Ann had drilled into me—after keeping my finger off the trigger unless I was about to fire—was to keep track of my ammo count.

It didn't take long to manually roll up the BearCat's window, but it was a pain. Why it didn't have powered windows like every other car these days was something I'd never understand. Once it was up, I double-checked the lock. It was set, so no shambler—or any of King Dale's men, for that matter—could slip inside.

It wouldn't be easy crawling into the back with Baby in hand, so I left the AR in the shotgun rack before making my way into the back of the vehicle. It took some effort to manuever around the empty gas cans and ammo crate we'd brought for Temple and me, but eventually I managed to squeeze fully into the back.

Temple wasn't up in the turret. Nor was he in one of the seats, reloading his beloved Garand. It took me a moment to find him. But when I did, I really wished I hadn't.

"Oh, Temple." I sighed softly as I spotted his still form. Sometime during our dash back into the maelstrom he'd slipped out of the BearCat's turret, laid down between the two rows of seats, and died quietly without making a fuss. His great, big heart had simply been unable to take it anymore.

He'd said his time was near. Many times, actually. He repeated it over and over again, and every time he said that everything after the brain cancer was borrowed time. He hadn't known what for until he'd had to take care of his grandchildren. I hadn't believed it but apparently he'd known. I gently closed his eyes and tried not to cry. Unfortunately, real life wasn't like the movies, and his eyelids refused to stay shut, and they slowly opened until his unseeing eyes were staring right at me once again.

"Temple...that is a little creepy, dude," I muttered, then hiccupped and sniffled before whispering a silent prayer for him. Even dead he seemed to have his sense of humor. On the plus side, at least he'd died exacting some sort of revenge for the death of his family. Looking away, I understood finally why they used to put coins on the eyes of the dead—besides paying the Ferryman, at least. I placed a hand over his heart, just to make sure. There was nothing there. "We'll take care of your grandbabies, sir. I swear on it."

"Is he...?" Sister Ann asked from the driver's seat.

"Yes, ma'am."

"And the world loses another good man," she stated and shifted the BearCat back into gear. There was a resignation in her voice I'd never heard before. It was disheartening and, for a moment, a hole in my stomach seemed to open and all my hope died in it. If Sister Ann was giving up, then what chance did we have? "Poor man. His grandchildren will be loved and cherished by all, and his memory will be honored. *Requiem aeternam dona ei, Domine. Et lux perpetua luceat ei. Requiescat in pace. Amen.*"

"Amen," I repeated quietly. I knew the *Requiem aeternam*, thanks to the sisters who had, once upon a time before the end of the world, taught at St. Dominic's. But hearing Sister Ann say it instead of my mangling of the prayer felt good for the soul. Her Latin was both effortless and flawless.

"Madison, do you want to—"

"There's still the other pen, ma'am," I interrupted, knowing what she was going to ask me before she'd even begun the question. There was no way we could head back now. I steeled myself. Even though I knew what was necessary, there was nothing more I wanted than to head back to campus, curl up in a ball, and sleep for ten days. "Temple was right. We can't let it stand. Those shamblers need to be put out of their misery."

There was nothing more I could do for Temple. Covering him with one of the spare blankets we'd brought for Governor Lenity-Jones, I moved back to the front seat. Sister Ann was staring straight ahead, her fingers gripping the steering wheel tightly. There were tears in her eyes. I didn't understand. We'd lost hundreds of students and teachers since the Pacific Flu outbreak, and I'd never seen her cry. Not even once. She'd always been our rock, the one person who was stoic through thick and thin. Nothing got to her.

"Ma'am?" I asked, almost hesitant. This was not something I knew how to handle. She'd never taught me how to comfort the one responsible for everyone else's well-being.

"I'm sorry," Sister Ann said and wiped her eyes.

"Why?" I asked, confused. "What for?"

She sniffled once and smiled. It was slight, but it was there. "You're right. What for, indeed?"

"You told me it's okay to cry for ourselves," I reminded her. "You said that when all this chaos and madness began, remember? It's always okay to cry for ourselves."

"I did."

"And we never apologize for our tears," I told her emphatically. "Your words."

"For a girl who I believed never listened to anyone, you seem to have picked up a lot of good advice somewhere along the line."

"Well . . . I had an excellent teacher."

The street was oddly quiet. For a town filled with shamblers running around, it seemed rather sedate. The larger of the two trucks that had been chasing us since the Ranbow Gap blockade hadn't followed when we'd turned down Commercial. With Temple gone and neither Sister Ann nor I knowing our way around Clifton Forge well enough, I was on the lookout for any sort of side street where they could pop out and sideswipe us.

While there were plenty of streets a truck that size could fit through on the driver's side, there was nothing interesting to be seen except for dark, empty homes. No streets for old King Dale to ambush us from there, though I could see one coming up.

"On the right," I warned Sister Ann. She slowed the vehicle down and kept us in the center of the road as we approached it. Once I saw no signs of a truck, I exhaled the breath I hadn't known I was holding. Looking past the street corner I spotted a large, three-story building farther up the road. Almost all of its windows were boarded up and the main doorway was bricked up. There was a flagpole sitting in the middle of a weed-filled parking lot. "Wait. Is that a school?"

It was. There weren't any signs out in front but every horror movie I'd seen where they featured a haunted, abandoned school looked just like this one—complete with the police tape covering a broken window with a KEEP OUT sign hanging in front of it.

Sister Ann slowly turned onto the street. On the left side across the parking lot there was a smaller building I hadn't seen originally. It looked more like some sort of gymnasium. After a few seconds I realized that this little dilapidated building had to be the armory Temple had spoken of.

Looking around, I couldn't see any sign of a pen to hold shamblers in. There was a baseball field up behind the abandoned school but, not seeing the usual press of bodies against the fence like down at the amphitheater, it was easy to dismiss it as a holding pen.

There simply wasn't any room down here for an outdoor area to keep the shamblers safely contained.

So where were they?

"No shamblers," I pointed out after another quick look around. "Weird."

"They're here," she said in a quiet voice. "You're just not looking at the right spot."

"Huh?"

She jerked her chin toward the front door of the armory. "There."

I followed the direction she indicated and blinked, confused. There was nothing but the front doors to the armory. Then I saw a flash of—what? A face? Watching the doors intently, a few seconds later I was rewarded with the unwashed, filthy face of a shambler—only this one was not clawing and chewing on the door to come out and attack us. This one looked . . . frightened?

Suddenly it clicked. I'd spent months tracking one of these shamblers around campus, to no avail. "These are those other shamblers. The betas."

"But what use are they to him?" Sister Ann mused.

"Who cares? Let's bust them out, too. He can chase them all over and deal with them."

"Maddie . . ." Sister Ann stopped, then sighed. "I miss the surety of youth sometimes."

"What's the problem?" I asked. "They're penned up. We let them out, and he's gotta deal with them. Or they run around until they die off. This is . . . not right."

"But is it any worse than releasing captive rabbits out into the wild? Pet bunnies?"

"Bunnies aren't dangerous," I reminded her.

"And they are?" she asked me, looking back at the wild eyes of the beta shamblers locked inside the armory. I looked away, confused. There were times when living with a nun drove me insane. Her moral compass was something I would never truly grasp. "You know they *can* be dangerous."

"When cornered . . ." I allowed, albeit grudgingly. Motioning toward the doors, I struggled to find the right words before continuing. "They're trapped in there . . . we don't know why, right? What if he's . . . I don't know . . . doing 'stuff' to them?"

Sister Ann sighed again. This was the worst possible time to be having a philosophical discussion about shamblers, yet here we were. "Madison, sometimes—"

I never got to hear the last bit of what she was going to say. Something large and heavy slammed into us. The back end of the BearCat was violently thrown to the side. Metal screeched as it ground against metal, and my head smacked into the metal doorframe as I found myself momentarily out of my seat. Sister Ann was thrown into the center console at the same time. The heavy shocks of the BearCat absorbed us landing back on the ground, though we bounced a few times before settling it. Faintly, I could hear the sound of a car horn over the loud ringing sound in my head.

Reaching up to touch my scalp, it came away wet. It took me a moment to realize that it was blood. My blood, to be precise. My head swam and I felt like I was still flying through the air. Struggling to get my bearings, I noticed that the front doors of the armory were *much* closer now than they had been before. And getting closer every second. It took me a moment to realize that the big armored vehicle was still in gear, and Sister Ann was no longer in control.

It was the gentlest tap in the history of car accidents, but 9,000 pounds of American steel against flimsy metal doors with a chain link and a cheap lock keeping them shut meant a very short contest of strength. The doors buckled in under the gentle but constant pressure of the BearCat's expanded brush guard and suddenly, the doors collapsed. I stared stupidly as our vehicle kept trying to go through the doorframe before it dawned on me that one of us needed to either hit the brakes or put it in reverse.

Reaching over, I threw the shifter up as far as I could. While the gears in the drive shaft didn't necessarily grind like my dad's used to when he was shifting into second, it was clear the BearCat was not designed for such a rapid transition from drive to reverse. Sluggishly it began to back out, creating a large opening in the doorway as it moved away from the armory.

"Are you okay?" I asked Sister Ann, who was slumped over in her seat, clutching her ribs. She wheezed something under her breath. "Sister?"

"O-okay," she managed, staying hunched. She was having a lot of trouble breathing. She was definitely hurt far worse than I had been. There was no other way to explain it but that her breathing sounded ... *wet.* "Ribs."

The BearCat suddenly dropped lower in the rear. Looking back, I could see that the back door was still intact. Temple was wedged between the seats still, looking comfortably asleep. If I hadn't known any better I could have believed it. With the exception of the boxes tossed about, the interior looked decent. There was no way for me to check out the rest of the damage from whatever had hit us without getting out—which I was not about to do.

The beta shamblers, sensing their freedom, were running out of the armory and scattering in all directions. Somewhere I could hear shouting, and someone was shooting a very loud handgun. I could hear a car horn continuously going off nearby. Confused, I leaned out the window to see what was going on behind us.

It was the big truck that I'd thought we lost during our initial thunder run through town. The entire front end of it was smashed and steam was coming out of the engine. Or maybe smoke, it was hard to tell. One of the wheels had fallen off and rolled away someplace. There was only one person in the back standing against the few shamblers that came close to him, and he was making short work of them with that monstrous handgun of his. His driver looked worse for wear but was moving inside the truck.

King Dale. I ground my teeth and grabbed Baby from the rack. I was about to go out and confront him, but Sister Ann laid a hand on my arm.

"Wait ..." she hissed and put the BearCat in park. She made a pained noise once she was able to lower her arm. Another shambler, a small female who looked frighteningly familiar for some reason, shot out of the armory and disappeared around the side of the building. "Dangerous."

Sister Ann was right, of course. Going out there now while King Dale was shooting every single shambler he could see was a recipe for being shot myself.

His face was a bloodied mess. He had a nasty cut on his forehead and more blood was trickling from his nose. There was no way to tell whether he hadn't been wearing his seatbelt when he ran the truck into us, or if this was his reward for wearing a seatbelt and he was simply lucky to be alive. I couldn't just get out and ask him. Well, I could, but random acts of gunfire.

Concussions are weird like that.

He paused shooting, probably to reload. It wasn't likely one of the beta shamblers had gotten him. This was our chance to make a break for it, only I wasn't sure just how bad the damage to our rear end was. Was there a flat tire? Had the rear been so badly damaged that we couldn't drive out of there? Was the truck blocking our only way out? To answer any of those questions, I'd have to poke my head up out of the turret or get out . . . and risk getting shot by the self-proclaimed King of Appalachia.

Or worse, eaten by a shambler.

Neither option appealed, but there really wasn't a choice because Sister Ann made the decision for us.

She opened the door and slid out of the driver's side, clutching her ribs with one hand. Moving slowly, she began to limp toward the rear of the vehicle. Not knowing what else to do, I quickly slung Baby across my chest and followed suit, making certain I closed my door after getting out. The last thing I wanted was for some shambler to think the BearCat was a great new home.

King Dale saw me as soon as I rounded the rear of the armored vehicle. Clearly, he'd already spotted Sister Ann. Knowing she was never armed, though, he wasn't really looking to exact violence on her. I knew this because the moment he recognized me he was raising that massive hand cannon and preparing to end my life. I started to raise Baby up, though it was clear he had the drop on me. The injured driver of the truck, meanwhile, had stumbled around the front and aimed his AR at me as well. The likelihood of my survival was pretty low.

"Stop!" Sister Ann commanded, then doubled over and groaned. She spit on the ground before standing back upright. Looking down, I noticed that it was all blood. I started toward her but Dale moved the barrel of his gun my direction. I froze, unsure. My desire to help Sister Ann almost outweighed my own survival instincts. She gave me a small head shake before raising a single hand toward him. "Stop. Please. No more. In the name of God, sir. Please."

"God?" Dale all but spat at that. He motioned at the ruined doors of the armory. "You think God exists here?"

"He does," she whispered, barely loud enough for me to hear. Coughing once and wincing, she straightened her back as much as she could and raised her voice. "He most definitely does."

"He has to," I added, since Sister Ann looked pale and ready to pass out. She needed to get back to campus and see Dr. Brittany. "You saying God can't be here means you put limits on God. That's . . . wrong."

He snorted. "I ain't got time for a philosophical discussion with a murderer."

Ouch. That hurt. "I didn't want to kill him!"

"Sure you didn't," he snarled back. He gestured at Baby. "You just bring it along because it's like a fashion accessory or something."

"Shamblers, you idiot!" I shouted back. "I carry it because of the freaking *zombie apocalypse* we're living in!"

"Please, stop," Sister Ann called out again as she moved between us. She shot me a look before trying to calm King Dale down. "Stop. There are so few lives left. We can't . . ."

"You can't keep these things locked up like this," I said, looking at Sister Ann to see if she was okay. She clearly wasn't. "It's not right! Just kill them and be done with it! This . . . this isn't right!"

"Kill them? Like you do? Kill them all? Going to shoot them in cold blood like you did with my brother?" King Dale nearly roared.

I froze at that. The man who'd grabbed Ulla had been his *brother*? Oh, *crap*. No wonder the man hated us—no, he hated *me*. In his eyes I'd gunned his brother down when he'd been behind, alone. Probably believed I shot him in the back or something, I don't know. Had King Dale gone back and grabbed the body and decided on his own what had gone down? We never went back to double-check to see if it was still there. Nobody had wanted to go that way again. Especially me.

There wasn't any part of the world I knew of where shooting someone's brother instantly triggered a blood feud. Here? In hillbilly central? If not for the zombie apocalypse, I'd probably already be dead. Or at least have half of the town out for my blood.

"I didn't mean to!" I protested, looking at Sister Ann for help. Unfortunately, she was doubled over again, her face deathly pale.

"You didn't mean to shoot my brother *multiple times*?" King Dale screamed at me. The barrel of his pistol looked *huge* from my point of view, and it was pointed directly at me now. Oddly enough, the driver with the AR felt like an afterthought. Still, I hesitated to bring Baby up. Neither man might shoot. I definitely did not want to shoot either of them. Killing shamblers was one thing. I'd already taken a man's life. That was not something I wanted to repeat.

"He tried to grab one of the girls I *swore* to protect!"

"Bullshit!" King Dale choked back a sob. "He'd changed! He swore he was different now! He promised! He was my *brother!*"

"He grabbed Ulla! She's a little girl who had to watch her sister get torn to shreds by a shambler!" I fairly screamed back at him. My temper was starting to rise, which was never a good thing. It made my skin flushed and my freckles stand out even more. Plus, I tended to rant when I became angry. "She can't talk now! She only does sign language! Your *brother* tried to take her from me!"

Out of the corner of my eye I saw something move toward King Dale. At first I thought it was one of his men but then recognized the shambler. It was the small female I'd chased around campus a few times. Somehow King Dale or his men had snatched her up sometime since I'd last seen her.

She was sniffing the air, almost like a threatened animal would, and moving slowly but steadily closer. This was unlike any other behavior I'd seen this shambler make before. It wasn't quite moving like one of the aggressive ones would, but it also was not running away like a timid rabbit. No, this was new behavior altogether.

The shambler was quietly stalking Appalachia Rex, and he had no idea.

The urge to remain quiet was a powerful one. Let the shambler do the deed for me so I could grab Sister Ann and get us both back to campus, and safety. It would be clean, though not merciful. Not that he'd earned a merciful death. No one would be the wiser. After all, someone like King Dale surely deserved that sort of karmic justice, right? Nobody would blame me even if they did ever learn the truth.

No. That's not who I was, not who I wanted to become. I was better than that. There might be some things in this world I would be willing to do—apparently killing a man to protect a child was one of them—but there was no way I would stay quiet and let someone die at the hands of a shambler.

"Dale? There's a shambler stalking you," I told him in as calm of a voice as I could manage. The shambler was creeping forward cautiously still, but its eyes were locked onto his back. It was barely twenty feet away now, and like a cautious predator unsure of its prey, the shambler paused every few steps to almost test the air. Slowly I began to raise Baby. "To your right, my left."

"Boss?" the driver wheezed. "I'm hurtin', boss."

He laughed at me and cocked the hammer back dramatically.

"I ain't falling for that!" He laughed—no, *cackled*, actually. The man was clearly teetering on the edge of sanity and was quickly losing his balance. "That's the oldest trick in the book! I turn to look, there's nothing there, and you shoot me!"

"I'm not playing around!"

I was torn. Part of me—an admittedly large part—wanted the shambler to attack. However, the words of Sister Ann rang in my head still. Noninfected life was precious to us now. So very few of us remained. Less than three percent of the world population survived. Less than that after everyone lost power and were thrown back to the Dark Ages, maybe.

As crazy as King Dale might seem, we'd have to be neighbors again when this was all over. A reckoning might happen but that wasn't up to us, but to the courts—if we ever got them back, that is. This man, and those who followed him, might be doing things wrong, but that didn't necessarily make them *bad*.

Except for the shambler holding pens. Keeping them penned up like animals was cruel. They were still people, in a twisted sort of way. Even if there was no cure, mercifully killing them was a far better option than imprisonment and cannibalism.

But all of this meant I had to save King Dale. I had to *try*.

Everything happened at once. I brought Baby up and took aim just to his left as the shambler lunged for him. The driver shouted and fired right as I did. Dale, caught off guard by my movements, hesitated just long enough for me to draw a bead on it. Sister Ann had somehow moved to my right despite her injuries, twisting and crying out. Taking a half second to make sure I had the shot, I squeezed off a round right as she latched onto his arm.

King Dale shrieked in either pain or fear, I'm not sure which. The giant revolver, which had been pointed directly at my chest, shifted away slightly when he was hit by the shambler. He fired and thankfully missed me by a mile. The driver screamed and fell to the ground as Dale's round punched into his stomach.

Appalachia Rex was a mess. Blood was pouring down his arm from the nasty bite but I could see that my aim had been true. There was a neat hole in the beta's shoulder. The only problem was, the shambler was merely wounded.

He pushed the shambler off, giving me just enough space for a better shot. This time I squeezed off two rounds, with both striking it in the upper chest. The shambler, tiny to begin with, staggered back from the impacts. The beta whined like a wounded dog before dropping to the ground, bleeding profusely.

"Shit!" Dale said, staring in my direction. The blood dripping from the bite had reached his hand already. The shambler had bit him *deep*. "Shit shit *shit!*"

For a moment, I thought he was going to shoot me. The odds of him surviving a bite from a shambler and not turning into one were slim to none. Blood transmission, they said, was always fatal. One way or the other. So why not take out the girl who'd been responsible for killing his brother? In a twisted sort of way, it made sense.

Only... he wasn't looking at his wound or the gun. Or even toward me, actually. Confused, I turned slightly to follow his gaze.

There was Sister Ann on the ground, bleeding from a gunshot wound. She'd taken it for me when the driver had panicked and fired. I couldn't think coherently. The one person left in this crazy, broken world who actually gave a damn was lying on the ground, dead.

I don't remember screaming or running over to her, of setting Baby down on the ground to try and stop the steady flow of blood coming from the bullet hole in her chest. The CPR was rough but serviceable, but it had no effect on her. I was robbed of her, not being allowed any final words of wisdom thanks to some jackass hillbilly. The shot had been perfect, killing her almost instantly.

She'd died as she'd lived—serenely.

It was pure bullshit. Sister Ann couldn't die. This was some horrid sick joke God was playing on me, on all of the survivors at the school. There was no way she could leave us like this. Not at the hands of some wannabe tinpot dictator who was a dead man anyway thanks to some random shambler I hadn't managed to kill months before when given the chance.

My throat was raw. It took me a second to realize I'd screamed long and hard when I saw her. The muscles on my arm were burning but I didn't know why. In my chest, my heart felt as if something was squeezing it tightly, trying to crush it in an icy grip. It hurt to breathe. Turning my face to the side, I promptly threw up. The act made me feel even worse.

All the while, King Dale said nothing. He simply stood there, mute. He was crying. Like I cared about his feelings. Not now. Not ever again. There would be no mercy for him, no. I was going to find great satisfaction in killing the murderous bastard.

There was no memory of picking Baby back up, turning, and aiming. It was simply a blink, and everything changed. I had Baby shifted right and trained on his chest before I even knew what I was doing.

I never understood before when someone said that their soul hurt when they lost a loved one, that a part of them was gone and there was no filling the gap. The sensation was simply something I'd never really understood. How could I? Before St. Dominic's and the Sisters of Notre Dame de Namur, I'd been a selfish, petty little girl. It was they who'd showed me how to be more.

It was Sister Ann who guided me to become what I was now.

"No ... I didn't ... wait ... no! I didn't!" Dale screamed as tears ran freely down his face. I swallowed, throat suddenly dry.

It would be so easy. The voice whispered from the depths of that dark part of me I'd always known about, and had willingly embraced a long time ago. A gentle squeeze of the trigger and I would have vengeance. Sister Ann would be avenged. The rage and hatred I felt was pure. There was nothing wrong with it. Hell, she'd told me it was okay when I'd shot that man to protect Ulla. What was one more death on this fucked-up day anyway?

No.

I didn't so much hear as *feel* the voice deep in my wounded heart. A balm on my soul, the voice whispered again. *No.* A simple, singular word that carried weight many times heavier than the slew of hate the other voice in my head had been raging at me. The last remnants of a good woman were still in me, the woman she'd intended for me to become. I wasn't gone quite yet. The darkness hadn't claimed me fully. I would never be *that* girl again. No, Sister Ann wouldn't let me. Not before, not ever.

The dark and evil voice inside me wailed. Sister Ann's love squashed it. Madison Coryell, president of the student council, remained.

I nodded slowly at him. A strange sense of calm came over me. For the first time in my life, I understood what Sister Ann meant about finding my inner peace. There was no other way to explain it.

"I didn't mean to!" King Dale was still protesting. "I never intended...I didn't...set out to be the villain!"

"You're definitely not the hero."

There was a weight on my hands. A light one, but definitely noticeable. Gentle and insistent. Exhaustion? It had to be. It was pushing the barrel of Baby downward. I really wanted to keep it up and pointed at his chest, but the weight was growing to be too much. Was the adrenaline of our insane chase finally wearing off? Made sense. It'd been a long, crazy pursuit.

The weight continued to carry Baby down. There was no strength left in my arms to keep it up. I was done. Dale still had his revolver, but it was down and at his hip. If he brought it up to shoot me, I was pretty sure he could put a round into me before I did anything.

"Your brother was trying to hurt one of the girls," I reminded him. My voice came out surprisingly gentle, which startled me a little. "I didn't know who he was, only that he was trying to hurt someone I swore to protect."

"You think I don't know that!" King Dale sobbed. Maybe this was the first person he'd ever killed? I know what it did to me. How would the murder of someone who had looked at him as leader, king even, affect an already damaged soul? "He just...Damn it!"

"I'm sorry for your loss." The worst thing about it was, I actually meant it.

His breaths came in small hitches as he struggled to regain his composure. "You're not sorry for shooting him, though. I can tell."

"No. I'm not. But I'm not shooting anyone else. Human, I mean. Shamblers don't count."

"No, I guess they don't." Dale half-turned and looked around at the wreckage. I did as well. The town was in rough shape, and though some of the blame could be laid at our feet, it was clear that a lot of the ruin had occurred since the Fall. Dale heaved a great sigh and wiped the tears from his face. Blood from the shambler's nasty bite was trickling slowly but steadily down his arm. "So much energy into building the wrong things. I wasn't rebuilding society, was I? No. I failed them. Failed my brother. What a . . . fucked-up world we live in. That I created here. Take care of your girls. Just like the nun would have wanted. You hear me, girl?"

"I've never done anything else."

"No," he looked at me, *truly* looked, for the first time. I could see the confusion in his eyes, and the sadness. There was a hurt there that had affected him to his very core.

Many people have traumatic events that shape who they become. We use those as either a crutch, or motivation. Spite is one hell of a motivator, but the past is as well. Blaming things on the past to excuse what we did in the present is cowardly, yet we do it. Every day. Dale had simply taken whatever trauma he'd suffered in the past and used it to excuse everything he did.

Dale coughed and rubbed his face with his empty hand. He looked like hell. I was willing to bet I didn't look much better. Not after the rolling gunfight we'd been in with all those shamblers. "Ain't gonna be no Kingdom of Appalachia. Not now."

"Not now, no." I affirmed this with a nod. "Governor's back in power. We've got a president again, too. America is hurt, but we're not dead yet."

"Well . . . shit."

"Language."

He chuckled at that. It was soft, but it was earnest. "You, too?"

"Sister Ann guided me through the worst of times," I told him. "Why risk ticking her off now that she can see everything? Besides, I still haven't worked off my demerits yet."

Now he did laugh. I don't know why, but it was both good to hear it, and terrifying. Perhaps it was scary to watch the harsh façade he'd portrayed for the past six months crumble away? Something about it was off, though I couldn't say what exactly. In better times, Dale might have been a good man. But these weren't better times, and it would take much to change this. Him and his friends had made certain of that.

"You're a smart girl. I wish . . . no. I knew how everything would end. To say otherwise would be lying. Lied to my brother. About him. I knew he was broken. Lied to myself about what he was trying to do. Damn. Blamed everyone but the person whose fault it really was. What happened? What the hell happened to me? Shit. Long live the king or some bullshit, I guess," Dale said wearily before bringing the revolver up and placing the barrel against his chin. There was no hesitation as he pulled the trigger.

There are no words to describe what went through my mind at that moment. The only thing I could really do was watch the body drop to the ground, my brain not really processing everything. It was as if my brain had decided to short-circuit at that very moment and was doing a hard reboot.

I stared at King Dale's still form for a long minute, not really comprehending what I'd just witnessed.

"To rule over a kingdom of ash and ruin," I murmured as a warm breeze brushed the hair from my face. Legacies were important to people. Older people, I mean. What people remember about them, and how they are perceived. Their successes and failures measured, and later seen as they stood the test of time. Sister Ann's was set in stone. Unassailable. When God made her, He shattered the mold.

Appalachia Rex? For King Dale, his legacy would not be a good one. There was no way to sugarcoat it. He'd been a man driven to incredible things because of his need to protect—or at least what he'd probably thought would keep people safe.

I understood him. Not completely, but enough. The darkness did not have qualms about who it attacked, only that it won. It was insidious, infecting our thoughts and minds, corrupting what was good, making even the sweetest memory turn to ash with bitter regret.

I shook my head and turned my face into the breeze. It felt good, wholesome. The stench of unwashed bodies and rot was gone. Momentarily, true. But not now. There were no shamblers in sight. Turning away from the mess of King Dale, I set Baby in the back of the BearCat—which surprisingly hadn't been too damaged by the impact of Appalachia Rex's truck—and knelt down next to Sister Ann.

It took some doing but I managed. Sister Ann, while heavier than I was, still wasn't more than Lucia. Lifting her while being gentle and respectful while keeping an eye out for any rogue shambler was the challenge. After lots of struggling, I finally got her inside. Once her and Temple were situated in the back, I covered them each with the emergency blankets. There wasn't much else I could do for either of them except make them comfortable.

Could the dead find comfort after the fact?

I had no answer to that. Climbing into the front seat, I checked the fuel gauge. Even with the crazy antics of driving all around Clifton Forge, I still had over half a tank of gas left. Plenty to reach the mountain. The doors were locked and the engine turned over without missing a beat. Slowly, I eased the BearCat out from beneath the destroyed fencing and turned back onto the street. I knew Commercial would take me eventually to Ridgeway, and out of town.

"I'm sorry," I whispered, though I don't really know who I was whispering to. The dead don't speak, but they might be able to listen to a girl who wasn't sure if she was ready to be what Sister Ann said I needed to become.

CHAPTER TWENTY-TWO

"Saying goodbye is hard. It's not what any of us wanted, but here we are. The zombies are almost gone. People still get sick, but we're prepared now. We have hope . . . but the cost . . . my God, the cost . . . only in a future after we rebuild will we be able to look back and ask if the cost was truly worth it. If we have said future, my fellow Americans? Then yes, yes it was worth the cost."

From: *Collected Radio Transmissions of the Fall,*
University of the South Press, 2053

On a freezing cold Easter morning just after sunrise, the memorial service for both Temple and Sister Ann was held at the top of the mountain. All who called St. Dominic's home now were in attendance.

The night before, I'd sat down with the student council and Governor Lenity-Jones. Together we talked about the path forward for the school, our collective responsibilities, and the state as a whole. After one meeting with the governor I understood why Sister Ann had thought so highly of her. She was almost as good as Sister Ann motivating us.

Unsurprisingly, her long-term goal was to reestablish Richmond as the state's capital. For now, and until the state of emergency ended, Governor Lenity-Jones decided that Covington would make a perfect temporary capital location, though the downtown city hall was still damaged from the flooding and needed repairs. Like Sister Ann, the governor wanted to begin rebuilding. The main difference was the where.

More and more updates were coming in by the shortwave. The president was officially sworn in, and the fight to reclaim Washington, D.C., from the shambler hordes there was *on*. Marines were slowly driving any shamblers away from the White House. The Tomb of the Unknown Soldier was apparently under constant watch once more, something that made Governor Lenity-Jones extremely happy.

Reclaiming the world was going to be a long, tough slog, but we were living proof that it could be done. Not only *could* it, but it *had* to. Like Sister Ann had said over and over again, survival was only half of what it meant to be a human being. The other half was why we were here on this earth in the first place: to build.

Or in our case, rebuild.

These thoughts clouded my mind as I stood near the back of the gathered crowd. It had been a half-mile hike to the peak, and while it wasn't the highest mountain around us, it definitely had the best views. From the top one could look and see West Virginia, the Blue Ridge Mountains to the south and east, and watch the Jackson River meander toward Clifton Forge in the distance. From up here, the world was peaceful, serene. The daily struggle to survive wasn't as big of a problem here as it was down below.

Sister Ann loved it up here.

Had loved it, rather.

I blinked at the sudden tears and listened as Governor Lenity-Jones gave them both a eulogy. While she hadn't known Temple outside of meeting him back at Deer Creek, his granddaughters had spent a lot of time in the subsequent week since talking about how he'd kept them alive and protected them. A few of the other locals knew him and also offered tales and anecdotes. None of the words mattered, really. Two more little girls had been left alone in this world, and no kind words would ever change that.

Stop it, I mentally chided myself.

Her story about how Sister Ann—then Gunnery Sergeant Tabitha Towers—had shown a fresh-faced second lieutenant just how things worked and turned her into a proper marine was funny, but also wrong. The gunnery sergeant had been gone long before Sister Ann died. The governor didn't understand, not really. I don't even know if I did for sure.

One thing I did know was that I couldn't give a speech. Everyone was expecting me to say something in her memory, but every time I tried to think of what I was going to say, I came up blank. How does one describe the person who helped save your life without even letting on what they were doing? Is there any way to properly share the tale of the woman who selflessly gave every last ounce of her being to protecting us, keeping us safe, and giving us a reason to become more than just a group of teenagers existing in a broken, shattered world?

The sun crested the Blue Ridge Mountains to the east. Clouds, streaked across the sky as though painted by God Himself in pinks, purples, and blues, made the entire scene surreal. Birds were starting to chirp nearby. Cardinals, from the sound of it, but I couldn't be certain.

It was a perfect sunrise for such an occasion. It was also wrong.

Sister Ann *should* have been here to lead the Easter service, not buried back in the cemetery on campus. There was no way I could do it. I was barely Catholic, after all. It'd been Sister Ann's faith in God, and in us, that had kept the girls of St. Dominic's alive. Her sheer will and determination had forced us to thrive.

The governor came to the final part of her speech. It was a nice one, heartfelt and honest. I hadn't paid much attention since I'd already known what she was going to say. She'd practically borrowed a page out of Sister Ann's playbook, talking about resiliency in the face of our future challenges, working together to overcome our past differences, blah blah blah. While she was a good orator, there was just something about the governor's words that felt *off* to me.

Listening to her, it dawned on my why they felt wrong. They were Sister Ann's words, but without the sincerity or conviction behind them. In the two weeks since we'd buried Sister Ann and Temple, I'd gotten to know the governor halfway well. A lot of what she said was honest, but she always kept an ear on any issues that seemed to be plaguing random people across campus. She acknowledged the fact that the student council was nominally in charge still, and didn't create any conflict. But to me, it felt like she was always halfway campaigning and always worried about making a misstep in her words.

Sister Ann never worried about those things. She wasn't afraid to make a mistake, or say the wrong thing. Honesty was her schtick, absolute and complete. Even if it was something we didn't want to hear but needed to. The governor? Again, everything was heartfelt, but it also felt massaged, cautious. There was none of Sister Ann's *energy* behind it. The governor treated this as a mission. Sister Ann approached everything as if it were her very life.

There was a divide here, amongst the survivors. I hadn't spotted it at first, since I'd been busy trying to grieve for Sister Ann while keeping the girls calm and secure. The governor had a few people who had latched onto her the same way we girls had to Sister Ann following the early days of the Fall. Locals mostly, and almost all newer arrivals to the mountain. Kayla was standing near *her* group— well, with Sammie more accurately. But deep down I knew that if everything was on the line, Kayla would have my back.

Glancing around, I was a bit surprised to find almost every other student of St. Dominic's clustered near me. I'd seen this before, back when Sister Ann was still alive. They needed me now, the same way we'd needed her. Only now it was Maddie, She Who Kills Shamblers, in charge of things.

Scary, that.

The twins pressed up against me, one on either side. Fiona and Finlay had been very quiet since we'd buried Sister Ann. Their Tannerite bomb had been perfectly placed, removing the obstacle blocking I-64 that King Dale had put up so we could pass through. I gave each of them a slight hug, partly to comfort them, but more to calm my own nerves. My speech was up next.

The governor's speech ended and I clapped politely along with everyone else, some more enthusiastically than others. None of my girls were clapping very hard. Like me, they'd all been deeply affected by Sister Ann's death. Some of the refugees who'd arrived after Temple might not have agreed one hundred percent with the way Sister Ann did things up on the mountain, but none of them would have denied her positive impact on the school, Covington, and Alleghany County as a whole.

"Maddie?" the governor asked once the applause quieted down. I swallowed and started to approach, but stopped as the lump in my throat grew. Looking around, I could see everyone staring at me expectantly. On the girls' faces I saw hope and expectation. They'd voted for me to lead them, and Sister Ann had given them her blessing in making this happen. On some of the others' faces I saw unease and nervousness. They didn't know me, and now they were expected to live on campus being ordered around by an eighteen-year-old?

All this was completely fair. It also wasn't.

The altar where Monsignor Dietrich had given the last Easter morning service—two years ago, since last year's was cancelled on account of the zombie apocalypse—was old and worn, donated a long time ago by someone who did stonemasonry. They'd used a local rock found around campus, nelsonite, to carve the altar out of a large, singular piece. I only know this because both Sisters Ann and Margaret had explained it to us on the hike back down to campus afterward.

Stepping behind the altar, I struggled to relax. The expectant faces of everyone around, waiting for me to say something, to screw it all up, was almost too much. The survivors looked at me with eagerness, fear, suspicion, and even dislike. I knew why... or at least, I thought I did.

We'd run our student council without any of the refugees' opinions. Kids, in their eyes, deciding what the school would do. Some probably harbored grudges against us for that. Sister Ann probably saw it coming, which was why she suggested setting up a commission to be run out of Covington. Get them off campus, since St. Dominic's was never intended to be a power base for anyone.

Breathe. I could almost hear Sister Ann's voice in my head. A surprisingly warm breeze brushed frizzy hair from my eyes, reminding me that I forgot to tie it back when I woke up this morning. Though it was a cold morning, the day promised to be warm and pleasant.

Which I didn't want. The weather should have been miserable, cold, and rainy. It should have been exactly what I was feeling at the moment. But no, nature had other ideas.

Lucia and Emily both threw me a thumbs-up. They both thought I could do it. And if they believed, then the others definitely thought so as well. I had to do it. The girls needed me to be strong for them. Now, and in the future.

What was a simple speech compared to standing tall in front of

Sister Ann and admitting I screwed up? One took guts, the other, courage. I shot Lucia and Emily a grateful smile. It was quick, but I knew they'd seen it.

"Thank you," I said, meeting Governor Lenity-Jones's gaze steadily. "Just a fair warning . . . I'm a terrible public speaker." There was a small titter of laughter from the younger girls of the school. Good. I continued, "She never lost faith in you . . . or any of us. Ever."

My heart felt like it was on fire. It was hammering against my ribs, threatening to burst through, each *thud* more painful than the last. I *suck* at giving speeches. Being in front of a group like this, talking about the one person who'd been my rock for the past year? The lone individual who kept us together, made us stronger, created a family amongst a bunch of girls who would have descended into chaos and probably died in the early days of the Fall without her?

This should have been her moment. A triumphant return to some normalcy, of her giving the Easter morning service with the usual solemnity. To celebrate the resurrection, not to mourn a death. Easter was about life. Things like this are what she was put on this earth for. She shouldn't have been lying in the cold ground while a bunch of teenage delinquents like us were still here. Setting the notes down on the stone, I let the words come directly from the heart.

"Sister Ann believed that the mission of St. Dominic's Preparatory School for Girls was to both teach and save young girls. Later, it became a refuge for those who survived the Fall. Again, the theme was saving and teaching. She also wanted to be a beacon of hope for everyone, and that's what we're going to be. She believed in us, and we believed in her. And we will continue to believe in her vision, and strive toward it. That is my promise to all the girls under my care. Sister Ann showed us the way, and we will not fail her."

There was nothing else to say. The speech had been exactly what Sister Ann would have done: short, sweet, and to the point. The governor was frowning slightly. Why, I didn't know. Not that I cared what she thought. My mission was to protect the girls, and the school. Let her focus on the problems that came with being the governor. I had no interest in anything like that. I turned and walked away.

Nobody tried to stop me. The walk rapidly turned into a run. I couldn't say how long I weaved my way across the mountaintop, only that it felt like forever. Pine branches whipped across my face as I fled through a particularly thick grove. Birds sang as the sky began shifting slowly from pinks and deep blues to lighter shades.

Eventually, I started figuring out where I wanted to go, to be. Though I hadn't been this particular way before, with direction I felt a little more confident. I wasn't worried about any shamblers here. Bears were a passing concern. The main worry for me was twisting an ankle on a hidden root or something in the darkness. Fortunately, I made it to where my subconscious wanted me to be without breaking my neck.

At the spot of our crucible, I stopped and stared. It'd been three years since I first climbed this rock. That angry little girl was gone, replaced by . . . who? I didn't know yet, but I figured Sister Ann would be pleased with the end of my journey.

The sun had climbed over the Blue Ridge Mountains to the east. It was cold now, but it promised to be warmer later. The lookout point was the one spot on the mountain where nothing obstructed the view. This had been the spot where I promised I would give my best effort to be the person God meant for me to be. During those first two days out in the wilderness, before the world ended and everything went to crap, Sister Ann had brought me and the other three girls here to watch the sunrise. There she had told us what her expectations of us were, what St. Dominic's was, and—most important of all—what *ours* should be.

I cried. It was the first time since Sister Ann had died that I allowed myself to cry. All the pain, anguish, and uncertainty that had built up since we returned from the Homestead was lanced like a poisonous boil with every sob. For the first time, I allowed myself to mourn what I'd lost. My family. My friends.

My mentor and role model.

Grieving is what we do. It's totally okay, too. There's nothing wrong with it. Sister Ann told me once that funerals were created to pay our final respects for the dead, but the grieving process is for our own soul, our loss. We are sad for what we lose when someone close dies. It's part of the process, she'd said. I'd believed her but hadn't really understood it. Not then, at least.

I finally did.

It didn't really help, though. Not that I expected it to. Crying was a waste of energy. Uncontrollable sobbing was selfish. I was weak. There was no way I could protect the girls now, not without Sister Ann. We'd failed. *I* would fail. It was only a matter of time now. Someone would come in, push me out, and then—

"It's okay," a soft, unfamiliar voice whispered behind me. Blinking through my tears, I turned to see who had managed to follow me through the forest. It was Ulla, all by herself. Nobody else had tried to follow. My little minion had tracked me through the forest to make sure I was okay. Or maybe she thought I would leave her? She leaned in and wrapped her arms around my waist. She sniffled and squeezed as she buried her face into my ribs. Her hesitant voice was music to my ears. "It's okay, Maddie."

Ulla. She was speaking. In spite of all the crap we'd gone through, with everything that had gone bad during the rescue, the little girl had never given up. She'd found the strength I'd known was inside her the whole time. A wave of emotions crashed over me. I smiled. Tears ran down my face, but damn it, I wasn't sobbing anymore. I'd saved her life. In return, she helped me find something I thought I'd lost—hope. I cried, but this time they were happy tears. Miracles do happen, every single day.

Sister Ann had been right all along. In a vast sea of darkness, a beacon of hope was what we needed to be. It was what St. Dominic's was supposed to stand for—a light on top of a mountain, surrounded by a sea of darkness, offering a chance for those who would take the opportunity. A lighthouse in the worst of storms. Even in death Sister Ann was teaching, striving to make us better women, better human beings. She'd shown us the way. It would be up to us now.

Oh, who was I kidding? It was always up to us if we wanted to be better. Our choice. And with her as an example, we would succeed. Sister Ann never taught us to fail, only to keep striving toward a goal. If we stumble, we push on. If we get knocked down, we stand back up. When we succeed, we do it with humility.

Not *if* we succeeded. Never if. Sister Ann wouldn't allow it.

I kissed the top of Ulla's head the same way Sister Ann had done for me once, so many months before. It was comforting for me then, and I knew Ulla found it to be the same for her now. A simple act of kindness, made out of love, could change the life of a child in the blink of an eye.

Straightening my back, I turned and held her hand. It was a long walk to the altar, and an even longer one down to campus, but I had a school to lead.

"I know it'll be okay, kiddo. We'll be all right. All of us. I'll protect you all. Sister Ann said we'd be okay."

And Sister Ann was never, ever wrong.

∞ The End ∞